NEW YORK REVIEW BOOKS
CLASSICS

BUTCHER'S CROSSING

JOHN WILLIAMS (1922–1994) was born and raised in
northeast Texas. Despite a talent for writing and acting,
Williams flunked out of a local junior college after his first
year. He reluctantly joined the war effort, enlisting in the
Army Air Corps, and managing to write a draft of his first
novel while there. Once home, Williams found a small
publisher for the novel and enrolled at the University of
Denver, where he was eventually to receive both his B.A.
and M.A., and where he was to return as an instructor in
1954. Williams was to remain on the staff of the writing pro-
gram at the University of Denver until his retirement in 1985.
During these years, he was an active guest lecturer and
writer, publishing two volumes of poetry and three novels,
Butcher's Crossing, Stoner (also published by NYRB Classics),
and the National Book Award–winning *Augustus*.

MICHELLE LATIOLAIS is a member of the Programs in
Writing at the University of California at Irvine where she is
associate professor of English. She is the author of the novel
Even Now.

OTHER BOOKS BY JOHN WILLIAMS
PUBLISHED BY NYRB CLASSICS

Augustus
Nothing but the Night
Stoner

BUTCHER'S CROSSING

JOHN WILLIAMS

Introduction by

MICHELLE LATIOLAIS

NEW YORK REVIEW BOOKS

New York

THIS IS A NEW YORK REVIEW BOOK
PUBLISHED BY THE NEW YORK REVIEW OF BOOKS
207 East 32nd Street, New York, NY 10016
www.nyrb.com

Copyright © 1960 by John Williams; copyright renewed © 1988 by John Williams
Introduction copyright © 2007 by Michelle Latiolais
All rights reserved.

Library of Congress Cataloging-in-Publication Data
Williams, John Edward, 1922–
  Butcher's Crossing / by John Williams.
      p. cm. — (New York Review Books classics)
  ISBN-13: 978-1-59017-198-1 (alk. paper)
  ISBN-10: 1-59017-198-5 (alk. paper)
  I. Title.
PS3545.I5286B8 2007
813'.54—dc22

                                        2006029210

ISBN 978-1-59017-198-1
Available as an electronic book; ISBN 978-1-59017-424-1

Printed in the United States of America on acid-free paper.
2 0 19 18 17 16 15 14 13

Introduction

In 1981 I began my graduate studies with John Williams at the University of Denver, where he had taught since 1954. After my first workshop, he came to my office—almost completely obscured by the stack of books he carried; he was not at all a tall man—and he set them on my desk. "Ignore all of what you just heard and sat through. Read these authors. They will be your teachers. You're a writer who can't be taught, who has to figure it out on her own." The rich timbre of his voice resounded in the tiny space. He walked out through the warren of graduate-student offices and down the dingy linoleum hall. He wore a blazer and slacks and a paisley ascot. I never saw him dressed any differently, not even when I visited him in Fayetteville, Arkansas, shortly before he died. I was dumbstruck, nor did I know what to be most dumbstruck by, the fact that a professor had come to me, or being told I could not be taught. I was used to simpering in doorways during office hours until a professor deigned to look up from his papers and acknowledge me; I was in graduate school *to be taught*, and to be taught by John Williams, who had received the National Book Award in 1973 for his novel *Augustus*.

I turned to the tower of novels above which had so recently been John Williams's gaunt, deeply lined face—he was an inveterate smoker and emphysema would kill him in 1994. There was Ford Madox Ford's perfectly structured *The Good Soldier* and Edith Wharton's *The House of Mirth* and

The Age of Innocence and *Ethan Frome*. *The Wife of Martin Guerre* and *The Trial of Sören Qvist* were finely wrought and beautifully atmospheric historical novels by Janet Lewis, whose career—Williams would later tell me—had been eclipsed by her husband, the poet and critic Yvor Winters. Vitally important to John Williams's own writing were the novels of Henry James, and so under Williams's tutelage I would learn to write the consciousness of a character by reading *Daisy Miller*, *The Portrait of a Lady*, *The Golden Bowl*, and *The Ambassadors*.

John Williams wrote three very fine novels, each within a specific genre, and each a production which significantly transcends the ghettoizing of genre fiction. *Butcher's Crossing* (1960) is a western; *Stoner* (1965) is an "academic novel," or rather a novel which unfolds within the walls of the academy; and *Augustus* (1972) is a historical novel constructed of documents and letters whose authors—each in one of Cicero's three oratorical styles—collectively fill out a picture of the adult life of Augustus Caesar. Not completely playfully, John Williams always refused to claim *Nothing but the Night* (1948), his first novel, written while serving with the U.S. Army Air Corps during World War II. Somewhat in deference to his evaluation, I have never read it.

John Williams did not necessarily embrace or even eschew genre convention so much as he found interest in exploring the mendacity that arises when convention starts to control material or story or, most problematically, character. Williams's examination of genre, even as he writes within it, is erudite, stately, illuminating. *The iconoclasm need not be loud and messy,* I can almost hear him saying, his eyes keenly on us in workshop and then his full head of slicked-back black hair tilting and the cigarette placed between his lips.

Butcher's Crossing. In his third year at Harvard College, and shortly after hearing a lecture by Ralph Waldo Emerson,

William Andrews leaves his studies to come west. The year is 1873 and fortune can be made in buffalo hides as the moneyed classes of America are all agog for buffalo robes, though later in the novel the hunters wonder at this craze as "you never can really get the stink out of them." But buffalo hides and the proceeds which can be had from them—smell or no smell—are not what Will Andrews seeks. His father is a Unitarian minister, as was Ralph Waldo Emerson's, and Andrews, like Emerson, is not a man who can find himself in the halls of academe:

> Sometimes after listening to the droning voices in the chapel and in the classrooms, he had fled the confines of Cambridge to the fields and woods that lay southwestward to it. There in some small solitude, standing on bare ground, he felt his head bathed by the clean air and uplifted into infinite space; the meanness and the constriction he had felt were dissipated in the wildness about him. A phrase from a lecture by Mr. Emerson that he had attended came to him: I become a transparent eyeball. Gathered in by field and wood, he was nothing; he saw all; the current of some nameless force circulated through him. And in a way that he could not feel in King's Chapel, in the college rooms, or on the Cambridge streets, he was a part and parcel of God, free and uncontained. Through the trees and across the rolling landscape, he had been able to see a hint of the distant horizon to the west; and there, for an instant, he had beheld somewhat as beautiful as his own undiscovered nature.

Andrews leaves Boston "crowded with carriages and walking men who toiled sluggishly beneath the arches of evenly spaced elms that had been made to grow, it seemed, out of the flat stone of sidewalk and roadway." He leaves his father's house on Clarendon Street near Beacon and the river

Charles "winding among plotted fields and villages and towns, carrying the refuse of man and city out to the great bay." Andrews wants to go where no man has gone before, and though he is leaving the house in which he was born and raised, he is not yet born, nor is he yet grown. It is a story you have heard before, an ur-story, one of self-discovery, a dream sought, and a setting-out fearlessly and confidently to achieve this realization, a young man going west...and therein begins what perhaps the reader has not encountered before: John Williams's intense scrutiny of this romantic tale, this unquestioned gloss of the manic energies underlying westward expansion, manifest destiny, the "American spirit" and its projection of an individualism which could only be sought and found in the wild open spaces of the American Frontier. Therein also begins Williams's goading of Emersonian Transcendentalism, its promise of the good and truth and beauty found only in nature. Even more deeply mordant is his examination of the intuitive spirituality thought to exist in nature, man's soul in profound correspondence with a divine oversoul, with God. Will Andrews as the tenderfoot, a stock character in the western, is perfect for Williams's purposes: a tenderfoot in search of what he has *read* about the wilderness. Irony in *Butcher's Crossing* is pervasive, but it is of the stinging variety, and not so very funny.

Andrews arrives in Butcher's Crossing, Kansas, and within hours has been talked into funding a hunting expedition into the Colorado Rockies. Miller, the experienced hunter and mountain man, has a few years earlier discovered a hidden valley with a tremendous herd of buffalo, and for some time now he has been trying to secure partners for an expedition which promises huge financial gain. There is a perfect glimmer of possibility in the novel that this hidden valley of buffalo bounty doesn't really exist, and that Miller is telling a tall tale, taking Andrews for a ride, as the expression goes, but, alas, all Andrews really wants is the ride, the experience of the wilderness and what this promises him by way of self-discovery.

Miller sets off with Andrews's money to Ellsworth, Kansas, meaning to hire a skinner, Fred Schneider, and to purchase provisions for the expedition. Left behind is the expectant Andrews and Miller's sidekick, Charley Hoge, who is to be the expedition's oxen drover and camp man. Hoge is a character replete with western cliché, except we understand in John Williams's deft treatment that the characterization is an excavation *of* cliché and not a participation *in* cliché. Hoge is one-handed, alcoholic, and hasn't a thing in the world to say and so spouts passages from the Bible and other common places ostensibly grounded in the Bible's unassailable wisdom. This might matter if anyone around Hoge cared about the Bible, but no one does, not even the educated Will Andrews who reflects at one point that he has more familiarity with Emerson than with the Bible, which he realizes—realizes mildly, very mildly—he has never read. Andrews seeks the wilderness so that he can be "a part and parcel of God, free and uncontained"; what he will later encounter in nature is more akin to the malice of an Old Testament God. It is the marvelous wry wit of Williams's writing that suggests Andrews would have been better served knowing—even if just from biblical verses—about floods and plagues and unleashed fury from above than this presumed benignity of oneness with God.

Andrews has a letter of introduction to a "hide man" in Butcher's Crossing named J. D. McDonald, who had years earlier known Andrews's father and attended his church in Boston. McDonald, reminded of this time by Andrews's letter, says querulously, "Listen, boy. I went to your father's church because I thought I might meet somebody that would give me a better job, and I started going to those little meetings your father had for the same reason. I never even knew what they were talking about, half the time."

This is a small scene very early in the novel, before Andrews has met Miller and funded the expedition, and it simultaneously underscores Andrews's discontent with formalized religious activity and what people seek from it as it presages Andrews's own incomprehension in the wilderness, that other house of God.

As Andrews and Hoge wait for Miller's return from Ellsworth, Andrews sits in the window of his hotel room as a child might, locked in his room, pining for the future, a time in which he can realize himself. Andrews may be Emersonian man, he may have set out seeking to know something profound, something spiritual, but the figurative language of the novel characterizes something far more fundamental, and that is a type of infancy or childhood from which Andrews must emerge, an infancy of mind. "In his mind were fragments of Miller's talk about the mountain country to which they were going, and those fragments glittered and turned and fell softly in accidental and strange patterns. Like the loose stained bits of glass in a kaleidoscope, they augmented themselves with their turning and found light from irrelevant and accidental sources." This is a mind filled with toys, John Williams might be saying, and later in the novel, after Miller has returned to Butcher's Crossing with all the provisions the expedition will need, and they have set off, Williams writes this passage:

> The passing of time showed itself in the faces of the three men who rode with him and in the changes he perceived within himself. Day by day he felt the skin of his face hardening in the weather; the stubble of hair on the lower part of his face became smooth as his skin roughened, and the backs of his hands reddened and then browned and darkened in the sun. He felt a leanness and a hardness creep upon his body; he thought at times that he was moving into a new body, or into a real body that had lain hidden beneath layers of unreal softness and whiteness and smoothness.

Baby fat is being shed and a man is emerging from beneath

the soft, white, smooth layers but this imagery will play in a different register later in the novel as the four men are trapped by the weather and buried for several months beneath blankets of white snow. They survive by constructing a shelter of buffalo hides and then by stitching hides together to make second skins for themselves. In the spring, when the men emerge, what they are and what has arisen from this gestation, shall we say, is equivocal at best.

At the precise center of *Butcher's Crossing* begins the buffalo hunt, a passage some forty pages long. The relative ease with which a herd of five thousand buffalo is picked off by Miller happens in odd, almost puzzling contrast to the hardship of the journey the four men endure getting to the secluded Colorado valley. Certainly as one reads one wants the deaths of these great beasts to matter more, to be more difficult. The mindlessness of this carnage is underscored—though it hardly needs to be—when Miller, the seasoned hunter, admonishes himself for having thought briefly about not getting a clean shot. This one brief flicker of perception— call it doubt; you cannot call it conscience—seems to break his concentration and destroys his aim. As the instinctual milling and bawling stand of the few remaining buffalo is broken, and they are led away out of the valley in a "thin dark stream" by the young bull, broken also is the mechanical loading and firing and reloading of Miller's rifle, this collective machine of which Andrews is a necessary cog. He loads the rifles, then cools them down after they've been fired, cleans them and reloads them and hands them back to Miller. It is not surprising to read that Andrews—in thrall to this machinery and unquestioning of his participation in it—"did not know who he was, or where he went." And afterwards, after the stand is broken, and the few living buffalo are gone down the valley, Andrews cannot count the dead buffalo much past thirty, cannot find the numbers, and once again in the novel infancy—an emergence from infancy or a return to such—is in contention. Is a man named William Andrews being formed, or is he being seriously regressed? He is now without his numbers in this blood-soaked valley, and at the end of the novel, he is without language for his fellow hunters: "The four men looked at one another, moving their eyes slowly and searchingly across the faces about them. They did not move, and they did not speak. We had something to say to each other, Andrews thought dimly, but we don't know what it is; we have something we ought to say."

There is a long list of fine contemporary writers who have taken up the western, perceiving it to be an important and quintessentially American genre, but they have most often done so parodically—hilariously. Read Richard Brautigan's *The Hawkline Monster: A Gothic Western* (1974) or Percival Everett's *God's Country* (1994)—these are fine rides!—or read Robert Coover's *Ghost Town* (1998) with its unrelenting drollery, but John Williams took the western seriously, and more importantly, he took the reasons behind the emergence of the genre seriously. What even the most knocked-off, hackneyed western satisfied in slews of American readers was an urge and a desire and a hunger worth contemplating, excavating.

The western—no matter the medium—satisfied something in the American spirit, and sure it was hokum, snake oil, but we are still slathering it on ourselves today. The western is a major American genre, one that goes to the heart of our famous patriotism. "Bring 'em on" is voiced from the Oval Office in reference to Iraqi militants. It is the cry of the cattle drive, the wagon train pulling out of St. Jo, the sharpshooters poised in the rock crevices, the fierce Indians below—the desire for a foe, a challenge which will reaffirm our national character.

I think it is worth mentioning that Williams was writing

Butcher's Crossing as his country advised and aided Ngo Dinh Diem, President of Vietnam, and that *Butcher's Crossing* was published as the first American troops landed on Vietnamese soil. Williams could not have known yet that millions would die soon in Laos and Cambodia—and that this blood would be on American hands, for no defensible reason.

Butcher's Crossing is a novel about a young man who sets out to "find himself," but it is also the story of a young country violently insisting on itself mindless of the consequences. Will Andrews retching in the tall grass of the valley where almost an entire herd of five thousand buffalo has been slaughtered embodies a historical America, initially young and gung ho, this new contest merely an opportunity to confirm all that supposed to be enduring and strong in the national character, but like this buffalo kill in a valley in Colorado, and like Vietnam and perhaps like Iraq, a sickening revelation of character is at hand. Or perhaps the absence of character. John Williams's unflinching attention in *Butcher's Crossing* to the mechanical madness of human behavior suggests man at one with nature—man's nature—to be a horrifying prospect.

In 1984, shortly after the summer Olympics in Los Angeles, I arrived at the University of California at Irvine to continue my graduate studies. Oakley Hall—himself the author of an important western titled *Warlock* and nominated for a Pulitzer Prize in 1958—leaned across his desk and said to me, "You studied with John Williams. He wrote the finest western ever written." A year later Cormac McCarthy's *Blood Meridian: Or the Evening Redness in the West* would be published to give *Butcher's Crossing* and *Warlock* some company in what was becoming a pantheon of western masterpieces.

—MICHELLE LATIOLAIS

BUTCHER'S CROSSING

. . . everything that has life gives sign of satisfaction, and the cattle that lie on the ground seem to have great and tranquil thoughts. These halcyons may be looked for with a little more assurance in that pure October weather which we distinguish by the name of the Indian summer. The day, immeasurably long, sleeps over the broad hills and warm wide fields. To have lived through all its sunny hours, seems longevity enough. The solitary places do not seem quite lonely. At the gates of the forest, the surprised man of the world is forced to leave his city estimates of great and small, wise and foolish. The knapsack of custom falls off his back with the first step he takes into these precincts. Here is sanctity which shames our religions, and reality which discredits our heroes. Here we find Nature to be the circumstance which dwarfs every other circumstance, and judges like a god all men that come to her.

Nature, Ralph Waldo Emerson

Aye, and poets send out the sick spirit to green pastures, like lame horses turned out unshod to the turf to renew their hoofs. A sort of yarb-doctors in their way, poets have it that for sore hearts, as for sore lungs, nature is the grand cure. But who froze to death my teamster on the prairie? And who made an idiot of Peter the Wild Boy?

The Confidence Man, Herman Melville

PART ONE

I

The coach from Ellsworth to Butcher's Crossing was a
dougherty that had been converted to carry passengers and
small freight. Four mules pulled the cart over the ridged,
uneven road that descended slightly from the level prairie
into Butcher's Crossing; as the small wheels of the dougherty entered and left the ruts made by heavier wagons, the
canvas-covered load lashed in the center of the cart shifted,
the rolled-up canvas side curtains thumped against the
hickory rods that supported the lath and canvas roof, and
the single passenger at the rear of the wagon braced himself
by wedging his body against the narrow sideboard; one hand
was spread flat against the hard leather-covered bench and
the other grasped one of the smooth hickory poles set in
iron sockets attached to the sideboards. The driver, separated from his passenger by the freight that had been piled
nearly as high as the roof, shouted above the snorting of the
mules and the creaking of the wagon:

"Butcher's Crossing, just ahead."

The passenger nodded and leaned his head and shoulders
out over the side of the wagon. Beyond the sweating rumps
and bobbing ears of the mules he caught a glimpse of a
few bare shacks and tents set in a cluster before a taller
patch of trees. He had an instantaneous impression of color
—of light dun blending into gray set off by a heavy splash of
green. Then the bouncing of the wagon forced him to sit
upright again. He gazed at the swaying mound of goods in
front of him, blinking rapidly. He was a man in his early
twenties, slightly built, with a fair skin that was beginning
to redden after the day's exposure to the sun. He had re-

moved his hat to wipe the sweat from his forehead and had not replaced it; his light brown hair, the color of Virginia tobacco, was neatly clipped, but it lay now in damp unevenly colored ringlets about his ears and forehead. He wore yellowish-brown nankeen trousers that were nearly new, the creases still faintly visible in the heavy cloth. He had earlier removed his brown sack coat, his vest, and his tie; but even in the breeze made by the dougherty's slow forward progress, his white linen shirt was spotted with sweat and hung limply on him. The blond nap of a two-day-old beard glistened with moisture; occasionally he rubbed his face with a soiled handkerchief, as if the stubble irritated his skin.

As they neared town, the road leveled and the wagon went forward more rapidly, swaying gently from side to side, so that the young man was able to relax his grasp on the hickory pole and slump forward more easily on the hard bench. The clop of the mules' feet became steady and muffled; a cloud of dust like yellow smoke rose about the wagon and billowed behind it. Above the rattle of harness, the mules' heavy breathing, the clop of their hooves, and the uneven creaking of the wagon could be heard now and then the distant shout of a human voice and the nickering of a horse. Along the side of the road bare patches appeared in the long level of prairie grass; here and there the charred, crossed logs of an abandoned campfire were visible; a few hobbled horses grazed on the short yellow grass and raised their heads sharply, their ears pitched forward, at the sound of the wagon passing. A voice rose in anger; someone laughed; a horse snorted and neighed, and a bridle jingled at a sudden movement; the faint odor of manure was locked in the hot air.

Butcher's Crossing could be taken in almost at a glance. A group of six rough frame buildings was bisected by a narrow dirt street; there was a scattering of tents beyond the buildings on either side. The wagon passed first on its left a loosely erected tent of army drab with rolled-up sides, which held from the roof flap a flat board crudely lettered in red, JOE LONG, BARBAR. On the opposite side of the road was a low building, almost square, windowless, with a flap of canvas for a door; across the bare front boards of this building were the more carefully executed letters, in black, BRADLEY DRY GOODS. In front of the next building, a long rectangular structure of two stories, the dougherty stopped. From within this building came a low, continuous murmur of voices, and there could be heard the regular clink of glass on glass. The front was shaded by a long overhang of roof, but there was discernible in the shadow over the entrance-way an ornately lettered sign, in red with black edging, which said: JACKSON'S SALOON. Upon a long bench in front of this place sat several men lethargically staring at the wagon as it came to a halt. The young passenger began to gather from the seat beside him the clothing he had doffed earlier in the heat of the day. He put on his hat and his coat and stuffed the vest and cravat into a carpetbag upon which he had been resting his feet. He lifted the carpetbag over the sideboard into the street and with the same motion lifted a leg over the boards and stepped onto the hanging iron plate that let him descend to the ground. When his boot struck the earth, a round puff of dust flew up, surrounding his foot; it settled on the new black leather and on the bottom of his trouser leg, making their colors nearly the same. He picked up his bag and walked under the projecting roof into the shade; behind him the driver's curses mingled with the clank of iron and the jingling of harness chain as he detached the rear doubletree from the wagon. The driver called plaintively:

"Some of you men give me a hand with this freight."

The young man who had got off the wagon stood on the rough board sidewalk watching the driver struggle with the reins that had tangled with the harness trace. Two of the men who had been sitting on the bench got up, brushed past him, and went slowly into the street; they contemplated the rope that secured the freight and began unhurriedly to tug at the knots. With a final jerk the driver managed to unsnarl the reins; he led the mules in a long diagonal across the street toward the livery stable, a low open building with a split-log roof supported by unpeeled upright logs.

After the driver led his team into the stable, another

stillness came upon the street. The two men were methodi-
cally loosening the ropes that held the covered freight; the
sounds from inside the saloon were muffled as if by layers
of dust and heat. The young man stepped forward carefully
upon the odd lengths of scrap board set directly on the
earth. Facing him was a half-dugout with a sharply slanting
roof at the near edge of which was a hinged covering, held
upright by two diagonal poles, which let down to cover the
wide front opening; inside the dugout, on benches and
shelves, were scattered a few saddles and a half dozen or
more pairs of boots; long strips of raw leather hung from a
peg that jutted out of the sod wall near the opening. To
the left of this small dugout was a double-storied structure,
newly painted white with red trimmings, nearly as long as
Jackson's Saloon and somewhat higher. In the dead center
of this building was a wide door, above which was a neatly
framed sign that read BUTCHERS HOTEL. It was toward
this that the young man slowly walked, watching the street
dust pushed forward in quick, dissipating jets by his moving feet.

He entered the hotel and paused just beyond the open
door to let his eyes become accustomed to the dimness. The
vague shape of a counter rose in front of him to his right;
behind it, unmoving, stood a man in a white shirt. A half
dozen straight leather-seated chairs were scattered about the
room. Light was given from square windows set regularly in
the three walls he could see; the squares were covered with
a translucent cloth that billowed slightly inward as if the
dimness and comparative coolness were a vacuum. He went
across the bare wood floor to the waiting clerk.

"I would like a room." His voice echoed hollowly in the
silence.

The clerk pushed forward an opened ledger and handed
him a steel-tipped quill. He signed slowly, William Andrews; the ink was thin, a pale blue against the gray page.

"Two dollars," the clerk said, pulling the ledger closer to
him and peering at the name. "Two bits extra if you want
hot water brought up." He looked up suddenly at Andrews.
"Be here long?"

"I'm not sure," Andrews said. "Do you know a J. D. McDonald?"

"McDonald?" The clerk nodded slowly. "The hide man? Sure. Everybody knows McDonald. Friend of yours?"

"Not exactly," Andrews said. "Do you know where I can find him?"

The clerk nodded. "He has an office down by the brining pits. About a ten-minute walk from here."

"I'll see him tomorrow," Andrews said. "I just got in from Ellsworth a few minutes ago and I'm tired."

The clerk closed the ledger, selected a key from a large ring that was attached to his belt, and gave the key to Andrews. "You'll have to carry your own bag up," he said. "I'll bring up the water whenever you want it."

"About an hour," Andrews said.

"Room fifteen," the clerk said. "It's just off the stairs."

Andrews nodded. The stairs were unsided treads without headers that pitched sharply up from the far wall and cut into a small rectangular opening in the center level of the building. Andrews stood at the head of a narrow hall that bisected the long row of rooms. He found his own room and entered through the unlocked door. In the room there was space only for a narrow rope bed with a thin mattress, a roughly hewn table with a lamp and a tin wash basin, a mirror, and a straight chair similar to those he had seen below in the lobby. The room had one window that faced the street; set into it was a light detachable wood frame covered with a gauzelike cloth. He realized that he had seen no glass windows since he had got into town. He set his carpetbag on the bare mattress.

After he had unpacked his belongings, he shoved his bag under the low bed and stretched himself out on the uneven mattress; it rustled and sank beneath his weight; he could feel the taut ropes which supported the mattress against his body. His lower back, his buttocks, and his upper legs throbbed dully; he had not realized before how tiring the journey had been.

But now the journey was done; and as his muscles loosened, his mind went back over the way he had come. For nearly two weeks, by coach and rail, he had let himself be carried across the country. From Boston to Albany, from Albany to New York, from New York— The names of the cities jumbled in his memory, disconnected from the route he had taken. Baltimore, Philadelphia, Cincinnati, St. Louis. He remembered the grinding discomfort of the hard coach chairs, and the inert waiting in grimy depots on slatted wooden benches. All the discomforts of his journey now seeped outward from his bones, brought to consciousness by his knowledge of the journey's end.

He knew he would be sore tomorrow. He smiled, and closed his eyes against the brightness of the covered window that he faced. He dozed.

Some time later the clerk brought up a wooden tub and a bucket of steaming water. Andrews roused himself and scooped up some of the hot water in the tin basin. He soaped his face and shaved; the clerk returned with two more buckets of cold water and poured them in the tub. When he had left the room, Andrews undressed slowly, shaking the dust from his garments as he drew them off; he laid them carefully on the straight chair. He stepped into the tub and sat down, his knees drawn up to his chin. He soaped himself slowly, made drowsy by the warm water and the late afternoon quiet. He sat in the tub until his head began to nod forward; when at last it touched his knees, he straightened himself and got out of the tub. He stood on the bare floor, dripping water, and looked about the room. Finding no towel, he took his shirt off the chair and dried himself.

A dimness had crept into the room; the window was a pale glow in the gathering murk, and a cool breeze made the cloth waver and billow; it appeared to throb like something alive, growing larger and smaller. From the street came the slowly rising mutter of voices and the sounds of boots clumping on the board walks. A woman's voice was raised in laughter, then abruptly cut off.

The bath had relaxed him and eased the increasing throb of his strained back muscles. Still naked, he pushed the folded linsey-woolsey blanket into a shape like a pillow and lay down on the raw mattress. It was rough to his skin. But he was asleep before it was fully dark in his room.

During the night he was awakened several times by sounds not quite identified on the edge of his sleeping mind. During these periods of wakefulness he looked about him and in the total darkness could not perceive the walls, the limits of his room; and he had the sensation that he was blind, suspended in nowhere, unmoving. He felt that the sounds of laughter, the voices, the subdued thumps and gratings, the jinglings of bridle bells and harness chains, all proceeded from his own head, and whirled around there like wind in a hollow sphere. Once he thought he heard the voice, then the laughter, of a woman very near, down the hall, in one of the rooms. He lay awake for several moments, listening intently; but he did not hear her again.

II

Andrews breakfasted at the hotel. In a narrow room at the rear of the first floor was a single long table, around which was scattered a number of the straight chairs that appeared to be the hotel's principal furniture. Three men were at one end of the table, hunched together in conversation; Andrews sat alone at the other end. The clerk who had brought his water up the day before came into the dining room and asked Andrews if he wanted breakfast; when Andrews nodded, he turned and went toward the small kitchen behind the three men at the far end of the table. He walked with a small limp that was visible only from the rear. He returned with a tray that held a large plate of beans and hominy grits, and a mug of steaming coffee. He put the food before Andrews, and reached to the center of the table for an open dish of salt.

"Where could I find McDonald this time of the morning?" Andrews asked him.

"In his office," the clerk said. "He's there most of the time, day and night. Go straight down the road, toward the creek, and turn off to your left just before you get to the patch of cottonwoods. It's the little shack just this side of the brining pits."

"The brining pits?"

"For the hides," the clerk said. "You can't miss it."

Andrews nodded. The clerk turned again and left the room. Andrews ate slowly; the beans were lukewarm and tasteless even with salt, and the hominy grits were mushy and barely warmed through. But the coffee was hot and bitter; it numbed his tongue and made him pull his lips tight along his even white teeth. He drank it all, as swiftly as the heat would allow him.

By the time he finished breakfast and went into the street, the sun had risen high above the few buildings of the town and was bearing down upon the street with an intensity that seemed almost material. There were more people about than there had been the afternoon before, when he first had come into the town; a few men in dark suits with bowler hats mingled with a larger number more carelessly dressed in faded blue levis, soiled canvas, or broadcloth. They walked with some purpose, yet without particular hurry, upon the sidewalk and in the street; amid the drab shades of the men's clothing there was occasionally visible the colorful glimpse—red, lavender, pure white—of a woman's skirt or blouse. Andrews pulled the brim of his slouch hat down to shade his eyes, and walked along the street toward the clump of trees beyond the town.

He passed the leather goods shop, the livery stable, and a small open-sided blacksmith shop. The town ended at that point, and he stepped off the sidewalk onto the road. About two hundred yards from the town was the turnoff that the clerk had described; it was little more than twin ribbons of earth worn bare by passing wheels. At the end of this path, a hundred yards or so from the road, was a small flat-roofed shack, and beyond that a series of pole fences, arranged in a pattern he could not make out at this distance. Near the fences, at odd angles, were several empty wagons, their tongues on the earth in directions away from the fences. A vague stench that Andrews could not identify grew stronger as he came nearer the office and the fences.

The shack door was open. Andrews paused, his clenched hand raised to knock; inside the single room was a great clutter of books, papers, and ledgers scattered upon the bare wood floor and piled unevenly in the corners and spilling out of crates set against the walls. In the center of this, apparently crowded there, a man in his shirt sleeves sat hunched over a rough table, thumbing with intense haste the heavy pages of a ledger; he was cursing softly, monotonously.

"Mr. McDonald?" Andrews said.

The man looked up, his small mouth open and his brows raised over protuberant blue eyes whose whites were of the same shaded whiteness as his shirt. "Come in, come in," he said, thrusting his hand violently up through the thin hair that dangled over his forehead. He pushed his chair back from the table, started to get up, and then sat back wearily, his shoulders slumping.

"Come on in, don't just stand around out there."

Andrews entered and stood just inside the doorway. McDonald waved in the direction of a corner behind Andrews, and said:

"Get a chair, boy, sit down."

Andrews drew a chair from behind a stack of papers and placed it in front of McDonald's desk.

"What do you want—what can I do for you?" McDonald asked.

"I'm Will Andrews. I reckon you don't remember me."

"Andrews?" McDonald frowned, regarding the younger man with some hostility. "Andrews. . . ." His lips tightened; the corners of his mouth went down into the lines that came up from his chin. "Don't waste my time, goddammit; if I'd remembered you I'd have said something when you first came in. Now—"

"I have a letter," Andrews said, reaching into his breast pocket, "from my father. Benjamin Andrews. You knew him in Boston."

McDonald took the letter that Andrews held in front of him. "Andrews? Boston?" His voice was querulous, distracted. His eyes were on Andrews as he opened the letter. "Why, sure. Why didn't you say you were— Sure, that preacher fellow." He read the letter intently, moving it about before his eyes as if that might hasten his perusal.

When he had finished, he refolded the letter and let it drop onto a stack of papers on the table. He drummed his fingers on the table. "My God! Boston. It must have been twelve, fourteen years ago. Before the war. I used to drink tea in your front parlor." He shook his head wonderingly. "I must have seen you at one time or another. I don't even remember."

"My father has spoken of you often," Andrews said.

"Me?" McDonald's mouth hung open again; he shook his head slowly; his round eyes seemed to swivel in their sockets. "Why? I only saw him maybe half a dozen times." His gaze went beyond Andrews, and he said without expression: "I wasn't anybody for him to speak of. I was a clerk for some dry goods company. I can't even remember its name."

"I think my father admired you, Mr. McDonald," Andrews said.

"Me?" He laughed shortly, then glowered suspiciously at Andrews. "Listen, boy. I went to your father's church because I thought I might meet somebody that would give me a better job, and I started going to those little meetings your father had for the same reason. I never even knew what they were talking about, half the time." He said bitterly, "I would just nod at anything anybody said. Not that it did a damn bit of good."

"I think he admired you because you were the only man he ever knew who came out here—who came west, and made a life for himself."

McDonald shook his head. "Boston," he half whispered. "My God!"

For another moment he stared beyond Andrews. Then he lifted his shoulders and took a breath. "How did old Mr. Andrews know where I was?"

"A man from Bates and Durfee was passing through Boston. He mentioned you worked for the Company in Kansas City. In Kansas City, they told me you had quit them and come here."

McDonald grinned tightly. "I have my own company now. I left Bates and Durfee four, five years ago." He scowled, and one hand went to the ledger he had closed when Andrews entered the shack. "Do it all myself, now.

. . . Well." He straightened again. "The letter says I should help you any way I can. What made you come out here, anyway?"

Andrews got up from the chair and walked aimlessly about the room, looking at the piles of papers.

McDonald grinned; his voice lowered. "Trouble? Did you get in some kind of trouble back home?"

"No," Andrews said quickly. "Nothing like that."

"Lots of boys do," McDonald said. "That's why they come out here. Even a preacher's son."

"My father is a lay minister in the Unitarian Church," Andrews said.

"It's the same thing." McDonald waved his hand impatiently. "Well, you want a job? Hell, you can have a job with me. God knows I can't keep up. Look at all this stuff." He pointed to the stacked papers; his finger was trembling. "I'm two months behind now and getting further behind all the time. Can't find anybody around here to sit still long enough to—"

"Mr. McDonald," Andrews said. "I know nothing about your business."

"What? You don't what? Why, it's hides, boy. Buffalo hides. I buy and sell. I send out parties, they bring in the hides. I sell them in St. Louis. Do my own curing and tanning right here. Handled almost a hundred thousand hides last year. This year—twice, three times that much. Great opportunity, boy. Think you could handle some of this paper work?"

"Mr. McDonald—"

"This paper work is what gets me down." He ran his fingers through the thin black strands of hair that fell about his ears.

"I'm grateful, sir," Andrews said. "But I'm not sure—"

"Hell, it's only a start. Look." With a thin hand like a claw he grasped Andrews's arm above the elbow and pushed him toward the doorway. "Look out there." They went into the hot sunlight; Andrews squinted and winced against the brightness. McDonald, still clutching at his arm, pointed toward the town. "A year ago when I came here there were three tents and a dugout over there—a saloon, a whorehouse, a dry goods store, and a blacksmith. Look at it now." He pushed his face up to Andrews and said in a hoarse whisper, his breath sweet-sour from tobacco: "Keep this to yourself —but this town's going to be something two, three years from now. I've got a half dozen lots staked out already, and the next time I get to Kansas City, I'm going to stake out that many more. It's wide open!" He shook Andrews's arm as if it were a stick; he lowered his voice, which had grown strident. "Look, boy. It's the railroad. Don't go talking this around; but when the railroad comes through here, this is going to be a *town*. You come in with me; I'll steer you right. Anybody can stake out a claim for the land around here; all you have to do is sign your name to a piece of paper at the State Land Office. Then you sit back and wait. That's all."

"Thank you, sir," Andrews said. "I'll consider it."

"*Consider* it!" McDonald released his arm and stepped back from him in astonishment. He threw up his hands and they fluttered as he walked around once in a tight, angry little circle. "Consider it? Why, boy, it's an opportunity. Listen. What were you doing back in Boston before you came out here?"

"I was in my third year at Harvard College."

"You see?" McDonald said triumphantly. "And what would you have done after your fourth year? You'd have gone to work for somebody, or you'd have been a schoolteacher, like old Mr. Andrews, or— Listen. There ain't many like us out here. Men with vision. Men who can think to tomorrow." He pointed a shaking hand toward the town. "Did you see those people back there? Did you talk to any of them?"

"No, sir," Andrews said. "I only got in from Ellsworth yesterday afternoon."

"Hunters," McDonald said. His dry thin lips went loose and open as if he had tasted something rotten. "All hunters and hard cases. That's what this country would be if it wasn't for men like us. People just living off the land, not knowing what to do with it."

"Are they mostly hunters in town?"

"Hunters, hard cases, a few eastern loafers. This is a

hide town, boy. It'll change. Wait till the railroad comes through."

"I think I'd like to talk to some of them," Andrews said.

"Who?" McDonald shouted. "Hunters? Oh, my God! Don't tell me you're like the other younguns that come in here. Three years at Harvard College, and you want to use it that way. I ought to have known it. I ought to have known it when you first came."

"I just want to talk to some of them," Andrews said.

"Sure," McDonald said bitterly. "And the first thing you know, you'll be wanting to go out." His voice became earnest. "Listen, boy. Listen to me. You start going out with those men, it'll ruin you. Oh, I've seen it. It gets in you like buffalo lice. You won't care any more. Those men—" Andrews clawed in the air, as if for a word.

"Mr. McDonald," Andrews said quietly, "I appreciate what you're trying to do for me. But I want to try to explain something to you. I came out here—" He paused and let his gaze go past McDonald, away from the town, beyond the ridge of earth that he imagined was the river bank, to the flat yellowish green land that faded into the horizon westward. He tried to shape in his mind what he had to say to McDonald. It was a feeling; it was an urge that he had to speak. But whatever he spoke he knew would be but another name for the wildness that he sought. It was a freedom and a goodness, a hope and a vigor that he perceived to underlie all the familiar things of his life, which were not free or good or hopeful or vigorous. What he sought was the source and preserver of his world, a world which seemed to turn ever in fear away from its source, rather than search it out, as the prairie grass around him sent down its fibered roots into the rich dark dampness, the Wildness, and thereby renewed itself, year after year. Suddenly, in the midst of the great flat prairie, unpeopled and mysterious, there came into his mind the image of a Boston street, crowded with carriages and walking men who toiled sluggishly beneath the arches of evenly spaced elms that had been made to grow, it seemed, out of the flat stone of sidewalk and roadway; there came into his mind the image of tall buildings, packed side by side, the ornately cut stone of which was grimed by smoke and city filth; there came into his mind the image of the river Charles winding among plotted fields and villages and towns, carrying the refuse of man and city out to the great bay.

He became aware that his hands were tightly clenched; the tips of his fingers slipped in the moisture of his palms. He loosened his fists and wiped his palms on his trousers.

"I came out here to see as much of the country as I can," he said quietly. "I want to get to know it. It's something that I have to do."

"Young folks," said McDonald. He spoke softly. Flat lines of sweat ran through the glinting beads of moisture that stood out on his forehead, and ran into his tangled eyebrows, which were lowered over the eyes that regarded Andrews steadily. "They don't know what to do with themselves. My God, if you'd start now—if you had the sense to start now, by the time you're forty, you could be—" He shrugged. "Ahhh. Let's get back out of the sun."

They re-entered the dim little shack. Andrews discovered that he was breathing heavily; his shirt was soaked with perspiration, and it clung to his skin and slid unpleasantly over it as he moved. He removed his coat and sank into the chair before McDonald's table; he felt a curious weakness and lassitude descend from his chest and shoulders to his fingertips. A long silence fell upon the room. McDonald's hand rested on his ledger; one finger moved aimlessly above the page but did not touch it. At last he sighed deeply and said:

"All right. Go and talk to them. But I'll warn you: Most of the men around here hunt for me; you're not going to have an easy time getting into a party without my help. Don't try to hook up with any of the men I send out. You leave my men alone. I won't be responsible. I won't have you on my conscience."

"I'm not even sure I want to go on a hunt," Andrews said sleepily. "I just want to talk to the men that do."

"Trash," McDonald muttered. "You come out here all the way from Boston, Massachusetts, just to get mixed up with trash."

"Who should I talk to, Mr. McDonald?" Andrews asked.

"What?"

"Who should I talk to?" Andrews repeated. "I ought to talk to someone who knows his business, and you told me to keep away from your men."

McDonald shook his head. "You don't listen to a word a man says, do you? You got it all figured out."

"No, sir," Andrews said. "I don't have anything figured out. I just want to know more about this country."

"All right," McDonald said tiredly. He closed the ledger that he had been fingering and tossed it on a pile of papers. "You talk to Miller. He's a hunter, but he ain't as bad as the rest of them. He's been out here most of his life; at least he ain't as bad as the rebels and the hard Yankees. Maybe he'll talk to you, maybe he won't. You'll have to find out for yourself."

"Miller?" Andrews asked.

"Miller," McDonald said. "He lives in a dugout down by the river, but you'll more likely find him in Jackson's. That's where they all hang out, day and night. Ask anybody; everybody knows Miller."

"Thank you, Mr. McDonald," Andrews said. "I appreciate your help."

"Don't thank me," McDonald said. "I'm doing nothing for you. I'm giving you a man's name."

Andrews rose. The weakness had gone into his legs. It is the heat, he thought, and the strangeness. He stood still for a moment, gathering his strength.

"One thing," McDonald said. "Just one thing I ask you." He appeared to Andrews to recede into the dimness.

"Of course, Mr. McDonald. What is it?"

"Let me know before you go out, if you decide to go. Just come back here and let me know."

"Of course," Andrews said. "I'll be seeing you often, I hope. It's just that I want to have a little more time before I decide anything."

"Sure," McDonald said bitterly. "Take all the time you can. You got plenty."

"Goodbye, Mr. McDonald."

McDonald waved his hand, angrily, and turned his attention abruptly to the papers on his desk. Andrews walked

slowly out of the shack, into the yard, and turned on the
wagon trail that led to the main road. At the main road,
he paused. Across from him and some yards to his left was
the clump of cottonwoods; beyond that, intersecting the
road, must be the river; he could not see the water, but he
could see the humped banks clustered with low-growing
shrub and weed winding off into the distance. He turned
and went back toward the town.

It was near noon when he arrived at the hotel; the tiredness that had come upon him in McDonald's shack remained. In the hotel dining room he ate lightly of tough
fried meat and boiled beans, and sipped bitter hot coffee.
The hotel clerk, who limped in and out of the dining room,
asked him if he had found McDonald; he replied that he
had; the clerk nodded and said nothing more. Soon Andrews left the dining room, went up to his room, and lay
on his bed. He watched the cloth screen at his window billow softly inward until he was asleep.

III

When he awoke his room was dark; the cloth screen at his
window let in a flickering brightness from the street below.
He heard distant shouts beneath the querulous murmur of
many voices, and the snorting of a horse and the clop of
hooves. For a moment he could not remember where he
was.

He got up abruptly and sat on the edge of his bed. The
mattress rustled beneath him; he relaxed, and ran his fingers through his hair, down over the back of his head and
neck, and stretched his head backward, welcoming the soreness that warmed pleasantly up between his shoulder
blades. In the darkness he walked across his room to the
small table, which was outlined dimly beside the window.
He found a match on the table and lit the lamp beside
the washbasin. In the mirror his face was a sharp contrast
of yellow brightness and dark shadow. He put his hands in
the lukewarm water of the basin and rinsed his face. He

dried his hands and face on the same shirt he had used the day before. By the flickering light of the lamp, he put on his black string tie and brown sack coat, which was beginning to smell of his own sweat, and stared at himself in the mirror as if he were a stranger. Then he blew the lamp out, and made his way out of the room.

The street lay in long shadows cast by the yellow lights that came from the open doors and windows of the few buildings of Butcher's Crossing. A lone light came from the dry goods store opposite the hotel; bulky figures moved about it, their sizes exaggerated by the shadows. More light, and the sound of laughter and heavily clumping feet came from the saloon next to it. A few horses were tethered to the roughly hewn hitching rail set out eight or ten feet from the sidewalk in front of Jackson's; they were motionless, but the moving lights glinted on their eyeballs and on the smooth hair of their flanks. Up the street, beyond the dugout, two lanterns hung on logs in front of the livery stable; just beyond the livery stable, a dull red glow came from the blacksmith shop, and there could be heard the heavy clank of hammer upon iron and the angry hissing as hot metal was thrust into water. Andrews went in a slow diagonal across the street toward Jackson's.

The room he entered was long and narrow; its length extended at a right angle from the street, and its width was such that four men could not stand with comfort shoulder to shoulder across it. Half a dozen lanterns hung from unpainted, sooty rafters; the light they gave was reflected sharply downward, so that the surface of everything in the room glinted with yellow light and everything beneath those surfaces fell into vague shadows. Andrews walked forward. To his right a long bar extended nearly the length of the room; the bar top was two thick-hewn planks placed side by side, and supported by unfinished split logs set directly on the unevenly planked floor. He breathed deeply, and the sharp mingled odor of burning kerosene, sweat, and liquor gathered in his lungs; he coughed. He went to the bar, which was only a little higher than his waist; the bartender, a short bald man with large mustaches and a yellow skin, looked at him without speaking.

"A beer," Andrews said.

The bartender drew a heavy mug from beneath the bar and turned to one of several kegs that stood on large wooden boxes. He turned a spigot and let the beer slide in white bubbles down the side of the mug. Setting the mug before Andrews, he said:

"That'll be two bits."

Andrews tasted the beer; it seemed warmer than the room, and its flavor was thin. He laid a coin on the table.

"I'm looking for a Mr. Miller," he said. "I was told I might find him here."

"Miller?" The bartender turned indifferently and looked at the far end of the room where, in the shadows, there were two small tables about which were seated half a dozen men drinking quietly. "Don't seem to be in here. You a friend of his?"

"I've never met him," Andrews said. "I want to see him on a matter of—business. Mr. McDonald said that I would probably find him here."

The bartender nodded. "You might find him in the big room." He indicated with his eyes a point behind Andrews; Andrews turned and saw that there was a closed door that must lead to another room. "He's a big man, clean shaved. Probably be sitting with Charley Hoge—little feller, gray-haired."

Andrews thanked the bartender, finished his beer, and went through the door on the narrow side of the saloon. The room he entered was large and more dimly lighted than the one he had left. Though many lanterns hung from hooks on the smoked rafters, only a few were lighted; the room lay in pools of light and larger irregular spaces of shadow. Rudely shaped tables were arranged so that there was an empty oval space in the center of the room; at the back a straight staircase led up to the second floor. Andrews walked forward, opening his eyes wide against the dimness.

At one of the tables sat five men playing cards; they did not look up at Andrews, nor did they speak among themselves. The slap of cards and the tiny click of poker chips came upon the quietness. At another table sat two girls.

their heads close together, murmuring; a man and a woman were seated together nearby; a few other groups were gathered at shadowed tables elsewhere in the large room. There was a quiet, slow fluidity to the scene which was strange to Andrews, and it absorbed him so that for a moment he did not remember why he had come here. At the far end of the room, through the dimness and the smoke, he saw seated at a table two men and a woman. They were somewhat apart from the others, and the larger of the men was looking directly at him. Andrews moved across the open space toward them.

When he stood before their table, all three of them were looking up at him. The four remained for several moments unmoving and silent; Andrews's attention was on the large man directly in front of him, but he was aware of the girl's rather pale plump face and yellow hair that seemed to flow from round bare shoulders, and of the smaller man's long nose and gray stubbled face.

"Mr. Miller?" Andrews asked.

The large man nodded. "I'm Miller," he said. His pupils were black and sharply distinct from the whites, and his brows were set closely above them in a frown that wrinkled the broad bridge of his nose. His skin was slightly yellowed and smooth like cured leather, and at the corners of his wide mouth deep ridges curved up to the thick base of his nose. His hair was heavy and black; it was parted at the side, and lay in thick ropes over half his ears. He said again, "I'm Miller."

"My name is Will Andrews. I—my family are old friends of J. D. McDonald. Mr. McDonald said you might be willing to talk to me."

"McDonald?" Miller's heavy, almost hairless lids came down over his eyes in a slow blink. "Sit down, son."

Andrews sat in the empty chair between the girl and Miller. "I hope I'm not interrupting anything."

"What does McDonald want?" Miller asked.

"I beg your pardon?"

"McDonald sent you over here, didn't he? What does he want?"

"No, sir," Andrews said. "You don't understand. I just

wanted to talk with someone who knew this country. Mr. McDonald was kind enough to give me your name."

Miller looked at him steadily for a moment, and then nodded. "McDonald's been trying to get me to head a party for him for two years now. I thought he was trying again."

"No, sir," Andrews said.

"You work for McDonald?"

"No, sir," Andrews said. "He offered me a job, but I turned it down."

"Why?" Miller asked.

Andrews hesitated. "I didn't want to be tied down. I didn't come out here for that."

Miller nodded, and shifted his bulk; Andrews realized that the man beside him had been motionless until this moment. "This here is Charley Hoge," Miller said, moving his head slightly in the direction of the gray man who sat opposite Andrews.

"I'm pleased to meet you, Mr. Hoge," Andrews said, and put his hand across the table. Hoge was grinning at him crookedly, his sharp face sunk down between narrow shoulder blades. He slowly raised his right arm, and suddenly thrust his forearm across the table. The arm ended at the wrist in a white nub that was neatly puckered and scarred. Involuntarily, Andrews drew his own hand back. Hoge laughed; his laughter was an almost soundless wheeze that seemed forced from his thin chest.

"Don't mind Charley, son," Miller said. "He always does that. It's his idea of fun."

"Lost it in the winter of sixty-two," Charley Hoge said, still gasping with his laughter. "It froze, and would have dropped clean off, if—" He shivered suddenly, and continued to shiver as if he felt the cold again.

"You might buy Charley a drink of whisky, Mr. Andrews," Miller said almost gently. "That's another one of his ideas of fun."

"Of course," Andrews said. He half rose from his chair. "Shall I—"

"Never mind," Miller said. "Francine will get the drinks." He nodded at the blonde girl. "This is Francine."

Andrews was still half raised above the table. "How do

you do," he said, and bowed slightly. The girl smiled, her pale lips parting over teeth that were very white and slightly irregular.

"Sure," Francine said. "Does anybody else want something?" She spoke slowly and with the trace of a Germanic accent.

Miller shook his head.

"A glass of beer," Andrews said. "And if you would like something?"

"No," Francine said. "I'm not working now."

She got up and moved away from the table; for a few moments Andrews's eyes followed her. She was heavy, but she moved with grace across the room; she wore a dress of some shiny material with broad white and blue stripes. The bodice was tight, and it pushed the fullness of her flesh upward. Andrews turned questioningly toward Miller as he sat down.

"Does she—work here?" Andrews asked.

"Francine?" Miller looked at him without expression. "Francine is a whore. There are nine, ten of them in town; six of them work here, and there are a couple of Indians that work the dugouts down by the river."

"A scarlet woman," Charley Hoge said; he was still shivering. "A woman of sin." He did not smile.

"Charley is a Bible man," Miller said. "He can read it pretty good."

"A—whore," Andrews said, and swallowed. He smiled. "Somehow, she doesn't look like—a—"

The corners of Miller's wide mouth lifted slightly. "Where'd you say you was from, son?"

"Boston," he said. "Boston, Massachusetts."

"Ain't they got whores in Boston, Massachusetts?"

Andrews's face warmed. "I suppose so," he said. "I suppose so," he said again. "Yes."

Miller nodded. "They got whores in Boston. But a whore in Boston, and a whore in Butcher's Crossing; now, there's two different things."

"I see," Andrews said.

"I don't reckon you do," Miller said. "But you will. In Butcher's Crossing, a whore is a necessary part of the economy. A man's got to have something besides liquor and food to spend his money on, and something to bring him back to town after he's been out on the country. In Butcher's Crossing, a whore can pick and choose, and still make a right smart amount of money; and that makes her almost respectable. Some of them even get married; make right good wives, I hear, for them that want wives."

Andrews did not speak.

Miller leaned back in his chair. "Besides, this is a slack time, and Francine ain't working. When a whore ain't working, I guess she looks just about like anybody else."

"Sin and corruption," Charley Hoge said. "She's got the taint within her." With his good hand, he grasped the edge of the table so tightly that the knuckles showed blue-white against the brown of his skin.

Francine returned to the table with their drinks. She leaned over Andrews's shoulder to set Charley Hoge's glass of whisky before him. Andrews was aware of her warmth, her smell; he shifted. She put his beer before him, and smiled; her eyes were pale and large, and her reddish-blond lashes, soft as down, made her eyes appear wide and un-blinking. Andrews took some coins from his pocket and put them in her palm.

"Do you want me to leave?" Francine asked Miller.

"Sit down," Miller said. "Mr. Andrews just wants to talk."

The sight of the whisky had calmed Charley Hoge; he took the glass in his hand and drank rapidly, his head thrown back and his Adam's apple running like a small animal beneath the gray fur of his bearded throat. When he finished the drink, he hunched himself back in his chair and remained still, watching the others with cold little gray eyes.

"What did you want to talk about, Mr. Andrews?" Miller asked.

Andrews looked uncomfortably at Francine and Charley Hoge. He smiled. "You put it kind of abruptly," he said.

Miller nodded. "I figured to."

Andrews paused, and said: "I guess I just want to know the country. I've never been out here before; I want to know as much as I can."

"What for?" Miller asked.

Andrews looked at him blankly.

"You talk like you're an educated man, Mr. Andrews."

"Yes, sir," he said. "I was three years at Harvard College."

"Well," Miller said, "three years. That's quite a spell. How long you been away from there?"

"Not long. I left to come out here."

Miller looked at him for a moment. "Harvard College." He shook his head. "I learned myself to read one winter I was snowed in a trapper's shack in Colorado. I can write my name on paper. What do you think you can learn from me?"

Andrews frowned, and suppressed a tone of annoyance he felt creep into his voice. "I don't even know you, Mr. Miller," he said with a little heat. "It's like I said. I want to know something about this country. Mr. McDonald said you were a good man to talk to, that you knew as much about this country as any man around. I had hoped that you would be kind enough to converse with me for an hour or so, to acquaint me with—"

Miller shook his head again, and grinned. "You sure talk easy, son. You do, for a fact. That what you learn to do at Harvard College?"

For a moment, Andrews stared at him stiffly. Then he smiled. "No, sir. I reckon not. At Harvard College, you don't talk; you just listen."

"Sure, now," Miller said. "That's reason enough for any man to leave. A body's got to speak up for his self, once in a while."

"Yes, sir," Andrews said.

"So you came out here. To Butcher's Crossing."

"Yes, sir."

"And when you learn what you want to learn, what'll you do? Go back and brag to your kinfolk? Write something for the papers?"

"No, sir," Andrews said. "It's not for any of those reasons. It's for myself."

Miller did not speak for several moments. Then he said, "You might buy Charley another glass of whisky; and I'll have a glass myself this time."

Francine rose. She spoke to Andrews: "Another beer?"

"Whisky," Andrews said.

After Francine left their table, Andrews was silent for some time; he did not look at either of the two men at the table with him.

Miller said: "So you didn't tie up with McDonald."

"It wasn't what I wanted."

Miller nodded. "This is a hunt town, boy. If you stay around, there ain't much choice about what you do. You can take a job with McDonald and make yourself some money, or you can start yourself some kind of little business and hope that the railroad does come through, or you can tie up with a party and hunt buffalo."

"That's about what Mr. McDonald said."

"And he didn't like the last idea."

Andrews smiled. "No, sir."

"He don't like hunters," Miller said. "And they don't like him either."

"Why?"

Miller shrugged. "They do the work, and he gets all the money. They think he's a crook, and he thinks they're fools. You can't blame either side; they're both right."

Andrews said, "But you're a hunter yourself, aren't you, Mr. Miller?"

Miller shook his head. "Not like these around here, and not for McDonald. He outfits his own parties, and gives them fifty cents a head for raw hides—summer hides, not much more than thin leather. He has thirty or forty parties out all the time; he gets plenty of skins, but the way it's split up, the men are lucky if they make enough to get through the winter. I hunt on my own or I don't hunt at all." Miller paused; Francine had returned with a quarter-filled bottle and fresh glasses and a small glass of beer for herself. Charley Hoge moved quickly toward the glass of whisky she set before him; Miller took his own glass in his large, hairless hand and cupped it; Andrews took a quick sip. The liquor burned his lips and tongue and warmed his throat; he could taste nothing for the burning.

"I come out here four years ago," Miller continued, "the same year McDonald did. My God! You should have seen this country then. In the spring, you could look out from here and see the whole land black with buffalo, solid as grass, for miles. There was only a few of us then, and it was nothing for one party to get a thousand, fifteen hundred head in a couple of weeks hunting. Spring hides, too, pretty good fur. Now it's hunted out. They travel in smaller herds, and a man's lucky to get two or three hundred head a trip. Another year or two, there won't be any hunting left in Kansas."

Andrews took another sip of whisky. "What will you do then?"

Miller shrugged. "I'll go back to trapping, or I'll do some mining, or I'll hunt something else." He frowned at his glass. "Or I'll hunt buffalo. There are still places they can be found, if you know where to look."

"Around here?" Andrews asked.

"No," Miller said. He moved his large, black-suited body restlessly in the chair and pushed his untasted drink precisely to the center of the table. "In the fall of sixty-three, I was trapping beaver up in Colorado. That was the year after Charley here lost his hand, and he was staying in Denver and wasn't with me. The beaver was late in furring out that year, so I left my traps near the river I was working and took my mule up towards the mountains; I was hoping to get a few bears. Their skin was good that year, I had heard. I climbed all over the side of that mountain near three days, I guess, and wasn't able to even catch sight of a bear. On the fourth day, I was trying to work my way higher and further north, and I come to a place where the mountain dropped off sharp into a little gorge. I thought maybe there might be a side stream down there where the animals watered, so I worked my way down; took me the best part of a day. They wasn't no stream down there. They was a flat bed of bare ground, ten, twelve foot wide, packed hard as rock, that looked like a road cut right through the mountain. Soon as I saw it, I knew what it was, but I couldn't believe what I saw. It was buffalo; they had tromped the earth down hard, going this way and coming back, for years. I followed the bed up the mountain the rest of that day, and near nightfall come out on a valley bed

flat as a lake. That valley wound in and out of the mountains as far as you could see; and they was buffalo scattered
all over it, in little herds, as far as a man could see. Fall
fur, but thicker and better than winter fur on the plains
grazers. From where I stood, I figured maybe three, four
thousand head; and they was more around the bends of
the valley I couldn't see." He took the glass from the center of the table and gulped quickly, shuddering slightly as
he swallowed. "I had the feeling no man had ever been in
that valley before. Maybe some Indians a long time ago,
but no man. I stayed around two days, and never saw a
human sign, and never saw one coming back out. Back near
the river, the trail curved out against the side of the mountain and was hid by trees; working up the river, a man
would never see it."

Andrews cleared his throat. When he spoke, his voice
sounded strange and hollow to himself: "Did you ever go
back there?"

Miller shook his head. "I never went back. I knew it
would keep. A man couldn't find it unless he knew where
it was, or unless he stumbled on it accidental like I did;
and that ain't very likely."

"Ten years," Andrews said. "Why haven't you gone
back?"

Miller shrugged. "Things ain't been right for it. One
year Charley was laid up with the fever, another year I
was promised to something else, another I didn't have a
stake. Mainly I haven't been able to get together the right
kind of party."

"What kind do you need?" Andrews asked.

Miller did not look at him. "The kind that'll let it be
my hunt. They ain't many places like this left, and I never
wanted any of the other hunters along."

Andrews felt an obscure excitement growing within him.
"How many men would it take for a party like this?"

"That would depend," Miller said, "on who was getting it
up. Five, six, seven men in most parties. Myself, on this
hunt, I'd keep it small. One hunter would be enough, because he'd have all the time he needed to make his kill;
he could keep the buffalo in the valley all the time he needs.

A couple of skinners and a camp man. Four men ought to be able to do the job about right. And the fewer the men, the bigger the take will be."

Andrews did not speak. On the edge of his sight, Francine moved forward and put her elbows on the table. Charley Hoge took a deep, sharp breath, and coughed gently. After a long while, Andrews said:

"Could you get up a party this late in the year?"

Miller nodded, and looked over Andrews's head. "Could be done, I suppose."

There was a silence. Andrews said: "How much money would it take?"

Miller's eyes lowered and met Andrews's; he smiled slightly. "Are you just talking, son, or have you got yourself interested in something?"

"I've got myself interested," Andrews said. "How much money would it take?"

"Well, now," Miller said. "I hadn't thought serious about going out this year." He drummed his heavy pale fingers on the table top. "But I suppose I could think about it, now."

Charley Hoge coughed again, and added an inch of whisky to his half-filled glass.

"My stake's pretty low," Miller said. "Whoever came in would have to put up just about all the money."

"How much?" Andrews said.

"And even so," Miller continued, "he'd have to understand that it would still be my hunt. He'd have to understand that."

"Yes," Andrews said. "How much would it take?"

"How much money you got, son?" Miller asked gently.

"A little over fourteen hundred dollars," Andrews said.

"You'd want to go along, of course."

Andrews hesitated. Then he nodded.

"To work, I mean. To help with the skinning."

Andrews nodded again.

"It would still be my hunt, you understand," Miller said.

Andrews said: "I understand."

"Well, it might be arranged," Miller said, "if you wanted to put up the money for the team and provisions."

"What would we need?" Andrews asked.

"We'd need a wagon and a team," Miller said slowly. "Most often the team is mules, but a mule needs grain. A team of oxen could live off the land, going and coming, and they pull a heavy enough load. They're slow, but we wouldn't be in a great hurry. You got a horse?"

"No," Andrews said.

"We'd need a horse for you, and maybe for the skinner, whoever he is. You shoot a gun?"

"Do you mean a—pistol?"

Miller smiled tightly. "No man in his right mind has any use for them little things," he said, "unless he wants to get killed. I mean a rifle."

"No," Andrews said.

"We ought to get you a small rifle. I'll need powder and lead—say a ton of lead and five hundred pounds of powder. If we don't use it all, we can get refunds. In the mountains, we can live off the land, but we have to have food going and coming back. Couple of sacks of flour, ten pounds of coffee, twenty of sugar, couple pounds of salt, a few sides of bacon, twenty pounds of beans. We'll need some kettles and a few tools. A little grain for the horses. I'd say five or six hundred dollars would do it easy."

"That's nearly half of all the money I have," Andrews said.

Miller shrugged. "It's a lot of money. But you stand to make a lot more. With a good wagon, we ought to be able to load in close to a thousand skins. They should bring us near twenty-five hundred dollars. If there's a big kill, we can let some of the hides winter over and go back in the spring and get them. I'll take 60 per cent and you get 40; I'm taking a bit more than usual, but it's my hunt, and besides I take care of Charley here. You'll take care of the other skinner. When we get back, you should be able to sell the team and wagon for about what you paid for it; so you'll make out all right."

"I ain't going," Charley Hoge said. "That's a country of the devil."

Miller said pleasantly, "Charley lost that hand up in the Rockies; he ain't liked the country since."

"Hell fire and ice," Charley Hoge said. "It ain't for human man."

"Tell Mr. Andrews about losing your hand, Charley," Miller said.

Charley Hoge grinned through his short, grizzled beard. He put the stump of his hand on the table and inched it toward Andrews as he spoke. "Miller and I was hunting and trapping early one winter in Colorado. We was up on a little rise just before the mountains when a blizzard come up. Miller and I got separated, and I slipped on a rock and hit my head and got knocked clean out of my senses. Don't know how long I laid there. When I come to, the blizzard was still blowing, and I could hear Miller calling."

"I'd been looking for Charley nearly four hours," Miller said.

"I must've knocked a glove off when I fell," Charley Hoge continued, "because my hand was bare and it was froze stiff. But it wasn't cold. It just kind of tingled. I yelled at Miller, and he come over, and he found us a shelter back in some rocks; they was even some dry logs, and we was able to keep a fire going. I looked at that hand, and it was blue, a real bright blue. I never seen anything like it. And then it got warmed up, and then it started to hurt; I couldn't tell whether it hurt like ice or whether it hurt like fire; and then it turned red, like a piece of fancy cloth. We was there two, three days, and the blizzard didn't let up. Then it turned blue again, almost black."

"It got to stinking," Miller said, "so I knew it had to come off."

Charley Hoge laughed with a wheezing, cracking voice. "He kept telling me it had to come off, but I wouldn't listen to him. We argued almost half a day about it, until he finally wore me down. He never would of talked me into it if I hadn't got so tired. Finally I just laid back and told him to cut away."

"My God," Andrews said, his voice barely a whisper.

"It wasn't as bad as you might think," he said. "By that time the hurt was so bad I could just barely feel the knife. And when he hit bone, I passed out, and it wasn't bad at all then."

"Charley got careless," Miller said. "He shouldn't have slipped on that rock. He ain't been careless since, have you, Charley?"

He laughed. "I been mighty careful since then."

"So you see," Miller said, "why Charley don't like the Colorado country."

"My God, yes!" Andrews said.

"But he'll go with us," Miller continued. "With only one hand, he's a better camp man than most."

"No," Charley Hoge said. "I ain't going. Not this time."

"It'll be all right," Miller said. "This time of year, it's almost warm up there; there won't be no snow till November." He looked at Andrews. "He'll go; all we'll need is a skinner. We'll need a good one, because he'll have to break you in."

"All right," Andrews said. "When will we be leaving?"

"We should hit the mountains about the middle of September; it'll be cool up there then, and the hides should be about right. We should leave here in about two weeks. Then a couple of weeks to get there, a week or ten days on the kill, and a couple of weeks back."

Andrews nodded. "What about the team and the supplies?"

"I'll go into Ellsworth for those," Miller said. "I know a man there who has a sound wagon, and there should be oxen for sale; I'll pick up the supplies there, too, because they'll be cheaper. I should be back in four, five days."

"You'll make all the arrangements," Andrews said.

"Yes. You leave it all to me. I'll get you a good horse and a varmint rifle. And I'll get us a skinner."

"Do you want the money now?" Andrews asked.

The corners of Miller's mouth tightened in a close smile. "You don't lose any time making up your mind, do you, Mr. Andrews?"

"No, sir," Andrews said.

"Francine," Miller said, "we all ought to have another drink on this. Bring us all some more whisky—and bring yourself some too."

Francine looked for a moment at Miller, then at Andrews; her eyes stayed upon Andrews as she rose and went away from the table.

"We can have a drink on it," Miller said, "and then you can give me the money. That will close it."

Andrews nodded. He looked at Charley Hoge, and beyond him; he was drowsy with the heat and with the warm effects of the whisky he had drunk; in his mind were fragments of Miller's talk about the mountain country to which they were going, and those fragments glittered and turned and fell softly in accidental and strange patterns. Like the loose stained bits of glass in a kaleidoscope, they augmented themselves with their turning and found light from irrelevant and accidental sources.

Francine returned with another bottle and placed it in the center of the table; no one spoke. Miller lifted his glass, poised it for a moment where the light from a lantern struck it with a reddish-amber glow. The others silently raised their glasses and drank, not putting the glasses down until they were empty. Andrews's eyes watered at the burning in his throat; through the moisture he saw Francine's face shimmering palely before him. Her own eyes were upon him, and she was smiling slightly. He blinked and looked at Miller.

"You got the money with you?" Miller asked.

Andrews nodded. He opened a lower button of his shirt and withdrew from his money belt a sheaf of bills. He counted six hundred dollars upon the scarred table and returned the other bills to his belt.

"And that's all there is to it," Miller said. "I'll ride into Ellsworth tomorrow and pick up what we need and be back in less than a week." He shuffled through the bills, selected one, and held it out to Charley Hoge. "Here. This will keep you while I'm gone."

"What?" Charley Hoge asked, his voice dazed. "Ain't I coming with you?"

"I'll be busy," Miller said. "This will take care of you for a week."

Charley Hoge nodded slowly, and then whipped the bill out of Miller's hand, crushed it, and thrust it into his shirt pocket.

Andrews pushed his chair back from the table and arose; his limbs felt stiff and reluctant to move. "I believe I'll turn in, if there's nothing else we need to talk about."

Miller shook his head. "Nothing that can't wait. I'll be pulling out early in the morning, so I won't see you till I get back. But Charley'll be around."

"Good night," Andrews said. Charley Hoge grunted and looked at him somberly.

"Good night, ma'am," Andrews said to Francine, and bowed slightly, awkwardly, from the shoulders.

"Good night, Mr. Andrews," Francine said. "Good luck."

Andrews turned from them and walked across the long room. It was nearly deserted, and the pools of light on the rough-planked floor and the hewn tables seemed sharper, and the shadows about those pools deeper and more dense than they had been earlier. He walked through the saloon and out onto the street.

The glow from the blacksmith shop had all but disappeared, and the lanterns hung on the poles in front of the livery stable had burned down so that only rims of yellow light spread from the bottoms of glass bulbs; the few horses that remained tethered in front of the saloon were still, their heads slumped down nearly between their legs. The sound of Andrews's boots upon the board walk was loud and echoing; he went into the street and walked across to his hotel.

IV

For the first few days after Miller left Butcher's Crossing for Ellsworth, Andrews spent much of his time in his hotel room; he lay on the thin mattress of his narrow bed and gazed at the bare walls, the roughly planked floor, the flat low ceiling. He thought of his father's house on Clarendon Street near Beacon and the river Charles. Though he had left there with his portion of an uncle's bequest less than a month before, he felt that the house, in which he had been born and in which he had lived his youth, was very distant in time; he could summon only the dimmest image of the tall elms that surrounded the house, and of the house itself. He remembered more clearly the great dim parlor and the sofa covered with dark red velvet upon which he had lain on summer afternoons, his cheek brushed by the heavy pile, his eyes following, until they were confounded, the intricately entwined floral design carved upon the walnut frame of the sofa. As if it were important, he strained his memory; beside the sofa there had been a large lamp with a round milk-white base encircled by a chain of painted roses, and beyond that, on the wall, neatly framed, was a series of water colors done by a forgotten aunt during her Grand Tour. But the image would not stay with him. Unreal, it thinned like blown fog; and Andrews came back to himself in a raw bare room in a crudely built frame hotel in Butcher's Crossing.

From that room he could see nearly all the town; when he discovered that he could take the gauze-covered frame out of the window, he spent many hours sitting there, his arms folded on the lower frame of the window opening, his chin resting on one forearm, gazing out upon the town. His gaze alternated between the town itself, which seemed to move in a sluggish erratic rhythm like the pulse of some brute existence, and the surrounding country. Always, when his gaze lifted from the town, it went westward toward the river, and beyond. In the clean early morning light, the horizon was a crisp line above which was the blue and cloudless sky; looking at the horizon, sharply defined and with a quality of absoluteness, he thought of the times when, as a boy, he had stood on the rocky coast of Massachusetts Bay, and looked eastward across the gray Atlantic until his mind was choked and dizzied at the immensity he gazed upon. Older now, he looked upon another immensity in another horizon; but his mind was filled with some of the wonder he had known as a child. As if it were an intimation of some knowledge he had long ago lost, he thought now of those early explorers who had set out upon another waste, salt and wide. He remembered hearing of the superstition that told them they would come to a sharp brink, and sail over it, to fall forever from the world in space and darkness. The legends had not kept them back, he knew; but he wondered how often, in their lonely sailing, they had intimations of depthless plunge, and how often they were repeated in their dreams. Looking at the horizon, he could see the line waver in the rising heat of the day; by late afternoon, with the rising winds, the line became indistinct, merged with the sky, and to the west was a vague country whose limits and extents were undefined. And as night came upon the land, creeping from the brightness sunk like a coal in the western haze, the little town that held him seemed to contract as the dark expanded; and he had, at moments, when his eye lost a point of reference, a sensation like falling, as the sailors must have had in their dreams in their deepest fears. But a light would flicker on the street below him, or a match would flare, or a door would open to let lantern light gleam on a passing boot; and he would again discover himself sitting before an open window in his hotel room, his muscles aching from inactivity and strain. Then he would let himself drop upon his bed and sleep in another darkness that was more familiar and more safe.

Occasionally he would interrupt his wait by the window and go down into the street. There the few buildings in Butcher's Crossing broke up his view of the land, so that it no longer stretched without limit in all directions—though at odd moments he had a feeling as if he were at a great distance above the town, and even above himself, gazing down upon a miniature cluster of buildings, about which crawled a number of tiny figures; and from this small center the land stretched outward endlessly, blotched and made shapeless by the point from which it spread.

But more usually, he wandered upon the street among the people who seemed to flow into and out of Butcher's Crossing as if by the impulse of an erratic but rhythmical tide. He went up and down the street, in and out of stores, paused, and went swiftly again, adjusting his motions to those of the people he moved among. Though he sought nothing in his mingling, he had odd and curious impressions that seemed to him important, perhaps because he did not seek them. He was not aware of these impressions as they occurred to him; but in the evening, as he lay in darkness on his bed, they came back to him with the force of freshness.

He had an image of men moving silently in the streets amidst a clatter of sound that was extraneous to them, that defined rather than dispersed their silence. A few of them wore guns thrust carelessly in their waistbands, though most of them went unarmed. In his image, their faces had a marked similarity; they were brown and ridged, and the eyes, lighter than the skin, had a way of looking slightly upward and beyond whatever they appeared to gaze at. And finally he had the impression that they moved naturally and without strain in a pattern so various and complex that his mind could not grasp it, a pattern whose secret passages could not be forced or opened by the will.

During Miller's absence, he spoke of his own volition to only three persons—Francine, Charley Hoge, and Mc-Donald.

Once he saw Francine on the street; it was at noon, when few people were about; she was walking from Jackson's Saloon toward the dry goods store, and they met at the entrance, which was directly across the street from the hotel. They exchanged greetings, and Francine asked him if he had got used to the country yet. As he replied, he noticed minute beads of sweat that stood out distinctly above her full upper lip and caught the sunlight like tiny crystals. They spoke for some moments, and an awkward silence fell between them; Francine stood solid and unmoving before him, smiling at him, her wide pale eyes blinking slowly. At last he muttered an apology and walked away from her, up the street, as if he had some place to go.

He saw her again early one morning as she descended the long stairway that came from the upper floor of Jackson's Saloon. She wore a plain gray dress with the collar unbuttoned at the throat, and she came down the stairs with great care; the stairs were steep and open, so that she watched her feet as she placed them precisely at the center of the thick boards. Andrews stood on the board sidewalk and watched her come down; she did not wear a hat, and as she came out of the shadow of the building, the morning brightness caught her loose reddish-gold hair and gave warmth to her pale face. Though she had not seen him as she came down, she looked up at him without surprise when she got to the sidewalk.

"Good morning," Andrews said.

She nodded and smiled; she remained facing him with one hand still on the rough wooden bannister of the stair; she did not speak.

"You're up early this morning," he said. "There's hardly anyone on the street."

"When I get up early, I take a walk sometimes."

"All alone?"

She nodded. "Yes. It's good to walk alone in the morning; it's cool then. Soon it'll be winter and too cold to walk, and the hunters will be in town, and I won't be alone at all. So in the summer and fall I walk when I can in the morning."

"This is a beautiful morning," Andrews said.

"Yes," Francine said. "It's very cool."

"Well," Andrews said doubtfully, and started to move away, "I suppose I'll leave you to your walk."

Francine smiled and put her hand on his arm. "No. It's all right. You walk with me for a while. We'll talk."

She took his arm, and they walked slowly up and down the street, speaking quietly, their voices distinct in the morning stillness. Andrews moved stiffly; he did not look often at the girl beside him, and he was conscious of every muscle that moved him with her. Though afterward he thought often about their walk, he could not remember anything they said.

He saw Charley Hoge more frequently. Usually their conversations were brief and perfunctory. But once, casually, in a remote connection, he mentioned that his father was a lay minister in the Unitarian Church. Charley Hoge's eyes widened, his mouth dropped incredulously, and his voice took on a new note of respect. He explained to Andrews that he had been saved by a traveling preacher in Kansas City, and had been given a Bible by that same man. He showed Andrews the Bible; it was a cheap edition, worn, with several pages torn. A deep brownish stain covered the corners of a number of the pages; Charley explained that this was blood, buffalo blood, that he had got on the Bible just a few years ago; he wondered if he had committed, even by accident, a sacrilege; Andrews assured him that he had not. Thereafter Charley Hoge was eager to talk; sometimes he even went to the effort of seeking Andrews out to discuss with him some point of fact or question of interpretation about the Bible. Soon, almost to his surprise, it occurred to Andrews that he did not know the Bible well enough to talk about it even on Charley Hoge's terms—had not, in fact, ever read it with any degree of thoroughness. His father had encouraged his reading of Mr. Emerson, but had not, to his recollection, insisted that he read the Bible. Somewhat reluctantly, he explained this to Charley Hoge; Charley Hoge's eyes became lidded with suspicion, and when he spoke to Andrews again it was in the tone of evangelicism rather than equality.

As he listened to Charley Hoge's exhortations, his mind wandered away from the impassioned words; he thought of the times, short months before, when he had been compelled to be present each morning at eight at King's Chapel in Harvard College, to listen to words much like the words to which he listened now. It amused him to compare the crude barroom that smelled of kerosene, liquor, and sweat to the austere dark length of King's Chapel where hundreds of soberly dressed young men gathered each morning to hear the mumbled word of God.

Listening to Charley Hoge, thinking of King's Chapel, he realized quite suddenly that it was some irony such as this that had driven him from Harvard College, from Boston, and thrust him into this strange world where he felt unaccountably at home. Sometimes after listening to the droning voices in the chapel and in the classrooms, he had fled the confines of Cambridge to the fields and woods that lay southwestward to it. There in some small solitude, standing on bare ground, he felt his head bathed by the clean air and uplifted into infinite space; the meanness and the constriction he had felt were dissipated in the wildness about him. A phrase from a lecture by Mr. Emerson that he had attended came to him: I become a transparent eyeball. Gathered in by field and wood, he was nothing; he saw all;

the current of some nameless force circulated through him. And in a way that he could not feel in King's Chapel, in the college rooms, or on the Cambridge streets, he was a part and parcel of God, free and uncontained. Through the trees and across the rolling landscape, he had been able to see a hint of the distant horizon to the west; and there, for an instant, he had beheld somewhat as beautiful as his own undiscovered nature.

Now, on the flat prairie around Butcher's Crossing, he regularly wandered, as if seeking a chapel more to his liking than King's or Jackson's Saloon. On one such sojourn, on the fifth day after Miller had left Butcher's Crossing, and on the day before he returned, Andrews went for the second time down the narrow rutted road toward the river, and on an impulse turned off the road onto the path that led to McDonald's shack.

Andrews walked through the doorway without knocking. McDonald was seated behind his littered desk; he did not move as Andrews came into the room.

"Well," McDonald said, and cleared his throat angrily, "I see you've come back."

"Yes, sir," Andrews said. "I promised I would tell you if—"

McDonald waved his hand impatiently. "Don't tell me," he said, "I already know. . . . Pull up a chair."

Andrews got a chair from the corner of the room and brought it up beside the desk.

"You know?"

McDonald laughed shortly. "Hell, yes, I know; everybody in town knows. You gave Miller six hundred dollars, and you're off on a big hunt, up in Colorado, they say."

"You even know where we're going," Andrews said.

McDonald laughed again. "You don't think you're the first one that Miller has tried to get in on this deal, do you? He's been trying for four years, maybe more—ever since I've known him, anyway. By this time, I thought he'd have stopped."

Andrews was silent for a moment. Finally, he said: "It doesn't make any difference."

"You'll lose your tail, boy. Miller saw them buffalo, if he

saw them at all, ten, eleven years ago. There's been a lot of hunting since then, and the herds have scattered; they don't all go where they used to go. You might find a few old strays, but that's all; you won't get your money back."

Andrews shrugged. "It's a chance. Maybe I won't."

"You could still back out," McDonald said. "Look." He leaned across the table and pointed a stiff index finger at Andrews. "You back out. Miller will be mad, but he won't make trouble; you can get four, five hundred dollars back on the stuff you've laid out for. Hell, I'll buy it from you. And if you really want to go out on a hunt, I'll fix you up; I'll send you out on one of my parties from here. You won't be gone more than three or four days, and you'll make more off of those three or four days than you will off the whole trip with Miller."

Andrews shook his head. "I've given my word. But it's kind of you, Mr. McDonald; I thank you very much."

"Well," McDonald said after a moment. "I didn't think you'd back out. Too stubborn. Knew it when I first saw you. But it's your money. None of my business."

They were silent for a long while. Andrews said at last, "Well, I wanted to see you before I left. Miller will be coming back tomorrow or the next day, and I won't know when we'll take off from here." He got up from the chair and put it back in its corner.

"One thing," McDonald said, not looking at him. "That's rough country you're going up into. You do what Miller tells you. He may be a son-of-a-bitch, but he knows the country; you listen to him, and don't go thinking you know anything at all."

Andrews nodded. "Yes, sir." He went forward until his thighs pressed against McDonald's desk and he was bent a little above McDonald's disheveled face. "I hope you do not think I am ungrateful in this matter. I know that you are a kind man, and that you have my best interests in mind. I am truly indebted to you." McDonald's mouth had slowly opened and now it hung incredulously wide, and his round eyes were watching Andrews. Andrews turned from him and walked out of the little shack into the sunlight.

In the sunlight he paused. He wondered if he wished to

go back to the town just now. Unable to decide, he let his feet carry him vaguely along the wagon tracks to the main road; there he hesitated for a moment, to turn first one way and another, as the needle of a compass, slow to settle, discovers its point. He believed—and had believed for a long time—that there was a subtle magnetism in nature, which, if he unconsciously yielded to it, would direct him aright, not indifferent to the way he walked. But he felt that only during the few days that he had been in Butcher's Crossing had nature been so purely presented to him that its power of compulsion was sufficiently strong to strike through his will, his habit, and his idea. He turned west, his back toward Butcher's Crossing and the towns and cities that lay eastward beyond it; he walked past the clump of cottonwoods toward the river he had not seen, but which had assumed in his mind the proportions of a vast boundary that lay between himself and the wildness and freedom that his instinct sought.

The mounded banks of the river rose abruptly up, though the road ascended less steeply in a gradual cut. Andrews left the road and went into the prairie grass, which whipped about his ankles and worked beneath his trouser legs and clung to his skin. He paused atop the mound and looked down at the river; it was a thin, muddy trickle over flat rocks where the road crossed it, but above and below the road deeper pools lay flat and greenish brown in the sun. He turned his body a little to the left so that he could no longer see the road that led back to Butcher's Crossing.

Looking out at the flat featureless land into which he seemed to flow and merge, even though he stood without moving, he realized that the hunt that he had arranged with Miller was only a stratagem, a ruse upon himself, a palliative for ingrained custom and use. No business led him where he looked, where he would go; he went there free. He went free upon the plain in the western horizon which seemed to stretch without interruption toward the setting sun, and he could not believe that there were towns and cities in it of enough consequence to disturb him. He felt that wherever he lived, and wherever he would live hereafter, he was leaving the city more and more, withdrawing

into the wilderness. He felt that that was the central meaning he could find in all his life, and it seemed to him then
that all the events of his childhood and his youth had led
him unknowingly to this moment upon which he poised, as
if before flight. He looked at the river again. On this side is
the city, he thought, and on that the wilderness; and
though I must return, even that return is only another
means I have of leaving it, more and more.

He turned. Butcher's Crossing lay small and unreal before him. He walked slowly back toward the town, on the
road, his feet scuffing in the dust, his eyes watching the
puffs of dust that his feet went beyond.

V

Late on the sixth day following his departure from Butcher's Crossing, Miller returned.

In his room, Andrews heard shouts on the street below
him and heard the thump of heavy feet; above these sounds,
muffled by the distance, came the crack of a whip and the
deep-throated howl of a driver. Andrews came to his feet
and strode to the window; he leaned out over the ledge and
looked toward the eastern approach to the town.

A great cloud of dust hung upon the air, moved forward,
and dissipated itself in its forward movement; out of the
dust plodded a long line of oxen. The heads of the lead
team were thrust downward, and the two beasts toed in
toward each other, so that occasionally their long curving
horns clashed, causing both beasts to shake their heads and
snort, and separate for a few moments. Until the team got
very near the town—the lead oxen passing Joe Long's barber
shop—the wagon was scarcely visible to the townspeople
who stood about the sidewalks and to Will Andrews who
waited above them.

The wagon was long and shallow, and it curved downward
toward the center so that it gave the fleeting appearance of
a flat-bottomed boat supported by massive wheels; faded
blue paint flecked the sides of the wagon, and the vestiges

of red paint could be seen on the slow-turning spokes near the centers of the scarred, massive wheels. A heavy man in a checked shirt sat high and erect on a wagon box seat clipped near the front; in his right hand was a long bull-whip which he cracked above the ears of the lead team. His left hand pulled heavily against an upright hand brake, so that the oxen, which moved forward under his whip, were restrained by the heavy weight of the wagon above its half-locked wheels. Beside the wagon, slouched in his saddle, Miller rode a black horse; he led another, a sorrel, which was saddled but riderless.

The procession passed the hotel and passed Jackson's Saloon. Andrews watched it go beyond the livery stable, beyond the blacksmith's shop, and out of town. He watched until he could see little but the moving cloud of dust made brilliant and impenetrable by the light of the falling sun, and he waited until the dust cloud stopped and thinned away down in the hollow of the river. Then he went back to his bed and lay upon it, his palms folded beneath the back of his head, and stared up at the ceiling.

He was still staring at the ceiling, at the random flickerings of light upon it, an hour later when Charley Hoge knocked at his door and entered without waiting for a reply. He paused just inside the room; his figure was shadowy and vague, enlarged by the dim light that came from the hall.

"What are you laying here in the dark for?" he asked.

"Waiting for you to come up and get me," Andrews said. He lifted his legs over the side of the bed and sat upright on its edge.

"I'll light the lamp," Charley Hoge said. He moved forward in the darkness. "Where is it?"

"On the table near the window."

He pulled a match across the wall beside the window; the match flared yellow. With the hand that held the match, he lifted the smoked chimney from the lamp, set it down on the table, touched the match to the wick, and replaced the chimney. The room brightened as the wick's burning grew steadier, and the flickerings from the out-of-doors were submerged. Charley Hoge dropped the burnt match to the floor.

"I guess you know Miller's back in town."

Andrews nodded. "I saw the wagon as it came past. Who was with him?"

"Fred Schneider," Charley Hoge said. "He's going to be our skinner. Miller's worked with him before."

Andrews nodded again. "I suppose Miller got everything he needed."

"Everything's ready," Charley Hoge said. "Miller and Schneider are at Jackson's. Miller wants you to come over so we can get everything settled."

"All right," Andrews said. "I'll get my coat."

"Your coat?" Charley Hoge asked. "Boy, if you're cold now, what are you going to do when we get up in the mountains?"

Andrews smiled. "I'm not cold. I'm just in the habit of wearing it."

"A man loses lots of habits in time," Charley Hoge said. "Come on, let's go."

The two men left the room and went down the stairs. Charley Hoge went a few steps in front of Andrews, who had to hurry to keep up with him; he walked with quick, nervous strides, and his thin, drawn-in shoulders jerked upward with his steps.

Miller and Schneider were waiting at the long narrow bar of Jackson's. They stood at the bar with glasses of beer in front of them; a light mantle of dust clung about the shoulders of Schneider's red-checked shirt, and the ends of his straight, bristling brown hair visible beneath a flat-brimmed hat were caked white with trail dust. The two men turned as Charley Hoge and Will Andrews came down the room toward them.

Miller's flat thin lips curved upward in a tight smile. A precise swath of black beard shadowed the heavy lower half of his face. "Will," he said softly. "Did you think I wasn't coming back?"

Andrews smiled. "No. I knew you'd be back."

"Will, this is Fred Schneider; he's our skinner."

Andrews extended his hand and Schneider took it. Schneider's handclasp was loose, indifferent; he shook Andrews's hand once with a quick pumping motion. "How do," he said. His face was round, and though the lower part was covered with a light brown stubble, the whole face gave the appearance of being smooth and featureless. His eyes were wide and blue, and they regarded Andrews from beneath heavy, sleepy lids. He was a man of medium height, thickly built; he gave the immediate impression of being at all times watchful, alert, and on his guard. He wore a small pistol in a black leather holster hung high on his waist.

Miller drained the last of his beer from his glass. "Let's go in the big room where we can sit down," he said, wiping a bit of foam from his lips with a forefinger.

The others nodded. Schneider stood aside and waited for them to pass through the side door; then he followed, closing the door carefully behind him. The group of four men, with Miller in the lead, went toward the back of the room. They took a table near the stairs; Schneider sat with his back to the stairs, facing the room; Andrews sat in front of him. Charley Hoge was at Andrews's left, and Miller was at his right.

Miller said, "On my way back from the river, I stopped in and saw McDonald. He'll buy our hides from us. That'll save us packing to Ellsworth."

"How much will he pay?" asked Schneider.

"Four dollars apiece for prime hides," Miller said. "He's got a buyer for prime hides back east."

Schneider shook his head. "How much for summer hides? You won't find any prime skins for another three months."

Miller turned to Andrews. "I haven't made any arrangements with Schneider, and I haven't told him where we're going. I thought I ought to wait till we all got together."

Andrews nodded. "All right," he said.

"Let's have a drink while we talk," Miller said. "Charley, see if you can find somebody to bring us back a pitcher of beer and some whisky."

Charley Hoge scraped his chair back on the floor, and went swiftly across the room.

"Did you make out all right at Ellsworth?" Andrews asked.

Miller nodded. "Got a good buy on the wagon. Some of

the oxen haven't been broken in, and a couple of them need to be shod; but the lead team is a good one, and the rest of them will be broke in after the first few days."

"Did you have enough money?"

Miller nodded again, indifferently. "Got a little left over, even. I found you a nice horse; I rode it all the way back. All we need to pick up here is some whisky for Charley, a few sides of bacon, and— Do you have any rough clothes?"

"I can pick some up tomorrow," Andrews said.

"I'll tell you what you need."

Schneider looked sleepily at the two men. "Where are we going?"

Charley Hoge came across the room; behind him, carrying a large tray with a pitcher, bottle, and glasses upon it, Francine weaved among the tables. Charley Hoge sat down, and Francine put the bottle of whisky and the pitcher of beer in the center of the table and put the glasses in front of the men. She smiled at Andrews, and turned to Miller. "Did you bring me what I asked for from Ellsworth?"

"Yeah," Miller said. "I'll give it to you later. You set at another table for awhile, Francine. We got business to talk over."

Francine nodded, and walked to a table where another girl and a man were sitting. Andrews watched her until she sat down; when he turned, he saw that Schneider's eyes were still upon her. Schneider blinked slowly once, and turned his eyes to Andrews. Andrews looked away.

All of the men except Charley Hoge filled their glasses with beer; he took the bottle of whisky before him, uncorked it, and let the pale amber liquor gurgle into his glass nearly to the brim.

"Where are we going?" Schneider asked again.

Miller set his glass of beer to his lips and drank in long even swallows. He put the glass on the table and turned it with his heavy fingers.

"We're going to the mountain country," Miller said.

"The mountain country," Schneider said. He put his glass on the table as if the taste of the beer had suddenly become unpleasant. "Up in the Colorado Territory."

"That's right," Miller said. "You know the country."

"I know it," Schneider said. He nodded for several moments without speaking. "Well, I guess I ain't lost much time. I can get a good night's sleep and start back for Ellsworth early tomorrow morning."

Miller did not speak. He took his glass up and finished his beer, and sighed deeply.

"Why in the hell do you figure to go clear across the country?" Schneider asked. "You can find plenty of buffalo thirty, forty mile from here."

"Summer hides," Miller said. "Thin as paper, and just about as strong."

Schneider snorted. "What the hell do you care? You can get good money for them."

"Fred," Miller said, "we've worked together before. I wouldn't lead you into something that wasn't good. I got a herd staked out; nobody knows anything about it except me. We can get back a thousand hides easy, maybe more. You heard McDonald; four dollars apiece for prime hides. That's four thousand dollars, six hundred dollars for your share, maybe more. That's a damn sight better than you'll do anywhere else around here."

Schneider nodded. "If there's buffalo where you say there is. How long has it been since you seen this herd?"

"It's been some time," Miller said. "But that don't worry me."

"It worries me," said Schneider. "I know for a fact you ain't been in the mountain country for eight, nine years; maybe longer."

"Charley's going," Miller said. "And Mr. Andrews here is going; he's even put up the money."

"Charley will do anything you tell him to," Schneider said. "And I don't know Mr. Andrews."

"I won't argue with you, Fred." Miller poured himself another glass of beer. "But it seems like you're letting me down."

"You can find another skinner who ain't got as much sense as I have."

"You're the best there is," Miller said. "And for this trip, I wanted the best."

"Hell," Schneider said. He reached for the pitcher of

beer; it was almost empty. He held it up and called to Francine. Francine got up from the table where she was sitting, took the pitcher, and left without speaking. Schneider took the bottle of whisky from in front of Charley Hoge and poured several fingers of it into his beer glass. He drank it in two gulps, grimacing at the burning.

"It's too much of a gamble," he said. "We'd be gone two months, maybe three; and we might have nothing to show for it. It's been a long time since you seen them buffalo; a country can change in eight or nine years."

"We won't be gone more than a month and a half, or two months," Miller said. "I got fresh, young oxen; they should make near thirty miles a day going, and maybe twenty coming back."

"They might make fifteen going and ten coming, if you pushed them right hard."

"The days are long this time of year," Miller said. "The country's nearly level right up to where we're going, and there's water all along the way."

"Hell," Schneider said. Miller did not speak. "All right," Schneider said. "I'll go. But no shares. I'm taking no chances. I'll take sixty dollars a month, straight, starting the day we leave here and ending the day we get back."

"That's fifteen dollars more than usual," Miller said.

"You said I was the best," Schneider said, "and you offered shares. Besides, that's rough country where you intend to go."

Miller looked at Andrews; Andrews nodded.

"Done," Miller said.

"Where's that gal with the beer?" Schneider asked.

Charley Hoge took the bottle of whisky from in front of Schneider and replenished his glass. He sipped the liquor delicately, appreciatively; his small gray eyes darted between Miller and Schneider. He grinned sharply, craftily at Schneider, and said:

"I knowed all along you'd give in. I knowed it from the first."

Schneider nodded. "Miller always gets what he's after."

They were silent. Francine came across the room with

their pitcher of beer and set it on the table. She smiled briefly at the group, and spoke again to Miller.

"You about finished with your business?"

"Almost," Miller said. "I left your package in the front room, under the bar. Why don't you run out and see if it's what you wanted. Maybe you can come back a little later and have a drink with us."

Francine said, "All right," and started to move away. As she moved, Schneider put out a hand and laid it on her arm. Andrews stiffened.

"Sprechen sie Deutsch?" he asked. He was grinning.

"Yes," she said.

"Ach," he said. "Ich so glaube. Du arbeitest jetzt, nicht wahr?"

"Nein," Francine said.

"Ja," Schneider said, still grinning. "Du arbeitest mit mir, nicht wahr?"

"All right," Miller said. "We've got things to talk about. Go on now, Francine."

Francine moved away from Schneider's hand and went quickly across the room.

"What was that all about?" asked Andrews. His voice was tight.

"Why, I just asked her if she wanted a little job of work," Schneider said. "I ain't seen a better looking whore since I was in St. Louis."

Andrews looked at him for a moment; his lips tingled with anger, and his hands, beneath the table, were tightly clasped. He turned to Miller. "When do we figure on leaving?"

"Three or four days," Miller said. He looked from Andrews to Schneider with faint amusement. "The wagon needs a little work, and like I said a couple of the oxen need to be shod. Nothing's going to hold us up."

Schneider poured himself a glass of beer. "You said there was water all the way. What route do we take?"

Miller smiled. "Don't worry about that. I have that all figured out. I've thought it over in my mind for a long time."

"All right," Schneider said. "Do I work alone?"

"Mr. Andrews will help you."

"He ever done any skinning before?" He looked at Andrews, grinning again.

"No," Andrews said shortly. His face grew warmer.

"I'd feel better about it if I worked with somebody I knew better," Schneider said. "No offense."

"I think you'll find that Mr. Andrews will be a lot of help, Fred." Miller's voice was gentle, and he did not look at Schneider.

"All right," Schneider said. "You're the boss. But I ain't got any extra knives."

"All of that's taken care of," Miller said. "All we need is to get Will some work clothes; we can do that tomorrow."

"You've got it all figured out, haven't you?" Schneider spoke indifferently; the sleepy look had come back into his pale eyes. Miller nodded.

Andrews finished the last dregs of his warm beer. "I take it, then, that there's nothing else we have to talk about tonight."

"Nothing that won't keep," Miller said.

"Then I think I'll go back to the hotel. I have a few letters I ought to write."

"All right, Will," Miller said. "But we ought to get those clothes tomorrow. Why don't you meet me at the dry goods store just after noon."

Andrews nodded. He said good night to Charley Hoge, and laid a bill on the table. "I'd be obliged if you'd all have another drink on me." He walked across the room, through the door into the smoky bar, and quickly onto the street.

The anger which had risen within him back in the room, listening to Schneider talk to Francine, began to subside. A light breeze came in from the river, and carried with it the odor of manure and the acrid smell of heated impure metal from the blacksmith shop across the street from him. A red glow from the shop filtered through the yellow light of a lantern hung within the doorway; the soft whoosh of bellows working could be heard among the clangs of metal on hot metal. He breathed deeply of the cooling night air, and started off the board sidewalk to cross the street to his hotel.

But he halted, with one foot in the dust of the street and the other still resting on the edge of a thick plank. He had heard, or thought he had heard, his name whispered behind him, somewhere in the darkness. He turned uncertainly, and heard more distinctly the voice that called to him:

"Mr. Andrews! Over here."

The whispered voice seemed to come from one corner of the long saloon building. He went toward it, his way lighted by the irregular glow that came from the half-door and the small high windows of Jackson's Saloon.

It was Francine. Though he had not expected to see her, he looked at her without surprise; she stood on the first step of the long steep stairway that led up the side of the building. Her face was made pale and vague by the darkness, and her body was a dark shadow in the darkness around her. She reached out her hand and laid it on his shoulder; on the step, she stood above him, and looked down at him when she spoke:

"I thought that was you. I've been waiting here for you to come out."

Andrews's voice came with difficulty. "I—I got tired of talking to them. I needed some fresh air."

She smiled and drew back a little, her hand still light on his shoulder; her face fell into shadow, and he could see only her eyes and her teeth revealed by her smiling in the reflection of dim light.

"Come upstairs with me," she said softly. "Come up for a while."

He swallowed, and tried to speak. "I—"

"Come on," she said. "It'll be all right."

She exerted a gentle pressure on his shoulder, and turned away from him; he heard the rustle of her clothes as she started up the stairs. He followed, groping for the rough handrail on his left, his eyes desperately trying to make out the shape that went softly and slowly above him, pulling him with her invisibly.

They paused at the small square landing at the top of the stairs. She stood in the dark shade of the doorway, fumbling with the latch; for an instant, Andrews looked out over Butcher's Crossing; what he could see of the town was a dark, irregular shadow like a blotch upon the glimmer of the plain. The thin edge of a new moon hung in the west. The door creaked open, Francine whispered something, and he followed her into the darkness of the doorway.

A small dim light burned in the distance; its illumination was thin and local, but he could make out that they were in a narrow hall. The muffled sounds of men's voices and the clump of boots on wood came from below; he realized that they were just above the large hall beside Jackson's Saloon, out of which he had walked a few moments before. He groped forward, and his hands touched the smooth stiff material of Francine's dress.

"Here," she whispered. She found his hand, and took it; her hand felt cool and moist to his own. "Down this way."

He went blindly after her, his feet sliding and catching on the rough boards of the floor. They stopped; dimly he made out a doorway. Francine opened the door, saying, "This is my room," and went in. Andrews followed, blinking against the light that came when the door was opened.

Inside the room, he closed the door and leaned against it, his eyes following Francine, who moved across the small room to a table upon which a lamp, its base milk-white and decorated with brightly painted roses, burned dimly. She turned the lamp up so that the room was more brightly illumined; the light revealed the smallness of the room, the neatly made iron bedstead, a small, curving sofa whose wooden frame was carved with twined flowers and upon which were cushions covered with dark red velvet. The walls of the room were newly papered; upon them hung several framed engravings of woodland scenes. Here and there on the walls the brightly flowered wallpaper curled and peeled, revealing naked wood. Though he did not know what he had expected, Andrews was taken aback and made slightly uncomfortable by the familiarity of the room. For a moment he did not move.

Francine, her back to the light, was smiling; again, he was aware of the light glinting from her eyes and teeth. She motioned to the couch. Andrews nodded and went across the floor; when he sat down, he looked at his feet;

there was a thin carpet, worn and stained, over the floor. Francine came across the room from the table beside the bed and sat on the couch beside him; she sat a little sideways, so that she was facing him; her back was straight, and she looked almost prim, there in the lamplight, with her hands folded in her lap.

"You—you have a nice place here," Andrews said.

She nodded, pleased. "I have the only carpet in town," she said. "I had it sent in from St. Louis. Pretty soon I'm going to get a glass window. The dust blows in and it's hard to keep a place clean."

Andrews nodded, and smiled. He drummed his fingers on his knees. "Have—you been here long? In Butcher's Crossing?"

"Two years," she said indifferently. "I was in St. Louis before that, but there were too many girls there. I didn't like it." Her eyes were upon him as if she had no interest in what she was saying. "I like it here. I can rest in the summer, and there aren't so many people."

He spoke to her, but he hardly knew what he said; for as he spoke, his heart went out to her in an excess of pity. He saw her as a poor, ignorant victim of her time and place, betrayed by certain artificialities of conduct, thrust from a great mechanical world upon this bare plateau of existence that fronted the wilderness. He thought of Schneider, who had caught her arm and spoken coarsely to her; and he imagined vaguely the humiliations she had schooled herself to endure. A revulsion against the world rose up within him, and he could taste it in his throat. Impulsively he reached across the sofa and took her hand.

"It—must be a terrible life for you," he said suddenly.

"Terrible?" She frowned thoughtfully. "No. It's better than St. Louis. The men are better, and there aren't so many girls."

"You have no family, no one you can go to?"

She laughed. "What would I do with a family?" She squeezed his hand, and raised it, and turned it palm upward. "So soft," she said. She caressed his palm with her thumb, which moved slowly and rhythmically in small circles. "That's the only thing I don't like about the men here. Their hands are so rough."

He was trembling. With his free hand he grasped the armrest of the sofa and held it tightly.

"What do they call you?" Francine asked softly. "Is it William?"

"Will," Andrews said.

"I'll call you William," she said. "It's more like you, I think." She smiled slowly at him. "You're very young, I think."

He removed his hand from the smooth caress of her fingers. "I am twenty-three."

She came closer to him, sliding across the sofa; the rustle of her stiff smooth dress sounded like soft cloth tearing. Her shoulder lightly pressed against his shoulder, and she breathed gently, evenly.

"Don't be angry," she said. "I'm glad you're young. I want you to be young. All of the men here are old and hard. I want you to be soft, while you can be. . . . When will you go with Miller and the others?"

"Three or four days," Andrews said. "But we will be back within the month. And then—"

Francine shook her head, though she continued smiling. "Yes, you'll be back; but you won't be the same. You'll not be so young; you will become like the others."

Andrews looked at her confusedly, and in his confusion cried: "I will only become myself!"

She continued as if he had not interrupted. "The wind and sun will harden your face; your hands will no longer be soft."

Andrews opened his mouth to reply; he had become vaguely angry at her words. But he did not speak his anger; and as he looked at her in the lamplight, his anger died. There was a simplicity and earnestness, a sweet but not profound sorrow in her expression, which disarmed him, and which raised a tenderness with the pity he had felt a moment earlier. At that instant it seemed to him incredible that she could be what her profession termed her. He extended the hand that he had withdrawn, and covered her hand.

"You are—" he began, and hesitated, and began again. "You are—" But he could not finish; he did not know what he wanted to say.

"But for a little while," Francine said, "you will be here; for three or four days you will be young and soft."

"Yes," Andrews said.

"You will stay here for those days?" Francine said softly. She ran her fingertips lightly over the back of his hand. "You will make love to me?"

He did not speak; he was aware of her fingers moving upon his hand, and he concentrated upon that sensation.

"I'm not working now," Francine said quickly. "It's for love; it's because I want you."

He shook his head numbly, not in refusal but in despair. "Francine, I—"

"I know," she said softly, smiling again. "You have not had a woman before, have you?" He did not speak. "Have you?"

He remembered several abortive experiments with a younger cousin of his, a small, petulant girl, some years before; he remembered his urgency, his embarrassment, and his eventual boredom; and he remembered his father's averted face and vague words after the visiting parents of the girl left their home. "No," he said.

"It's all right," Francine said. "I'll show you. Here." She stood up, and extended her hands down to him. He grasped them and stood up before her. She came close to him, almost touching him; he felt her soft stomach come against him; his muscles contracted, and he flinched slightly away.

"It's all right," Francine said, her breath warm against his ear. "Don't think of anything." She laughed softly. "Are you all right?"

"Yes," he said shakily.

She pulled away from him a little and looked at his face; it seemed to him that her lips had grown thicker, and that her eyes had darkened. She moved her body against him. "I wanted you the first time I saw you," she said. "Without you even touching me, or talking to me." She moved away, her eyes still dark upon him; she reached her arms up behind her neck and began unsnapping her dress. He watched her numbly, his arms held awkwardly at his sides. Suddenly, she shook her body and the dress fell in a gray heap at her feet. She was nude; her body gleamed in the lamplight. Delicately she stepped out of the dress, and her flesh quivered with the movement; her heavy breasts swung slowly as she walked toward him.

"Now," she said, and lifted her lips up to him. He kissed her with dry lips, tasting wetness; she whispered against his lips, and her hands fumbled with his shirt front; he felt her hands go inside his shirt, go lightly over the tensed muscles of his chest. "Now," she said again; it was a bruised sound, and it seemed to echo in his head.

He pulled away from her a little to look at her soft heavy body that clung to him like velvet, held there of its own nature; there was a serenity on her face, almost as if it were asleep; and he felt that she was beautiful. But suddenly there came into his mind the words that Schneider had used, back in the saloon—he had said he hadn't seen a better looking whore since he had left St. Louis; and the look of her face changed, though he could not tell in what respect. He was assailed by the knowledge that others had seen this face as he was seeing it now; that others had kissed her on her wet lips, had heard the voice he was hearing, had felt the same breath he was feeling upon his own face, now. They had quickly paid their money, and had gone, and others had come, and others. He had a quick and irrational image of hundreds of men, steadily streaming in and out of a room. He turned, pulled away from her, suddenly dead inside himself.

"What is it?" Francine said sleepily. "Come back."

"No!" he said hoarsely, and flung himself across the room, stumbling on the edge of the rug. "My God! . . . No. I'm —I'm sorry." He looked up. Francine stood dumbly in the center of the room; her arms were held out as if to describe a shape to him; there was a look of bewilderment in her eyes. "I can't," he said to her, as if he were explaining something. "I can't."

He looked at her once more; she did not move, and the look of bewilderment did not leave her face. He pulled open the door and let the knob fly violently from his hand;

he ran into the dark hall and stumbled down its length, opened the door to the landing, and stood for a moment on the landing, breathing air in deep, famished gulps. When his legs regained some of their strength, he went down the stairs, feeling his way by the rough bannister.

He stood for a moment on the rough sidewalk, and looked up and down the street. He could not see much of Butcher's Crossing in the darkness. He looked across the street at his hotel; a dim light came from the doorway. He went across the dusty street toward it. He did not think of Francine, or of what had happened in the room above Jackson's Saloon. He thought of the three or four days that he would have to wait in this place before Miller and the others were ready. He thought of how he might spend them, and he wondered how he might press them into one crumpled bit of time that he could toss away.

PART TWO

I

In the early dawn, on the twenty-fifth day of August, the four men met behind the livery stable where their wagon, loaded with six weeks' provisions, waited for them. A sleepy stable man, scratching his matted hair and cursing mechanically under his breath, yoked their oxen to the wagon; the oxen snorted and moved uneasily in the faint light cast by a lantern set on the ground. His task completed, the stable man grunted and turned away from the four men; he shambled back toward the livery stable, swinging the lantern carelessly beside him, and dropped upon a pile of filthy blankets that lay on the open ground outside. Lying on his side, he raised the globe of the lantern and blew out the flame. In the darkness, three of the men mounted their horses; the fourth clambered into the wagon. For a few moments none of them spoke or moved. In the silence and darkness the heavy breathing of the stable man came regular and deep, and the thin squeak of leather upon wood sounded as the oxen moved against their yokes.

From the wagon Charley Hoge cleared his throat and said: "Ready?"

Miller sighed deeply, and answered, his voice muffled and quiet: "Ready."

Upon the silence came the sudden pop of braided leather as Charley Hoge let his bull-whip out above the oxen, and his voice, shrill and explosive, cracked: "Harrup!"

The oxen strained against the weight of the wagon, their hooves pawing and thudding dully in the earth; the wheels groaned against the hickory axles; for a moment there was a jumble of sound—wood strained against its grain, raw-hide and leather slapped together and pulled in high thin screeches, and metal jangled against metal; then the sound gave way to an easy rumble as the wheels turned and the wagon slowly began to move behind the oxen.

The three men preceded the wagon around the livery stable and into the wide dirt street of Butcher's Crossing. Miller rode first, slouched in his saddle; behind him, form-ing a broad-based triangle, rode Schneider and Andrews. Still, no one spoke. Miller looked ahead into the darkness that was gradually beginning to lift; Schneider kept his head down, as if he were asleep in his saddle; and Andrews looked on either side of him at the little town that he was leaving. The town was ghostly and dim in the morning darkness; the fronts of the buildings were gray shapes that rose out of the earth like huge eroded stones, and the half-dugouts appeared to be piles of rubble thrown carelessly about open holes. The procession passed Jackson's Saloon, and soon it was past the town. In the flat country beyond the town, it seemed to be darker; the clopping of the horses' hooves became dull and regular in the ears of the men, and the thin clogging odor of dust clung about their nos-trils, and was not blown away in the slowness of their passage.

Beyond the town the procession passed on its left Mc-Donald's small shack and the pole-fenced brining pits; Miller turned his head, grunted something inaudible to himself, and chuckled. A little past the clump of cotton-wood trees, where the road began to go upward over the mounded banks of the stream, the three men on horseback came to a pause and the wagon behind them creaked to a halt. They turned and looked back, widening their eyes against the darkness. As they looked at the vague sprawling shape of Butcher's Crossing, a dim yellow light, disem-bodied and hanging casually in the darkness, came on; from somewhere a horse neighed and snorted. With one accord, they turned again on their horses and began to de-scend the road that led across the river.

Where they crossed, the river was shallow; its trickling around the flat rocks that had been laid in the soft mud as

a bed for crossing had a murmurous sound that was intensified by the darkness; the dim light from the filling moon
caught irregularly upon the water as it flowed, and there was
visible upon the stream a constant glitter that made it appear wider and deeper than it was. The water barely came
above their horses' hooves, and flowed unevenly over the
turning rims of the wagon wheels.

A few moments after they crossed the stream, Miller
again pulled his horse to a halt. In the dimness, the other
men could see him raise himself in the saddle and lean
toward the lifting darkness in the west. As if it were heavy,
he lifted his arm and pointed in that direction.

"We'll cut across country here," he said, "and hit the
Smoky Hill trail about noon."

The first pink streaks of light were beginning to show in
the east. The group turned off the road and set across the
flat land; in a few minutes, the narrow road was no longer
visible to them. Will Andrews turned in his saddle and
looked back; he could not be sure of the point where they
had left the road, and he could see no mark to guide them
in their journey westward. The wagon wheels went easily
and smoothly through the thick yellow-green grass; the
wagon left narrow parallel lines behind it, which were
quickly swallowed up in the level distance.

The sun rose behind them, and they went more quickly
forward, as if pushed by the increasing heat. The air was
clear, and the sky was without clouds; the sun beat against
their backs and brought sweat through their rough clothing.

Once the group passed a small hut with a sod roof. The
hut was set on the open plain; behind it a small plot of
ground had been cleared once, but now it was going back
to the yellow-green grass that covered the land. A broken
wagon wheel lay near the front entrance, and a heavy
wooden plow was rotting beside it. Through the wide door,
at the side of which hung a scrap of weathered canvas,
they could see an overturned table and the floor covered
with dust and rubble. Miller turned in his saddle and spoke
to Andrews:

"Gave it up." His voice had a thin edge of satisfaction.

"Lots of them have tried it, but don't many make it. They pull out when it gets a little bad."

Andrews nodded, but he did not speak. As they went past the hut, his head turned; he watched the place until his view of it was cut off by the wagon that came behind them.

By noon the horses' hides were shining with sweat, and white flecks of foam covered their mouths and were sent flying into the air as they shook their heads against the bits. The heat throbbed against Andrews's body, and his head pounded painfully with the beat of his pulse; already the flesh on his upper thighs was tender from rubbing against the saddle flaps, and his buttocks were numb on the hard leather of the seat. Never before had he ridden for more than a few hours at a time; he winced at the thought of the pain he would feel at the end of the day.

Schneider's voice broke upon him: "We ought to be getting to the river about this time. I don't see no sign of it yet."

His voice was directed to no one in particular, but Miller turned and answered him shortly. "It ain't far. The animals can hold out till we get there."

Hardly had he finished speaking when Charley Hoge, behind them in the wagon, perched higher on his wagon seat than they in their saddles, called in his high voice: "Look ahead! You can see the trees from here."

Andrews squinted and strained his eyes against the noon brightness. After a few moments he was able to make out a thin dark line that slashed up through the yellow field.

Miller turned to Schneider. "Shouldn't be more than ten minutes from here," he said, and smiled a little. "Think you can hold out?"

Schneider shrugged. "I ain't in no hurry. I was just wondering if we was going to find it as easy as you thought."

Miller rapped his horse gently across the rump with one hand, and the horse went forward a bit more rapidly. Behind him Andrews heard the sharp crack of Charley Hoge's whip, and heard his wordless cry to the oxen. He turned. The oxen lumbered forward more swiftly, as if they had been awakened from a reverie. A light breeze came toward them, ruffling the grass in a soft sweep. The horses' ears pitched forward; beneath him Andrews felt a sudden stiffening and a surge of movement as his horse went ahead.

Miller pulled back on his reins and called to Andrews: "Hold him hard. They smell water. If you ain't careful, he'll run away with you."

Andrews grasped the reins tightly and pulled hard against the forward movement of the horse; the horse's head came back, the black eyes wide and the coarse black mane flying. He heard behind him the thin squeak of leather straining as Charley Hoge braked against the oxen, and heard the oxen lowing as if in agony at their restraint.

By the time they got to the Smoky Hill, the animals were quieter, but tense and impatient. Andrews's hands were sore from pulling against the reins. He dismounted; hardly had he got his feet on the ground when his horse sprang away from him and tore through the low underbrush that lined the river.

His legs were weak. He took a few steps forward and sat shakily in the shade of a scrub oak; the branches scratched against his back, but he did not have the will to move. He watched dully as Charley Hoge set the brake on the wagon and unyoked the first team of oxen from the heavy single-tree. With his one hand pulling hard against the yoke, his body slanted between the oxen, Charley Hoge let himself be pulled toward the stream. He returned in a few moments and led another pair to the stream, while the remaining oxen set up a deep and mindless lowing. Miller dropped upon the ground beside Andrews; Schneider sat across from them, his back to another tree, and looked about indifferently.

"Charley has to lead them down two at a time, yoked together," Miller said. "If he let them all go down together, they might trample each other. They ain't got much more sense than buffalo."

By the time the last oxen were released from the wagon, the horses began to amble back from the river. The men removed the bits from their horses' mouths and let them graze. Charley got some dried fruit and biscuits from the wagon, and the men munched on them.

"Might as well take it easy for a while," Miller said. "The stock will have to graze; we can take it easy for a couple of hours."

Small black flies buzzed about their damp faces, and their hands were busy slapping them away; the slow gurgle of the river, hidden by the dense brush, came to their ears. Schneider lay on his back and placed a dirty red handkerchief over his face and folded his bare hands under his armpits; soon he was asleep, and the center of the red handkerchief rose and fell gently with his breathing. Charley Hoge wandered along the grassy outer bank of the river toward the grazing animals.

"How far have we come this morning?" Andrews asked Miller, who sat erect beside him.

"Pretty near eight miles," Miller answered. "We'll do better when the team is broke in. They ain't working together like they ought to." There was a silence. Miller continued: "A mile or so ahead, we run into the Smoky Hill trail; it follows the river pretty close all the way into the Colorado Territory. It's easy traveling; should take us less than a week."

"And when we get into the Colorado?" Andrews asked.

Miller grinned briefly and shook his head. "No trail there. We'll just travel on the country."

Andrews nodded. The weakness in his body had given way to a lassitude. He stretched his limbs and lay on his stomach, his chin resting on his folded hands. The short grass, green under the trees and moist from the seepage of the river, tickled his nostrils; he smelled the damp earth and the sweet sharp freshness of the grass. He did not sleep, but his eyes drooped and his breath came evenly and deeply. He thought of the short distance they had come, and he tensed muscles that were growing sore. It was only the beginning of the journey; what he had seen this morning—the flatness, the emptiness, the yellow sea of undisturbed grass—was only the presentiment of the wilderness. Another strangeness was waiting for him when they left the trail and went into the Colorado Territory. His half-closed eyes nearly recaptured the sharp engravings he had seen in books, in magazines, when he was at home in Boston; but the thin black lines wavered upon the real grass before him, took on color, then faded. He could not recapture the strange sensations he had had, long ago, when he first saw those depictions of the land he now was seeking. Among the three men who waited beside the river, the silence was not broken until Charley Hoge began leading the oxen back to the wagon to yoke them for the resumption of the afternoon trip.

The trail upon which they went was a narrow strip of earth that had been worn bare by wagon wheels and hooves. Occasionally deep ruts forced the wagon off into the tall grass, where the land was often more level than on the trail. Andrews asked Miller why they stuck to the trail, and Miller explained that the sharp grass, whipping all day against the hooves and fetlocks of an ox, could make him footsore. For the horses, which lifted their hooves higher even in a slow walk, there was less danger.

Once, along the trail, they came upon a wide strip of bare earth that intersected their path. In this strip the earth was packed tightly down, though its surface was curiously pocked with regular indentations. It extended away from the river almost as far as the eye could see, and gradually merged into the prairie grass; on the other side of the men, it led toward the river, gradually increasing in width to the very edge of the river, which at this point was bare of brush and tree.

"Buffalo," Miller said. "This is their watering place. They come across here—" he pointed to the plain, "in a straight line, and spread out at the river. No reason for it. I've seen a thousand buffalo lined up in ruts like this, one behind another, waiting for water."

Along the trail they saw no other signs of the buffalo that day, though Miller remarked that they were getting into buffalo country. The sun whitened the western sky and threw its heat against their movement. Their horses bowed their heads and stumbled on the flat land, their sleek coats shining with sweat; the oxen plodded before the wagon, their breathing heavy and labored. Andrews pulled his hat down to shade his face, and bent his head so that he saw only the horse's curved black mane, the dark brown pommel of his saddle, and the yellow land moving jerkily beneath him. He was soaked with sweat, and the flesh of his thighs and buttocks was raw from its chafing against the saddle. He shifted his position until the shifting offered him no relief, and then he tethered his horse on the tailgate of the wagon and clambered upon the spring seat beside Charley Hoge. But the hard wood of the seat pained him more than the saddle, and the dust from the oxen's hooves choked him and made his eyes burn; he had to sit rigid and tense upon the narrow board to hold himself erect against the slow swaying of the wagon. Soon, with a few words to Charley Hoge, who had not spoken to him, he got off the wagon and once again resumed his shifting position in his saddle. For the rest of the afternoon he rode in a kind of pain that approached numbness but never achieved it.

When the sun descended beyond the vast curve of the horizon, reddening the sky and the land, the animals lifted their heads and went forward more swiftly. Miller, who had ridden all day ahead of the party, turned and shouted to Charley Hoge:

"Whip them up! They can stand it, now the day's turned cool. We need to make another five miles before we set camp."

For the first time since early in the morning, the sharp crack of Charley Hoge's whip sounded above the creaking of the wagon and the thud of the oxen's hooves. The men stirred their horses to a fast walk that occasionally broke into a slow jarring trot.

After the sun went down the darkness came swiftly; and still the group moved forward. The moon rose thinly behind them; it seemed to Andrews that their motion carried them nowhere, that they were agitated painfully upon a small dim plateau that moved beneath them as they had the illusion of going forward. In the near darkness, he grasped the horn of his saddle and raised himself up by pressing his unsteady feet upon the stirrups.

About two hours later, Miller, a vague shape that seemed a part of the animal he rode, halted and shouted back to them in a voice clear and sharp in the darkness:

"Pull her up at that clump of willows, Charley. We camp here."

Andrews went cautiously toward Miller, holding his reins tightly against the movement of his horse. Dark against the lesser darkness, the brush of the river bank sprang up before him. He tried to remove one foot from a stirrup to dismount but his leg was so stiff and numb that he was unable to do so. Finally he reached down and grasped the stirrup by its strap and tugged until he could feel the stirrup swing free. Then he threw the weight of his body to one side and half fell from his horse; he supported himself for a few moments on the ground by holding hard to his saddle.

"Rough day?" The voice was low but close to his ear. He turned; Miller's broad white face hung in the darkness.

Andrews swallowed and nodded, not trusting himself to speak.

"It takes some getting used to," Miller said. "A couple days' riding, then you'll be all right." He untied Andrews's bedroll from behind his saddle and gave the horse a heavy slap on the rump. "We'll bed down in that little draw on the other side of the willows. Think you can manage now?"

Andrews nodded and took the bedroll from him. "Thanks," he said. "I'm all right." He walked unsteadily in the direction that Miller had indicated, though he could see nothing beyond the dark clump of the willow. Dim shapes moved around him, and he realized that Charley Hoge had already unyoked the oxen and they were crashing their way to the river. He heard the sound of a shovel pushing into earth and grating on rock, and saw the glint of moonlight on the blade as it was turned. He went nearer; Charley Hoge was digging a small pit. With his good hand he held the handle of the shovel, while with one foot he thrust the blade into the ground; then, bending over, he cradled the handle in the bend of his other arm and levered the shovel up, spilling the earth beside the pit he was digging. Andrews dropped his bedroll to the ground and sat upon it, his arms thrust between his legs, his fingers curled loosely on the ground.

After a few moments, Charley Hoge stopped his digging

and went away into the darkness, returning with a bundle of twigs and small branches. He dropped them into the pit and struck a match, which flamed fretfully in the darkness, and thrust the match among the small twigs. Soon the fire was burning brightly, leaping up into the darkness. Not until then did Andrews notice Schneider lounging across from him on the other side of the fire. Schneider grinned at him once, sardonically, his face flickering in the flame-light; then he lay back on his bedroll and pulled his hat over his face.

For the next hour or two, in his exhaustion, Andrews was only vaguely aware of what happened around him. Charley Hoge came in and out of his sight, feeding the fire; Miller came up near him, spread out his bedroll, and lay upon it, his gaze directed at the fire; Andrews dozed. He came awake with a start at the aroma of brewing coffee, and looked about him with a sudden bewilderment; for a moment all he could see was the small glowing patch of coals in front of him, which sent an intense heat against his face and arms. Then he was aware of the bulky figures of Schneider and Miller standing near the pit; painfully he raised himself from the bedroll and joined them. In silence the men drank their coffee and ate the scalding beans and side pork that Charley Hoge had prepared. Andrews found himself eating wolfishly, in great gulps, though he was not aware of any hunger. The men scraped the large pot clean of the food, and sopped the liquid in their tin plates with crumbs of dried biscuit. They drained the blackened coffee-pot to the dregs, and sat on their bedrolls with their hot coffee, sipping slowly, while Charley Hoge carried the utensils down to the river.

Without removing his shoes, Andrews folded his bed-roll over him and lay on the ground. Mosquitoes buzzed about his face, but he did not brush them away. Just before he went to sleep, he heard in the distance the sound of horses' hooves and the faint squeal of rapidly turning wagon wheels; the far sound of a man's voice shouting indistinguishable words rose above the other noises. Andrews lifted himself on an elbow.

Miller's voice came to him, very close, out of the dark-

ness. "Buffalo hunters. Probably one of McDonald's outfits." His voice was edged with contempt. "They're going
too fast; can't have many hides."

The sounds faded into the distance. For a while, Andrews remained on his elbow, his eyes straining in the direction that the sounds had come from. Then his arm tired
and he lay down and slept almost immediately.

II

The great plain swayed beneath them as they went steadily
westward. The rich buffalo grass, upon which their animals
fattened even during the arduous journey, changed its color
throughout the day; in the morning, in the pinkish rays of
the early sun, it was nearly gray; later, in the yellow light
of the midmorning sun, it was a brilliant green; at noon it
took on a bluish cast; in the afternoon, in the intensity of
the sun, at a distance, the blades lost their individual character and through the green showed a distinct cast of yellow,
so that when a light breeze whipped across, a living color
seemed to run through the grass, to disappear and reappear
from moment to moment. In the evening after the sun had
gone down, the grass took on a purplish hue as if it absorbed
all the light from the sky and would not give it back.

After their first day's journey, the country lost some of
its flatness; it rolled out gently before them, and they traveled from soft hollow to soft rise, as if they were tiny chips
blown upon the frozen surface of a great sea.

Upon the surface of this sea, among the slow hollows and
crests, Will Andrews found himself less and less conscious
of any movement forward. During the first few days of the
journey he had been so torn with the raw agony of movement that each forward step his mount took cut itself upon
his nerves and upon his mind. But the pain dulled after
the first days, and a kind of numbness took its place; he
felt no sensation of his buttocks upon the saddle, and his
legs might have been of wood, so stiffly and without feeling
did they set about the sides of his horse. It was during

this numbness that he lost the awareness of any progression forward. The horse beneath him took him from hollow to crest, yet it seemed to him that the land rather than the horse moved beneath him like a great treadmill, revealing in its movement only another part of itself.

Day by day the numbness crept upon him until at last the numbness seemed to be himself. He felt himself to be like the land, without identity or shape; sometimes one of the men would look at him, look through him, as if he did not exist; and he had to shake his head sharply and move an arm or a leg and glance at it to assure himself that he was visible.

And the numbness extended to his perception of the others who rode with him on the empty plain. Sometimes in his weariness he looked at them without recognition, seeing but the crudest shapes of men. At such times he knew them only by the positions they occupied. As at the beginning of the journey, Miller rode ahead and Andrews and Schneider formed the base of a triangle behind him. Often, as the group approached out of a hollow a slight rise of land, Miller, no longer outlined against the horizon, seemed to merge into the earth, a figure that accommodated itself to the color and contour of the land upon which it rode. After the first day's journey, Miller spoke very little, as if hardly aware of the men who rode with him. Like an animal, he sniffed at the land, turning his head this way and that at sounds or scents unperceived by the others; sometimes he lifted his head in the air and did not move for long moments, as if waiting for a sign that did not come.

Beside Andrews, but across from him by thirty feet or more, rode Schneider. His broad hat pulled low over his eyes and his stiff hair bristling beneath his hat like a bundle of weathered straw, he slumped in his saddle. Sometimes his eyes were closed and he swayed in the saddle, dozing; at other times, awake, he stared sullenly at a spot between his horse's ears. Occasionally he took a chew of tobacco from a square black plug that he kept in his breast pocket, and spat contemptuously at the ground as if at something that had offended him. Seldom did he look at any of the others, and he did not speak unless it was necessary.

Behind the men on horses, Charley Hoge rode high on the clip seat of the wagon. Covered by the light dust that the horses and the oxen lifted and through which he passed, Charley Hoge held his head erect, his eyes raised above the oxen and the men before him. Sometimes he called out to them in a thin, mocking, cheerful voice; sometimes he hummed tunelessly to himself, keeping time with the stump of his right wrist; and sometimes his toneless voice cracked into a quavering hymn that jarred the hearing of all three men, who turned and looked back upon Charley Hoge's oblivious, contorted face with the open mouth and squinted eyes that saw none of them. At night, after the men were fed and the animals hobbled, Charley Hoge would open his worn and filthy Bible and mouth silently to himself by the dying light of the campfire.

On their fourth day out of Butcher's Crossing, for the second time Andrews saw the sign of buffalo.

It was Miller who made him see it. The group had come out of one of the interminable hollows that rolled through the Kansas plains; Miller, on top of the small rise, halted his horse and beckoned. Andrews rode up beside him.

"Look out yonder," Miller said, and lifted his arm.

Andrews followed the direction that Miller indicated. At first he could see only the rolling land that he had seen before; then, in the distance, his gaze settled upon a patch of white that gleamed in the late morning sun. At the distance from which he regarded it the patch had no shape, and barely had the substance to make itself visible in the blue-green grass that surrounded it. He turned back to Miller. "What is it?" he asked.

Miller grinned. "Let's ride over and get a closer look."

They let their horses go in an easy lope across the ground; Schneider came more slowly behind them, while Charley Hoge turned the ox team slightly so that he followed, far behind them, in the same direction.

As they drew nearer to the spot Miller had indicated, Andrews began to see that it was more than a patch of white; whatever it was spread over a relatively large area of ground, as if strewn there carelessly by a huge, inhuman hand. Near the area Miller pulled his horse up abruptly and dismounted, winding the reins around the saddle horn so that the horse's neck was arched downward. Andrews did the same, and walked up beside Miller, who stood unmoving, looking out over the scattered area.

"What is it?" Andrews asked again.

"Bones," Miller said, and grinned at him once more. "Buffalo bones."

They walked closer. In the short prairie grass, the bones gleamed whitely, half-submerged in the blue-green grass, which had grown up around them. Andrews walked among the bones, careful not to disturb them, peering curiously as he passed.

"Small kill," Miller said. "Must not have been more than thirty or forty. Fairly recent, too. Look here."

Andrews went to him. Miller stood before a skeleton that was almost intact. From the curving, notched spine, which showed upon its top regular indentations of a grayish color, depended the broad-bowed blades of the rib cage. The rib bones were very broad and sweeping at the front, but nearer the flanks of the animal they sharply decreased in breadth and length; near the flank, the ribs were only nubs of white held to the spinal column by dried cords of sinew and gristle. Two broad flanges of bone at the end of the spine nestled in the grass; trailing behind these flanges, flat in the grass, were the two wide and sharply tapering bones of the rear legs. Andrews walked around the skeleton, which lay upright on what had once been its belly, peering closely at it; but he did not touch it.

"Look here," Miller said again. He pointed to the skull, which lay directly before the open oval front of the rib cage. The skull was narrow and flat, curiously small before the huge skeleton, which at its largest point reached slightly higher than Andrews's waist. Two short horns curved up from the skull, and a wisp of dried fur clung to the flat top of the skull.

"This carcass ain't more than two years old," Miller said. "It's still got a stink to it."

Andrews sniffed; there was the faint rank odor of dried and crumbling flesh. He nodded, and did not speak.

"This here fellow was a big one," Miller said. "Must have been near two thousand pound. You don't see them around here that big very often."

Andrews tried to visualize the animal from the remains that rested stilly on the prairie grass; he called to his memory the engravings that he had seen in books. But that uncertain memory and the real bones would not merge; he could not imagine the animal as it had been.

Miller kicked at one of the broad ribs; it snapped from the spine and fell softly in the grass. He looked at Andrews and moved his arm in a broad gesture to the country around them. "There was a time, in the days of the big kills, when you could look a mile in any direction and see the bones piled up. Five, six years ago, we'd have been riding through bones from Pawnee Fork clean to the end of the Smoky Hill. This is what the Kansas hunt has come to." He kicked again, contemptuously, at another rib. "And these won't be here long. Some dirt farmer will run across these and load them in a wagon and cart them off for fertilizer. Though there ain't enough here to hardly bother with."

"Fertilizer?" Andrews asked.

Miller nodded. "Buffalo's a curious critter; there ain't a part of him you can't use for something." He walked the length of the skeleton, bent, and picked up the broad bone of a hind leg; he swung it in the air as if it were a club. "The Indians used these bones for everything from needles to war clubs—knives so sharp they could split you wide open. They'd glue pieces of the bone together with pieces of horn for their bows, and use another piece, whittled down, for an arrowhead. I've seen necklaces carved so pretty out of little pieces of this, you'd think they was made in St. Louis. Toys for the little ones, combs for the squaws' hair—all out of this here bone. Fertilizer." He shook his head, and swung the bone again, flung it away from him; it sailed high in the air; catching the sun, it fell in the soft grass, bounced once, and was still.

Behind them a horse snorted; Schneider had ridden up near them.

"Let's get going," he said. "We'll see plenty of bones before we're through with this trip—leastways, if there's the
kind of herd up in them mountains that there's supposed
to be."

"Sure," Miller said. "This is just a little pile anyway."

The wagon came near them; in the hot noon air, Charley Hoge's voice raised quaveringly; he sang that God was
his strong salvation, that he feared no foe, nor darkness
nor temptation; he stood firm in the fight, with God at
his right hand. For a moment the three men listened to
the tortured voice urging its message upon the empty land;
then they pushed their horses before the wagon and resumed their slow course across the country.

The signs of the buffalo became more frequent; several
times they passed over packed trails left by great herds that
went down to the river for water, and once they came
upon a huge saucerlike depression, nearly six feet in depth
at its deepest point and over forty feet across; grass grew
to the very edge of this shallow pit, but in the pit itself
the earth had been worked to a fine dust. This, Miller explained to Andrews, was a buffalo wallow, where the great
beasts found relief from the insects and lice that plagued
them by rolling about in the dust. No buffalo had been
there for a long time; Miller pointed out that there were
no buffalo chips about and that the grass around the pit
was green and uncropped.

Once they saw the dead body of a buffalo cow. It lay
stiffly on its side in the thick green grass; its belly was distended, and a foul stench of decaying flesh spread from it.
At the approach of the men, two vultures that had been
tearing at the flesh rose slowly and awkwardly into the air,
and circled high above their carrion. Miller and Andrews
rode near the carcass and dismounted. Upon the still, awkward shape the fur was a dull umber roughed to black in
spots; Andrews started to go nearer, but the stench halted
him. His stomach tightened; he pulled back, and circled the
beast so that the wind carried the full force of the odor
away from him.

Miller grinned at him. "Kind of strong, ain't it?" Still
grinning, he went past Andrews and squatted down be-

side the buffalo, examining it carefully. "Just a little cow," he said. "Whoever shot her, missed the lights; more than likely, this one just plain bled to death. Probably left behind by the main herd." He kicked at the stiff, extended lower leg. The flesh thudded dully, and there was a light ripping sound as if a piece of stiff cloth had been torn. "Ain't been dead more than a week; it's a wonder there's any meat left." He shook his head, turned, and walked back to his horse, which had shied away from the odor. When Miller approached, the horse's ears flattened and it leaned backward away from him; but Miller spoke soothingly and the horse stilled, though the muscles around its forelegs were tense and trembling. Miller and Andrews mounted and rode past the wagon and past Schneider, who had taken no notice of their stopping. The odor of the rotting buffalo clung in Miller's clothes, and even after he had gone ahead of Andrews, occasionally a light breeze would bring the odor back and cause Andrews to pull his hand across his nostrils and his mouth, as if something unclean had touched them.

Once, also, they saw a small herd; and again it was Miller who pointed it out to Andrews. The herd was little more than clustered specks of blackness in the light green of the prairie; Andrews could make out no shape or movement, though he strained his eyes against the bright afternoon sun and raised himself high in the saddle.

"It's just a little herd," Miller said. "The hunters around here have cut them all up into little herds."

The three of them—Andrews, Miller, and Schneider—were riding abreast. Schneider said impartially, to no one: "A body has sometimes got to be satisfied with a little herd. If that's the way they run, that's the way a body has got to cut them."

Miller, his eyes still straining at the distant herd, said: "I can recollect the day when you never saw a herd less than a thousand head, and even that was just a little bunch." He swept his arm in a wide half-circle. "I've stood at a place like this and looked out, and all I could see was black—fifty, seventy-five, a hundred thousand head of buffalo, moving over the grass. Packed so tight you could walk on their backs, walk all day, and never touch the ground. Now all you see is stragglers, like them out there. And grown men hunt for them." He spat on the ground.

Again Schneider addressed the air: "If all you got is stragglers, then you hunt for stragglers. I ain't got my hopes up any longer for much more."

"Where we're going," Miller said, "you'll see them like we used to in the old days."

"Maybe so," Schneider said. "But I ain't got my hopes up too high."

From the wagon behind them came the high crackle of Charley Hoge's voice. "Just a little bitty herd. You never saw nothing that little in the old days. The Lord giveth and the Lord taketh away."

At the sound of Charley Hoge's voice, the three men had turned; they listened him out; when he finished, they turned again; but they could no longer find the tiny smudge of black in the expanse of the prairie. Miller went on ahead, and Schneider and Andrews dropped back; none of them spoke again of what they had seen.

Such interruptions of their journey were few. Twice on the trail they passed small parties going in their direction. One of these parties consisted of a man, his wife, and three small children. Grimed with dust, their faces drawn and sullen with weariness, the woman and children huddled in a small wagon pulled by four mules and did not speak; the man, eager to talk and almost breathless in his eagerness, informed them that he had driven all the way from Ohio where he had lost his farm, and that he planned to join a brother who had a small business in California; he had begun the journey with a group of other wagons, but the lameness of one of his mules had so slowed his progress that he was now nearly two weeks behind the main party, and he had little hope of ever catching up. Miller examined the lame mule, and advised the man to swing up to Fort Wallace, where he could rest his team, and wait for another wagon train to come through. The man hesitated, and Miller told him curtly that the mule could not make it farther than Fort Wallace, and that he was a fool to continue on the trail alone. The man shook his head stubbornly. Miller said nothing more; he motioned to Andrews and Schneider, and the party pulled around the man and woman and the children and went ahead. Late in the evening the dust from the small mule-drawn wagon could be seen in the distance, far behind them. Miller shook his head.

"They'll never make it. That mule ain't good for two more days." He spat on the ground. "They should of turned off where I told them."

The other party they passed was a larger one of five men on horseback; these men were silent and suspicious. Reluctantly, they informed Miller that they were on their way to Colorado where they had an interest in an undeveloped mining claim, which they intended to work. They refused Charley Hoge's invitation to join them for supper, and they waited in a group for Miller's party to pass. Late that night, after Miller, Andrews, Schneider, and Hoge had bedded down, they heard the muffled clop of hooves circling around and passing them.

Once, where the trail skirted close to the river, they came upon a wide bluff, from the side of which had been excavated a series of crude dugouts. On the flat hard earth in front of the dugouts several brown, naked children were playing; behind the children, near the openings of the dugouts, squatted half a dozen Indians; the women were shapeless in the blankets they held about them despite the heat, and the men were old and wizened. As the group passed, the children ceased their play and looked at them with dark, liquid eyes; Miller waved, but none of the Indians gave any sign of response.

"River Indians," Miller said contemptuously. "They live on catfish and jack rabbits. They ain't worth shooting anymore."

But as their journey progressed such interruptions came to seem more and more unreal to Andrews. The reality of their journey lay in the routine detail of bedding down at night, arising in the morning, drinking black coffee from hot tin cups, packing bedrolls upon gradually wearying horses, the monotonous and numbing movement over the prairie that never changed its aspect, the watering of the horses and oxen at noon, the eating of hard biscuit and dried fruit, the resumption of the journey, the fumbling setting up of camp in the darkness, the tasteless quantities of beans and bacon gulped savagely in the flickering darkness, the coffee again, and the bedding down. This came to be a ritual, more and more meaningless as it was repeated, but a ritual which nevertheless gave his life the only shape it now had. It seemed to him that he moved forward laboriously, inch by inch, over the space of the vast prairie; but it seemed that he did not move through time at all, that rather time moved with him, an invisible cloud that hovered about him and clung to him as he went forward.

The passing of time showed itself in the faces of the three men who rode with him and in the changes he perceived within himself. Day by day he felt the skin of his face hardening in the weather; the stubble of hair on the lower part of his face became smooth as his skin roughened, and the backs of his hands reddened and then browned and darkened in the sun. He felt a leanness and a hardness creep upon his body; he thought at times that he was moving into a new body, or into a real body that had lain hidden beneath layers of unreal softness and whiteness and smoothness.

The change that he saw in the others was less meaningful to him, and less extreme. Miller's heavy, evenly shaped beard thickened on his face and began to curl at the extreme ends; but the change was more readily apparent in the way he sat his saddle, in his stride upon the ground, and in the look of his eyes that gazed on the opening prairie. An ease, a familiarity, a naturalness began to replace the stiff and formal attitude that Andrews had first encountered in Butcher's Crossing. He sat his saddle as if he were a natural extension of the animal he rode; he walked in such a way that it appeared his very movement was caressing the contours of the ground; and his gaze upon the prairie seemed to Andrews as open and free and limitless as the land that occasioned his regard.

Schneider's face seemed to recede and hide in the slowly growing beard that bristled like straw upon his darkening skin. Day by day Schneider withdrew into himself; he spoke to the others less frequently, and in his riding he appeared to be almost attempting to disassociate himself from them: he looked always in a direction that was away from them, and at night he ate his food silently, turned sideways from the campfire, and bedded down and was asleep long before the others.

Of them all, Charley Hoge showed the least change. His gray beard bristled a bit more fully, and his skin reddened but did not brown in the weather; he looked about him impartially, slyly, and spoke abruptly and without cause to all of them, expecting no answer. When the trail was level, he took out his worn and tattered Bible and thumbed through its pages, his weak gray eyes squinting through the dust. At regular intervals throughout the day he reached beneath the wagon seat and drew out a loosely corked bottle of whisky; he pulled the cork out with his yellowed teeth, dropped it into his lap, and took long noisy swallows. Then, in his high, thin, quavering voice he sang a hymn that floated faintly through the dust and died in the ears of the three men who rode before him.

On the sixth day of their traveling, they came to the end of the Smoky Hill Trail.

I I I

The dark green line of trees and brush that they had followed all the way from Butcher's Crossing turned in a slow curve to the south. The four men, who came upon the turning in the midmorning of their sixth day of journey, halted and gazed for some moments at the course of the Smoky Hill River. From where they halted, the land dropped off so that in the distance, through the brush and trees of the banks, they could see the slow-moving water. In the distance it lost its muddy green hue; the sunlight silvered its surface, and it appeared to them clear and cool. The three men brought their horses close together; the oxen turned their heads toward the river and moaned softly; Charley Hoge called them to a halt, and set the brake handle of the wagon; he jumped off the spring seat, clambered from the wagon, and walked briskly over to where the others waited. He looked up at Miller.

"Trail turns here with the river," Miller said. "Follows it all the way up to the Arkansas. We could follow it and be sure of plenty of water, but it would put us near a week off getting where we're aiming at."

Schneider looked at Miller and grinned; his teeth were white in his dust-encrusted face.

"I take it you don't aim to go by the trail."

"It'd put us a week off, maybe more," Miller said. "I've gone across this country before." He waved toward the flat country in the west that lay beyond the Smoky Hill Trail. "They's water there, for a body that knows where it is."

Schneider, still grinning, turned to Andrews. "Mr. Andrews, you don't look like you ever been thirsty in your life; real thirsty, I mean. So I guess it won't do much good to ask you what you want to do."

Andrews hesitated; then he shook his head. "I have no right to speak. I don't know the country."

"And Miller does," Schneider said, "or at least that's what he tells us. So we go where Miller says."

Miller smiled and nodded. "Fred, you sound like you want an extra week's pay. You ain't afraid of a little dry stretch, are you?"

"I've had dry stretches before," Schneider said. "But I never have got over feeling put out when I saw horses and bull-oxes being watered and me with a dry throat."

Miller's smile widened. "It takes the grit out of a man," he said. "It's happened to me. But they's water less than a day from here. I don't think it'll come to that."

"Just one thing more," Schneider said. "How long did you say it's been since you went over this bit of land?"

"A few years," Miller said. "But some things don't leave a man." Though the smile remained on his face, his voice stiffened. "You don't have no serious complaints yet, do you, Fred?"

"No," Schneider said. "I just thought there was a few things I ought to say. I said I'd go along with you back at

Butcher's Crossing, and I'll go along with you now. It don't matter to me one way or another."

Miller nodded, and turned to Charley Hoge. "Reckon we'd better rest the stock and water them up good before we go on. And we'd better carry along as much water as we can, just in case. You take care of the team, and we'll get what water we can back up to the wagon."

While Charley Hoge led the oxen down to the river, the others went to the wagon and found what containers they could for carrying water. From a broad square of canvas that covered their provisions, Miller fashioned a crude barrel, held open and upright by slender green saplings that he cut at the river bank. Two of the more slender saplings he tied together and bent into a circle, and tied again; this he attached near the four corners of the square canvas with leather thongs. The shorter and stubbier saplings he cut to a length, notched, and attached to the circled saplings, thus forming a receptacle some five feet in diameter and four feet in height. With buckets and kettles that Charley Hoge used for cooking and with one small wooden keg, the three men filled the canvas barrel three-quarters full; it took them the better part of an hour to do so.

"That's enough," Miller said. "If we put any more in, it would just slosh out."

They rested in the shade beside the Smoky Hill, while the hobbled oxen wandered along the banks, grazing on the rich grass that grew in the moisture. Because of the intense heat, and because of the dry country over which they would be traveling, Miller told them, they would begin their second drive somewhat later; so Charley Hoge had time to cook up some soaked beans, sowbelly, and coffee. Until the afternoon sun pushed the shade beyond them, they lay wearily on the grassy bank of the river, listening to the rustle of the water that flowed past them smoothly, coolly, effortlessly, that flowed back through the prairie through which they had worked their way, past Butcher's Crossing, and onward to the east. When the sun touched his face, Andrews sat up. Miller said: "Might as well get started." Charley Hoge gathered his oxen, yoked them in pairs, and put them to the wagon. The party turned to the flat land upon which they could see neither tree nor trail to guide them, and went forward upon it. Soon the line of green that marked the Smoky Hill River was lost to them; and in the flat unbroken land Andrews had to keep his eyes firmly fixed on Miller's back to find any direction to go in.

Twilight came upon them. Had it not been for his tiredness, and the awkward, shambling weariness of the horses beneath the weight they carried forward, Andrews might have thought that the night came on and held them where they started, back at the bend of the Smoky Hill. During the afternoon's drive he had seen no break in the flat country, neither tree, nor gully, nor rise in the land that might serve as a landmark to show Miller the way he went. They camped that night without water.

Few words were exchanged as they broke the packs from their horses and set up the night's camp on the open prairie. Charley Hoge led the oxen one by one to the back of the wagon; Miller held the large canvas receptacle erect while the oxen drank. By the light of a lantern he kept careful watch on the level of water; when an ox had drunk its quota, Miller would say sharply: "That's enough," and kick at the beast as Charley Hoge tugged its head away. When the oxen and the horses had drunk, the tank remained one-fourth full.

Much later, around the campfire, which Charley Hoge had prepared with wood gathered at their noon stop, the men squatted and drank their coffee. Schneider, whose tight impassive face seemed to twitch and change in the flickering firelight, said impersonally:

"I never cared for a dry camp."

No one spoke.

Schneider continued: "I guess there's a drop or two left in the tank."

"It's about a fourth full," Miller said.

Schneider nodded. "We can make one more day on that, I figure. It'll be a mite dry, but we should make one more day."

Miller said, "I figure one more day."

"If we don't come across some water," Schneider said.

"If we don't come across some water," Miller agreed.

Schneider lifted his tin cup and drained the last dreg of coffee from it. In the firelight, his raised chin and throat bristled and quivered. His voice was cool and lazy. "I reckon we'd better hit some water tomorrow."

"We'd better," Miller said. Then: "There's plenty of water; it's just there for the finding." No one answered him. He went on. "I must have missed a mark somewhere. There should have been water right along here. But it's nothing serious. We'll get water tomorrow, for sure."

The three men were watching him intently. In the dying light, Miller returned each of their stares, looking at Schneider at length, coolly. After a moment he sighed and put his cup carefully on the ground in front of Charley Hoge.

"Let's get some sleep," Miller said. "I want to get an early start in the morning, before the heat sets in."

Andrews tried to sleep, but despite his tiredness he did not rest soundly. He kept being awakened by the low moaning of the oxen, which gathered at the end of the wagon, pawed the earth, and butted against the closed tailgate that protected the little store of water in the open canvas tank.

Andrews was shaken from his uneasy sleep by Miller's hand on his shoulder. His eyes opened on darkness, and on the dim hulk of Miller above him. He heard the others moving about, stumbling and cursing in the early morning dark.

"If we can get them going soon enough, they won't miss the watering," Miller said.

By the time the false light shone in the east, the oxen were yoked; the party again moved westward.

"Give your horses their heads," Miller told them. "Let them set their own pace. We'll do better not to push any of them till we get some water."

The animals moved sluggishly through the warming day. As the sun brightened, Miller rode far ahead of the main party; he sat erect in his saddle and moved his head constantly from one side to another. Occasionally he got off his horse and examined the ground closely, as if it concealed some sign that he had missed atop his horse. They continued their journey well into the middle of the day, and past it. When one of the oxen stumbled and in getting to its feet gashed at its fellow with a blunt horn, Miller called the party to a halt.

"Fill your canteens," he said. "We've got to water the stock and there won't be any left."

Silently, the men did as they were told. Schneider was the last to approach the canvas tank; he filled his canteen, drank from it in long, heavy gulps, and refilled it.

Schneider helped Charley Hoge control the oxen as, one by one, they were led to the rear of the wagon and the open tank of water. When the oxen were watered and tethered at some distance from the wagon, the horses were allowed to finish the water. After the horses had got from the tank all that they were able, Miller broke down the saplings that gave the canvas its shape, and with Charley Hoge's help drained the water that remained in the folds of the canvas into a wooden keg.

Charley Hoge untethered the oxen and let them graze on the short yellowish grass. Then he returned to the wagon and broke out a package of dried biscuits.

"Don't eat too many of them," Miller said. "They'll dry you out."

The men squatted in the narrow shade cast by the wagon. Slowly and delicately, Schneider ate one of the biscuits and took a small sip of water after it.

Finally he sighed, and spoke directly to Miller: "What's the story, Miller? Do you know where there's water?"

Miller said: "There was a little pile of rocks a piece back I think I remember. Another half-day, and we ought to hit a stream."

Schneider looked at him quizzically. Then he stiffened, took a deep breath, and asked, his voice soft: "Where are we, Miller?"

"No need to worry," Miller said. "Some of the landmarks have changed since I was here. But another half-day, and I'll get us fixed."

Schneider grinned, and shook his head. He laughed softly and sat down on the ground, shaking his head.

"My God," he said. "We're lost."

"As long as we keep going in that direction," Miller

pointed away from their shadows, toward the falling sun, "we're not lost. We're bound to run into water tonight, or early in the morning."

"This is a big country," Schneider said. "We're not bound to do anything."

"No need to worry," Miller said.

Schneider looked at Andrews, still grinning. "How does it feel, Mr. Andrews? Just thinking about it makes you thirsty, don't it?"

Andrews looked away from him quickly, and frowned; but what he said was true. The biscuit in his mouth felt suddenly dry, like sun-beat sand; he had swallowed against the dryness. He noticed that Charley Hoge put his half-eaten biscuit into his shirt pocket.

"We can still cut south," Schneider said. "Another day, at the most a day and a half, we'll run into the Arkansas. The stock might just hold up for a day and a half."

"It would put us a week off," Miller said. "And besides, there's no cause for it; we may get a little dry, but we'll make it all right. I know this country."

"Not so well you don't get lost in it," Schneider said. "I say, we turn to the Arkansas. We'll be sure of water there." He pulled up a tuft of the dry, yellow grass that surrounded them. "Look at this. There's been a drought in this country. How do we know the streams ain't dried up? What if the ponds are empty?"

"There's water in this country," Miller said.

"Seen any sign of buffalo?" Schneider looked at each of them. "Not a sign. And you won't find buffalo where there ain't no water. I say, we ought to head for the Arkansas."

Miller sighed and smiled distantly at Schneider. "We'd never make it, Fred."

"What?"

"We'd never make it. We've been heading at an angle ever since we left the Smoky Hill. With watered stock, it would take us two and a half days—almost as bad as going back to the Smoky Hill. Dry, this stock would never make it."

"God damn it," Schneider said quietly, "you ought to have let us know."

Miller said: "There's nothing to worry about. I'll get you to water, if I have to dig for it."

"God damn it," Schneider said. "You son of a bitch. I'm half a mind to cut out on my own. I might just make it."

"And you might not," Miller said. "Do you know this country, Fred?"

"You know damn well I don't," Schneider said.

"Then you'd better stick with the party."

Schneider looked from one of them to another. "You're pretty sure the party's going to stick with you?"

Miller's tight face relaxed, and the loose ridges came again about the corners of his mouth. "I'm going ahead, just like I've been going. I just have to get the feel of the land again. I've been watching too close, trying too hard to remember. Once I get the feel of the country again, I'll be all right. And the rest of you will be all right, too."

Schneider nodded. "Hoge will stick with you, I guess. That right, Charley?"

Charley Hoge lifted his head abruptly, as if startled. He rubbed the stump of his wrist. "I go where God wills," he said. "He will lead us to where water is when we are athirst."

"Sure," Schneider said. He turned to Andrews. "Well, that leaves us, Mr. Andrews. What do you say? It's your wagon and your team. If you say we go south, Miller would have a hard time going against you."

Andrews looked at the ground; between the dry thin blades of grass the earth was powdery. Though he did not look up, he felt the eyes of the others upon him. "We've come this far," he said. "We might as well keep on with Miller."

"All right," Schneider said. "You're all crazy. But it looks like I've got no choice. Do whatever you want to do."

Miller's thin flat lips lengthened in a slight smile. "You worry too much, Fred. If it gets that bad, we can always get by on Charley's whisky. There must be nine or ten gallons of it left."

"The horses will be glad to hear that," Schneider said. "I can see us walking out of here on ten gallons of whisky."

"You worry too much," Miller said. "You'll live to be a hundred and five."

"I've had my say. I'll go along with you. Now let me get some rest." He lay on his side, rolled under the shade of the wagon, and came to rest with his back to them.

"We all might as well try to get some sleep," Miller said. "It won't do to travel in the heat. We'll rest ourselves, and get the drive started this evening."

Lying on his side, his folded arm supporting his head, Andrews looked out of the shade across the level prairie. As far as he could see, the land was flat and without identity. The blades of grass that stood up stiffly a few inches from his nose blurred and merged into the distance, and the distance came upon him with a rush. He closed his eyes upon what he saw, and his vague fingers pushed at the grass until they parted it, and he could feel the dry powdery earth upon his fingertips. He pressed his body against the ground, and did not look at anything, until the terror that had crept upon him from his dizzying view of the prairie passed, as if through his fingertips, back into the earth whence it had come. His mouth was dry. He started to reach for his canteen, but he did not. He forced thirst away from him, and put thought from his mind. After a while, his body, tense against the earth, relaxed; and before the afternoon was over, he slept.

When the edge of the sun cut into the far horizon they resumed their journey.

Night came on rapidly. In the moonlight, Miller, ahead of them, was a frenzied, hunched figure, whose body swayed this way and that in his saddle. Though Andrews and Schneider let their horses go at their own paces, Miller spurred in an erratic zigzag across the land that seemed to glow out of the night. To no apparent purpose, Miller would cut at a sharp angle from a path they took, and follow the new course for half an hour or so, only to abandon it and cut in another direction. For the first few hours, Andrews tried to keep their course in his mind; but weariness dulled his attention, and the stars in the clear sky, and the thin moon, whirled about his head; he closed his eyes and slumped forward in the saddle, letting his horse trail Schneider and Miller. Even in the cool of the night, thirst gnawed at him, and occasionally he took a small sip of water from his canteen. Once they paused to let the oxen graze; Andrews remained in his saddle, sleepily aware of what was going on.

They traveled into the next morning, and into the heat of the day. The oxen moved slowly; they moaned almost constantly, and their breaths were dry and rasping. Even Andrews could see that their coats were growing dull, and that the bones were showing sharply along their ribs and flanks.

Schneider rode up beside him and jerked his head back in the direction of the oxen. "They look bad. Their tongues will start swelling next. Then they won't be able to breathe and pull at the same time. We should have headed south. With luck, we might have made it."

Andrews did not answer. His throat felt unbearably dry. Despite himself he reached behind his saddle for his canteen and took two long swallows of water. Schneider grinned and drew his horse away. With an effort of will Andrews closed his canteen and replaced it behind his saddle.

Shortly before noon Miller pulled his horse to a halt, dismounted, and walked back toward the slowly moving wagon. He motioned to Charley Hoge to stop.

"We'll wait the heat out here," he said shortly. He walked into the shade of the wagon; Schneider and Andrews came up to him. "They look bad, Miller," Schneider said. He turned to Charley Hoge: "How do they drive?"

Charley Hoge shook his head.

"Their tongues are beginning to swell. They won't last out the day. And the horses. Look at them."

"Never mind that," Miller said. His voice was low and toneless, almost a growl. The black pupils of his eyes were shining and blank; they were fixed upon the men without appearing to see them. "How much water's left in the canteens?"

"Not much," Schneider said. "Maybe enough to get us through the night."

"Get them," Miller said.

"Now look," Schneider said. "If you think I'm going to use water for anything except myself, you—"

"Get them," Miller said. He turned his eyes to Schneider.

Schneider cursed softly, got to his feet, and returned with his own and Andrews's canteens. Miller gathered them, put his with them, and said to Charley Hoge: "Charley, get the keg and bring your canteen down here."

Schneider said: "Now, look, Miller. Those oxen will never make it. No use wasting what little water we got. You can't—"

"Shut up," Miller said. "Arguing about it will just make us drier. Like I said, we still have Charley's whisky."

"My God!" Schneider said. "You were serious."

Charley Hoge returned to the shade beside the wagon and handed Miller a canteen and the wooden keg. Miller set the keg carefully on the ground, rotating it a few times under the pressure of his hands so that it rested level on the stubby grass. He unscrewed the tops of the canteens, one by one, and carefully poured the water into the keg, letting the canteens hang above it for several minutes, until the last globules of water gathered on the mouths, hung, and finally dropped. After the last canteen was emptied, about four inches of water was in the keg.

Schneider picked up his empty canteen, looked at it carefully, and then looked at Miller. With all his strength, he flung the canteen against the side of the wagon, from where it rebounded back toward him, past him, and fell into the grass.

"God damn it!" he shouted; his voice was startling in the hot prairie quiet. "What good do you expect to do with that little bit of water? You're throwing it away!"

Miller did not look at him. He spoke to Charley Hoge: "Charley, unyoke the oxen and lead them around here one at a time."

While the three men waited—Miller and Andrews still, Schneider quivering and turning in an impotent rage—Charley Hoge singly detached the oxen and led them around to Miller. Miller took a rag from his pocket, soaked it in the water, and squeezed it gently, holding it carefully above the keg so that no water was lost.

"Fred, you and Will get a hold of his horns; hold him steady."

While Schneider and Andrews grasped each of the horns,

Charley Hoge circled the beast's bony and corded neck with his good arm, digging his heels in the ground and pulling against the forward surge of the ox. With the wet rag, Miller bathed the dry lips of the ox; then he put the rag into the water again and squeezed it so that no water was wasted.

"Pull up on the horns," he said to Schneider and Andrews.

When the ox's head was up, Miller grasped the upper lip of the beast and pulled upward. The tongue, dark and swollen, quivered in its mouth. Again with care, Miller bathed the rough distended flesh; his hand and wrist were thrust out of sight up into the ox's throat. Withdrawing his hand, he squeezed hard on the wet rag, and a few drops of water trickled on the tongue, which absorbed them like a dark dry sponge.

One by one the oxen's mouths were bathed. Sweatless and hot, the three men held the beasts and dug their feet into the earth; Schneider cursed steadily, quietly; Andrews breathed in heavy gasps the dry air that was rough like a burr in his throat, and tried to keep his arms from trembling loose from the smooth hot horns of the oxen. After each ox had been treated, Charley Hoge led it back to its yoke and returned with another. Despite the haste with which they worked, it was the better part of an hour before they finished with the last animal.

Miller leaned against the side of the wagon; his dry, leatherlike skin stood out from his black beard with a faint yellowish cast.

"They ain't so bad," he said breathing heavily. "They'll last to nightfall; and we still got a bit of water left." He pointed to the muddy inch or so of water that remained in the keg.

Schneider laughed; it was a dry sound that turned into a cough. "A pint of water for eight oxen and three horses."

"It'll keep the swelling down," Miller said. "It's enough for that."

Charley Hoge returned from the front of the wagon. "Do we unyoke them now and take a rest?"

"No," Miller said. "Their tongues'll swell as bad standing

here as they will if we keep on. And we can keep them from grazing better if we're on the move."

"On the move where?" Schneider said. "How long you think them cows can pull this here wagon?"

"Long enough," Miller said. "We'll find water."

Schneider moved suddenly, and whirled to Miller. "I just thought," he said. "How much lead and powder you got in that wagon?"

"Ton and a half, two tons," Miller said, not looking at him.

"Well, my God," Schneider said. "No wonder them animals is dry. We could go twice as far if we'd dump the stuff."

"No," Miller said.

"We can find water, and maybe come back and pick it up. It ain't as if we intended to just leave it here."

"No," Miller said. "We get there like we started out, or we don't get there at all. There ain't no need to get in a panic."

"You crazy son of a bitch," Schneider said. He kicked one of the heavy hickory wheel spokes. "God damn it. Crazier'n hell." He kicked the spoke again, and pounded a fist on the rim of the wheel.

"Besides," Miller said calmly, "it wouldn't make all that difference. On this land, a full wagon can pull almost as easy an an empty one, once the team gets started."

"It's no good talking to him," Schneider said. "No good at all." He strode out of the shade and went to his horse, which had been tethered to the end of the wagon, its head held high so that it could not graze. Andrews and Miller followed him more slowly.

"It does Fred good to blow off now and then," Miller said to Andrews. "He knows if we left the load here we might be a week finding it again, if we found it at all. Looking for it might put us in as bad shape as we are now. We don't leave a heavy enough trail to follow back, and you can't mark a trail very well in land like this."

Andrews looked behind him. It was true. The wheels of the wagon in the short stiff grass, on the baked earth, left hardly an impression; even now the grass over which they had driven was springing erect to hide the evidence of their passage. Andrews tried to swallow, but the contraction of his muscles was stopped by his dry throat.

Their horses moved sluggishly; and beneath Charley Hoge's cracking whip and before his thin sharp voice, the oxen moved weakly against the pull of the wagon. They shambled unsteadily forward, working not as a team but as separate beasts struggling from the whip and the sound of the driving voice behind them. Once in the afternoon the party came near a shallow depression in the earth, the bottom of which was cracked in an intricate pattern of dried mud. They looked sullenly at the dried-up pond and did not speak.

In the middle of the afternoon, Miller forced each of them to take a short swallow of Charley Hoge's whisky.

"Don't take much," he warned. "Just enough to get your throat wet. More than that will make you sick."

Andrews gagged on the liquor. It seared his dry tongue and throat as if a torch had been thrust into his mouth; when he ran his tongue over his cracked dry lips, they burned with a pain that lingered for many minutes later. He closed his eyes and clung to his saddle horn as the horse went forward; but the darkness upon his closed eyelids was shot with spears of light that whirled dizzily; he was forced to open them again and observe the trackless and empty way they went.

By sundown the oxen again were breathing with sharp grunting moans; their tongues were so swollen that they moved with their mouths half open; their heads were down, swinging from side to side. Miller called the wagon to a halt. Again Schneider and Andrews held the horns of the beasts; but even though both men were much weaker than they had been earlier, their task was easier. The oxen dumbly and without resistance let themselves be pulled around, and did not even show interest in the water with which Miller bathed their mouths.

"We won't stop," Miller said. His voice was a heavy flat croak. "Better to keep them moving while they're still on their feet."

He stood the bucket on its edge and sopped up the last

of the water with the rag. He bathed the mouths of the horses; when he finished, the rag was almost dry.

After the sun dropped beneath the flat horizon before them, darkness came on quickly. Andrews's hands clung to the saddle horn; they were so weak that again and again they slipped from it, and he hardly had the strength to pull them back. Breathing was an effort of agony; slumped inertly in his saddle, he learned to snuffle a little air through his nostrils and to exhale it quickly, and to wait several seconds before he repeated the process. Sometime during the night he discovered that his mouth was open and that he could not close it. His tongue pushed between his teeth, and when he tried to bring them together a dull dry pain spread in his mouth. He remembered the sight of the oxen's tongues, black and swollen and dry; and he pushed his mind away from that image, away from himself, and tried to push his mind into a place as dark and unbounded as the night in which he traveled. Once, an ox stumbled and would not get back upon its feet; the three men had to dismount and with their little remaining strength pull and tug and prod the beast upright. Then the oxen would not or could not summon strength to get the wagon into motion, so the three pushed against the wagon spokes, while Charley Hoge's whip cracked above the oxen, until the wheels began to move and the beasts took up the forward movement in a slow shamble. Andrews tried to wet his mouth with a little of Charley Hoge's whisky, but most of the liquid ran off his lips down the corners of his mouth. He rode most of the night in a state that alternated between a mild delirium and intense pain. Once he came to his senses and found himself alone in the darkness; he had no sense of place, no knowledge of direction. In a panic he whirled one way and another in his saddle; he looked upward into the immense bowl of the sky, and downward at the earth upon which he rode; and the one seemed as far away as the other. Then he heard faintly the creak of the wagon, and prodded his horse in that direction. In a few moments he was back with the others, who had not noticed his lagging behind. Even with them, he shivered for a long while, the panic he had felt when he thought himself abandoned still upon him; for a long while the panic kept him alert, and he followed Miller's dim movements, not as if those movements might lead him where he wished to go, but as if they might save him from wandering into a nothingness where he would be alone.

Shortly after dawn, they found water.

Afterward Andrews remembered as if from a dream the first sign they had that water was near. In the early light from the east Miller stiffened in his saddle and raised his head like an alert animal. Then, almost imperceptibly, he pulled his horse in a slightly northerly direction, his head still raised and alert. A few moments later he reined his horse more sharply north, so that Charley Hoge had to dismount from the wagon and prod the oxen toward Miller's horse. Then, as the first small edge of the sun came above the flat line in the east, Andrews was aware that his horse had begun to quiver beneath him. He saw that Miller's horse, too, was straining impatiently; its ears were pitched sharply forward, and it was held by Miller's taut reins. Miller twisted in his saddle and faced those behind him. In the soft yellow light that fell upon Miller's face, Andrews could see the cracked lips, raw and slightly bleeding from the distended cracks, parted in a grotesque smile.

"By God," Miller called; his voice was rasping and weak, but it held a deep note of triumph. "By God, we found it. Hold your horses back, and—" Turning still farther around, he raised his voice, "Charley, hold on to them oxen as hard as you can. They'll smell it in a few minutes, and they're like to go crazy."

Andrews's horse bolted suddenly; startled, he pulled back with all his strength on the reins, and the horse reared upward, its front hooves pawing the air. Andrews leaned frantically forward, burrowing his face in the horse's mane, so that he would not topple off.

By the time they came in sight of the stream, which wound in a flat treeless gully cut on the level land, the animals were quivering masses of flesh held back by the tiring muscles of the men. When the sound of the stream came to their ears, Miller called back to them: "Jump off, and let 'em go!"

Andrews lifted one foot from a stirrup; as he did so, the horse, relieved of the pressure of the reins, lunged forward, spilling Andrews to the ground. By the time he got to his feet, the horses were at the stream, on their knees, their heads thrust down into the shallow trickle.

Charley Hoge called from the wagon: "Somebody come here and give me a hand with this brake!" With his hand and with the crook of the elbow of his other arm, he was pulling against the large hand brake at the side of the wagon; the locked wheels of the wagon tore through the short grass, raising dust. Andrews stumbled across the ground and climbed upon the wagon by way of the unmoving wheel spokes. He took the hand brake from Charley Hoge's grasp.

"Got to get them unyoked," Charley Hoge said. "They'll kill theirselves if they go at this much longer."

The brake jerked and trembled under Andrews's grasp; the smell of scorched wood and leather came to his nostrils. Charley Hoge jumped from the wagon and ran to the lead team. With deft movements, he knocked the pins from an oxbow, and jerked the oxbow from the yoke, jumping aside as the ox lunged forward, past him, toward the stream. Miller and Schneider stood on either side of the team, trying to quiet the oxen as Charley Hoge unyoked them. When the last ox was unyoked, the three men went in a stumbling trot across the ground to a spot a few feet upstream from where the animals were lined.

"Take it easy," Miller said, when they had flung themselves down on their stomachs beside the narrow, muddy stream. "Just get your mouths wet at first. Try to drink too much, and you'll make yourselves sick."

They wet their mouths and let a little of the water trickle down their throats, and then lay for a few moments on their backs, letting their hands remain behind their heads, the water trickling softly and coolly over them. Then they drank again, more deeply; and rested again.

They stayed at the stream all that day, letting the animals have their fill of water, and grazing them on the short dry grass. "They've lost a lot of strength," Miller said. "They'll be a full day getting even part of it back."

Shortly before noon, Charley Hoge gathered some drift-wood that he found along the stream, and started a fire. He put some dry beans on to cook, and fried some side meat, which they wolfed immediately with the last of the dried biscuits, washing it all down with quantities of coffee. They slept the afternoon through; while they slept, the fire died down beneath the beans, and Charley Hoge had to start it again. Later, in the darkness, they ate the beans, under-cooked and hard, and drank more coffee. They listened for a while to the slow, contented movement of the livestock around them; and themselves contented, they lay on their bedrolls around the embers of the campfire and slept, hear-ing in their sleep the quiet thin gurgle of the stream they had found.

They resumed their journey before dawn the next morn-ing, only a little weak from the ordeal of thirst they had endured. Miller led the party with more confidence, now that water had been found. He spoke of the water as if it were a live thing that attempted to elude him. "I've found it, now," he had said back at the camp beside the stream. "It won't get away from me again."

And it did not get away. They made their way westward in an erratic course over the featureless land, finding water always at their day's end; usually they came upon it in darkness, when to Schneider and Andrews it seemed im-possible that it could be found.

On the fourteenth day of their journey, they saw the mountains.

For much of the previous afternoon, they had traveled toward a low bank of clouds that distantly shrouded the western horizon, and they had traveled into the night be-fore they found water. So they rose late that morning.

By the time they awoke, the sky was steel-blue and the sun was burning heavily in the east. Andrews rose from his bedroll with a start; they had not remained so late in camp during all the journey. The other men were still in their bedrolls. He started to call to them; but his eyes were caught by the brilliant clearness of the sky. He let his eyes wander unfocused over the high clear dome; and as they settled to the west, as they always settled, he stiffened and looked more closely. A small low uneven hump of dark blue rose on the farthest extremity of land that he could see. He sprang up and went a few steps forward, as if those few steps would enable him to see more closely. Then he turned back to the sleeping men; he went to Miller and shook his shoulder excitedly.

"Miller!" he said. "Miller, wake up."

Miller stirred and opened his eyes, and came quickly to a sitting position, instantly awake.

"What is it, Will?"

"Look." Andrews pointed to the west. "Look over there."

Not looking where Andrews pointed, Miller grinned. "The mountains. I reckoned we should be in sight of them sometime today."

By this time the others were awake. Schneider looked once at the thin far ridge, shrugged, got his bedroll together and lashed it behind his saddle. Charley Hoge gave the mountains a quick glance and turned away, busying himself with the preparations for the morning meal.

Late in the morning they began again their long trek westward. Now that their goal was visible, Andrews found that the land upon which they traveled took on features that he had not been able to recognize before. Here the land dipped into a shallow gully; there a small cropping of stone stood out from the earth; elsewhere in the distance a scrubby patch of trees smudged the greenish-yellow of the landscape. Before, his eyes had remained for most of the time fixed upon Miller's back; now they strained into the distance, toward the uneven hump of earth, now sharp, now blurred, upon the far horizon. And he found that he hungered after them much as he had thirsted after the water; but he knew the mountains were there, he could see them; and he did not know precisely what hunger or thirst they would assuage.

The journey to the foothills took them four days. Gradually, with their going, the mountains spread and reared upon the land. As they came nearer Miller grew more impatient; when they nooned at a stream (the number of which increased as they traveled), he was hardly able to wait for the stock to water and graze. He urged them on, more and more swiftly, until at last the crack and hiss of Charley Hoge's whip was regular and steady and the oxen's lips were flecked and dripping with white foam. They drove late into each night, and were on the move again before the sun rose.

Andrews felt that the mountains drew them onward, and drew them with increasing intensity as they came nearer, as if they were a giant lodestone whose influence increased to the degree that it was more nearly approached. As they came nearer he had again the feeling that he was being absorbed, included in something with which he had had no relation before; but unlike the feeling of absorption he had experienced on the anonymous prairie, this feeling was one which promised, however vaguely, a richness and a fulfillment for which he had no name.

Once they came upon a broad trail running north and south. Miller paused upon it, got off his horse, and examined the path that had been worn in the grass.

"Cattle trail, looks like. They must have started running cattle up from Texas." He shook his head. "It wasn't here the last time I come through."

Late in the afternoon, just before dark, Andrews saw in the distance the long thin parallel lines of a railroad, which found a level course by winding among the gentle hillocks that were beginning to swell upon the land; but Miller had already seen it.

"My God!" Miller said. "A railroad!"

The men increased the paces of their mounts, and in a few minutes halted beside the humped foundation of the road. The tops of the rails gleamed dully in the last light of the sun. Miller got off his horse and stood unmoving for a moment. He shook his head, knelt, and ran his fingers over the smooth steel of the tracks. Then, his hand still upon the metal, he raised his eyes to the mountains, which now loomed high and jagged in the orange and blue light of the afternoon sky.

"My God!" he said again. "I never thought they'd get a railroad in this country."

"Buffalo," Schneider said. He remained on his horse, and

spat at the rails. "Big herd. I never seen big herds yet, where a railroad's been in a few years."

Miller did not look up at him. He shook his head, and then rose to his feet and mounted his horse.

"Come on," he said abruptly. "We got a long way to go before we set up camp."

Though they passed several clear streams, Miller forced them to travel for nearly three hours after dark. The travel was slow, for as they approached the mountains the land was more broken; frequently, they had to skirt large groves of trees that grew near the streams, and had to bypass several sharp hills that rose vaguely out of the darkness. Once, in the distance, they saw the glimmering of a light that might have come from the open door of a house. They continued their drive until they were out of its sight, and for some time afterward.

Early the next morning, they were in the foothills. A few pines were scattered on the sharply rising sides of the hills that cut off their view of the mountains. Miller, riding ahead, guided the wagon along the land that gently rose up to the hills; he pointed to a sharp strip of pines that descended from one of these, and they made in that direction. The hills dropped sharply into a valley; at the bottom of the cut, the land leveled on either side of a small stream. They followed this draw onto a broad flat valley, which stretched to the very base of the mountains.

"We should hit the river by noon," Miller said. "Then we start to climb."

But it was shortly after noon when they came upon the river. The land on the side from which they approached was clear; a few sumacs, already tinged with yellow, and a few clumps of scrub willow straggled along the bank. The bed of the river was wide; it was perhaps two hundred yards from the rise on their side to a steep ledge on the other. But for many yards beyond either bank, and in the bed itself, grass was growing, and even a few small trees and shrubs. Through the years, the river had cut away at earth and solid stone; now it ran thin and shallow at the center of its path in a swath no more than thirty feet in width. It ran smoothly and clearly among rocks, some flat and some thrust sharply up from the bed, here and there breaking into whirling eddies and white-topped riffles.

They nooned at the point at which they had first approached the river. While the other stock was grazing, Miller mounted his horse and rode away in a northeasterly direction, following the river's flow. Andrews wandered away from Charley Hoge and Schneider, who were resting beside the wagon, and sat on the bank. The mountain was a mass of pines. On the far bank the heavy brown trunks raised thirty or forty feet before the boughs spread to hold deep green clusters of pine needles. In the spaces between the huge trunks were only other trunks, and others, on and on, until the few trees that he could see merged into an image of denseness, impenetrable and dark, compounded of tree and shadow and lightless earth, where no human foot had been. He raised his eyes, and followed the surface of the mountain as it jutted steeply upward. The image of the pines was lost, and the image of the denseness, and indeed even the image of the mountain itself. He saw only a deep green mat of needle and bough, which became in his gaze without identity or size, like a dry sea, frozen in a moment of calm, the billows regular and eternally still— upon which he might walk for a moment or so, only to sink as he moved upon it, slowly sink into its green mass, until he was in the very heart of the airless forest, a part of it, darkly alone. He sat for a long time upon the bank of the river, his eyes and his mind caught in the vision he had.

He was still sitting on the bank when Miller returned from his downstream journey.

Miller rode silently up to the resting men, who gathered around him as he drew his horse to a halt and dismounted.

"Well," Schneider said, "you been gone long enough. Did you find what you were looking for?"

Miller grunted. His eyes went past Schneider, and ranged up and down the line of the river that he could see from where he stood.

"I don't know," Miller said. "It seems like the country has changed." His voice was quietly puzzled. "It seems like everything is different from what it was."

Schneider spat on the ground. "Then we still don't know where we are?"

"I didn't say that." Miller's eyes continued to range the line of the river. "I been here before. I been all over this country before. I just can't seem to get things straight."

"If this ain't the damndest chase I ever been on," Schneider said. "I feel like we're looking for a pin in a stack of hay." He walked angrily away from the little group. He sat down at the wagon, his back against the spokes of a rear wheel, and looked sullenly out over the flat valley across which they had traveled.

Miller walked to the bank of the river where Andrews had sat during his absence. For several minutes he stared across the river into the forest of pines that thrust up through the side of the mountain. His legs were slightly spread, and his large shoulders slumped forward; his head drooped, and his arms hung loosely at his sides. Every now and then one of his fingers twitched, and the slight movements turned his hands this way and that. At last he sighed, and straightened.

"Might as well get started," he said, turning to the men. "We ain't going to find nothing as long as we sit here."

Schneider protested that there was no use for them all to join in the search, since only Miller would know the spot he wanted (if even Miller would know it) when he came upon it. Miller did not answer him. He directed Charley Hoge to yoke the oxen; soon the party was making its way in a southwesterly direction, opposite to the way that Miller had taken alone earlier in the afternoon.

All afternoon they made their way upriver. Miller went near the riverbank; sometimes, when the bank became too brushy, he rode his horse into the river itself, where the horse stumbled over the stones that littered the bed nearly to the edge of either bank. Once a thick grove of pines, which grew up to the very bank of the river, deflected the course of the wagon; the men in the main party skirted the grove, while Miller kept to the river bed. Andrews, with Schneider and Charley Hoge, did not see Miller for more than an hour; when finally the wedge-shaped grove was skirted, he saw Miller far ahead of them, upriver, leaning out from his saddle to inspect the far bank.

They made camp early that night, only an hour or so after the sun went down behind the mountains. With darkness, a chill came in the air; Charley Hoge threw more branches on the fire and dragged upon the branches a sizable log, which Schneider, in an excess of energy and anger, had cut from a pine tree whose top had been snapped the winter before by the weight of snow and wind. The fire roared violently in the quiet, driving the men back from it and lighting their faces a deep red. But after the fire died down to large embers the chill came again; Andrews got an extra blanket from the wagon and added it to his thin bedroll.

In the morning, silently, they broke camp. Andrews and Charley Hoge worked together; Schneider and Miller, apart from each other, stood apart from the two who worked. Schneider whittled savagely on a slender bough of pine; the shavings piled up on the ground where he was sitting, between his upraised knees. Miller stood again at the bank of the river, his back to the others, and gazed into the shallow flow of clear water that came from the direction in which they were to travel.

The morning's journey began lethargically. Schneider slumped in his saddle; when he looked up from the ground, his eyes came to rest sullenly upon Miller's back. Charley Hoge snapped the long whip perfunctorily over the ears of the lead oxen, and drank frequently from one of the bottles he kept in the box under his spring seat. Only Miller, who seemed to Andrews to become less and less a part of the group, kept restlessly ahead, now on the bank, now on the edge of the river bed, now in the water itself, which flowed whitely around the fetlocks of his horse. Miller's restlessness began to affect Andrews, and he found himself gazing with an increasing intensity at the anonymous green forest that edged the river and defined the course of their passage.

In the middle of the morning, ahead of them, Miller halted his horse. The horse stood near the center of the river bed; as the others came up close to him, Andrews could see that Miller was gazing thoughtfully, but without real interest, at a spot on the bank opposite them. When the wagon halted, Miller turned to the group and said quietly:

"This is the place. Charley, turn your wagon down here and come straight across."

For a moment, none of them moved. Where Miller pointed was no different from any of the places along the unchanging stretch of mountainside that they had passed that morning or the previous afternoon. Miller said again:

"Come on. Turn your wagon straight across."

Charley Hoge shrugged. He cracked his whip above the left ear of the off-ox, and set the hand brake for the descent down the heavily sloping riverbank. Schneider and Andrews went ahead, following closely behind Miller, who turned his horse straight into the thick forest of pines.

For a moment, as he and Schneider and Miller pressed their horses directly into the face of the forest, Andrews had a sensation of sinking, as if he were being absorbed downward into a softness without boundary or mark. The sound of their horses' breathing, the clop of their hooves, and even the few words the men spoke, all were absorbed in the quiet of the forest, so that all sound came muted and distant and calm, one sound much the same as another, whether it was the snort of a horse or a spoken word; all was reduced to soft thuds which seemed to come, not from themselves, but from the forest, as if there beat within it a giant heart, for anyone to hear.

Schneider's voice, made soft and dull and unconcerned by the forest, came from beside Andrews: "Where the hell are we going? I don't see no sign of buffalo here."

Miller pointed downward. "Look what we're on."

The horses' hooves, Andrews saw, were sliding the smallest bit upon what he had thought was the grayish-green bed of the forest; a closer look showed him that they were riding over a series of long flat stones that grew up from the base of the mountain and wound among the trees.

"They don't leave no track here that a man would notice," Miller said. Then he leaned forward in the saddle. "But look up there."

The stone trail ended abruptly ahead of them, and a natural clearing widened among the trees and wound gradually up the side of the mountain. The bed of this clearing held a broad, regular swath of earth worn bare of grass; raw earth and stones showed the boundaries of the path. Miller kicked his horse up to the point where it began, and dismounted; he squatted in the middle of the path and inspected it carefully.

"This is their road." His hand caressed the hard-packed contours of the earth. "There's been a herd over it not too long ago. Looks like a big one."

"By God!" Schneider said. "By God!"

Miller rose. "It's going to be hard climbing from now on. Better tie your horses to the tail of the wagon; Charley'll be needing our help."

The buffalo trail went up the mountainside at an irregular angle. The wagon made its way up the steeply pitched incline; it went slowly upward, and then dipped sharply down in a hollow, and then went upward again. Andrews, after he had hitched his horse to the tailgate, strode beside the wagon with long, strong steps. The fresh high air filled his lungs, and gave him a strength he was not aware of having felt before. Beside the wagon, he turned to the two men, who were lagging some distance behind.

"Come on," he called in an excess of exuberance and strength; he laughed a little, excitedly. "We'll leave you behind."

Miller shook his head; Schneider grinned at him. Neither man spoke. They shuffled awkwardly over the rough trail; their movements were slow and resigned and deliberate, as if made by old men walking to no purpose and with great reluctance.

Andrews shrugged and turned away from them. He looked ahead at the trail, eagerly, as if each turn would bring him a new surprise. He went in front of the wagon, striding along easily and swiftly; he loped down the small hollows, and climbed the rises with long, heavy thrusts of his legs. At a high rise, he paused; for a moment the wagon was out of his sight; he stood on a large stone that jutted up between two pines, and looked down; the mountain fell off sharply from the trail, and he could see for miles in either direction the river they had crossed only a few minutes before, and the land stretching level to the foothills that lay behind them. The land looked calm and undisturbed; he wondered idly at the half-submerged fear he had had of it during their crossing. Now that they were over it, it had the appearance of a friend known for a long while—it offered him a sense of security, a sense of comfort, and a knowledge that he could return to it and have that security and comfort whenever he wished. He turned. Above him, before him, the land was shrouded and unknown; he could not see it or know where they went. But his view of the other country, the level country behind him, touched upon what he was to see; and he felt a sense of peace.

He heard his name called. The sound came to him faintly from the trail below where the wagon was making its way upward. He leaped down from the rock, and trotted back to the wagon, which had halted before a sharp rise of the trail. Miller and Schneider were standing at the rear wheels; Charley Hoge sat on the clip seat, holding the hand brake against the backward roll of the wagon.

"Give us a hand here," Miller said. "This pull's a little steep for the oxen."

"All right," Andrews said. He noticed that his breath was coming rapidly, and that there was a slight ringing in his ears. He set his shoulder to the lower rear wheel, as Schneider had to the one pitched at a higher level on the other side of the trail. Miller faced him, and pulled at a large round wheel spoke, as Andrews pushed. Charley Hoge's whip whistled behind them, and then cracked ahead of them, over the oxen's heads, as his voice raised in a long, loud "Harrup!" The oxen inched forward, straining; Charley Hoge released the hand brake, and for an instant the men at the wheels felt a heavy, sickening, backward roll; then the weight of the oxen took hold; and as the men strained at the wheels, the wagon slowly began to move forward and upward on the trail.

The blood pounded in Andrews's head. Dimly, he saw muscles like large ropes coil around Miller's forearms, and saw the veins stand out heavily on his forehead. As the

wheel turned, he found another spoke and put his shoulder
to it; his breath came in gasps that sent sharp pains in his
throat and chest. Bright points lighted the dimness in his
eyes, and the points whirled; he closed his eyes. Suddenly
he felt air in front of his hands, and then the sharp stones
of the trail were digging in his back.

As from a great distance, he heard voices.

Schneider said: "He looks kind of blue, don't he?"

He opened his eyes; the brightness danced before him,
and the dark green needles of the pines were very close,
then very far away, and a patch of blue sky was revealed
above the needles. He heard the rasping sound of his own
breath; his arms lay helplessly at his sides, and the heaving
of his chest pushed the back of his head against a rock;
otherwise he did not move.

"He'll be all right." Miller's voice was slow and measured
and easy.

Andrews turned his head. Schneider and Miller were
squatting to his left; the wagon was some distance away,
atop the rise which had momentarily halted it.

"What happened?" Andrews's voice was thin and weak.

"You passed out," Miller told him. Schneider chuckled.
"In these mountains, you got to take it easy," Miller continued. "Air's thinner than what a body's used to."

Schneider shook his head, still chuckling. "Boy, you was
sure going great there for a while. Thought you'd get clean
over the mountain before it hit you."

Andrews smiled weakly, and raised himself on one elbow;
the movement caused his breath, which had quieted somewhat, again to come rapidly and heavily. "Why didn't you
slow me down?"

Miller shrugged. "This is something a body's got to find
out for his self. It don't do no good to tell him."

Andrews got to his feet, and swayed dizzily for a moment;
he caught at Miller's shoulder, and then straightened and
stood on his own strength. "I'm all right. Let's get going."

They walked up the rise to the wagon. Andrews was
breathing heavily again and his hands were shaking by the
time they had gone the short distance.

Miller said: "I'd tell you to ride your horse for a while

till you get your strength back, but it wouldn't be a good idea. Once you get your wind broke, it's better to keep on going afoot. If you rode your horse now, you'd just have it all to do over again."

"I'm all right," Andrews said.

They started off again. This time, Andrews kept behind Miller and Schneider and tried to imitate their awkward, stumbling gait. After a while he discovered that the secret was to keep his limbs loose and let his body fall forward, and to use his legs only to keep his body from the ground. Though his breath still came in shallow gasps, and though after a slightly steep ascent the lights still whirled before his eyes, he found that the peculiar shambling rhythm of the climb prevented him from becoming too tired. Every forty-five minutes Miller called for a halt and the men rested. Andrews noticed that neither Miller nor Schneider sat when they rested. They stood upright, their chests heaving regularly; at the instant the heaving subsided they started off again. After discovering the agony of getting up from a sitting or lying position, Andrews began standing with them; it was much easier and much less tiring to resume the climb from a standing position than from a sitting one.

Throughout the afternoon the men walked beside the wagon; and when the trail narrowed they walked behind it, putting their shoulders to the wheels when a slope caused the hooves of the oxen to slip and slide on the hard trail.

By midafternoon, they had pushed and tugged halfway up the side of the mountain. Andrews's legs were numb, and his shoulder burned from repeated pushings against the wagon wheel. Even when he rested, the sharp thin air, cool and dry, pricked against his throat and caused sharp pains in his chest. He longed to rest, to sit on the ground, or to lie on the soft pine needles just off the trail; but he knew what the pain of rising would be; so he stood with the others when they rested, and looked up the trail to where it disappeared among the thick pines.

Late in the afternoon the trail made a turning so abrupt that Charley Hoge had to back the wagon up several times, angling it more to his right each time, so that finally it could negotiate the angle, its right wheels brushing against the pines, the left coming dangerously close to the brink of a sheer gully that descended three or four hundred feet. Past the turning, the party halted. Miller pointed ahead; the trail went steeply up to a point between two rough peaks, dark and jagged against the bright afternoon sky.

"There it is," Miller said. "Just beyond them peaks."

Charley Hoge cracked his whip above the oxen's ears, and whooped. Startled, the oxen lurched forward and upward; their hooves dug into the earth, and slipped; the men again put their shoulders against the wheels of the wagon.

"Don't push them too hard," Miller called to Charley Hoge. "It's a long pull, all the way to the top."

Foot by foot, they pulled and pushed the wagon up the last steep ascent. Sweat came out on their faces, and was instantly dried by the high, cool air. Andrews heard the groaning sound of air pulled into lungs, and realized that the sound he heard was his own, so loud that it almost drowned out the breathing of the other men, the creak of the wagon as it strained unnaturally upward, and the heavy sounds of the oxen's breathing and plodding and slipping on the trail. He gasped for air, as if he were drowning; his arms, hanging loose as his shoulder ground against the spokes, wanted to flail, as if they might raise him to more air. The numbness of his legs intensified, and suddenly they were numb no longer; he felt that hundreds of needles were pricking into his flesh, and that the needles warmed, became white-hot, and burned outward from his bone to his flesh. He felt that the sockets of his bones—ankle, knee, and hip—were being crushed by the weight they impelled forward. Blood pounded in his head, throbbed against his ears, until even the sound of his own breathing was submerged; and a red film came over his eyes. He could not see before him; he pushed blindly, his will supplanting his strength, becoming his body, until his pain submerged them both. Then he pitched forward, away from the wagon; the sharp stones on the path cut into his hands, but he did not move. He stayed for several moments on his hands and knees, and watched with a detached curiosity the blood from his cut palms seeping out and darkening the earth upon which they rested.

After a few moments, he was aware that the wagon had come to a halt just as he had pitched away from it, and that it was standing level now, no longer at an angle from the trail. On his right the sheer side of a rock thrust upward; to his left, above the wagon, no more than thirty feet away, was another very like it. He tried to get to his feet, but he slipped to his knees and remained there for a moment more. Still on his hands and knees, he saw Charley Hoge sitting erect on the wagon seat, looking out before him, not moving; Miller and Schneider were hanging on the wheels they had pushed; they, too, were looking before them, and they were silent. Andrews crawled a few feet forward, and pushed himself upright; he wiped his bloody hands on his shirt.

Miller turned to him. "There it is," he said quietly. "Take a look."

Andrews walked up to him, and stood looking where he pointed. For perhaps three hundred yards, the trail cut down between the pines; but at that point, abruptly, the land leveled. A long narrow valley, flat as the top of a table, wound among the mountains. Lush grass grew on the bed of the valley, and waved gently in the breeze as far as the eye could see. A quietness seemed to rise from the valley; it was the quietness, the stillness, the absolute calm of a land where no human foot had touched. Andrews found that despite his exhaustion he was holding his breath; he expelled the air from his lungs as gently as he could, so as not to disturb the silence.

Miller tensed, and touched Andrews's arm. "Look!" He pointed to the southwest.

A blackness moved on the valley, below the dark pines that grew on the opposite mountain. Andrews strained his eyes; at the edges of the patch, there was a slight ripple; and then the patch itself throbbed like a great body of water moved by obscure currents. The patch, though it appeared small at this distance, was, Andrews guessed, more than a mile in length and nearly a half mile in width.

"Buffalo," Miller whispered.

"My God!" Andrews said. "How many are there?"

"Two, three thousand maybe. And maybe more. This valley winds in and out of these hills; we can just see a little part of it from here. No telling what you'll find on farther."

For several moments more, Andrews stood beside Miller and watched the herd. He could, at the distance from which he viewed, make out no shape, distinguish no animal from another. From the north a cool wind began to rise; it came through the pass; Andrews shivered. The sun had fallen far below the mountain opposite them, and its shadow darkened the place where they stood.

"Let's get down and set up camp," Miller said. "It'll be dark soon."

Slowly, as if a procession, the group made its way down the incline to the valley. They were at the level ground before dark rolled from the mountain.

IV

They set up camp near a small spring. The spring water flashed in the last light as it poured thinly over smooth rock into a pool at the base of the mountain, and thence overflowed into a narrow stream half hidden by the thick grass of the valley.

"There's a little lake a few miles to the south," Miller said. "That's where the buff'll go to water."

Charley Hoge unyoked the oxen and set them to graze on the valley grass. With the help of Andrews, he dragged the large sheet of canvas from the wagon; then he cut several slender boughs from a young pine, and the two men constructed a box frame, over which they stretched the canvas, securing it carefully and tucking it so that the edges made a floor upon the grass. Then, from the wagon, they lugged the boxes of gunpowder and placed them within the small square tent.

"If I got this powder wet," Charley Hoge chuckled, "Miller would kill me."

After he had finished helping Charley Hoge, Andrews

got an ax and went with Schneider a little way up the side of the mountain and began cutting a supply of wood for the camp. They let the logs remain where they were felled, hacking off the smaller branches and piling them beside the trees. "We'll get the horses and drag them down later," Schneider said. By dark, they had felled half a dozen fair-sized trees. Each returned to the camp with an armload of branches; and they dragged between them the trunk of a small tree.

Charley Hoge had built a fire against a huge boulder, which was twice the height of any of the men and so deeply creviced at one point that it formed a natural draft for the smoke. Though the fire was blazing high, he already had the coffeepot resting at one edge of the fire, and on another he had set the familiar pot of soaked beans. "Last night we'll have to eat beans," Charley Hoge said. "Tomorrow we'll have buffalo meat; maybe I'll even get a little small game, and we'll have a stew."

Across the trunks of two close-set pines, he had nailed a heavy straight bough; upon this bough, neatly hung, were his utensils—a large skillet, two pans, a ladle, several knives whose handles were discolored and scarred but whose blades gleamed in the leaping flame, a small hatchet, and an ax. Resting on the ground was a large iron kettle, the outside black but the inside gleaming a dull grayish-silver. Beside this, against the trunk of one of the trees, was the large box that contained the other provisions.

After the men finished eating, they hollowed long oval depressions in the loose pine needles; in these depressions they laid crisscross small branches, and upon the branches leveled the pine needles they had scooped out, so that they could put their bedrolls upon a springy mattress that held their bodies lightly and comfortably. They placed their bedrolls close to the fire, near the boulder; thus, they were partially protected from weather coming from the north or west across the valley; the forest would hold off the weather from the east.

By the time their beds were made, the fire had died to gray-coated embers. Miller watched the coals intently, his face a dark red in their glow. Charley Hoge lighted the lantern that hung on the bough beside his cooking utensils; the feeble light was lost in the darkness. He carried the lantern to the fire where the men sat. Miller rose and got the heavy iron kettle from the ground and set it squarely in the bed of coals. Then he took the lantern and handed it to Charley Hoge, who followed him to the large box of provisions beside the tree. From the box Miller removed two large bars of lead and carried them to the fire; he stuck them into the kettle, crossing them so that their weight did not upset it. Then he went to the little square tent that Charley Hoge and Will Andrews had constructed, and took from it a box of powder and a smaller box of caps; he carefully tucked the canvas back around the remaining powder before he left.

At the campfire he knelt beside his saddle, which rested near his bedroll, and took from his saddlebag a large loose sack which was secured at the mouth by a leather thong. He untied the thong, and spread the cloth on the ground; hundreds of dully gleaming brass shell cases descended in a loose mound. Andrews edged closer to the two men.

The lead in the blackened kettle shifted above the heat. Miller inspected the kettle, and moved it so that the heat came through more evenly. Then, with a hatchet, he opened the box of gunpowder and tore open the heavy paper that protected the black grains. Between his thumb and fore-finger, he took a pinch and threw it on the fire where it blazed for an instant with a blue-white flame. Satisfied, Miller nodded, and dug again into his saddlebag; he with-drew a bulky flat object, hinged on one side, that opened to disclose a number of shallow depressions evenly spaced and connected to each other by tiny grooves. He carefully cleaned this mold with a greased rag; when Miller closed it, Andrews could see a tiny cuplike mouth at its top.

Again Miller reached into his bag and took out a large ladle. He inserted it in the now-bubbling kettle of lead, and delicately spooned the molten lead into the mouth of the bullet mold. The hot lead crackled on the cool mold; a drop spattered on Miller's hand, which held the mold, but he did not flinch. After the mold was filled, Miller thrust it into a bucket of cold water that Charley Hoge had brought up to him; the mold hissed in the water, which bubbled in white froth. Then Miller withdrew the mold, and spilled the bullets on the cloth beside the cartridge cases.

When the pile of lead bullets was about equal in size to the pile of brass cartridges, Miller put the mold aside to cool. Quickly but carefully he examined the molded bullets; occasionally he smoothed the base of one with a small file; more rarely he tossed a defective one back into the iron kettle, which he had set back from the fire. Before he put the bullets into a new pile beside the empty brass shells, he rubbed the base of each pellet in a square of beeswax. From the square container beside the powder box, he took the tiny caps and thrust them easily into the empty shells, tamping them carefully with a small black tool.

Again from his saddlebag he drew out a narrow spoon and a crumpled wad of newspaper. With the spoon he measured a quantity of gunpowder; over the opened box of gunpowder, he held a shell casing and filled it three-quarters full of the black gunpowder. He tapped the casing sharply on the edge of the box to level the powder, and with his free hand tore a bit from the crumpled newspaper and wadded that into the shell. Finally he picked up one of the lead bullets and jammed it into the loaded shell case with the heel of his palm. Then with his strong white teeth, he crimped the edge of the brass casing where it held the butt of the bullet, and threw the bullet carelessly into yet a third pile.

For several minutes the three men watched Miller reload the shell casings. Charley Hoge watched delightedly, grinning and nodding his head at Miller's skill; Schneider watched sleepily, indifferently, yawning now and then; Andrews watched with intent interest, trying to impress in his memory the precise nature of each of Miller's movements.

After a while Schneider roused himself and spoke to Andrews:

"Mr. Andrews, we got work to do. Get your knives, and let's sharpen them up."

Andrews looked at Miller, who jerked his head in the direction of the large provisions box. In the dim light of the lantern Andrews pawed through the box; at last he found the flat leather case that Miller had got for him back in Butcher's Crossing. He took the case back to the fire, which was now leaping in the flame of a fresh log that Charley Hoge had thrown on. He opened the case. The knives gleamed brightly in the firelight; the bone handles were clean and unscarred.

Schneider had got his knives from his saddlebag; he removed one from its case and tested its edge against his calloused thumb. He shook his head, and spat heartily on a long grayish-brown whetstone, whose center was worn away so that the surface of the stone described a long curve; with the flat of his knife he distributed the spittle evenly on the surface. Then he worked the blade on the stone in a long oval, holding the blade at a careful angle, and managing the oval movement so that the stone bit equally into each part of the blade. Andrews watched him for a few moments; then he selected a knife and tested his own blade on his thumb. The edge pressed into the soft hump of flesh, but it did not bite.

"You'll have to sharpen them all," Schneider said, glancing up at him; "a new knife's got no cutting edge."

Andrews nodded and took from his case a new whetstone; he spat on it, as he had seen Schneider do, and spread the spittle upon the surface.

"You ought to soak your stone in oil for a day or two before you use it," Schneider said. "But I guess it don't make no difference this time."

Andrews began rotating the blade upon the stone; his movements were awkward, and he could not find the rhythm which would allow every part of the blade to be equally whetted.

"Here," Schneider said, dropping his own knife and stone. "You got the blade pitched too high. You might get a sharp edge like that, but it wouldn't last more than one or two skins. Give it to me."

Schneider skillfully ran the blade over the stone, whipping it back and forward so swiftly that Andrews could hardly see it. Schneider turned the blade over and showed Andrews the angle at which he held it to the stone.

"You get a long cutting edge like this," Schneider said. "It'll last you near a full day's skinning without sharpening again. You make your cut too narrow, you'll ruin your knife." He handed the knife butt-first to Andrews. "Try it."

Andrews touched the blade to his thumb; he felt a hot little pain. A thin line of red appeared diagonally across the ball of his thumb; he watched it dumbly as it widened, and as the blood ran irregularly in the tiny whorls of his thumb.

Schneider grinned. "That's the way a knife should cut. You got a good set of knives."

Under Schneider's supervision, Andrews sharpened the other knives. As he sharpened each knife of a different shape or size, Schneider explained its use to him. "This one here's for long work," Schneider said. "You can slit a bull from throat to pecker without taking it out of the skin." And: "This one's for close work, around the hooves. This one's good for dressing your meat down, once the bull's skinned. And this one's for scraping the skin, once she's off."

When at last Schneider was satisfied with the knifes, Andrews returned them to their cases. From the new movement to which he had been introduced, his arm was tired; from the tightness with which he had held the knives while sharpening them, his right hand was numb. A chill wind blew from the pass; Andrews shivered, and moved closer to the fire.

Miller's voice came from the darkness behind the three men who sat silently around the campfire. "Everything ready for tomorrow?" The men turned. The firelight caught the buttons on Miller's shirt and the fringes of his opened buckskin jacket, and glinted on his heavy nose and forehead; his dark beard blended into the darkness so that Andrews had the momentary impression of a head floating above the merest suggestion of a body. Then Miller came up to them and sat down.

"Everything's ready," Schneider said.

"Good." Miller drew a bullet from one of the bulging pockets of his jacket. On a flat rock near the fire he marked with the lead tip a long irregular oval that curved nearly into a semicircle.

"Near as I can remember," Miller said, "this is the shape of the valley. We only saw a little bit of it this afternoon. A few miles on, around this first bend, it widens out to maybe four, five miles across; and it goes on twenty or twenty-five miles. It don't look like a lot of ground, but the grass is thick and rich, and it grows back almost as fast as it's cropped; it'll feed a hell of a lot of buffalo."

In the fire, a burned-through log fell and sent into the air a shower of sparks that glowed and died in the darkness.

"Our job is easy," Miller went on. "We start our kill with the little herd we saw this morning, and then we work down the valley. Nothing to worry about; there ain't no way out of this canyon except the way we came through. Leastways, there's no way for buffalo. Mountains steepen around the first bend; lots of places there's nothing up but sheer rock."

"This'll be the main camp?" Schneider asked.

Miller nodded. "As we work down the valley, Charley'll follow us with the wagon to pick up the hides; we'll bale them back here. We might have to make a few camps away from here, but not many; when we get to the end of the valley, if there are any buffalo left, we can herd them back up toward here. In the long run, it'll save us time."

"Just one thing," Schneider said. "Start us off easy. Mr. Andrews, here, is going to need a few days before he'll be much help. And I don't want to have to skin stiff buffalo."

"The way this is set up," Miller said, "there's no hurry. If we had to, we could stay here all winter picking them off."

Charley Hoge threw another log on the already blazing fire. In the intense heat, the log flared instantly into flame. For that moment, the faces of the four men gathered around the fire were lighted fully, and each could see the other as if in daylight. Then the outer bark of the log burned away, and the firelight died to a steady flame. Charley Hoge waited for several minutes; then, with a shovel, he banked the flames with dead ashes, so that in the yellow light of the lantern the men could see only the whitish-yellow smoke struggling upward through the ashes. Without further words, they turned into their bedrolls.

For a long time after he had bedded down, Will Andrews listened to the silence around him. For a while the acrid smell of the smothered pine log's burning warmed his nostrils; then the wind shifted and he could no longer smell the smoke or hear the heavy breaths of the sleeping men around him. He turned so that he faced the side of the mountain over which they had traveled. From the darkness that clung about the earth he lifted his gaze and followed the dim outlines of particular trees as they rose from the darkness and gradually gained distinctness against the deep blue cloudless sky that twinkled with the light of the clear stars. Even with an extra blanket on his bedroll, he was chilled; he could see the gray cloud of his breath as he breathed the sharp night air. His eyes closed upon the image of a tall conical pine tree outlined blackly against the luminous sky, and despite the cold he slept soundly until morning.

V

When Andrews awoke, Charley Hoge was already up and dressed; he huddled over the fire, adding twigs to the coals that had been kept overnight by the banking. Andrews lay for a moment in the comparative warmth of his bedroll, and watched his breath fog the air. Then he flung the blankets aside, and, shivering, got into his boots, which were stiff and hard from the cold. Without lacing them, he clumped over to the fire. The sun had not yet come over the mountain against which their camp was set; but on the opposite mountain, at the top, a mass of pine trees was lighted by the early sun; a patch of turning aspen flamed a deep gold in the green of the pines.

Miller and Schneider arose before Charley Hoge's coffee began to boil. Miller beckoned to Andrews; the three men trudged out of their cover of trees onto the level valley, where a hundred yards away their hobbled horses were grazing. They led the animals back to the camp and saddled them before the coffee, the side meat, and the fried mush were ready.

"They ain't moved much," Miller said, pointing through the trees. Andrews saw the thin black line of the herd strung out around the bend of the valley. He drank his coffee hurriedly, scalding his mouth. Miller ate his breakfast calmly, slowly. After he finished, he went a little way into the forest and from a low branch selected a forked bough and chopped it off about two feet from the fork; with his knife, he trimmed the fork so that the two small branches protruded from the main branch about six inches; then he sharpened the thick base of the main branch. From his pile of goods beside his bedroll, he got his gun and unwrapped the oilskin which protected it from the night dampness. He inspected the gun carefully, and thrust it into the long holster attached to his saddle. The three men mounted their horses.

In the open valley, Miller pulled his horse up and spoke to the two men on either side of him. "We'll go straight to them. Point your horses behind mine, and don't let them swerve out. As long as we keep straight at them they won't scare."

Andrews rode behind Miller, his horse at a slow walk. His hands ached; he looked at his knuckles; the skin was stretched white across the bones. He relaxed his grip on the reins, and let his shoulders slump; he was breathing heavily.

By the time they had gone halfway across the width of the valley, the herd, slowly grazing, had rounded the bend. Miller led the two men up near the base of the mountain.

"We'll have to go easy from here," he said. "You never know how the wind will be blowing in these mountains. Tie your horses up; we'll go on foot."

Walking one behind the other with Miller in the lead, the men made their way around the blunt rocky base of the mountain. Miller halted suddenly, and held up one hand. Without turning his head, he spoke to those behind him in the normal tones of conversation: "They're just ahead, not more than three hundred yards away. Go easy, now." He squatted and ripped off a few blades of grass and with his hand held high let them fall to the ground. The wind carried the blades back toward him. He nodded. "Wind's right." He rose and went forward more slowly.

Andrews, carrying over one shoulder the bag containing Miller's ammunition, shifted his burden; and as he shifted it, he saw a movement in the herd in front of him.

Again without turning his head, Miller said: "Just keep walking straight. As long as you don't move out of the line, they won't get scared."

Now Andrews could see the herd clearly. Against the pale yellow-green of the grass, the dark umber of the buffalo stood out sharply, but merged into the deeper color of the pine forest on the steep mountainside behind them. Many of the buffalo were lying at ease upon the soft valley grass; those were mere humps, like dark rocks, without identity or shape. But a few stood at the edges of the herd, like sentinels; some were grazing lightly, and others stood unmoving, their huge furry heads slumped between their forelegs, which were so matted with long dark fur that their shapes could not be seen. One old bull carried thick scars on his sides and flanks that could be seen even at the distance where the three men walked; the bull stood somewhat apart from the other animals; he faced the approaching men, his head lowered, his upward curving ebony horns shining in the sunlight, bright against the dark mop of hair that hung over his head. The bull did not move as they came nearer.

Miller paused again. "No need for all of us to go on. Fred, you wait here; Will, you follow me; we'll have to try to skirt them. Buffalo always face downwind; can't get a good shot from this angle."

Schneider dropped to his knees and let himself down to a prone position; with his chin resting on his folded hands, he regarded the herd. Miller and Andrews cut to their left. They had walked about fifteen yards when Miller raised his hand, palm outward; Andrews halted.

"They're beginning to stir," Miller said. "Go easy."

Many of the buffalo at the outer edges of the herd had got to their feet, raising themselves stiffly on their forelegs, and then upon their hind legs, wobbling for a moment until they had taken a few steps forward. The two men remained still.

"It's the moving that stirs them up," Miller said. "You could stand right in front of them all day and not bother them, if you could get there without moving."

The two men began again their slow movement forward. When the herd showed another sign of restlessness, Miller dropped to his hands and knees; Andrews came up behind him, awkwardly dragging the sack of ammunition at his side.

When they were broadside to the herd and about a hundred and fifty yards away from it, they stopped. Miller stuck into the ground the forked branch he had been carrying, and rested his gun barrel on the fork. Andrews crawled up beside him.

Miller grinned at him. "Watch the way I do it, boy. You aim just a little behind the shoulder blade, and about two-thirds of the way down from the top of the hump; that is, if you're shooting from behind, the way we are. This is the heart shot. It's better to get them a little from the front, through the lights; that way, they don't die so quick, but they don't run so far after they're shot. But with a wind, you take a chance, trying to get in front of them. Keep your eye on the big bull, the one with the scars all over him. His hide ain't worth a damn, but he looks like the leader. You always try to pick out the leader of a herd and get him first. They ain't apt to run so far without a leader."

Andrews watched intently as Miller lined his gun upon the old bull. Both of Miller's eyes were open along the sights of his gun barrel. The stock was tight against his cheek. The muscles of his right hand tensed; there was a heavy *crrack* of the rifle; the stock kicked back against Miller's shoulder, and a small cloud of smoke drifted away from the mouth of the gun barrel.

At the sound of the gun, the old bull jumped, as if startled by a sharp blow on his rump; without hurry, he began loping away from the men who lay on their bellies.

"Damn," Miller said.

"You missed him," Andrews said; there was amazement in his voice.

Miller laughed shortly. "I didn't miss him. That's the trouble with heart-shot buffalo. They'll go a hundred yards sometimes."

The other buffalo began to be aroused by the movement of their leader. Slowly at first, a few raised themselves on their thick forelegs; and then suddenly the herd was a dark mass of moving fur as it ran in the direction its leader had taken. In the closely packed herd, the humps of the animals bobbed rhythmically, almost liquidly; and the roar of the hooves came upon the two men who lay watching. Miller shouted something that Andrews could not distinguish in the noise.

The buffalo passed their wounded leader, and ran beyond him some three hundred yards, where their running gradually spent itself, and where they stood, milling uneasily about. The old bull stood alone behind them, his massive head sunk below his hump; his tail twitched once or twice, and he shook his head. He turned around several times, as another animal might have done before sleeping, and finally stood facing the two men who were more than two hundred yards away from him. He took three steps toward them, and paused again. Then, stiffly, he fell on his side, his legs straight out from his belly. The legs jerked, and then he was still.

Miller rose from his prone position and brushed the grass off the front of his clothing. "Well, we got the leader. They won't run so far the next time." He picked up his gun, his shooting stick, and a long wire-handled cleaning patch that he had laid beside him. "Want to go over and take a look?"

"Won't we scare the rest of them?"

Miller shook his head. "They had their scare. They won't be so spooky now."

They walked across the grass to where the dead buffalo lay. Miller glanced at it casually and scuffed its fur with the toe of his boot.

"Ain't worth skinning," he said. "But you have to get the leader out of the way, if you're going to do any good with the rest of them."

Andrews regarded the felled buffalo with some mixture of feeling. On the ground, unmoving, it no longer had that kind of wild dignity and power that he had imputed to it only a few minutes before. And though the body made a huge dark mound on the earth, its size seemed somehow diminished. The shaggy black head was cocked a little to one side, held so by one horn that had fallen upon an unevenness of the ground; the other horn was broken at the tip. The small eyes, half-closed, but still brightly shining in the sun, stared gently ahead. The hooves were surprisingly small, almost delicate, cloven neatly like those of a calf; the thin ankles seemed incapable of having supported the weight of the great animal. The broad swelling side was covered with scars; some were so old that the fur had nearly covered them, but others were new, and shone flat and dark blue on the flesh. From one nostril, a drop of blood thickened in the sun, and dropped upon the grass.

"He wasn't good for much longer anyway," Miller said. "In another year he would have weakened, and been picked off by the wolves." He spat on the grass beside the animal. "Buffalo never dies of old age. He's either killed by a man or dragged down by a wolf."

Andrews glanced across the body of the buffalo and saw the herd beyond. It had settled; a few of the animals were still milling about; but more of them were grazing or resting on the grass.

"We'll give them a few minutes," Miller said. "They're still a mite skittish."

They walked around the buffalo that Miller had killed and made their way in the direction of the herd. They walked slowly but with less caution than they had during their first approach. When they came within two hundred and fifty yards, Miller stopped and tore off a small handful of grass-blades; he held them up and let them fall. They fell slowly downward, scattering this way and that. Miller nodded in satisfaction.

"Wind's died," he said. "We can get on the other side, and run them back toward camp; less hauling of the skins that way."

They made a wide circle, approached, and stopped a little

more than a hundred yards away from the closely bunched
herd. Andrews lay on his stomach beside Miller, who ad-
justed his Sharps rifle in the crotch of his shooting stick.

"Should get two or three this time, before they run," he
said.

He examined the disposition of the herd with some care
for several minutes. More of the buffalo lowered themselves
to the grass. Miller confined his attention to the buffalo
milling around the edges of the herd. He leveled his rifle
toward a large bull that seemed more active than the others,
and squeezed gently on the trigger. At the noise of his shot,
a few of the buffalo got to their feet; they all turned their
heads in the direction from which the shot came; they
seemed to stare at the little cloud of smoke that rose from
the barrel of the gun and thinned in the still air. The bull
gave a start forward and ran for a few steps, stopped, and
turned to face the two men who lay on the ground. Blood
dropped slowly from both nostrils, and then dropped more
swiftly, until it came in two crimson streams. The buffalo
that had begun to move away at the sound of the shot,
seeing their new leader hesitate, stopped in wait for him.

"Got him through the lights," Miller said. "Watch." He
reloaded his rifle as he spoke, and swung it around in search
of the most active of the remaining buffalo.

As he spoke, the wounded bull swayed unsteadily, staggered, and with a heavy lurch fell sideways. Three smaller
animals came up curiously to the fallen bull; for a few
seconds they stared, and sniffed at the warm blood. One
of them lifted its head and bawled, and started to trot
away. Immediately, beside Andrews, another shot sounded;
and the younger bull jumped, startled, ran a few feet, and
paused, the blood streaming from its nostrils.

In quick succession, Miller shot three more buffalo. By
the time he had shot the third, the entire herd was on its
feet, milling about; but the animals did not run. They
wandered about in a loose circle, bawling, looking for a
leader to take them away.

"I've got them," Miller whispered fiercely. "By God,
they're buffaloed!" He upended his sack of ammunition so
that several dozen shells were quickly available to him.

When he could reach them, Andrews collected the empty cartridges. After he had downed his sixth buffalo, Miller opened the breech of his rifle and swabbed out the powder-caked barrel with the cleaning patch tied on the end of the long stiff wire.

"Run back to the camp and get me a fresh rifle and some more cartridges," he said to Andrews. "And bring a bucket of water."

Andrews crawled on his hands and knees in a straight line away from Miller. After several minutes, he looked back over his shoulder; he got to his feet and trotted in a wide circle around the herd. When he turned around the bend in the valley, he saw Schneider sitting with his back propped against a rock, his hat pulled low over his eyes. At the sound of Andrews's approach, Schneider pushed his hat back and looked up at him.

"Miller has them buffaloed," Andrews said, panting. "They just stand there and let him shoot them. They don't even run."

"God damn it," Schneider said quietly. "He's got a stand. I was afraid of it. Sounded like the shots was coming too regular and close."

From the distance, they heard the sound of a shot; it was faint and inoffensive where they heard it.

"They just stand there," Andrews said again.

Schneider pulled his hat over his eyes and leaned against his rock. "You better hope they run pretty soon. Else we'll be working all night."

Andrews went toward the horses, which were standing close together, their heads erect and their ears pitched forward at the sound of Miller's gunfire. He got on his own horse, and set it at a gallop across the valley to their camp.

At his approach, Charley Hoge looked up from his work; he had spent the morning of the other men's absence felling a number of slender aspens and dragging them to the scattered trees at the edge of their camp.

"Give me a hand with some of these poles," Charley called to him as he dismounted. "Trying to set up a corral for the livestock."

"Miller's got a stand of buffalo," Andrews said. "He wants a fresh rifle and some cartridges. And some water."

"'I God," Charley Hoge said. "His name be praised." He dropped the aspen pole that with the crook of his bad arm he had half lifted up across the trunk of a pine, and scurried toward the canvas-covered store of goods near the rock chimney. "How many head?"

"Two hundred fifty, three hundred. Maybe more."

"'I God," Charley Hoge said. "If they don't scatter, it'll be as big a stand as he ever had." From the covered framework of pine boughs, Charley Hoge pulled an ancient rifle whose stock was nicked and stained and split at one point, the split being closed by tightly wound wire. "This here's just an old Ballard—nothing like the Sharps—but it's a Fifty, and he can use it enough to cool his good gun off. And here's some shells, two boxes—all we got. With what he filled last night, ought to be enough."

Andrews took the gun and the shells, in his haste and nervousness dropping a box of the latter. "And some water," Andrews said, stopping to retrieve the box of shells.

Charley Hoge nodded and went across the spring, where he filled a small wooden keg. Handing it to Andrews, he said: "Get a little of this warm before you use it on a rifle barrel; or don't let the barrel get too hot. Cold water on a real hot barrel can ruin it mighty quick."

Andrews, mounted on his horse, nodded. He clasped the keg to his chest with one arm, and reined the horse away from the camp. He pointed his horse toward the sound of the gunfire, which still came faintly across the long flat valley, and let the horse have its head; his arms tightly clasped the water keg and the spare rifle, and he held the reins loosely in one hand. He pulled his horse to a halt near the bend of the valley where Schneider was still dozing, and dismounted awkwardly, nearly dropping the keg of water in his descent. He wrapped the reins about a small tree and made his way in a wide half-circle around the valley bend to where Miller, enveloped now in a light gray haze of gunsmoke, lay on the ground and fired every two or three minutes into the milling herd of buffalo. Andrews crawled up beside him, carrying the water keg with one arm and sliding the rifle over the slick grass with his other hand, which supported him.

"How many of them have you got?" Andrews asked.

Miller did not answer; he turned upon him wide, black-rimmed eyes that stared at, through him, blankly, as if he did not exist. Miller grabbed the extra rifle, and thrust the Sharps into Andrews's hands; Andrews took it by the stock and the barrel, and immediately dropped it. The barrel was painfully hot.

"Clean her out," Miller said in a flat, grating voice. He thrust the cleaning rod toward him. "She's getting caked inside."

Careful not to touch the metal of the barrel, Andrews broke the rifle and inserted the cleaning patch into the mouth of the barrel.

"Not that way," Miller told him in a flat voice. "You'll foul the firing pin. Sop your patch in water, and go through the breech."

Andrews opened the keg of water and got the tufted end of the cleaning rod wet. When he inserted the rod into the breech of the barrel the hot metal hissed, and the drops of water that got on the outside of the barrel danced for a moment on the blued metal and disappeared. He waited for a few moments, and reinserted the patch. Drops of smoke-blackened water dripped from the end of the barrel. After cleaning the fouled gun, he took a handkerchief from his pocket, dipped it into the still-cool spring water, and ran it over the outside of the barrel until the gun was cool. Then he handed it back to Miller.

Miller shot, and reloaded, and shot, and loaded again. The acrid haze of gunsmoke thickened around them; Andrews coughed and breathed heavily and put his face near the ground where the smoke was thinner. When he lifted his head he could see the ground in front of him littered with the mounded corpses of buffalo, and the remaining herd—apparently little diminished—circling almost mechanically now, in a kind of dumb rhythm, as if impelled by the regular explosions of Miller's guns. The sound of the guns firing deafened him; between shots, his ears throbbed dully, and he waited, tense in the pounding silence, almost dreading the next shot which would shatter his deafness with a quick burst of sound nearly like pain.

Gradually the herd, in its milling, moved away from them; as it moved, the two men crawled toward it, a few yards at a time, maintaining their relative position to the circling buffalo. For a few minutes, beyond the heavy cloud of gunsmoke, they could breathe easily; but soon another haze formed and they were breathing heavily and coughing again.

After a while Andrews began to perceive a rhythm in Miller's slaughter. First, with a deliberate slow movement that was a tightening of the arm muscles, a steadying of his head, and a slow squeeze of his hand, Miller would fire his rifle; then quickly he would eject the still-smoking cartridge and reload; he would study the animal he had shot, and if he saw that it was cleanly hit, his eyes would search among the circling herd for a buffalo that seemed particularly restless; after a few seconds, the wounded animal would stagger and crash to the ground; and then he would shoot again. The whole business seemed to Andrews like a dance, a thunderous minuet created by the wildness that surrounded it.

Once during the stand, several hours after Miller had felled the first of the buffalo, Schneider crawled up behind them and called Miller's name. Miller gave no sign that he heard. Schneider called again, more loudly, and Miller jerked his head slightly toward him; but still he did not answer.

"Give it up," Schneider said. "You got seventy or eighty of them already. That's more than enough to keep Mr. Andrews and me busy half the night."

"No," Miller said.

"You got a good stand already," Schneider said. "All right. You don't have to—"

Miller's hand tightened, and a shot boomed over Schneider's words.

"Mr. Andrews here won't be much help; you know that," Schneider said, after the echoes of the gunshot had drifted away. "No need to keep on shooting more than we'll be able to skin."

"We'll skin all we shoot, Fred," Miller said. "No matter if I shoot from now till tomorrow."

"God damn it!" Schneider said. "I ain't going to skin no stiff buff."

Miller reloaded his gun, and swung it around restlessly on the shooting stick. "I'll help you with the skinning, if need be. But help you or not, you'll skin them, Fred. You'll skin them hot or cold, loose or hard. You'll skin them if they're bloated, or you'll skin them if they're froze. You'll skin them if you have to pry the hides loose with a crowbar. Now shut up, and get away from here; you'll make me miss a shot."

"God *damn* it!" Schneider said. He pounded the earth with his fist. "All right," he said, raising himself up to a crouching position. "Keep them as long as you can. But I ain't going to—"

"Fred," Miller said quietly, "when you crawl away from here, crawl away quiet. If these buffalo spook, I'll shoot you."

For a moment Schneider remained in his low crouch. Then he shook his head, dropped to his knees, and crawled away from the two men in a straight line, muttering to himself. Miller's hand tightened, his finger squeezed, and a shot cracked in the thudding quietness.

It was the middle of the afternoon before the stand was broken.

The original herd had been diminished by two-thirds or more. In a long irregular swath that extended beyond the herd for nearly a mile, the ground was littered with the dark mounds of dead buffalo. Andrews's knees were raw from crawling after Miller, as they made their way yard by yard in slow pursuit of the southward list of the circling herd. His eyes burned from blinking against the gunsmoke, and his lungs pained him from breathing it; his head throbbed from the sound of gunfire, and upon the palm of one hand blisters were beginning to form from his handling of the hot barrels. For the last hour he had clenched his teeth against any expression of the pain his body felt.

But as the pain of his body increased, his mind seemed to detach itself from the pain, to rise above it, so that he could see himself and Miller more clearly than he had before. During the last hour of the stand he came to see Miller as a mechanism, an automaton, moved by the moving herd; and he came to see Miller's destruction of the buffalo, not as a lust for blood or a lust for the hides or a lust for what the hides would bring, or even at last the blind lust of fury that toiled darkly within him—he came to see the destruction as a cold, mindless response to the life in which Miller had immersed himself. And he looked upon himself, crawling dumbly after Miller upon the flat bed of the valley, picking up the empty cartridges that he spent, tugging the water keg, husbanding the rifle, cleaning it, offering it to Miller when he needed it—he looked upon himself, and did not know who he was, or where he went.

Miller's rifle cracked; a young cow, hardly more than a calf, stumbled, got to its feet, and ran erratically out of the circling herd.

"Damn it," Miller said without emotion. "A leg shot. That will do it."

While he was speaking, he was reloading; he got another shot off at the wounded buffalo; but it was too late. On the second shot, the cow wheeled and ran into the milling herd. The circle broken, the herd halted and was still for a moment. Then a young bull broke away, and the herd followed, the mass of animals pouring out of their own wide circle like water from a spout, until Miller and Andrews could see only a thin dark stream of bobbing humps thudding away from them down the winding bed of the valley.

The two men stood erect. Andrews stretched his cramped muscles, and almost cried aloud in pain as he straightened his back.

"I thought about it," Miller said, speaking away from Andrews toward the dwindling herd. "I thought about what would happen if I didn't get a clean shot. So I didn't get a clean shot. I broke a leg. If I hadn't thought about it, I could have got the whole herd." He turned to Andrews; his eyes were wide and blank, the pupils unfocused and swimming in the whites. The unbearded skin of his face was black with the ash of gunpowder, and his beard was caked with it. "The whole herd," he said again; and his eyes focused upon Andrews and he smiled a little with the corners of his mouth.

"Was it a big stand?" Will Andrews asked.

"I never had a bigger," Miller said. "Let's count them down."

The two men began to walk back down the valley, following the loose, spread-out trail of felled buffalo. Andrews was able to keep the numbers straight in his mind until he had counted nearly thirty; but his attention was dissipated by the sheer quantity of the dead beasts, and the numbers he repeated to himself spread in his mind and whirled as in a pool; and he gave up his effort to count. Dazedly he walked beside Miller as they threaded their way among the buffalo, some of which had fallen so close together that their bodies touched. One bull had dropped so that its huge head rested upon the side of another buffalo; the head seemed to watch them as they approached, the dark blank shining eyes regarding them disinterestedly, then staring beyond them as they passed. The hot cloudless sun beat down upon them as they plodded over the thick spongy grass, and the heat raised from the dead animals a rank odor of must and wildness; the smooth swishing sound that their boots made in the tall grass intensified the silence around them; the dull pulsations in Andrews's head began to subside, and after the acrid smell of gunpowder, the strong odor of the buffalo was almost welcome. He hitched the empty water keg to a more comfortable position on his shoulder, and strode erect beside Miller.

Schneider was waiting for them where the long swath of buffalo ended. He sat on the mounded side of a large bull; his feet barely reached the ground. Behind him, their horses grazed quietly, their reins knotted loosely together and trailing.

"How many?" Schneider asked sadly.

"A hundred and thirty-five," Miller said.

Schneider nodded somberly. "About what I figured." He slid off the side of the buffalo and picked up his case of skinning knives, which he had put on the ground beside the felled bull. "Might as well get started," he said to An-

drews; "we got a long afternoon and a long night ahead
of us." He turned to Miller. "You going to help?"

For a moment, Miller did not answer. His arms hung
long at his sides, his shoulders drooped, and there was on
his face an expression of emptiness; his mouth hung slightly
open, and his head swung from side to side as he gazed upon
the receding field of dead buffalo. He swung his body
around to Schneider.

"What?" he asked dully.

"You going to help?"

Miller brought his hands up, chest-high, and opened
them. The forefinger of his right hand was puffed and
swollen and curved inward toward his palm; slowly he
straightened it. Across the palm of his left hand a long
narrow blister, pale against the grained blackness of the
surrounding flesh, extended diagonally from the base of the
forefinger to the heel of the palm near the wrist. Miller
flexed his hands and grinned, standing erect.

"Let's get started," he said.

Schneider beckoned to Andrews. "Get your knives, and
come with me."

Andrews followed him to a young bull; the two men
knelt together before it.

"You just watch me," Schneider said.

He selected a long curving blade and grasped it firmly in
his right hand. With his left hand he pushed back the
heavy collar of fur around the buffalo's neck; with his other
hand he made a small slit in the hide, and drew his knife
swiftly from the throat across the belly. The hide parted
neatly with a faint ripping sound. With a stubbier knife,
he cut around the bag that held the testicles, cut through
the cords that held them and the limp penis to the flesh;
he separated the testicles, which were the size of small
crab-apples, from the other parts of the bag, and tossed
them to one side; then he slit the few remaining inches of
hide to the anal opening.

"I always save the balls," he said. "They make mighty
good eating, and they put starch in your pecker. Unless they
come off an old bull. Then you better just stay away from
them."

With still another knife, Schneider cut around the neck of the animal, beginning at that point where he had made the belly slit and lifting the huge head up and supporting it on one knee so that he could cut completely around the throat. Then he slit around each of the ankles, and ripped down the inside of each leg until his knife met the first cut down the belly. He loosened the skin around each ankle until he could get a handhold on the hide, and then he shucked the hide off the leg until it lay in loose folds upon the side of the buffalo. After he had laid the skin back on each leg, he loosened the hide just above the hump until he could gather a loose handful of it. Upon this, he knotted a thin rope that he got from his saddlebag; the other end he tied to his saddle horn. He got in the saddle, and backed his horse up. The hide peeled off the buffalo as the horse backed; the heavy muscles of the bull quivered and jerked as the hide was shucked off.

"And that's all there is to it," Schneider said, getting down from his horse. He untied the rope from the bullhide. "Then you spread it out flat on the ground to dry. Fur side up, so it won't dry out too fast."

Andrews estimated that it had taken Schneider a little over five minutes to complete the job of skinning. He looked at the buffalo. Without its hide, it seemed much smaller; yellowish white layers of fat thinned upon the smooth blue twists of muscle; here and there, where flesh had come off with the skin, dark clots of blood lay on the flesh. The head, with its ruff of fur and its long beard beneath the chin, appeared monstrously large. Andrews looked away.

"Think you can do it?" Schneider asked.

Andrews nodded.

"Don't try to hurry it," Schneider said. "And don't pick an old bull; stick to the young light ones at first."

Andrews selected a bull about the same size as the one Schneider had skinned. As he approached it, it seemed to him that he shrank inside his clothes, which were suddenly stiff upon him. Gingerly he pulled from his case a knife similar to the one Schneider had used, and forced his hands to go through the motions he had seen a few moments be-

fore. The hide, apparently so soft on the belly, offered a
surprising resistance to his knife; he forced it, and felt it
sink into the hide and deeper into the flesh of the animal.
Unable to draw the knife in the smooth easy sweep that he
had observed Schneider use, he hacked an irregular cut
across the belly. He could not make his hands touch the
testicles of the buffalo; instead he cut carefully around the
bag on both sides.

By the time he had slit the hide on the legs and around
the throat, he was sweating. He pulled at the hide on one
of the legs, but his hands slipped; with his knife, he
loosened the flesh from the hide and pulled again. The
hide came from the leg with large chunks of flesh hanging
upon it. He managed to get enough hide gathered at the
hump to take the knot of his rope, but when he backed
his horse up to pull it loose, the knot slipped, and the horse
almost sat back on its haunches. He pulled a bit more of
the hide loose and knotted the rope more firmly. The horse
pulled again. The hide ripped from the flesh, half spinning
the buffalo around; he backed his horse up, and the hide
split, coming off the side of the buffalo and carrying with it
huge hunks of meat.

Andrews looked helplessly at the ruined hide. After a
moment, he turned to seek out Schneider, who was busily
engaged some hundred feet away ripping at the belly of a
large bull. Andrews counted six carcasses that Schneider
had stripped during the time of his own work with a single
one. Schneider looked in his direction, but he did not pause
in his work. He knotted his rope about the hide, backed
his horse up, and spread the shucked skin on the grass.
Then he walked over to where Andrews waited. He looked
at the ruined hide that still was attached to the rump of
the buffalo.

"You didn't get a clean pull," he said. "And you didn't
cut even around the neck. If you cut too deep, you get into
the meat, and that part pulls loose too easy. Might as well
give this one up."

Andrews nodded, loosened the knot around the hide, and
approached another buffalo. He made his cuts more carefully this time; but when he tried to shuck the hide, again

the hide split away as it had done before. Tears of rage came to his eyes.

Schneider came up to him again.

"Look," he said, not unkindly, "I don't have time to fool with you today. If Miller and I don't get these hides off in a few hours, these buffs will be stiff as boards. Why don't you drag a calf back to camp and dress it down? We need some meat, anyhow; and you can work on the carcass, get the feel of it. I'll help you fix up a rig."

Not trusting himself to speak, Andrews nodded; he felt a hot, irrational hatred for Schneider welling up in his throat.

Schneider selected a young cow, hardly more than a calf, and looped a rope around its chin and neck; he pulled the rope short, and knotted it around Andrews's saddle horn, so that with the pull of the horse the head of the buffalo did not drag on the ground.

"You'll have to walk your horse back," Schneider said. "He'll have enough to do dragging this cow."

Andrews nodded again, not looking at Schneider. He pulled the reins, and the horse leaned forward, its hooves slipping in the turf; but the carcass of the young buffalo slid a little, and the horse gained its footing and began to strain its way across the valley. Andrews plodded tiredly before the horse, loosely pulling it forward by the reins.

By the time he got back to the camp, the sun had gone behind the western range of mountains; there was a chill in the air that went through his clothing and touched his sweaty skin. Charley Hoge trotted out from the camp to meet him.

"How many?" Charley Hoge called.

"Miller counted a hundred and thirty-five," Andrews said.

"'I God," Charley Hoge said. "A big one."

Near the camp, Andrews halted his horse and untied the rope from the saddle horn.

"Nice little calf you got," Charley Hoge said. "Make good eating. You going to dress her down, or you want me to?"

"I'll dress her," Andrews said. But he made no movement. He stood looking at the calf, whose open transparent eyes were filmed over blankly with a layer of dust.

After a moment, Charley Hoge said: "I'll help you fix up a scaffold."

The two men went to the area where earlier Charley Hoge had been working on the corral for the livestock. The corral, roughly hexagonal in shape, had been completed; but there were still a few long aspen poles lying about. Charley Hoge pointed out three of equal length and they dragged them back to where the buffalo calf lay. They pounded the ends of the poles into the ground, and arranged them in the form of a tripod. Andrews mounted his horse, and lashed the poles together at the top. Charley Hoge threw the rope, which was still attached to the calf's head, over the top of the tripod, and Andrews tied the loose end to his saddle horn. He backed his horse up until the calf was suspended, its hooves barely brushing the short grass. Charley Hoge held the rope until Andrews returned to the tripod and secured the rope firmly to the top, so that the buffalo would not drop.

The buffalo hung; they surveyed it for a moment without speaking. Charley Hoge went back to his campfire; Andrews stood before the hung calf. In the distance, across the valley, he saw a movement; it was Schneider and Miller returning. Their horses went in a swift walk across the valley bed. Andrews took a deep breath, and put his knife carefully to the exposed belly of the calf.

He worked more slowly this time. After he had made the cuts in the belly, around the throat, and around the ankles, he carefully peeled the hide back so that it hung loosely down the sides of the animal. Then, reaching high above the hump, he ripped the hide from the back. It came off smoothly, with only a few small chunks of the flesh adhering to it. With his knife he scraped the largest of these chunks off, and spread the skin on the grass, flesh side downward, as he had seen Schneider do. While he stood back, looking down at his hide, Miller and Schneider rode up beside him and dismounted.

Miller, his face streaked with the black residue of powder smoke and smears of brownish-red blood, looked at him dully for a moment, and then looked at the hide spread on the ground. He turned and shambled unsteadily toward the campsite.

"Looks like a clean job," Schneider said, walking around the hide. "You won't have no trouble. Course, it's easier when your carcass is hanging."

"How did you and Miller do?" Andrews asked.

"We didn't get halfway through. We'll be working most of the night."

"I wish I could help," Andrews said.

Schneider walked over to the skinned calf and slapped the naked rump of it. "Nice fat little calf. She'll make good eating."

Andrews went to the calf and knelt; he fumbled among the knives in his case. He raised his head to Schneider, but he did not look at him.

"What do I do?" he asked.

"What?"

"What do I do first? I've never dressed an animal before."

"My God," Schneider said quietly. "I keep forgetting. Well, first you better de-gut her. Then I'll tell you how to cut her up."

Charley Hoge and Miller came around the tall chimney rock and leaned against it, watching. Andrews hesitated for a moment, then stood up. He pushed the point of his knife against the breastbone of the calf, and poked until he found the softness of the stomach. He clenched his teeth, and pushed the knife in the flesh, and drew the knife downward. The heavy, coiled blue-and-white guts, thicker than his forearm, spilled out from the clean edge of the cut. Andrews closed his eyes, and pulled the knife downward as quickly as he could. As he straightened up, he felt something warm on his shirtfront; a gush of dark, half-clotted blood had dropped from the opened cavity. It spilled upon his shirt and dripped down upon the front of his trousers. He jumped backward. His quick movement sent the calf rocking slowly on the rope, and made the thick entrails slowly emerge from the widening cut. With a heavy, liquid, sliding thud they spilled upon the ground; like something alive, the edge of the mass slid toward Andrews and covered the tops of his shoes.

Schneider laughed loudly, slapping his leg. "Cut her loose!" he shouted. "Cut her loose before she crawls all over you!"

Andrews swallowed the heavy saliva that spurted in his mouth. With his left hand he followed the thick slimy main gut up through the body cavity; he watched his forearm disappear into the wet warmth of the body. When his left hand came upon the end of the gut, he reached his other hand with the knife up beside it, and sliced blindly, awkwardly at the tough tube. The rotten smell of the buffalo's half-digested food billowed out; he held his breath, and hacked more desperately with his knife. The tube parted, and the entrails spilled down, gathering in the lower part of the body. With both arms, he scooped the guts out of the cavity until he could find the other attachment; he cut it away and tore the insides from the calf with desperate scooping motions, until they spread in a heavy mass on the ground around his feet. He stepped back, pale, breathing heavily through his opened mouth; his arms and hands, held out from his body, dripping with blood, were trembling.

Miller, still leaning against the chimney rock, called to Schneider: "Let's have some of that liver, Fred."

Schneider nodded, and took a few steps to the swinging carcass. With one hand he steadied it, and with the other reached into the open cavity. He jerked his arm; his hand came out carrying a large piece of brownish purple meat. With a few quick strokes of his knife, he sliced it in two, and tossed the larger of the pieces across to Miller. He caught the liver in the scoop of his two hands, and clutched it to his chest so that it would not slide out of his grasp. Then he lifted it to his mouth, and took a large bite from it; the dark blood oozed from the meat, ran down the sides of his chin, and dropped to the ground. Schneider grinned and took a bite from his piece. Still grinning, chewing slowly, his lips dark red from the meat, he extended the meat toward Andrews.

"Want a chew?" he asked, and laughed.

Andrews felt the bitterness rise in his throat; his stomach contracted in a sudden spasm, and the muscles of his throat pulled together, choking him. He turned and ran a few paces from the men, leaned against a tree, doubled over, and retched. After a few moments, he turned to them.

"You finish it up," he called to them. "I've had enough."

Without waiting for a reply, he turned again and walked toward the spring that trickled down some seventy-five yards beyond their camp. At the spring he removed his shirt; the blood from the buffalo was beginning to stiffen on his undershirt. As quickly as he could, he removed the rest of his clothing and stood in the late afternoon shadow, shivering in the cool air. From his chest to below his navel was the brownish red stain of buffalo blood; and in removing his clothing, his arms and hands had brushed against other parts of his body so that he was blotched with stains hued from a pale vermilion to a deep brownish crimson. He thrust his hands into the icy pool formed by the spring. The cold water clotted the blood, and for a moment he feared that he could not remove it from his skin. Then it floated away in solid tendrils; and he splashed water on his arms, his chest, and his stomach, gasping at the cold, straining his lungs to gather air against the repeated shocks of it.

When he had removed from his naked body the last flecks of blood he could see, he knelt on the ground and wrapped his arms around his body; he was shivering violently, and his skin had a faintly bluish cast. He took his clothing, article by article, and immersed it in the tiny pool; he scrubbed it as hard as he could, wringing each article out thoroughly and resubmerging it several times, until the water was muddied and tinged with a dirty red. Finally, with bits of fine gravel and soil gathered from the thin banks of the pool, he scrubbed at his blood-stained boots; but the blood and slime from the buffalo had entered into the pores of the leather and he could not scrub the stain away. He put the wet and wrinkled clothing back on and walked back to the camp. By this time it was nearly dark; and his clothing was stiff with the cold by the time he got to the campfire.

The buffalo had been dressed; the innards, the head, the

hooves, and the lean bony sides had been dragged away from the campsite and scattered. On a spit over the fire, which was smoking and flaming higher than it should have been, was impaled a large chunk of the hump meat; beside the fire on a square of dirty canvas, in a dark irregular pile, was the rest of the meat. Andrews went up to the fire, and put his body against the heat; from the wrinkles of his clothing rose little wisps of steam. None of the men spoke to him; he did not look directly at them.

After a few moments, Charley Hoge took a small box from the canvas-covered cache and examined it by the light of the fire; Andrews saw that it contained a fine white powder. Charley Hoge went around the chimney rock toward the scattered remains of the buffalo, muttering to himself as he went.

"Charley's out wolfing," Miller said to no one. "I swear, he thinks a wolf is the devil himself."

"Wolfing?" Andrews spoke without turning.

"You sprinkle strychnine over raw meat," Miller said. "You keep it up a few days around a camp, you won't have any trouble with wolves for a long time."

Andrews turned so that his back received the heat of the campfire; when he turned, the front of his clothing immediately cooled and the still-wet cloth was icy on his skin.

"But that ain't the reason Charley does it," Miller said. "He looks at a dead wolf like it was the devil his self, killed."

Schneider, squatting on his haunches, rose and stood beside Andrews, sniffing hungrily at the meat, which was beginning to blacken around the edges.

"Too big a piece," Schneider said. "Won't be done for an hour. A body gets a hunger, skinning all day; and he needs food if he's going to skin all night."

"It won't be so bad, Fred," Miller said. "There's a moon, and we'll get a little rest before the meat's done."

"It gets any colder," Schneider said, "and we'll be prying loose stiff hides."

Charley Hoge came into sight around the chimney rock, which now loomed dark against the light sky. He carefully placed the box of strychnine back in its cache, dusted his hands off on his trouser legs, and inspected the buffalo roast. He nodded, and set the coffeepot on the edge of the fire, where some coals were beginning to glow dully. Soon the coffee was boiling; the aroma of the coffee and the rich odor of the meat dripping and falling into the fire blended and came across to the men who waited for their food. Miller smiled, Schneider cursed lazily, and Charley Hoge cackled to himself.

Instinctively, remembering his revulsion earlier at the sight and odor of the buffalo, Andrews turned away from the rich smells; but he realized suddenly that they struck him pleasantly. He hungered for the food that was being prepared. For the first time since he had returned from his cold bath at the spring, he turned and looked at the other men.

He said sheepishly: "I guess I didn't do so good, dressing the buffalo."

Schneider laughed. "You tossed everything you had, Mr. Andrews."

"It's happened before," Miller said. "I've seen people do worse."

The moon, nearly full, edged over the eastern range; as the fire died, its pale bluish light spread through the trees and touched the surfaces of their clothing, so that the deep red glow cast by the coals was touched by the cold pale light where the two colors met on their bodies. They sat in silence until the moon was wholly visible through the trees. Miller measured the angle of the moon, and told Charley Hoge to take the meat, done or not, off the spit. Charley Hoge sliced great chunks of the half-done roast onto their plates. Miller and Schneider picked the meat up in their hands and tore at it with their teeth, holding it sometimes in their mouths while they snapped their fingers from the heat. Andrews sliced his meat with one of his skinning knives; the meat was tough but juicy, and it had the flavor of strong, undercooked beef. The men washed it down with gulps of scalding bitter coffee.

Andrews ate only a part of the meat that Charley Hoge had given him. He put his plate and cup down beside the fire, and lay back on his bedroll, which he pulled up near the fire, and watched the other men wordlessly gorge them-

selves on the meat and coffee. They finished what Charley
Hoge had given them, and ate more. Charley Hoge, himself, ate almost delicately from a thin slice of the roast
which he cut into very small pieces. He washed down the
small bites he took with frequent sips of coffee that he had
strongly laced with whisky. After Miller and Schneider had
finished the last bit of the hump roast, Miller reached for
Charley Hoge's jug, took a long swallow, and passed the jug
to Schneider, who turned the jug up and let the liquor
gurgle long in his throat; he swallowed several times before
he handed the jug to Andrews, who held the mouth of the
jug against his closed lips for several seconds before taking
a small, cautious swallow.

Schneider sighed, stretched, and lay on his back before
the fire. He spoke from deep in his throat, his voice a soft,
slow growl: "A belly full of buffalo meat, and a good drink
of whisky. All a body would need now is a woman."

"There ain't no sin in buffalo meat nor corn whisky," said
Charley Hoge. "But a woman, now. That's a temptation of
the flesh."

Schneider yawned, and stretched again on the ground.
"Remember that little whore back in Butcher's Crossing?"
He looked at Andrews. "What was her name?"

"Francine," Andrews said.

"Yeah, Francine. My God, that was a pretty whore.
Wasn't she kind of heated up for you, Mr. Andrews?"

Andrews swallowed, and looked into the fire. "I didn't
notice that she was."

Schneider laughed. "Don't tell me you didn't get into
that. My God, the way she kept looking at you, you could
have had it for damn near nothing—or nothing, come to
think of it. She said she wasn't working. . . . How was it,
Mr. Andrews? Was it pretty good?"

"Leave it be, Fred," Miller said quietly.

"I want to know how it was," Schneider said. He raised
himself on one elbow; his round face, red in the dull glow
of the coals, peered at Andrews; there was a fixed, tight
smile on his face. "All soft and white," he said hoarsely, and
licked his lips. "What did you do? Tell me what—"

"That's enough, Fred," Miller said sharply.

Schneider looked at Miller angrily. "What's the matter? I got a right to talk, ain't I?"

"You know it's no good thinking about women out here," Miller said. "Thinking about what you can't have will drive you off your feed."

"Jezebels," Charley Hoge said, pouring another cup of whisky, which he warmed with a bit of coffee. "The work of the devil."

"What you don't think about," Miller said, "you don't miss. Come on. Let's get after those hides while we have some good light."

Schneider got up and shook himself as an animal might after having been immersed in water. He laughed, clearing his throat. "Hell," he said, "I was just having me some fun with Mr. Andrews. I know how to handle myself."

"Sure," Miller said. "Let's get going."

The two men walked away from the campfire to where their horses were tethered at a tree. Just before they went beyond the dim circle of light cast by the campfire, Schneider turned and grinned at Andrews.

"But the first thing I'm going to do when we get back to Butcher's Crossing is hire myself a little German girl for a couple of days. If you get in too much of a hurry, Mr. Andrews, you might just have to pull me off."

Andrews waited until he heard the two men ride away, and watched as they loped across the pale bed of the valley, until their dark bobbing shapes merged into the darker rise of the western range of mountains. Then he slid into his bedroll and closed his eyes; he listened for a long while as Charley Hoge cleaned the utensils he had used for cooking, and tidied the camp. After a while there was silence. In the darkness Andrews ran his hand over his face; it was rough and strange to his touch; the beard, which he was constantly surprised to feel upon his face, distracted his hands and made his features unfamiliar to him; he wondered how he looked; he wondered if Francine would recognize him if she could see him now.

Since the night when he had gone up to her room in Butcher's Crossing, he had not let himself think of her. But with Schneider's mention of her name earlier in the evening, thoughts of her flooded upon him; he was not able to keep her image away. He saw her as he had seen her in those last moments in her room before he had turned and fled; seeing her in his mind, he turned restlessly upon his rough bed.

Why had he run away? From where had come that deadness inside him that made him know he must run away? He remembered the sickness in the pit of his stomach, the revulsion which had followed hard upon the vital rush of his blood as he had seen her stand naked and swaying slowly, as if suspended by his own desire, before him.

In the moment before sleep came upon him, he made a tenuous connection between his turning away from Francine that night in Butcher's Crossing, and his turning away from the gutted buffalo earlier in the day, here in the Rocky Mountains of Colorado. It came to him that he had turned away from the buffalo not because of a womanish nausea at blood and stench and spilling gut; it came to him that he had sickened and turned away because of his shock at seeing the buffalo, a few moments before proud and noble and full of the dignity of life, now stark and helpless, a length of inert meat, divested of itself, or his notion of its self, swinging grotesquely, mockingly, before him. It was not itself; or it was not that self that he had imagined it to be. That self was murdered; and in that murder he had felt the destruction of something within him, and he had not been able to face it. So he had turned away.

Once again, in the darkness, his hand came from beneath the covers and moved across his face, sought out the cold, rough bulge of his forehead, followed the nose, went across the chapped lips, and rubbed against the thick beard, searching for his features. When sleep came upon him his hand was still resting on his face.

VI

The days grew shorter; and the green grass of the flat mountain park began to yellow in the cool nights. After the first

day the men spent in the valley, it rained nearly every afternoon, so that they soon got in the habit of leaving their
work at about three and lying about the camp under a
tarpaulin stretched from the high sides of the wagon and
pegged into the ground. They talked little during these
moments of rest; they listened to the light irregular patter
of the rain, broken by the sheltering pines, as it dropped
on the canvas tarpaulin; and they watched beneath the high
belly of the wagon the small rain. Sometimes it was misty
and gray like a heavy fog that nearly obscured the opposite
rise of tree-grown mountain; and sometimes it was bright
and silvery, as the drops, caught by the sun, flashed like
tiny needles from the sky into the soft earth. After the rain,
which seldom lasted for an hour, they would resume their
chase and slaughter of the buffalo, working usually until
late in the evening.

Deeper and deeper into the valley the herd was pushed,
until Andrews, Miller, and Schneider were rising in the
morning before the sun appeared so that they could get in
a good day; by the middle of the first week they had to
ride more than an hour to get to the main herd.

"We'll chase them once clean to the end of the valley,"
Miller said when Schneider complained of their long rides.
"And then we'll chase them back up this way. If we keep
them going back and forth, they'll break up in little herds,
and we won't be able to get at them so easy."

Every two or three days Charley Hoge hitched the oxen
to the wagon and followed the trail of the slaughter, which
was marked by a bunched irregular line of stretched skins.
Andrews and Schneider, and sometimes Miller, went with
him; and as the wagon moved slowly along, the three men
flung the stiff flintskins into the wagon. When all the skins
were picked up, the wagon returned them to the main
camp, where they were again tossed from the wagon upon
the ground. Then the men stacked them one upon another,
as high as they could reach. When a stack was between
seven and eight feet in height, green thongs, stripped from
the skin of a freshly killed buffalo, were passed through the
cuts on the leg-skins of the top and bottom hides, and
pulled tight and tied. Each stack contained between sev-

enty-five and ninety hides, and each was so heavy that it took the combined strength of the four to boost it under the shelter of the trees.

At the skinning, Will Andrews's skill slowly increased. His hands toughened and became sure; his knives lost their new brightness, and with use they cut more surely so that soon he was able to skin one buffalo to Schneider's two. The stench of the buffalo, the feel of the warm meat on his hands, and the sight of clotted blood came to have less and less impact upon his senses. Shortly he came to the task of skinning almost like an automaton, hardly aware of what he did as he shucked the hide from an inert beast and pegged it to the ground. He was able to ride through a mass of skinned buffalo covered black with feeding insects, and hardly be aware of the stench that rose in the heat from the rotting flesh.

Occasionally he accompanied Miller in his stalking, though Schneider habitually stayed behind and rested, waiting for enough animals to be slaughtered for the skinning to begin. As he went with him, Andrews came to be less and less concerned with Miller's slaughter of the beasts as such; he came to notice the strategy that Miller employed at keeping the buffalo confined to a reasonable area, and at keeping the felled animals in such a pattern that they might be easily and economically skinned.

Once Miller allowed Andrews to take his rifle and attempt a stand. Lying on the ground on his stomach, as he had so often seen Miller do, Andrews chose his buffalo and caught him cleanly through the lungs. He killed three more before he shot badly and the small herd dispersed. When it was over he let Miller go ahead while he remained on his stomach, toying with the empty cartridges he had used, trying to fix the feelings he had had at the kill. He looked at the four buffalo that lay nearly two hundred yards away from him; his shoulder tingled from the heavy recoil of the Sharps rifle. He could feel nothing else. Some grassblades worked their way into his shirt front and tickled his skin. He got up, brushed the grass away, and walked slowly away from where he had lain, away from Miller, and went to where Schneider lay on the grass, near where their horses were tethered to one of the pines that stood down from the mountainside, slightly into the valley. He sat down beside Schneider; he did not speak; the two men waited until the sound of Miller's rifle became faint. Then they followed the trail of dead buffalo, skinning as they went.

At night the men were so exhausted that they hardly spoke. They wolfed the food that Charley Hoge prepared for them, drained the great smoked coffeepot, and fell exhausted upon their bedrolls. In their increasing exhaustion, to which Miller drove them with his inexorable pursuit, their food and their sleep came to be the only things that had much meaning for them. Once Schneider, desiring a change of food, went into the woods and managed to shoot a small doe; another time Charley Hoge rode across the valley to the small lake where the buffalo watered and returned with a dozen fat foot-long trout. But they ate only a small part of the venison, and the taste of the trout was flat and unsatisfying; they returned to their steady diet of rich, strong buffalo meat.

Every day Schneider cut the liver from one of the slain buffalo; at the evening meal, almost ritually, the liver was divided into roughly equal portions and passed among them. Andrews learned that the taking of the raw liver was not an ostentation on the part of the three older men. Miller explained to him that unless one did so, one got what he called the "buff sickness," which was a breaking out of the skin in large, ulcerous sores, often accompanied by fever and general weakness. After learning this, Andrews forced himself to take a bit of the liver every evening; he did not find the taste of it pleasant, but in his tiredness the faintly warm and rotten taste and the slick fiberless texture did not seem to matter much.

After a week in the valley, there were ten thonged stacks of hides set close together in a small grove of pines, and still Andrews could see no real diminution of the herds that grazed placidly on the flat bed of the valley.

The days slid one into another, marked by evening exhaustion and morning soreness; as it had earlier, on their overland voyage when they searched for water, time again seemed to Andrews to hold itself apart from the passing of the days. Alone in the great valley high in the mountains the four men, rather than being brought close together by their isolation, were thrust apart, so that each of them tended more and more to go his own way and fall upon his own resources. Seldom did they talk at night; and when they did, their words were directed to some specific business concerned with the hunt.

In Miller especially Andrews perceived this withdrawal. Always a man whose words were few and direct, he became increasingly silent. At evening, in the camp, he was by turns restless, his eyes going frequently from the camp to across the valley, as if he were trying to fix the buffalo herd and command it even though he could not see it; and indifferent, almost sullen, staring lethargically into the campfire, often not answering for minutes after his name was spoken or a question was asked of him. Only during the hunt, or when he was helping Andrews and Schneider with the skinning, was he alert; and even that alertness seemed to Andrews somehow unnaturally intense. He came to have an image of Miller that persisted even when Miller was not in his sight; he saw Miller's face, black and dull with powder smoke, his white teeth clenched behind his stretched-out leathery lips, and his eyes, black and shining in their whites, surrounded by a flaming red line of irritated lids. Sometimes this image of Miller came into his mind at night, in his dreams; and more than once he came awake with a start and thrust himself upward out of his bedroll, and found that he was breathing quickly, shallowly, as if in fright, as the sharp image of those eyes upon him dulled and faded and died in the darkness around him. Once he dreamed that he was some kind of animal who was being pursued; he felt a relentless presence that chased him from cover to cover, and at last penned him in a corner of blackness from which there was no retreat; before he awoke in fear, or at a dreamed explosion of violence, he thought he caught a glimpse of those eyes burning at him from the darkness.

A week passed, and another; the stacks of hides beside their camp grew in number. Both Schneider and Charley Hoge became increasingly restless, though the latter did not give direct voice to his restlessness. But Andrews saw it in

the looks that Charley Hoge gave to the sky in the afternoon when it clouded for the rain that Andrews and Schneider had grown to expect and welcome; he saw it in Charley
Hoge's increased drinking—the empty whisky crocks grew in
number almost as fast as did the ricks of buffalo hides; and
he saw it also at night when, against the growing cold,
Charley Hoge built the fire to a roaring furnace that drove
the rest of them away and covered himself when he bedded
down with a pressing number of buffalo hides that he had
managed to soften by soaking them in a thick soup of water
and wood ash.

One evening, near the end of their second week, while
they were taking their late evening meal, Schneider took
from his plate a half-eaten buffalo steak and threw it in the
fire, where it sizzled and curled and threw up a quantity
of dark smoke.

"I'm getting damned sick of buffalo meat," he said, and
for a long moment afterward was silent, brooding at the
fire until the steak was a black, twisted ash that dulled the
red coals upon which it lay. "Damn sick of it," he said again.

Charley Hoge sloshed his coffee and whisky in his tin
cup, inspected it for a second, and drank it, his thin gray-
fur-covered neck twisting as he swallowed. Miller looked at
Schneider dully and then returned his gaze to the fire.

"God damn it, didn't you hear me?" Schneider shouted,
to any or all of them.

Miller turned slowly. "You said you were getting tired of
buffalo meat," he said. "Charley will cook up a batch of
beans tomorrow."

"I don't want no more beans, and I don't want no sowbelly, and I don't want no more sour biscuits," Schneider
said. "I want some greens, and some potatoes; and I want
me a woman."

No one spoke. In the fire a green knot exploded and sent
a shower of sparks in the air; they floated in the darkness
and the men brushed them off their clothes as they settled.

Schneider said more quietly: "We been here two weeks
now; that's four days longer than we was supposed to be.
And the hunting's been good. We got more hides now than

we can load back. What say let's pack out of here to-morrow?"

Miller looked at him as if he were a stranger. "You ain't serious, are you, Fred?"

"You're damn right I am," Schneider said. "Look. Charley's ready to go back; ain't you, Charley?" Charley Hoge did not look at him; he quickly poured some more coffee into his cup, and filled it to the brim with whisky. "It's getting on into fall," Schneider continued, his eyes still on Charley Hoge. "Nights are getting cold. You can't tell what kind of weather you're going to get, this time of year."

Miller shifted, and brought his intense gaze directly upon Schneider. "Leave Charley alone," he said quietly.

"All right," Schneider said. "But just tell me. Even if we do stay around here, how are we going to load all the hides back?"

"The hides?" Miller said, his face for a moment blank. "The hides? . . . We'll load what we can, leave the others; we can come back in the spring and pack them out. That's what we said we'd do, back in Butcher's Crossing."

"You mean we're going to stay here till you've wiped out this whole herd?"

Miller nodded. "We're going to stay."

"You're crazy," Schneider said.

"It'll take another ten days," Miller said. "Two more weeks at the outside. We'll have plenty of time before the weather turns."

"The whole god damned herd," Schneider said, and shook his head wonderingly. "You're crazy. What are you trying to do? You can't kill every god damned buffalo in the whole god damned country."

Miller's eyes glazed over for a moment, and he stared toward Schneider as if he were not there. Then the film slid from his eyes, he blinked, and turned his face toward the fire.

"It won't do no good to talk about it, Fred. This is my party, and my mind's made up."

"All right, god damn it," Schneider said. "It's on your head. Just remember that."

Miller nodded distantly, as if he were no longer interested in anything that Schneider might want to say.

Angrily Schneider gathered his bedroll and started to walk away from the campfire. Then he dropped it and came back.

"Just one more thing," he said sullenly.

Miller looked up absently. "Yes?"

"We been gone from Butcher's Crossing now just a little over a month."

Miller waited. "Yes?" he said again.

"A little over a month," Schneider said again. "I want my pay."

"What?" Miller said. His face was puzzled for a moment.

"My pay," Schneider said. "Sixty dollars."

Miller frowned, and then he grinned. "You thinking of spending it right soon?"

"Never mind that," Schneider said. "You just give me my pay, like we agreed."

"All right," Miller said. He turned to Andrews. "Mr. Andrews, will you give Mr. Schneider his sixty dollars?"

Andrews opened his shirt front and took some bills from his money belt. He counted out sixty dollars, and handed the money to Schneider. Schneider took the money, and went to the fire, knelt, and carefully counted it. Then he thrust the bills into a pocket and went to where he had dropped his bedroll. He picked it up and went out of sight into the darkness. The three men around the fire heard the snapping of branches and the rustle of pine needles and cloth as Schneider put his bedroll down. They listened until they heard the regular sound of his breath, and then his angry snoring. They did not speak. Soon they, too, bedded down for the night. When they woke in the morning a thin rind of frost crusted the grass that lay on the valley bed.

In the morning light Miller looked at the frosted valley and said:

"Their grass is playing out. They'll be trying to get through the pass and down to the flat country. We'll have to keep pushing them back."

And they did. Each morning they met the buffalo in a frontal attack, and pushed them slowly back toward the sheer rise of mountains to the south. But their frontal assault was little more than a delaying tactic; during the night the buffalo grazed far beyond the point they had been turned back from the day before. On each succeeding day the main herd came closer and closer to the pass over which it had originally entered the high park.

And as the buffalo pressed dumbly, instinctively, out of the valley, the slaughter grew more and more intense. Already withdrawn and spare with words, Miller became with the passing days almost totally intent upon his kill; and even at night, in the camp, he no longer gave voice to his simplest needs—he gestured toward the coffeepot, he grunted when his name was spoken, and his directions to the rest of them became curt motions of hands and arms, jerks of the head, and guttural growlings deep in his throat. Each day he went after the buffalo with two guns; during the kill, he heated the barrels to that point just shy of burning them out.

Schneider and Andrews had to work more and more swiftly to skin the animals Miller left strewn upon the ground; almost never were they able to finish their skinning before sundown, so that nearly every morning they were up before dawn hacking tough skins from stiff buffalo. And during the day, as they sweated and hacked and pulled in a desperate effort to keep up with Miller, they could hear the sound of his rifle steadily and monotonously and insistently pounding at the silence, and pounding at their nerves until they were raw and bruised. At night, when the two of them rode wearily out of the valley to the small red-orange glow that marked their camp in the darkness, they found Miller slouched darkly and inertly before the fire; except for his eyes he was as still and lifeless as one of the buffalo he had killed. Miller had even stopped washing off his face the black powder that collected there during his firing; now the powder smoke seemed a permanent part of his skin, ingrained there, a black mask that defined the hot, glaring brilliance of his eyes.

Gradually the herd was worn down. Everywhere he looked Andrews saw the ground littered with naked corpses of buffalo, which sent up a rancid stench to which he had become so used that he hardly was aware of it; and the remaining herd wandered placidly among the ruins of their fellows, nibbling at grass flecked with their dry brown blood. With his awareness of the diminishing size of the herd, there came to Andrews the realization that he had not contemplated the day when the herd was finally reduced to nothing, when not a buffalo remained standing—for unlike Schneider he had known, without questioning or without knowing how he knew, that Miller would not willingly leave the valley so long as a single buffalo remained alive. He had measured time, and had reckoned the moment and place of their leaving, by the size of the herd, and not —as had Schneider—by numbered days that rolled meaninglessly one after another. He thought of packing the hides into the wagon, yoking the oxen, which were beginning to grow fat on inactivity and the rich mountain grass, to the wagon, and making their way back down the mountain, and across the wide plains, back to Butcher's Crossing. He could not imagine what he thought of. With a mild shock, he realized that the world outside the wide flat winding park hemmed on all sides by sheer mountain, had faded away from him; he could not remember the mountain up which they had labored, or the expanse of plain over which they sweated and thirsted, or Butcher's Crossing, which he had come into and left only a few weeks before. That world came to him fitfully and unclearly, as if hidden in a dream. He had been here in the high valley for all of that part of his life that mattered; and when he looked out upon it—its flatness, and its yellow-greenness, its high walls of mountain wooded with the deep green of pine in which ran the flaming red-gold of turning aspen, its jutting rock and hillock, all roofed with the intense blue of the airless sky—it seemed to him that the contours of the place flowed beneath his eyes, that his very gaze shaped what he saw, and in turn gave his own existence form and place. He could not think of himself outside of where he was.

On their twenty-fifth day in the mountains they arose late. For the last several days, the slaughter had been going more slowly; the great herd, after more than three weeks, seemed to have begun to realize the presence of their killers and to have started dumbly to prepare against them; they began to break up into a number of very small herds; seldom was Miller able to get more than twelve or fourteen buffalo at a stand, and much time was wasted in traveling from one herd to another. But the earlier sense of urgency was gone; the herd of some five thousand animals was now less than three hundred. Upon these remaining three hundred, Miller closed in—slowly, inexorably—as if more intensely savoring the slaughter of each animal as the size of the herd diminished. On the twenty-fifth day they arose without hurry; and after they had taken breakfast they even sat around the fire for several moments letting their coffee cool in their tin cups. Though they could not see it through the thick forest of pines behind them, the sun rose over the eastern range of mountains; through the trees it sent diffused mists of light that gathered on their cups, softening their hard outlines and making them glow in the semishade. The sky was a deep thin blue, cloudless and intense; crevices and hollows on the broad plain and in the sides of the mountain sent up nearly invisible mists which could be seen only as they softened the edges of rock and tree they surrounded. The day warmed, and promised heat.

After finishing their coffee, they loitered around the camp while Charley Hoge led the oxen out of the aspen-pole corral and yoked them to the empty wagon. For several days hides had been drying where Andrews and Schneider had pegged them; it was time for them to be gathered and stacked.

Schneider scratched his beard, which was tangled and matted like wet straw, and stretched his arms lazily. "Going to be a hot day," he said, pointing to the clear sky. "Probably won't even get a rain." He turned to Miller. "How many of the buff do you think's left? Couple of hundred?"

Miller nodded, and cleared his throat.

Schneider continued: "Think we'll be able to clean them up in three or four more days?"

Miller turned to him, as if only then aware that he had spoken. He said gruffly: "Three or four more days should do it, Fred."

"God damn," Schneider said happily. "I don't know

whether I can last that long." He punched Andrews on the arm. "What about you, boy? Think you can wait?"

Andrews grinned. "Sure," he said.

"A pocketful of money, and all the eats and women you can hold," Schneider said. "By God, that's living."

Miller moved impatiently. "Come on," he said. "Charley's got the team yoked. Let's get moving."

The four men moved slowly from the camp area. Miller rode ahead of the wagon; Andrews and Schneider wound their reins about their saddle horns and let their horses amble easily behind it. The oxen, made lazy and irritable by their inactivity, did not pull well together; the morning silence was broken by Charley Hoge's half-articulated, shouted curses.

Within half an hour the little procession had arrived at where the first buffalo had been killed and skinned more than three weeks before. The meat on the corpses had dried to a flintlike hardness; here and there the flesh had been torn away by the wolves before they had been killed or driven away by Charley Hoge's strychnine; where the flesh was torn, the bones were white and shining, as if they had been polished. Andrews looked ahead of him into the valley; everywhere he looked he saw the mounded bodies. By next summer, he knew, the flesh would be eaten away by vultures or rotted away by the elements; he tried to imagine what the valley would look like, spread about with the white bones. He shivered a little, though the sun was hot.

Soon the wagon was so thickly surrounded by corpses that Charley Hoge was unable to point it in a straight direction; he had to walk beside the lead team, guiding it among the bodies. Even so, the huge wooden wheels now and then passed over an outthrust leg of a buffalo, causing the wagon to sway. The increasing heat of the day intensified the always present stench of rotting flesh; the oxen shied away from it, lowing discontentedly and tossing their heads so wildly that Charley Hoge had to stand many feet away from them.

When they had made their slow way to where a wide space was covered with pegged-out skins and fresh corpses,

Andrews and Schneider got down from their horses. They tied large handkerchiefs about the lower parts of their faces, so that they could work without being disturbed by the horde of small black flies that buzzed about the rank meat.

"It's going to be hot working," Schneider said. "Look at that sun."

Above the eastern trees, the sun was a fiery mass at which Andrews could not look directly; unhindered by mist or cloud, it burned upon them, instantly drying the sweat that it pulled from their faces and hands. Andrews let his eyes wander about the sky; the cool blueness soothed them from the burning they had from his brief glance toward the sun. To the south, a small white cloud had formed; it hung quiet and tiny just above the rise of the mountains.

"Let's get going," Andrews said, kicking at a small peg that held a skin flat against the earth. "It doesn't look like it'll get any cooler."

A little more than a mile away, a slight dark movement was visible among the low mounds of corpses; a small herd was grazing quietly and moving slowly toward them. Miller abruptly reined his horse away from the three men who were busy loading the hides, and galloped toward the herd.

As the men worked, Charley Hoge led the oxen between them, so that neither would have to take more than a few steps to fling his hides upon the wagon bed. Shortly after Miller rode off, Andrews and Schneider heard the distant boom of his rifle; they lifted their heads and stood for a few moments listening. Then they resumed their work, unpegging and tossing the hides into the moving wagon more slowly, in rhythm with the booming sound of Miller's rifle. When the sound ceased, they paused in their work and sat on the ground, breathing heavily.

"Don't sound like we're going to have to do much skinning today," Schneider panted, pointing in the direction of Miller's firing. "Sounds like he only got twelve or fourteen so far."

Andrews nodded and lay back in a half-reclining position, resting his body on his elbows and forearms; he removed the large red bandana from his lower face so that his flesh might have the coolness of a faint breeze that had come up

during their rest. The throbbing of his head gradually subsided as the breeze became stronger and cooled him. After
about fifteen minutes, Miller's rifle sounded again.

"He found another little herd," Schneider said, rising to
his feet. "We might as well try to keep up with him."

But as they worked, they noticed that the rifle shots no
longer came with the same regularity, marking a rhythm by
which they could kick the stakes, raise the hides, and sail
them onto the wagon. Several shots came briefly spaced, in
a sharp flurry; there was a silence of several minutes; then
another brief flurry of shots. Andrews and Schneider looked
at each other in puzzlement.

"It don't sound right," Schneider said. "Maybe they're
getting skittish."

The closely-spaced shots were followed by the brief
sharp thunder of pounding hooves; in the distance could be
seen a light cloud of dust raised by the running buffalo. The
men heard another burst of rifle fire, and they saw the cloud
of dust turn and go away from them, back into the depths
of the valley. A few minutes later they heard another faint
rumbling of hooves, and saw another cloud of dust rise at
a different spot some distance east of the earlier stampede.
And again they heard the brief, close explosions of Miller's
rifle, and saw the dust cloud veer and go back beyond the
point from which it had begun.

"Miller's got himself some trouble," Schneider said.
"Something's got into them buff."

In the minutes that the men had been standing still,
listening to the gunshots and watching the dust trails, the
burning heat had lessened perceptibly. A thin haze had
come between them and the sun, and the breeze from the
south had grown stronger.

"Come on," Andrews said. "Let's get these hides loaded
while we've got a breeze."

Schneider lifted his hand. "Wait." Charley Hoge had left
the oxen, and now stood near Schneider and Andrews. The
rapid drumming of a running horse came to them; among
the scattered flayed bodies of the buffalo Miller appeared,
galloping toward them. When he came near the standing

men, he pulled his horse so abruptly to a halt that it reared,
its forehooves for a moment pawing the air.

"They're trying to get out of the valley," Miller's voice
came in a croaking rasp. "They've broke up in ten or twelve
little herds, and I can't turn them back fast enough; I need
some help."

Schneider blew his nose contemptuously. "Hell," he said
wearily, "let them go. There are only a couple of hundred
of them left."

Miller did not look at Schneider. "Will, you get on your
horse and wait over there." He pointed west to a spot two
or three hundred yards from the side of the mountain.
"Fred, you ride over there—" He pointed in the opposite
direction, to the east. "I'll stay in the middle." He spoke
to both Andrews and Schneider. "If a herd comes in your
direction, head it off; all you have to do is shoot into it
two or three times. It'll turn."

Schneider shook his head. "It's no good. If they're broke
up in little herds, we can't turn them all back."

"They won't all come at once," Miller said. "They'll
come two or three at a time. We can turn them back."

"But what's the use?" said Schneider, his voice almost a
wail. "What the hell's the use? It ain't going to kill you to
let a few of them get away."

"Hurry it up," said Miller. "They're liable to start any
minute."

Schneider raised his hands to the air, shrugged his shoulders, and went to his horse; Miller spurred toward the middle of the valley. Andrews mounted his horse, started to
ride in the direction that Miller had pointed to him, and
then rode up to the wagon to which Charley Hoge had
returned.

"You got a rifle, Charley?" Andrews asked.

Charley Hoge turned nervously. He nodded and drew a
small rifle from beneath the clip seat. "It's just your little
varmint rifle," he said as he handed it to him, "but it'll
turn them."

Andrews took the rifle and rode toward the side of the
mountain. He pointed his horse in the direction that the
buffalo would come from, and waited. He looked across the

valley; Miller had stationed himself in the center, and he leaned forward on his horse toward the herds that none of them could see. Beyond Miller, small in the distance, Schneider slouched on his horse as if he were asleep. Andrews turned again to the south and listened for the pounding of hooves which would mark the run of a herd.

He heard nothing save the soft whistling of the wind around his ears, which were beginning to tingle from the coolness. The southern reaches of the valley were softening in a faint mist that was coming down from the mountains; the small cloud that had earlier hovered quietly above the southern peaks now extended over the boxed end of the valley; the underside of the cloud was a dirty gray, above which the sunlit white vapor twisted and coiled upon itself before a thrusting wind that was not felt on the ground here in the valley.

A heavy rumble shook the earth; Andrews's horse started backward, its ears flattened about the sides of its head. For an instant Andrews searched the upper air about the southern mountains, thinking that he had heard the sound of thunder; but the rumbling persisted beneath him. Directly in front of him, in the distance, a faint cloud of dust arose, and blew away as soon as it had arisen. Then suddenly, out of the shadow, onto that part of the valley still flooded in sunlight, the buffalo emerged. They ran with incredible swiftness, not in a straight line toward him, but in swift swerves and turns, as if they evaded invisible obstacles suddenly thrust before them; and they swerved and turned as if the entire herd of thirty or forty buffalo were one animal with one mind, a single will—no animal straggled or turned in a direction that was counter to the movement of the others.

For several moments Andrews sat motionless and stiff on his horse; he had an impulse to turn, to flee the oncoming herd. He could not believe that a few shots from the small varmint rifle that he cradled in his right arm could be heard or even felt by a force that came onward with such speed and strength and will; he could not believe they could be turned. He twisted in the saddle, moving his neck stiffly so that he could see Miller. Miller sat still, watching him;

after a moment Miller shouted something that was drowned in the deepening rumble of the buffalo's stampede, and pointed toward them, motioning with his hand and arm as if he were throwing stones at them.

Andrews dug his heels into his horse's sides; the horse went forward a few steps and then halted, drawing back on its haunches. In a kind of desperation and fear, Andrews dug his heels again into the heaving sides of his mount, and beat with his rifle butt upon the quivering haunches. The horse leaped forward, almost upsetting him; it galloped for a moment wildly, throwing its head against the bit that Andrews held too tightly; then, soothed by its own motion, it steadied and ran easily forward toward the herd. The wind slapped into Andrews's face and swept tears from his eyes. For an instant he could not see where he was going.

Then his vision cleared. The buffalo were less than three hundred yards away from him, swerving and turning erratically, but heading toward him. He pulled his horse to a halt and flung his rifle to his shoulder; the stock was cold against his cheek. He fired once into the midst of the rushing herd; he barely heard the rifle shot above the thunder of hooves. He fired again. A buffalo stumbled and fell, but the others came around it, flowed over it like tumbling water. He fired again, and again. Suddenly, the herd swerved to his left, cutting across the valley toward Miller. Andrews heeled his horse and ran alongside the fleeing herd, firing into its rushing mass. Gradually the herd turned, until it was running with unabated speed back in the direction from which it had come.

Andrews pulled his horse to a stop; panting, he looked after the running herd and listened to the diminishing roar of pounding hooves. Then, upon that sound, faintly, came another similar to it. He looked across the valley. Another herd, slightly smaller than the first, sped across the flat land toward Schneider. He watched as Schneider fired into it, followed it as it swerved, and turned it back.

In all, the three of them turned back six rushes of the buffalo. When at last no sound of running hooves broke the silence, and after they had waited for many minutes in anticipation of another rush, Miller beckoned them to ride toward him in the center of the valley.

Andrews and Schneider rode up to Miller quietly, letting their horses walk so that they could hear a warning if the buffalo decided to charge again. Miller was looking across the valley, squinting at where the buffalo had run.

"We got them," Miller said. "They won't try to break out again like that."

A tremor of elation that he could not understand went through Andrews. "I never thought anything like that was possible," he said to Miller. "It was almost as if they were doing it together, as if they'd planned it." It seemed to him that he had not really thought of the buffalo before. He had skinned them by the hundreds, he had killed a few; he had eaten of their flesh, he had smelled their stench, he had been immersed in their blood; but he had not thought of them before as he was thinking of them now. "Do they do things like that very often?"

Miller shook his head. "You might as well not try to figure them out; you can't tell what they might do. I've been hunting them for twenty years and I don't know. I've seen them run clean over a bluff, and pile up a hundred deep in a canyon—thousands of them, for no reason at all that a man could see. I've seen them spooked by a crow, and I've seen men walk right in the middle of a herd without them moving an inch. You think about what they're going to do, and you get yourself in trouble; all a man can do is not think about them, just plow into them, kill them when he can, and not try to figure anything out." As he spoke, Miller did not look at Andrews; his eyes were on the valley, which was still now, and empty, save for the trampled bodies of the buffalo they had killed. He took a deep breath and turned to Schneider. "Well, Fred, we got us some cool weather anyhow. It won't be so bad working, now."

"Wait a minute," Schneider said. His eyes were fixed on nothing; he held his head as if he were listening.

"You hear them again?" Miller asked.

Schneider motioned with his hand for quiet; he sat in

his saddle for a few minutes more, still listening; he sniffed twice at the air.

"What is it?" Miller asked.

Schneider turned to him slowly. "Let's get out of here." His voice was quiet.

Miller frowned, and blinked. "What's wrong?"

"I don't know," Schneider said. "But something is. Something don't feel right to me."

Miller snorted. "You're spooked easier than a buffalo. Come on. We got half a day in front of us. They'll quiet down in a while and I can get a good number before it's dark."

"Listen," Schneider said.

The three men sat in their saddles, quiet, listening for something they did not know. The wind had died, but a slight chill remained in the air. They heard only silence; no breeze rustled through the pines, no bird called. One of their horses snorted; someone moved in the saddle, and there came the thin sound of leather creaking. To break the silence, Miller slapped his leg; he turned to Schneider and said loudly:

"What the hell—"

But he did not continue. He was silenced by Schneider's outstretched arm and hand and finger, which seemed to point at nothing. Puzzled, Andrews looked from one of them to another; and then his gaze halted in the air between them. Out of the air, large and soft and slow, like a falling feather, drifted a single snowflake. As he watched, he saw another, and another.

A grin broke out on his face, and a nervous bubble of laughter came up in his throat.

"Why, it's snowing," he said, laughing, looking again from one of them to the other. "Did you ever think this morning that—"

His voice died in his throat. Neither Miller nor Schneider looked at him, and neither gave any sign that they knew he had spoken. Their faces were tense and strained at the thickening sky from which the snow was falling more and more rapidly. Andrews looked quickly at Charley Hoge, who was sitting motionless some yards from the others on his high wagon seat. Charley Hoge's face was raised upward, and his arms were clasped together over his chest; his eyes rolled wildly, but he did not move his head or unclasp his arms.

"Let's go," Miller said quietly, still looking at the sky. "We might just make it before it gets too bad."

He pulled his horse around and rode a few steps up to Charley Hoge. He leaned from the saddle and shook Charley Hoge roughly by the shoulder.

"Let's haul, Charley."

For a moment, Charley Hoge did not seem to know Miller's presence; and when he turned to face him, he did not appear to recognize the large black-bearded face, which was beginning to glisten from the melting snowflakes. Then his eyes focused, and he spoke in a trembling voice:

"You said it would be all right." His voice gained strength, became accusing: "You said we'd make it out before the snows came."

"It's all right, Charley," Miller said. "We got plenty of time."

Charley Hoge's voice rose: "I said I didn't want to come. I told you—"

"Charley!" Miller's voice cracked. And then he said more softly: "We're just wasting time. Get your team headed back to camp."

Charley Hoge looked at Miller, his mouth working, but moving upon words that did not become sound. Then he reached behind him and took from its clip the long bull-whip, the braided leather of which trailed from the heavy butt. He whistled it over the ears of the lead team, in his fright letting the tip come too low, and drawing blood from the ear of the right lead ox. The ox threw his head around wildly and jumped forward, pulling the surprised weight of the other animals; for a moment the team floundered, each member pulling in a different direction. Then they settled together and pulled steadily. Charley Hoge cracked his whip again and the team broke into a lumbering run; he made no effort to guide the animals among the corpses of the buffalo. The wagon wheels, passing over the bodies,

pitched the wagon wildly about. Stiff hides slithered off and
fell to the ground; no one paused to retrieve them.

The three men on horseback rode close to the wagon;
they had to pull back on their reins to keep the animals
from bolting and running ahead. Within a few minutes the
air was white with snow; dimly, on either side, they could
see the veiled green of the mountainside; but they could
not see ahead to their camp. The shadowy pine trees on
either side of them guided their movement upon the flat
bed of the valley. Andrews squinted ahead toward their
camp, but all he could see was snow, the flakes circling and
slowly falling, one against another and another and another;
in his riding, they came at him, and if he looked at them,
his head whirled as they did and he became dizzy. He
fixed his eyes upon the moving wagon and saw the snow
unfocused, a general haze that surrounded him and isolated
him from the others, though he could see them dimly as
they rode. His bare hands, holding the reins and clutching
his saddle horn as his horse trotted and loped unevenly
among the corpses of the buffalo, reddened in the cold;
he tried to thrust one of them in a pocket of his trousers,
but the rough stiff cloth was so painful that he removed his
hand and kept it in the open.

After the first few minutes the ground was covered white
with snow; the wagon wheels, cutting easily through it, left
thin parallel ribbons of darkness behind them. Andrews
glanced back; within seconds after the wheels cut the snow,
the shallow ruts began to fill and only a few feet behind
them were whitened so that he could not tell where they
had been; despite their movement and the pitching of the
wagon, he had the feeling that they were going nowhere,
that they were caught on a vast treadmill that heaved them
up but did not carry them forward.

The breeze that had died when the first snowflakes began to fall came up again; it swirled the snow about them,
whipping it into their faces, causing them to squint their
eyes against its force. Andrews's jaws began to ache; he realized that for some moments he had been clenching his
teeth together with all the strength he had; his lips, drawn
back over his teeth in an aimless snarl, smarted and pained

him as the cold pushed against the tiny cracks and rawness there. He relaxed his jaws and dropped his head, hunching his shoulders against the cold which drove through the thin clothing upon his flesh. He looped the reins about his saddle horn and grasped it with both hands, letting his horse find its own way.

The wind grew stronger and the snow came in thick flurries. For an instant Andrews lost sight of the wagon and of the other men; a numb, vague panic made him lift his head; somewhere to his left he heard, above the whistle of the wind, the creak and thump of the wagon wheels. He pulled his horse in the direction of the sound, and after a moment saw the heavy shape of the wagon careening over the littered ground and dimly saw the hunched figure of Charley Hoge swaying on the high clip seat, lashing the thick air with his bull-whip; softly, muffled by the snow and drowned by the wind, its wet crack sounded.

And still the wind increased. It howled over the mountains and blew the snow into stinging pellets; in great sheets, it lifted the snow off the ground and spread it again; it thrust the fine white freezing powder into the crevices of their clothing where it melted from their bodies' warmth; and it hardened the moisture so that their clothing hung heavy and stiff upon them and gathered the cold to their flesh. Andrews clutched his saddle horn more firmly; there was no sensation in his hands. He removed one hand stiffly from the horn and flexed it, and beat it against the side of his leg until it began to throb painfully; then he did the same with the other hand. By then the first had grown numb again. A small pile of snow gathered in his saddle in the sharp V formed by his legs.

Above the wind he heard a faint shout; the wagon loomed up suddenly before him; his horse halted, pitching him forward. He heard the shout again and thought it was his name that was called. He guided his horse along the side of the wagon, hunching himself against the wind and peering out of his half-closed eyes every second or so, trying to see who had called him. Miller and Schneider, their horses close together facing the wind, waited for him at the front of the wagon. When he came up to them, he saw Charley Hoge huddled between the two horses, his back hunched to the wind.

Stiffly, leaning against the wind, their faces turned down so that the brims of their hats were blown against their cheeks, the men dismounted from their horses, and, crouching against the wind, thrusting themselves at an angle through it, came toward Andrews; Miller beckoned him to get down. As he dismounted, the force of the wind pushed his unsupported body forward and he stumbled, one foot for a moment caught in the stirrup.

Miller staggered up to him, grasped him by the shoulders, and put his bearded face—which was now stiff and icy in spots, where snow had melted and frozen—to Andrews's ear. He shouted: "We're going to leave the wagon here; it slows us up too much. You hold on to the horses while Fred and I unyoke the team."

Andrews nodded and pulled the reins with him as he went toward the horses. His own horse pulled back, almost dislodging the reins from his numb hand; he jerked heavily on the reins and the horse followed him. Still holding the reins in one hand, he stooped and fumbled in the snow, which lifted and swirled about his feet as if disturbed by a long explosion, until he found the knotted reins of the other horses. As he straightened, Charley Hoge, whose back had been toward him, turned; the stump of his forearm was thrust inside his light coat, and his good arm pressed it close to his body as his body hunched over it. For a moment Charley Hoge looked at Andrews without seeing him; his pale eyes were open and unblinking against the stinging wind and snow, and they focused on nothing. His mouth was moving rapidly and his lips twitched one way and another, causing the beard about his mouth to jerk unevenly. Andrews shouted his name but the wind tore the word from his lips; Charley Hoge's eyes did not move. Andrews came a little closer; shifting all three reins to one hand, he reached out his other to touch Charley Hoge on the shoulder. At his touch, Charley Hoge jerked back away and cowered, his eyes still glazed and his lips still working. Andrews shouted again:

"It'll be all right, Charley. It'll be all right."

He was barely able to hear what Charley Hoge repeated over and over, to the wind, the snow, and the cold:

"God help me. Lord Jesus Christ help me. God help me."

At a thump behind him, Andrews turned; a dim dark bulk loomed out of the whiteness and lumbered past him. The first of the oxen had been unyoked by Miller and Schneider. As the shape lumbered into the whiteness and disappeared, the horses which Andrews held bolted. Their quick movement caught him by surprise, and before he could throw his weight against the reins, one of the horses' bellies had brushed heavily against Charley Hoge, knocking him to the ground. Andrews started involuntarily toward him, and as he did so the three horses moved together, pulling him around and forward, so that he was off balance; his feet flew into the air behind him, and he landed heavily on his stomach and chest in the snow. Somehow he managed to hold on to the reins. Flat on the snow, he grinned foolishly at his blue-red hands that clutched the thin strips of leather. Snow flew around him, and he was aware of the heavy lift and fall of hooves on either side of his head; he realized slowly and almost without surprise that he was being dragged along the ground on his stomach.

He pulled his weight against the moving reins and managed to get his knees under his body; then he pulled harder, so that his knees went before him as he leaned backward and sawed on the reins. The rear leg of one of the horses brushed against his shoulder, and he nearly lost his balance; but he regained it and lifted himself upward again, thrusting his legs down in a desperate leap, stumbling to his feet, and running along with the horses for several yards. Then he dug his heels into the snow and sawed again on the reins; he felt himself being carried along, but less swiftly. His heels went beneath the snow, caught on the grass, and plowed shallowly into the earth. The horses slowed, and halted. He stood for a moment panting; he was still smiling foolishly, though his legs were trembling and his arms were without strength, as he turned and looked behind him.

Whiteness met his eyes. He could not see the wagon, or
the oxen, or the men who stood near them. He listened,
trying to hear a sound to guide him; nothing came above
the increasing moan of the wind. He knelt and looked behind him at the path he had scraped in the snow; a narrow,
rough depression showed shallowly. He pulled the horses
with him as he followed the path, stooping close to the
ground and brushing at the snow with his free hand. After
a few yards the trail began to fill, and soon it disappeared
before the gusts of wind and blown snow. As nearly as he
could guess, he continued to walk in the direction from
which he had been pulled. He hoped that he had been
carried away from the wagon in a straight line, but he could
not be sure. Every now and then he shouted; his voice was
whipped from his mouth and carried behind him by the
wind. He hurried, and stumbled in the snow; from his feet
and hands, numbness crept toward his body. He looked
about him wildly. He tried to walk forward slowly and
steadily, conserving his strength; but his legs jerked beneath him and carried him forward in an uneven gait that
was half trot, half run. The horses, whose reins he carried,
seemed an intolerable burden, though they moved docilely
behind him; he had to use all his will to keep from dropping the reins and running blindly in the snow. He sobbed,
and fell to his knees. Awkwardly, with the reins still
clutched in his right hand, he crawled forward.

Distantly, he heard a shout; he paused and lifted his
head. To his right, a little closer, the sound came again.
He got to his feet and ran toward it, his sobbing breath
becoming a rasping laugh. Suddenly, out of the white and
gray of the driving snow, the blurred shape of the wagon
loomed; and he saw three figures huddled beside it. One
of them detached itself and walked toward him. It was
Miller. He shouted something that Andrews did not understand, and took the reins that Andrews still held. When
he lifted the reins, Andrews's hand was lifted stiffly to chest
level; he looked at it and tried to loose the fingers. He could
not make them move. Miller took his hand and pried the
fingers back from the leather. His hand empty, Andrews

worked his fingers, opening and closing his hand until the cramp was gone.

Miller came near him and shouted in his ear: "You all right?"

Andrews nodded.

"Let's get going," Miller shouted. Bending against the wind, the two men struggled toward the wagon and Charley Hoge and Schneider. Miller drew Schneider's and Andrews's heads together and shouted again: "I'll put Charley on with me. You two stay close."

Beside the wagon the men mounted their horses. Miller pulled Charley Hoge up behind him; he tightly grasped Miller around the stomach and buried his head against Miller's back; his eyes were screwed shut, and his mouth still worked upon the words that none of them could hear. Miller moved his horse away from the wagon; Andrews and Schneider followed. In a few moments the wagon was blotted from their sight by a solid wall of falling snow.

Shortly they passed beyond the ground that was curved by the white mounds of buffalo carcasses; Miller pushed his horse to a gallop, and the others followed. The gaits of their horses were awkward, jolting them in their saddles so that they had to hang on to their saddle horns with both hands. Now and then they came upon stretches of ground where the snow lay in heavy drifts; there the horses slowed to a walk and plowed through the snow which covered their forelegs halfway up to their knees.

Andrews's sense of direction had become numbed by the swirling white vortex of snow. The faint gray-green of the pine trees that blanketed the opposing mountainsides, which had earlier guided them in the general direction of the valley's mouth, had long been shrouded from the views of all of them; beyond the horses and the figures huddled upon them, Andrews could not see any mark that showed him where they went. The same whiteness met his eyes wherever he looked; he had the sensation that, dizzily, they were circling around and around in a circle that gradually decreased, until they were spinning furiously upon a single point.

And still Miller spurred his horse, and beat its flanks,

which glistened with sweat even in the driving, bitter cold. The three horses were grouped closely together; with a kind of vague horror that he could not understand, Andrews saw that Miller had closed his eyes against the stinging gale, and kept them closed, his head turned downward and to the side so that it was visible to Andrews even in their heavy gallop. Miller kept a tight hold on the reins, guiding the horse in a direction that he did not see. The others followed him blindly, trusting his blindness.

Suddenly, out of the storm, a dark wall reared up before them; it was the mountainside of trees, upon which the snow, driven by the fierce wind, could not settle. The ghostly shape of the large chimney rock where they had built their fires loomed vaguely, a dirty yellow-gray against the white snow. Miller slowed his horse to a walk, and led the others to the aspen-pole corral that Charley Hoge had built. Trying to keep their backs to the wind, they dismounted and led their horses into the corral, tethering them close together in the farthest corner. They left their saddles on, hooking the stirrups over the horns so that in the wind they would not beat against the horses' sides. Miller motioned for them to follow him; bent almost double in the face of the wind, they made their way out of the corral toward the spot where they had stacked and baled the buffalo hides. The stacks of hides were drifted high with snow; some of them had blown over, and rested lengthwise on the ground; others swayed sharply before the strong gusts of wind; the corners of two or three loose hides, scattered over the ground, protruded from the snow; Andrews realized that this was what remained of an unthonged pile of hides, half as high as the completed ricks. Most of them had been blown away by the powerful wind. For a few moments, the men stood still, huddled close together beside a stack of hides.

Half leaning against it, a great weariness came over Andrews; despite the cold, his limbs loosened and his eyelids dropped. Dimly he remembered something that he had been told, or that he had read, about death by freezing. With a shiver of fright he stood up away from the hides. He flailed his arms, beating them against his sides until he could feel the blood run through them more swiftly; and he began to jog around in a small circle, lifting his knees as he ran.

Miller pushed himself away from the rick of hides where he had been resting and stood in his path; he put both hands on Andrews's shoulders, and said, his face close and his voice loud: "Be still. You want to get yourself froze to death, just keep moving around; that'll do it right quick."

Andrews looked at him dully.

"You work up a sweat," Miller continued, "and it'll freeze around you as soon as you're still for a minute. You just do what I tell you and you'll be all right." He returned to Schneider. "Fred, cut some of them hides loose."

Schneider fumbled in one of the pockets of his canvas coat and brought out a small pocketknife. He sawed at the frozen thongs until they parted and spilled the compressed hides out of their confines. Immediately, the wind caught half a dozen of them, lifted them high, and sailed them in various directions; some of them landed high in the branches of the pines, and others scudded along the snow toward the open valley and disappeared.

"Grab yourselves three or four of them," Miller shouted; and he fell upon a small pile that slid from the larger stack. Quickly Andrews and Schneider did the same; but Charley Hoge did not move. He remained huddled, half crouching. Miller, on his stomach, carrying the hides with him, crawled across the snow to where a few of the skins remained in the unbound pile. He pulled at the stiff thong that Schneider had hacked and managed to extricate a length of it from the bottom hide, where it was fastened to the small hole in the skin of what had been a buffalo leg. He cut this length into a number of pieces of equal length. Schneider and Andrews crawled across the snow and watched him as he worked.

With his short knife, Miller punched holes in each of the legs of the hides which he secured beneath him. Then, turning two of the skins against each other, so that fur touched fur, he thonged the legs together. The two other furs he turned so that the fur of each was to the weather, and placed them crosswise, one above and one beneath the crude open-ended and open-sided sack he had fashioned. When he had thonged the legs of the last two skins, there lay on the ground a rough but fairly effective protection against the weather, a bag whose ends were open but whose sides were loosely closed, into which two men could crawl and protect themselves against the main fury of the wind and hurtling snow. Miller dragged the heavy bag across the snow, pulled it among some of the fallen ricks, and jammed one open end against a bank of snow that was collecting against the fallen pile. Then he helped Charley Hoge crawl into the bag, and returned to Andrews and Schneider. Andrews lifted himself a little off the ground, and Miller pulled two of the hides from beneath him and began thonging the legs together.

"This will keep you from freezing," he shouted above the wind. "Just keep close together in this, and don't let yourselves get wet. You won't be warm, but you'll live." Andrews got to his knees and tried to grasp the edges of the hides, to pick them up and carry them to Miller, who had almost finished the first part of the shelter; but his fingers were so numb that he could not make them move with any precision; they hung at the ends of his hands and moved feebly and erratically over the frozen fur, without strength or sensation. Bending his hands from the wrists, shoving them through the snow under the hides, he staggered to his feet; pressing the hides against his lower body, he started to walk with them to Miller; but a gust of wind caught him, thrusting the hides heavily against him, and nearly lifted him off his feet. He fell to the ground again, near Miller, and pushed the hides through the snow to him.

Schneider had not moved. He lay on his stomach, on his small stack of hides, and looked at Miller and Andrews; through the snow and ice that glittered and stiffened his tangled hair and beard, his eyes gleamed.

After Miller had crossed the hides and as he was tying the last thong to hold them together, he shouted to Schneider: "Come on! Let's drag this over to where Charley and me are laying."

For a moment, through the ice and snow white on his face, Schneider's bluish lips retracted in what looked like a grin. Then slowly, from side to side, he shook his head.

"Come on!" Miller shouted again. "You'll freeze your ass off if you lay out here much longer."

Strongly through the howling wind came Schneider's voice: "No!"

Dragging the shelter between them, Andrews and Miller came closer to Schneider. Miller said:

"You gone crazy, Fred? Come on, now. Get inside this with Will, here. You're going to get froze stiff."

Schneider grinned again, and looked from one of them to another.

"You sons-of-bitches can go to hell." He closed his mouth and worked his jaws back and forth, trying to draw spittle; bits of ice and flakes of snow worked loose from his beard and were whipped away by the wind. He spat meagerly on the snow in front of him. "Up to now, I've done what you said. I went with you when I didn't want to go, I turned away from water when I knew they was water behind me, I stayed up here with you when I knew I hadn't ought to stay. Well, from now on in, I don't want to have nothing to do with you. You sons-of-bitches. I'm sick of the sight of you; I'm sick of the smell of you. From here on in, I take care of myself. That's all I give a damn about." He reached one hand forward to Miller; the fingers clawed upward, and trembled from his anger. "Now give me some of them thongs, and leave me be. I'll manage for myself."

Miller's face twisted in a fury that surpassed even Schneider's; he pounded a fist into the snow, where it sank deep to the solid ground.

"You're crazy!" he shouted. "Use your head. You'll get yourself froze. You never been through one of these blizzards."

"I know what to do," Schneider said. "I been thinking about it ever since this started. Now give me them thongs, and leave me be."

The two men stared at each other for several moments. The tiny snowflakes, thick and sharp as blowing sand, streamed between them. Finally Miller shook his head and handed the remaining thongs to Schneider. His voice became quieter. "Do what you have to do, Fred. It don't matter a damn to me." He turned a little to Andrews and jerked his head back toward the fallen bales. "Come on, let's get out of this." They crawled across the snow away from Schneider, pulling Andrews's shelter with them. Once Andrews looked back; Schneider had begun to lash his hides together. He worked alone and furiously in the open space of storm, and did not look in their direction.

Miller and Andrews placed the shelter beside the one which was humped with Charley Hoge's body, and shoved its open end against the bale of hides. Miller held the other end open and shouted to Andrews:

"Get in and lay down. Lay as quiet as you can. The more you move around, the more likely you are to get froze. Get some sleep if you can. This is liable to last for some time."

Andrews went into the bag feet first. Before his head was fully inside, he turned and looked at Miller.

Miller said: "You'll be all right. Just do what I said." Then Andrews put his head inside, and Miller closed the flap, stamping it into the snow so that it would stay closed. Andrews blinked against the darkness; the rancid smell of the buffalo came into his nostrils. He thrust his numb hands between his thighs, and waited for them to warm. They were numb for a long time and he wondered if they were frozen; when they finally began to tingle and then to pain him with their slowly growing warmth, he sighed and relaxed a little.

The wind outside found its way through the small openings of the bag and blew snow in upon him; the sides of the bag were thrust against him by the wind as it came in heavy gusts. As it lessened, the sides of the bag moved away from him. He felt movement in the shelter next to his own, and over the wind he thought he heard Charley Hoge cry out in fear. As his face warmed, the rough hair of the buffalo hide irritated his skin; he felt something crawl over it, and tried to brush it away; but the movement opened the sides of his shelter and a stream of snow sifted in upon him. He lay still and did not attempt to move again, though he realized that what he had felt on his cheek was one of the insects parasitic upon the buffalo—a louse, or a flea, or a tick. He waited for the bite into his flesh, and when it came he forced himself not to move.

After a time, the stiff hide shelter pressed upon him with an increasing weight. The wind seemed to have lessened, for no longer did he hear the angry snarl and moan about his ears. He raised the flap of his shelter, and felt the weight of the snow above him; in the darkness he saw only the faintest suggestion of light. He moved his hand toward it; it met the dry, crumbling cold of solidly banked snow.

Under the snow, between the skins that had only a few days before held together the flesh of the buffalo, his body rested. Slowly its sluggish blood generated warmth, and sent the warmth to his body's skin, and out to the close hide of the buffalo; thence his body gathered its own small warmth, and loosened within it. The shrill drone of the wind above him lulled his hearing, and he slept.

For two days and three nights the storm roared about the high valley where the men were trapped; they lay hidden under drifts of snow and did not move beneath them, except to emerge to relieve themselves, or to poke holes in the drifted banks to allow fresh air into their close dark caves of skin. Once Andrews had to come out into the weather to release water that he had held inside him until his groin and upper thighs throbbed with pain. Weakly he pushed the snow aside from his head-flap, and crawled into the bitter cold, blinking his eyes; he emerged into a darkness that was absolute. He felt the snow sting against his cheeks and forehead; he winced at the cold air that cut into his lungs; but he could see nothing. Afraid to move, he crouched where he had merged and made water into the night. Then he fumbled back through the snow and squirmed into his close shelter, which still held a bit of the body warmth that he had left.

Much of the time he slept; when he did not sleep, he lay motionless on his side, knees drawn up on his chest, so that his body would give warmth to itself. Awake, his mind was torpid and unsure, and it moved as sluggishly as his blood. Thoughts, unoccasioned and faint, drifted vaguely into his mind and out. He half remembered the comforts of his home in Boston; but that seemed unreal and far away, and of those thoughts there remained in his mind only thin ghosts of remembered sensation—the feel of a feather bed at night, the dim comfortable closeness of a front parlor, the sleepy hum of unhurried conversation below him after he had gone to bed.

He thought of Francine. He could not bring her image to his mind, and he did not try; he thought of her as flesh, as softness, as warmth. Though he did not know why (and though it did not occur to him to wonder why), he thought of her as a part of himself that could not quite make another part of himself warm. Somehow he had pushed that part away from him once. He felt himself sinking toward that warmth; and cold, before he met it, he slept again.

VII

On the morning of the third day, Andrews turned weakly under the weight of the snow and burrowed through the long drift that had gathered at his head. Though he had grown somewhat used to the cold, which even in sleep enveloped the thin edge of warmth his body managed to maintain, he flinched and closed his eyes, hunching his neck into his shoulders as his flesh came against the packed coldness of the snow.

When he came from under the snow, his eyes were still closed; he opened them upon a brilliance that seared them over for an instant with a white hotness. Though melting snow clung in patches to his hands, he clapped them over his eyes and rubbed them until the pain subsided. Gradually, by squinting his eyelids open a little at a time, he accustomed his eyes to daylight. When at last he was able to look around him, he viewed a world that he had not seen before.

Under a cloudless sky, and glittering coldly beneath a high sun, whiteness spread as far as he could see. It lay thickly drifted about the site of their camp and lay like movement frozen, in waves and hillocks over the broad sweep of the valley. The mountainside, which had defined the valley's winding course, now was softened and changed; in a gentle curve the snow lay in drifts about the dark pines that straggled from the mountain into the flat valley, so that only the tips of the trees showed dark against the whiteness of the snow. The snow was gathered high upon the mountainside, so that no longer did his eyes meet a solid sheet of green; now he saw each tree sharply defined against the snow which surrounded it. For a long time he stood where he had come out of his shelter and looked about him wonderingly, and did not move, reluctant to push through the snow which bore no mark of anything save itself. Then he stooped and poked one finger through the thin crust in front of him. He made his hand into a fist and enlarged the hole his finger had made. He scooped a handful of the snow, and let it trickle through his fingers in a small white pile beside the hole from which he had scooped it. Then, weak from lack of food and dizzy from his days and nights of lying in darkness, he stumbled forward a few steps through the waist-high drift; he turned around and around, looking at the land which had become so familiar to him that he had got out of the habit of noticing it, and which now was suddenly strange to him, so strange that he could hardly believe that he had looked upon it before. A clear and profound silence rose from the valley, above the mountains, and into the sky; the sound of his breathing came loudly to him; he held his breath to gather the quality of the silence. He heard the slither and drop of the snow as it fell from his trouser legs into the harder snow packed around his feet; in the distance there came the soft echoing snap of a branch that gave beneath its weight of snow; across the camp, from the drifted corral, came the sharp snort of a horse, so loud that Andrews imagined for a moment that it was only a few feet away. He turned toward the corral, expelling his clouded breath; beyond the drifted snow he saw the horses move.

Gathering air into his lungs, he shouted as loudly as he could; and after he had shouted, he remained with his mouth open, listening to the sound of his own voice that boomed as it grew fainter, and after what seemed to him a long time, trailed into the silence, dispersed by distances and absorbed by the snow. He turned to the mounds of snow, under one of which he had lain for two days; under the other Miller and Charley Hoge still lay. He saw no movement; a sudden fear caught him, and he took a few steps through the snow. Then he saw a tremor, saw the snow break from above the mound, and saw the break lengthen toward him. Miller's head—black and rough against the smooth whiteness from which it emerged—came into sight; the heavy arms, like those of a swimmer, flailed the snow aside and Miller stood upright, blinking furiously. After a moment he squinted at Andrews and said hoarsely, his voice wavering and unsure: "You all right, boy?"

"Yes," Andrews said. "You and Charley?"

Miller nodded. He looked across the expanse of their campsite. "I wonder how Fred made out. Likely as not he froze to death."

"The last I saw, before we settled in, he was over there," Andrews said, and pointed toward the chimney rock around which they had earlier arranged their camp. They walked toward it, their going uncertain; they sometimes plowed through drifted snow that came above their waists, and sometimes easily in snow that barely reached the middle of their calves. They went around the high rock, poking cautiously into the snow with their boots.

"No telling where he is now," Miller said. "We might not find him till the spring thaw."

But as he spoke, Andrews saw the snow move and break very close to him, beside the chimney rock.

"Here he is!" he shouted.

Between Miller and Andrews a rough shape came up through the snow. Great chunks of white ice clung to the matted hair of the buffalo hide and fell away, revealing the flat umber color; for an instant, Andrews drew back in fear, thinking irrationally that somehow a buffalo was rearing itself upward to confront them. But in the next instant, Schneider had thrown aside the skins in which he had wrapped himself like a mummy, and was standing blindly between them, his eyes screwed shut, an expression of pain furrowing the flesh between his eyebrows and pulling his mouth to one side.

"Jesus Christ, it's bright," Schneider said, his voice an unclear croak. "I can't see a thing."

"Are you all right?" Andrews asked.

Schneider opened his eyes to a slit, recognized Andrews, and nodded. "I think my fingers got a little frostbit, and my feet are damn near froze off; but I managed all right. If I ever get thawed out, I'll know for sure."

As well as they could—with their hands, their feet, and the folded buffalo hides that Schneider had discarded—the three men scraped away a large area of snow from around the chimney rock; upon the frozen ground, and over the charred, ice-coated remains of an old campfire, they piled what dry twigs they could strip from the snow-weighted lower branches of the pine trees. Miller dug into their cache of goods and found an old tinderbox, some crumpled paper that had not been wetted by the snow, and several unused cartridges. He laid the paper under the dry branches, worked the lead bullets loose from the cartridges, and poured the gunpowder upon the paper, crumpling more paper on the powder. He struck the tinderbox and ignited the powder, which flared powerfully, igniting the paper. Soon a small fire blazed, melting the snow that clung to the inward side of the rock.

"We'll have to keep this going," Miller said. "It's mighty hard to start a fire in a blowing wind with wet wood."

As the fire grew stronger, the men dug into the snow for logs and piled them, wet, upon the fire. They huddled about the warmth, so close that steam rose from their damp clothing; Schneider sat on his buffalo skins and thrust his boots close to the fire, almost into it. The smell of scorching leather mixed with the heavier smell of the burning logs.

After he had warmed himself, Miller walked across the campsite, following the irregular path that he and Andrews had made earlier, toward the place between the bales where Charley Hoge still lay. Andrews watched him go, following his progress with eyes that moved in a head that did not turn. The heat from the fire bit into his skin and pained him, and still he had the urge to get closer, to hover over the fire, to take the fire inside himself. He bit his lips with the pain of the heat, but he did not move away. He remained before the fire until his hands were a bright red, and until his face burned and throbbed. Then he backed away and instantly he was cold again.

Miller led Charley Hoge back across the snow toward the fire. Charley Hoge went before Miller, shambling loosely in the broken path, his head down, stumbling to his knees now and then. Once, when the path turned, he plowed into the unbroken snow, and halted and turned only when Miller caught at him and turned him gently back. When the two men came up before the fire, Charley Hoge stood inertly before it, his head still down, his face hidden from the others.

"He don't quite know where he is yet," Miller said. "He'll be all right in a little while."

As the fire warmed him, Charley Hoge began to stir. He looked dully at Andrews, at Schneider, and back at Miller; then he returned his gaze to the flames, and moved closer to them; he thrust the stump of his wrist close to the heat, and held it there for a long time. Finally he sat before the fire and rested his chin on his knees, which he cradled close to his chest with arms folded tightly around them; he gazed steadily into the flames, and blinked slowly, unseeingly, every now and then.

Miller went to the corral and inspected the horses; he returned leading his own horse, and reported to the men around the fire that the others seemed to be in good shape, considering the weather they had gone through. Digging again into the cache of their goods, he found the half-filled sack of grain that they had brought along to supplement the grass diet of the horses; he measured out a small quantity and fed it slowly to his horse. He told Schneider to feed the others after a while. He let his own horse wander about the area for a few moments until its muscles were loosened and it had gained strength from its food. Then, scraping the ice and snow off the saddle and tightening the cinch around its belly, he mounted.

"I'm going to ride up toward the pass and see how bad

it is," he said. He rode slowly away from them. His horse walked with head down, delicately lifting its forehooves out of the neat holes they made, and more delicately placing them on the thin crust and letting them sink, as if only by their own weight, through the snow.

After several minutes, when Miller was out of hearing, Schneider said to the fire: "It ain't no use for him to go look. He knows how bad it is."

Andrews swallowed. "How bad is it?"

"We'll be here for a while," Schneider said, and chuckled without humor; "we'll be here for a spell."

Charley Hoge raised his head and shook it, as if to clear his mind. He looked at Schneider, and blinked. "No," he said loudly, hoarsely. "No."

Schneider looked at Charley Hoge and grinned. "You come alive, old man? How did you like your little rest?"

"No," Charley Hoge said. "Where's the wagon? We got to get hitched up. We got to get out of here."

Charley Hoge got to his feet and swayed, looking wildly about him. "Where is it?" He took a step away from the fire. "We can't lose too much time. We can't—"

Schneider rose and put a hand on Charley Hoge's arm. "Take it easy," he said, gruffly and soothingly. "It's all right. Miller'll be back in a minute. He'll take care of everything."

As suddenly as he had arisen, Charley Hoge sat back on the ground. He nodded at the fire and mumbled: "Miller. He'll get us out of here. You wait. He'll get us out."

A heavy log, thawed to wetness by the heat, fell into the bed of coals; it hissed and cracked, sending up heavy plumes of blue-gray smoke. The three men squatted in the little circle of bare ground, which was soggy from the snow that had turned to water and seeped from the closely surrounding drifts. Waiting for Miller to return, they did not speak; torpid from the heat of the fire and weak from the two-day lack of food, they did not think of moving or feeding themselves. Every now and then Andrews reached over to the thinning bank beside him and lethargically took a handful of snow, stuffed it into his mouth, and let it melt on his tongue and trickle down his throat. Though he did not look beyond the campfire, the whiteness of the snow over the valley, caught and intensified by the brilliant sun, burned into his averted face, causing his eyes to smart and his head to throb.

Miller was gone from the camp nearly two hours. When he returned, he rode past the campsite without looking at anyone. He left his trembling and winded horse in the snow-banked corral and slogged wearily through the snow up to where they waited around the fire. He warmed his hands—blue-black from the cold and ingrained powder smoke that remained on them—and turned around several times to warm himself thoroughly before he spoke.

After a minute of silence, Schneider said harshly: "Well? How does it look?"

"We're snowed in good," Miller said. "I couldn't get within half a mile of the pass. Where I turned back, the snow was maybe twelve foot deep in places; and it looked like it was worse farther on."

Schneider, squatting, slapped his knees, and rose upright. He kicked at a charred log that had fallen from the fire and was sizzling on the wet ground.

"I knowed it," Schneider said dully. "By God, I knowed it before you told me." He looked from Miller to Andrews and back again. "I told you sons-of-bitches we ought to get out of here, and you wouldn't listen to me. Now look what you got yourselves into. What are you going to do now?"

"Wait," Miller said. "We get ourselves fixed up against another blow, and we wait."

"Not this feller," Schneider said. "This feller's going to get his self out of here."

Miller nodded. "If you can figure any way, Fred, you go to it."

Andrews rose, and said to Miller: "Is the pass we came over the only way out?"

"Unless you want to walk up over the mountain," Miller said, "and take your chances that way."

Schneider spread his arms out. "Well, what's wrong with that?"

"Nothing," Miller said, "if you're fool enough to try it. Even if you rigged up some snowshoes, you couldn't carry anything with you. You'd sink down in the first soft snow you came to. And you can't live off the land in the high country in the winter."

"A man with belly could do it," Schneider said.

"And even if you was fool enough to try that, you take a chance on another blow. Did you ever try to wait out a blizzard on the side of a mountain? You wouldn't last an hour."

"It's a chance," Schneider said, "that could be took."

"And even if you was fool enough to take that chance, without knowing the country you came out in, you might walk around for a week or two before you saw somebody to set you straight. There ain't nothing between here and Denver, to speak of; and Denver's a long way off."

"You know the country," Schneider said. "You could point us the way to go."

"And besides," Miller said. "We'd have to leave the goods here."

For a moment Schneider was silent. Then he nodded, and kicked at the wet log again. "That's it," he said in a tight voice. "I might of knowed. It's the goddamned hides you won't let go of."

"It's more than the hides," Miller said. "We couldn't take anything with us. The horses would run wild, and the cattle would go off with the buffalo that's still here. We'd have nothing to show for the whole try."

"That's it," Schneider said again, his voice raising. "That's what's behind it. Well, the goods don't mean that much to me. I'll go over by myself if need be. You just point out a route to me and give me a few landmarks, and I'll chance it on my own."

"No," Miller said.

"What?"

"I need you here," Miller said. "Three—" He glanced at Charley Hoge, who was rocking himself before the fire, humming tunelessly under his breath. "Two men can't manage the wagon and the hides down the mountain. We'll need you to help."

Schneider stared at him for a long moment. "You son-of-a-bitch," he said. "You won't even give me a chance."

"I'm giving you your chance," Miller said quietly. "And

that's to stay here with us. Even if I told you a route and some signs, you'd never make it. Your chance to stay alive is here with the rest of us."

Again Schneider was silent for several moments. At last he said: "All right. I should have knowed better than to ask. I'll sit here on my ass all winter and draw my sixty a month, and you sons-of-bitches can go to hell." He turned his back to Miller and Andrews, and thrust his hands angrily toward the fire.

Miller looked at Charley Hoge for a moment, as if to speak to him. Then he abruptly turned to Andrews. "Dig around in our goods and see if you can find a sack of beans. And find one of Charley's pots. We got to get some food in us."

Andrews nodded, and did as he was ordered. As he was poking through the snow, Miller left the campsite and returned a few minutes later dragging several stiff buffalo hides. He made three trips back and forth between the campsite and the place where the hides rested, returning each time with more. After he had made a pile of about a dozen, he poked in the snow until he found the ax. Then, with the ax on his shoulder, he trudged away from the camp, up the mountain, among the great forest of pine trees, the lower branches of which curved downward under the weight of the snow. The tips of many of them touched the whitened earth, so that the snow that held them down and the snow upon which they rested appeared to be the same, eccentric and bizarre curves to which the trees conformed. Under the arches thus formed Miller walked, until it appeared, as he went into the distance, that he was walking into a cave of dark green and blinding crystal.

In his absence Andrews threw several handfuls of dried beans into the iron kettle he had dug out of the snow. After the beans he scooped in several masses of snow, and placed the pot at the back of the fire, so that the kettle rested against one side of the rock. He had not been able to find the bag of salt in the snow, but he had found a small rind of salt pork wrapped in oilskin and a can of coffee. He dropped the rind into the kettle and searched again until he found the coffeepot. By the time Miller returned from the forest, the kettle of beans was bubbling and the faint aroma of coffee was beginning to rise from the pot.

On his shoulders Miller balanced several pine boughs, thick and heavy at the raw yellow butts where they had been chopped, narrowing behind him where the smaller branches and pine needles swept a heavy trail in the snow, roughing it and covering the tracks he made as he stumbled down the side of the mountain. Bent beneath the weight of the boughs, Miller staggered the last few steps up to the fire and let the boughs crash to the snow on either side of him; a fine cloud like white dust exploded up from the ground and whirled for several minutes in the air.

Beneath the grime and dirt Miller's face was blue-gray from cold and exhaustion. He swayed for several minutes where he had dropped the logs and then he walked with unsteady straightness to the fire and, still standing, warmed himself. He stood so, without speaking, until the coffee bubbled up over the sides of the pot and hissed on the coals.

His voice weak and empty, he said to Andrews: "Find the cups?"

Andrews moved the pot to the edge of the fire; his hand burned on the hot handle, but he did not flinch. He nodded. "I found two of them. The others must have blown away."

Into the two cups he poured the coffee that he had brewed. Schneider walked up. Andrews handed one of the cups to Miller, and one to Schneider. The coffee was thin and weak, but the men gulped at the scalding liquid without comment. Andrews threw another small handful of coffee into the steaming pot.

"Go easy on that," Miller said, holding the tin cup in both his hands, juggling it to prevent his hands from burning and cupping it to gather its heat. "We ain't got enough coffee now to last us; just let it boil longer."

With his second cup of coffee Miller seemed to regain some of his strength. He sipped from a third cup and passed it along to Charley Hoge, who sat still before the fire and did not look at any of the men. After his second cup, Schneider returned to the edge of the circle, beyond

Charley Hoge, and stared gloomily into the coals, which glowed faintly and grayly against the blinding whiteness that filtered through the trees, intensifying the shadow in which they sat.

"We'll build a lean-to here," Miller said.

Andrews, his mouth loose and tingling from the hot coffee, said indistinctly: "Wouldn't it be better out in the open, in the sun?"

Miller shook his head. "In the daytime, maybe; not at night. And if another blow came up, no lean-to we could build would last more than a minute on open ground. We build here."

Andrews nodded and drank the last of his coffee, tilting the cup up and throwing his head back so that the warm rim of the cup touched the bridge of his nose. The beans, softening in the boiling water, sent up a thin aroma. Though he was not aware of hunger, Andrews's stomach contracted at the odor and he bent over at the sudden pain.

Miller said: "Might as well get to work. Beans won't be ready to eat for two or three hours, and we have to get this up before night."

"Mr. Miller," Andrews said; and Miller, who had started to rise, paused and looked at him, crouched on one knee.

"Yes, boy?"

"How long will we have to be here?"

Miller stood up, and bent to brush off the black peat mud and wet pine needles that clung to his knees. From his bent head and under his black, tangled brows, he raised his eyes and looked directly at Andrews.

"I won't try to fool you, boy." He jerked his head toward Schneider, who had turned in their direction. "Or Fred either. We'll be here till that pass we come over thaws out."

"How long will that take?" Andrews asked.

"Three, four weeks of good warm weather would do it," Miller said. "But we ain't going to have three or four weeks before winter sets in hard. We're here till spring, boy. You might as well set your mind to it."

"Till spring?" Andrews said.

"Six months at the least, eight months at the most. So

we might as well dig in good, and get ourselves set for a long wait."

Andrews tried to realize how long six months would be, but his mind refused to move upon the figure. How long had they been here now? A month? a month and a half? Whatever it was, it had been so filled with newness and work and exhaustion, that it seemed like no period that could be measured, thought about, or put up against anything else. Six months. He spoke the words, as if they would mean more coming aloud from his lips. "Six months."

"Or seven, or eight," Miller said. "It won't do no good thinking about them. Let's get to work before this coffee wears off."

The rest of the day Andrews, Miller, and Schneider spent in constructing the lean-to. They stripped the smaller branches from the slender pine logs and piled them in a neat bundle near the fire. As Miller and Andrews worked on the logs, Schneider hacked from a stiff hide, the smallest and youngest he could find, a number of uneven but relatively slender thongs. His knives blunted quickly on the stonelike hides, and he had to sharpen a knife several times before it would peel off a single thong. After he had hacked a large number of thongs, he bent them so that they would fit into a huge kettle that he found among Charley Hoge's things buried in the snow. From around the fire he raked what dead ashes he could and put them in the kettle with the thongs. Then he called Miller and Andrews over to where he stood and told them to urinate in the kettle.

"What?" Andrews said.

"Piss in it," Schneider said, grinning. "You know how to piss, don't you?"

Andrews looked at Miller. Miller said: "He's right. That's the way the Indians do it. It helps draw the stiffness out of the hide."

"Woman piss is best," Schneider said. "But we'll have to make do with what we got."

Solemnly the three men made water into the iron kettle. Schneider inspected the level to which the ashes had risen; shaking his head regretfully, he threw several handfuls of snow into the kettle to bring the sooty mixture up to a level that would cover the thongs. He set the kettle on the fire, and joined Andrews and Miller in their work.

They cut the stripped logs to lengths, and set four of them—two short and two long—in a rectangle before the fire. To secure the logs, they dug into the soggy ground, cutting through the spreading roots of the trees and breaking through scattered subterranean rock, to a depth of nearly two feet. Into these holes they set the logs, so that the taller ones were facing the fire. The more slender and longer boughs they notched so that they would fit firmly, and lashed them to the thick uprights set into the ground, thus forming a sturdy boxlike frame that slanted from the foot-high stubs at the rear to the height of a man's shoulders at the front. They lashed the branches with the urine-and-ash-soaked thongs that were still so stiff they were barely workable. By that time it was midafternoon, and they paused, nearly exhausted, to eat the hard beans that had been boiling in the iron kettle. The four men ate out of a common pot, using whatever utensils they could salvage out of the snow, beneath which they lay scattered. The beans, without salt, were tasteless and lay heavy on their stomachs; but they worked them down and cleaned the heavy pot of its last morsel. When Miller, Schneider, and Andrews returned to their frame, the buffalo-hide thongs had hardened and contracted, and held the logs together like bands of iron. They spent the rest of the afternoon stringing buffalo hides to the frame, using the thongs which had softened in their bath of urine and wood ash. All around the frame they dug a shallow trench, into which they stuffed the ends of the hides, and covered them over with moist earth and peat, so that no air or moisture could run inside the shelter.

Before darkness came, the shelter was finished. It was a sturdy structure, walled and floored with buffalo skins, which were thonged and overlaid so that from the back and sides, at least, it was virtually water- and wind-proof. From the broad front, several hides were suspended loosely and arranged so that in a wind they could be secured by long pegs thrust into the ground. The men dug what remained of their bedrolls out of the snow, divided the remaining blankets equally, and spread them before the fire to dry. In the last light of the sun, which threw the snow-wrapped land into a glittering cold blue and a brilliant orange, Andrews looked at the shelter of log and buffalo hide that they had spent the day constructing. He thought: this will be my home for the next six or eight months. He wondered what it would be like, living there. He dreaded boredom; but that expectation was not fulfilled.

Their days were occupied with work. They cut narrow strips of softened hide in two-foot lengths, scraped the fur from them, made four-inch slits in the center of each, and wore these like masks over their eyes to cut down the blinding glare of the snow. From the pile of small branches of pine they selected lengths which they soaked and bent in oval shapes, and tied upon them a latticework of hide strips, using them as crude snowshoes to walk upon the thin hard crust of the snow without sinking down into it. From the softened hide they fashioned clumsy stockinglike boots, which they secured to the calves of their legs with thongs, and which kept their feet from freezing. They cured several hides to supplement the blankets that had blown away during the blizzard, and they even made for themselves loosely fitting robes which served in lieu of greatcoats. They cut wood for the fire, dragging the huge logs through the snow until the area around the camp was packed and hard, and they could slide them along the iced surface with little effort. They kept the fire going night and day, taking turns during the night getting up and walking into the sharp cold to thrust logs beneath the banked ashes. Once, during a heavy wind that lasted half the night, Andrews watched the campfire consume a dozen thick logs without once breaking into flame, the embers kept at a glowing intense heat by the wind.

On the fourth day after the blizzard, as Schneider and Andrews took axes and started into the woods to increase the stockpile of logs that grew beside the chimney rock, Miller announced that he would ride into the valley and shoot a buffalo; their meat was low, and the day promised to be fair. Miller mounted the lone horse in the corral—the other two had been turned loose to live with the oxen as best they could on what grass might be found in the

valley—and rode slowly away from the campsite. He returned nearly six hours later, and slid wearily off his horse.
He tramped through the snow to the three men who waited
for him around the campfire.

"No buffalo," he said. "They must have got out during
the blow, before the pass was snowed in."

"We ain't got much meat left," Schneider said. "The
flour's ruined, and we only got one more sack of beans."

"This ain't so high that game will be hard to find," Miller said. "I'll go out again tomorrow and maybe get us a
deer. If the worst comes, we can live on fish; the lake's froze
over, but not so thick a body can't chop through."

"Did you see the stock?" Schneider asked.

Miller nodded. "The oxen came through. The snow's
blowed away enough in spots so they'll manage. The horses
are looking poorly, but with luck they'll get through."

"With luck," Schneider said.

Miller leaned back from the fire, stretched, and grinned
at him.

"Fred, I swear you ain't got a cheerful bone in your body.
Why, this ain't bad; we're set now. I recollect one winter
I got snowed in up in Wyoming, all by myself. Clean
above timber line, and no way to get down. So high they
was no game; I lived all winter off my horse and one mountain goat, and the only shelter I had was what I made out
of that horseskin. This is good living. You got no call to
complain."

"I got call," Schneider said, "and you know it."

But as the days passed, Schneider's complaining became more and more perfunctory, and at last ceased alto-
gether. Though he slept at night in the hide shelter with
the other men, he spent more and more time alone, speaking to the others only when he was directly addressed, and
then as briefly and noncommittally as he could. Often when
Miller was off hunting for meat, Schneider would leave the
campsite and remain away until late in the afternoon, returning with nothing to show for his absence. Through his
apparent resolve to have little to do with the others of the
party, he got into the habit of talking to himself; once Andrews came upon him and heard him speaking softly, croon-

ingly, as if to a woman. Embarrassed and half-afraid, Andrews backed away from him; but Schneider heard him, and turned to face him. For a moment, the two men looked at each other; but it was as if Schneider saw nothing. His eyes were glazed and empty, and after a moment they turned dully away. Puzzled and concerned, Andrews mentioned Schneider's new habit to Miller.

"Nothing to worry about," Miller said. "A man by his self gets to doing that. I've done it myself. You got to talk, and for four men cooped together like we are, it ain't good to talk too much among their selves."

Thus, much of the time, Andrews and Charley Hoge were left to themselves at the camp while Miller hunted and Schneider wandered alone, speaking to whatever image floated before his mind.

Charley Hoge, after the first numb shock that came with his emergence from the snow, began slowly to recognize his surroundings and even to accept them. Among the debris of the camp that remained after the fury of the blizzard had spent itself, Miller had managed to find two gallon crocks of whisky that were unbroken; day by day he doled this out to Charley Hoge, who drank it with the weak thin bitter coffee made by boiling over and over the grounds used the previous day. Warmed and loosened by repeated doses of the coffee and whisky, Charley Hoge began to stir a little about the campsite—though at first he would not go beyond the wide circle between their shelter and the campfire which had been melted of the snow by the heat and their tramping upon it. One day, however, he stood bolt upright before the campfire, so suddenly that he sloshed and spilled a bit of his coffee-and-whisky. He looked around him wildly; dropping his cup to the ground, he slapped his hand about his chest, and thrust it into his jacket. Then he ran into the snow. Falling to his knees near the large tree where he had kept his goods, he began scrabbling in the snow, poking his hand downward and throwing the snow aside in small furious flurries. When Andrews went up to him and asked him what the matter was, Charley Hoge croaked only, over and over: "The book! The book!", and dug more furiously into the snow.

For nearly an hour he dug, every few minutes running back to the campfire to warm his hand and the blue puckered stump at his wrist, whimpering like a frightened animal. Realizing what he was after, Andrews joined him in his search, though he had no way of knowing where he ought to look. Finally, Andrews's numbed fingers, pushing aside a cake of snow, encountered a soft mass. It was Charley Hoge's Bible, opened and soaked, in a bed of snow and ice. He called to Charley Hoge and lifted the Bible, holding it like a delicate plate in his hands, so that the soaked pages would not tear. Charley Hoge took it from him, his hand trembling; the rest of the afternoon and part of the next morning he spent drying the book page by page, before the campfire. In the days thereafter, he filled his idleness by sipping a weak mixture of coffee and whisky and leafing through the blurred, soiled pages. Once Andrews, tense and near anger because of his inactivity and the silence that came upon the camp in Miller's absence, asked Charley Hoge to read him something. Charley Hoge looked at him angrily and did not answer; he returned to his Bible and thumbed through it dully, his forefinger laboriously tracing the lines and his brows drawn together in concentration.

Miller was most at ease in his isolation. Away from the camp in search of food during the day, he always returned shortly before twilight, appearing sometimes behind the men who waited for him, sometimes in front of them—but always appearing suddenly, as if he had thrust himself up out of the landscape. He would walk toward them silently, his dark bearded face often shagged and glittering with snow and ice, and drop whatever he had killed upon the snow near the campfire. Once he killed a bear and butchered it where it fell. When he appeared with the huge hindquarters of the bear balanced on each shoulder, staggering beneath their weight, it seemed to Andrews for an instant that Miller himself was some great animal, grotesquely shaped, its small head hunched between tremendous shoulders, bearing down upon them.

As the others weakened on their steady diet of wild meat, Miller's strength and endurance increased. After a full day of hunting, he still dressed his own kill and pre-

pared the evening meal, taking over most of the duties that
Charley Hoge seemed no longer capable of performing.
And sometimes, late, on clear nights, he went into the
woods with an ax, and the men who stayed by the warmth
of the campfire could hear the sharp hard ring of cold metal
biting into cold pine.

He spoke infrequently to the others; but his silence was
not of that intentness and desperation that Andrews had
seen during the hunt and slaughter of the buffalo. In the
evenings, hunched before the fire that reflected upon the
shelter behind them and returned the warmth to their
backs, Miller stared into the yellow flames whose light flickered over his dark, composed features; upon his flat lips
there was habitually a smile that might have been of con-
tentment. But the pleasure he took was not in the company,
even silent, of the other men; he looked at the fire and
beyond it into the darkness that was here and there lightened by the pale glow of moon or stars upon the drifted
snow. And in the mornings before he set out for his hunting,
as he fixed breakfast for the men and himself, he performed his tasks with neither pleasure nor annoyance but
as if they were only a necessary prelude for his leaving.
When he left the camp his movements seemed to flow into
the landscape; and on his snowshoes of young pine and buffalo thongs, he glided without effort and merged into the
dark forest upon the snow.

Andrews watched the men around him, and waited.
Sometimes at night, crowded with the others in the close
warm shelter of buffalo hide, he heard the wind, that often
suddenly sprang up, whistle and moan around the corners
of the shelter; at such moments the heavy breathing and
snoring of his companions, the touch of their bodies against
his own, and their body stench gathered in the closeness
of the shelter seemed almost unreal. At such times he felt
a part of himself go outward into the dark, among the wind
and the snow and the featureless sky where he was whirled
blindly through the world. Sometimes when he was near
sleep he thought of Francine, as he had thought of her when
he had been alone beneath the great storm; but he thought
of her more precisely now; he could almost bring her im-

age before his closed eyes. Gradually he let the remembrance of that last night with her come to him; and at last he came to think of it without shame or embarrassment. He saw himself pushing away from him her warm white flesh, and he wondered at what he had done, as if wondering at the actions of a stranger.

He came to accept the silence he lived in, and tried to find a meaning in it. One by one he viewed the men who shared that silence with him. He saw Charley Hoge sipping his hot thin mixture of coffee and watered whisky, warding off the bitter edge of cold that pressed against him at all times, even as he hunched over a blazing fire, and saw his blurred, rheumy eyes fixed upon the ruined pages of his Bible, as if desperately to keep those eyes from looking beyond into the white waste of snow that diminished him. He saw Fred Schneider withdraw into himself, away from his fellows, as if his lone sullen presence were the only defense he had against the great cold whiteness all around. Schneider tramped brutally through the snow, throwing as wide and rough a swath as his feet could make; through the thin slits in the narrow buffaloskin that he wore almost constantly tied over his eyes, he looked at the snow, Andrews thought, as if it were something alive, as if it were something against which he was waiting to spring, biding his time. He had taken to wearing again the small pistol that Andrews had first noticed back at Butcher's Crossing; sometimes when he muttered and mumbled to himself, his hand would creep up to his waistband, and gently caress the stock of the pistol. As for Miller—Andrews always paused when he thought of the shape that he wished Miller to take. He saw Miller rough and dark and shaggy against the whiteness of the snow; like a distant fir tree, he was distinct from the landscape, and yet an inevitable part of it. In the mornings he watched Miller go into the deep forest; and he always had the feeling that Miller did not so much go out of his sight as merge and become so intrinsic to the landscape that he could no longer be seen.

He was unable to view himself. Again, as if he were a stranger, he thought of himself as he had been a few months before at Butcher's Crossing, looking westward

from the river at the land he was now in. What had he
thought then? What had he been? How had he felt? He
thought of himself now as a vague shape that did nothing,
that had no identity. Once, on a bright cloudless day that
threw blindingly dark shadows over himself and Charley
Hoge and Schneider as they sat around the pale campfire,
he had a restless urge, a necessity to get away from the two
silent hulks on either side of him. Without a word to either,
he strapped his seldom-used snowshoes to his feet and
trudged away from the camp into the valley. For a long
time he walked, his eyes upon his feet that shuffled sibi-
lantly through the crusted snow. Though his feet were cold
to numbness above the snow, the back of his neck burned
beneath the unshadowed sun. When his legs began to ache
from the constant awkward shuffling forward, he stopped
and raised his head. All around him was whiteness which
glittered with needlelike points of fire. He gasped at the
immensity of what he saw. He raised his eyes a little more,
and saw in the distance the wavering dark points of pine
trees that lifted up the mountainside toward the pure blue
sky; but as he looked at the dark-and-bright rim of the
mountain that cut into the blue of the sky, the whole
mountainside shimmered and the edge of the horizon
blurred; and suddenly all was whiteness—above, below, all
around him—and he took an awkward backward step as a
sharp burning pain started in his eyes. He blinked and
cupped his hands over his eyes; but even upon his closed
lids he saw only whiteness. A small inarticulate cry came
from his lips; he felt that he had no weight in the whiteness, and for a moment he did not know whether he remained upright or whether he had gone down into the
snow. He moved his hands upon air, and then bent his
knees and moved his hands downward. They touched the
crusted softness of the snow. He dug his fingers into the
snow, gathering small handfuls, and thrust his hands
against his eyes. It was not until then that he realized that
he had come away from the camp without his snow-
blinders, and that the sun, reflected against the unbroken
snow, had seared his eyes so that he could not see. For
a long while he knelt in the snow, massaging his closed

lids with the snow he scraped under his fingers. Finally,
through barely-spread fingers that he kept over his eyes, he
was able to make out what he thought was the dark mass
of tree and rock that marked the campsite. With his eyes
closed, he trudged toward it; in his blindness, he sometimes
lost his balance and tumbled into the snow; when he did
so, he risked quick glimpses through his fingers so that he
could correct the direction in which he traveled. When he
finally arrived at the camp, his eyes were so burned that
he could see nothing, not even in brief glimpses. Schneider
came out to meet him and guided him into the shelter,
where he lay in darkness for the better part of three days,
while his eyes healed. Thereafter, he did not look upon the
snow again without his rawhide blinders to protect him;
and he did not go again into the great white valley.

Week by week, and at last month by month, the men
endured the changing weather. Some days were hot and
bright and summery, so still that no breeze dislodged a
flake of snow hanging on the tip of a pine bough; some
days a cold gray wind whistled through the valley, funneled
by the long reach of mountain on either side. Snow fell,
and on quiet days it made the air a solid mass that moved
gently downward from a gray-white sky; and sometimes it
was driven hard by various winds, which piled it in thick
banks about their shelter, so that from the outside it appeared that they lived in a hollowed cave of snow. The
nights were desperately, bitterly cold; no matter how closely
they put their bodies together, and no matter how heavily
they weighted themselves down with buffalo hides, they
slept in a tense discomfort. Day slipped into indistinguishable day, and week into week; Andrews had no sensation
of passing time, nothing against which to measure the coming thaw of spring. Every now and then he looked at the
notches in a stripped pine branch that Schneider had made
to keep track of the days; dully, mechanically, he counted
them, but the number had no meaning for him. He was
made aware of the passing of the months by the fact that
at regular intervals Schneider came up to him and asked
him for his month's pay. At such times, he solemnly
counted from his money belt the money Schneider de-

manded, wondering vaguely where he kept it after he got
it. But even this gave him no consciousness of passing time;
it was a duty he performed when Schneider asked him; it
had nothing to do with the time that did not pass, but
which held him unmoving where he was.

VIII

Late in March and early in April, the weather settled; and
day by day, with an agonizing slowness, Andrews watched
the snow melt in the valley. It melted first where it had
drifted most thinly, so that the once level valley became a
patchwork of bleached grass and humped banks of dirtying
snow. The days became weeks; and from the moisture that
seeped into the earth from the melting snow, and from the
steadying heat of the season, new growth poked up among
the matted winter grass. A light film of green overlaid the
grayish yellow of last year's growth.

As the snow melted and seeped into the quickening soil,
game became more plentiful; deer wandered into the valley
and cropped the fresh young blades of grass, and grew so
bold that often they grazed within a few hundred yards of
the camp; at a sound they would raise their heads, and
their small conical ears would pitch upward as their bodies
lowered and tensed, ready for flight; then, if the sound were
not repeated, they would resume their grazing, their tawny
necks bent in a delicate curve toward the earth. Mountain
quail whistled among the treetops above them and lighted
beside the deer, and fed with them, their mottled gray-
and-white-and-buff bodies blending into the earth upon
which they moved. With game so close and available, Miller no longer wandered in the forest; almost contemptuously, cradling Andrews's small repeater in the crook of his
elbow, he walked a few steps away from the camp, and
throwing the rifle butt casually to his shoulder brought
down as much game as they needed. The men were replete
with venison, quail, and elk; what dressed game they
could not eat spoiled in the growing warmth. Every

day, Schneider trudged through the melting snow toward
the pass to inspect the snow mass slowly melting between
them and the outside world. Miller looked at the sun and
calculated with his somber glances the widening patches of
bare earth that were beginning to eat toward the mountainside, and did not speak. Charley Hoge kept to his worn
Bible; but every now and then, as if with surprise, he lifted
his head and gazed upon the changing land. They gave less
care to the fire they had attended all winter long; several
times they let it go out, and had to start it again with the
tinderbox that Miller carried in his shirt pocket.

Even though the valley was almost cleared, the snow still
lay in heavy drifts where the flat land rose upward into tree
and mountain. Miller let out to graze the horse they had
kept corralled all winter; gaunt from its meager supply of
grain and what little forage it had been able to find, the
horse cropped the new grass to the bare earth around the
area that fronted their campsite. When it had regained
some of its lost strength, Miller saddled it and rode away
from the camp into the valley, and returned after several
hours with the two horses that had run loose during the
winter. After their long freedom, they were nearly wild;
when Miller and Schneider tried to hobble them, so that
they would not stray from the camp, they reared and turned
their heads, manes flying and eyes rolling upward so that
the whites were visible. After a few days of grazing on the
young grass their coats began to take on a faint shine and
their wildness decreased. At last the men were able to saddle them; the cinches they passed under their bellies could
not be tightened, so gaunt had they become during their
lean winter.

"A few more days of bad weather," Miller said bleakly,
"and we wouldn't have had any horses. We'd of had to walk
back to Butcher's Crossing."

The horses saddled and tamed, Miller, Andrews, and
Schneider rode into the valley. They paused at the wagon,
which had endured on the open plain the fury of the winter;
a few of the floor boards had warped and the metal fittings
showed thin layers of rust.

"It'll be all right," Miller said. "Needs a little grease here and there, but she'll do the job we need her to do." He leaned from his horse and touched with his forefinger the heavy metal band that encircled the wagon wheel; he looked at the bright rust on his fingertip and wiped his finger on his dirt-stiffened trousers.

From where the wagon rested, the men rode off in search of the oxen that had been loosed during the storm.

They found them all alive. Not so gaunt and bony as the horses had been, they were much wilder. When the men approached them, they broke into motion and pounded away in clumsy fright. The three men spent four days rounding up the eight oxen and leading them back to the camp, where they were hobbled and set to graze. As their bellies filled on the rapidly growing grass, they too lost some of their wildness; and before the week was out, the men were able to yoke them to the wagon and work them for a few hours aimlessly about the valley, among the wasted corpses of the buffalo killed in the fall. In the growing warmth, these corpses began to give off a heavy stench, and around them the grass grew thick and green.

As the weather warmed, the chill that had been in his bones all winter began to leave Andrews. His muscles loosened as he worked with the stock; his sight sharpened upon the greening earth; and his hearing, accustomed winter-long to noises absorbed in heavy layers of snow, began to take in the myriad sounds of the valley—the rustling of breezes through stiff pine boughs, the slither of his feet through the growing grass, the creak of the leather as his saddle moved on his horse, and the sound of the men's voices carrying across distances and diminishing into space.

As the stock fattened and became once again used to working under human hands, Schneider spent more and more time moving between the camp and the snow-packed pass that would let them out of the high valley and down the mountain into the flat country. On some days he returned, excited and eager, going up to each of them and speaking in a rapid, hoarsely whispering voice.

"It's going fast," he would say. "Underneath the rind, it's all hollow and mushy. Just a few days, now, and we can get through."

At other times he came back glumly.

"The god damned crust keeps the cold in. If we could just have a warm night or two, it might loosen up."

And Miller would look at him with a cool, not unfriendly amusement, and say nothing.

One day Schneider rode back from an inspection of the snow pack with more excitement than was usual.

"We can get through, men!" he said, his words running upon each other. "I went clean through, to the other side of the pack."

"On horseback?" Miller asked, not rising from the buffalo skin on which he lay.

"On foot," Schneider said. "Not more than forty or fifty yards of deep snow, and it's clean as a whistle from there on."

"How deep?" Miller asked.

"Not deep," Schneider said. "And it's soft as meal mush."

"How deep?" Miller asked.

Schneider raised his hand, palm downward, a few inches over his head. "Just a mite over a body's head. We could go through it easy."

"And you walked through it, you say?"

"Easy," Schneider said. "Clean to the other side."

"You god damned fool," Miller said quietly. "Did you stop to think what would happen if that wet snow caved in on you?"

"Not Fred Schneider," he said, and pounded himself on the chest with a closed fist. "Fred Schneider knows how to take care of his self. He takes no chances."

Miller grinned. "Fred, you're so hot for some soft living and easy tail, you'd burn your ass through hell if it would get you to it quick."

Schneider waved his fist impatiently. "Never mind about that. Ain't we going to get loaded?"

Miller stretched himself more comfortably on the buffalo hide. "No hurry," he said lazily. "If it's as deep as you say it is—and I know it ain't any less—we still got a few days."

"But we can get through *now!*" Schneider said.

"Sure," Miller said. "And take a chance on a cave-in. Get those oxen buried under a couple of ton of wet snow, not to say anything about ourselves, and then where would we be?"

"Ain't you even going to look?" Schneider wailed.

"No need to," said Miller. "Like I said, if it's anywhere near as deep as you say, we still got a few days. We'll just wait for a while."

So they waited. Charley Hoge, coming slowly out of his long dream during the winter, worked the oxen with the wagon for an hour or so every day, until they pulled, without a load at least, as easily as they had the previous fall. Under Charley Hoge's direction, Andrews smoked quantities of foot-long trout and great strips of venison to sustain them on their journey down the mountain and across the plain. Miller took to wandering again upon the mountainside, which was still drifted heavily in softening snow, with two rifles—his own Sharps and Andrews's varmint rifle —cradled in the crook of his arm. Frequently the men who remained at camp heard the booming of the Sharps or the smart crack of the small rifle; sometimes Miller brought his kill back to camp with him; more often he let it lie where it had dropped. At camp, his eyes constantly roved over the long valley and about the rising contours of surrounding mountainside; when he had to look away for one reason or another, he seemed to do so with reluctance.

Schneider's sullenness, which followed upon Miller's first refusal to leave the valley, turned into a kind of silent ferocity, of which Miller was the apparently unaware object. Schneider spoke to Miller only to insist that he accompany him to the pass, virtually every day, to inspect the snow pack that remained. When Schneider asked, Miller complied, neither good-naturedly nor bad-naturedly. He rode impassively away with Schneider, and returned impassively, his face set in calm untroubled lines beside Schneider's anger-reddened features. And to Schneider's half-articulate insistence, he replied only:

"Not yet."

To Andrews, though he said nothing, the last few days were the most difficult to endure. Again and again, at the imminent prospect of leaving, he found his hands clenched into fists, his palms sweaty; yet he could not have said where his eagerness to be gone came from. He could understand Schneider's impatience—he knew of Schneider's simple desire to fill his belly with civilized food, to surround his body with the softness of a clean bed, and to empty his gathered lust into the body of any waiting woman. But his own desire, though it may have included in some way all of those, was at once more intense and more vague. To what did he wish to return? From where did he wish to go? And yet the desire remained, for all its vagueness, sharp and painful within him. Several times he followed the trampled path in the snow that Miller and Schneider took to the pass, and stood where the snow lay thickly drifted in the narrow cut between the twin peaks that marked the entrance to the valley. Above the drifts, the raw brown-red rock of the peaks cut into the blue sky. He peered down the narrow open trench that Schneider had worn in the snow, but it twisted so that he could not see through it to the open country beyond.

Helpless before Miller's calm, they waited. They waited even when the snow, gathered in the solid shadow of the forest, began to melt and run in narrow rivulets past their campsite. They waited until late in April. Then one night before the campfire, suddenly Miller spoke:

"Get a good night's sleep. We load up and pull out tomorrow."

After he spoke, there was a long silence. Then Schneider rose to his feet, jumped in the air, and let out a loud whoop. He slapped Miller on the back. He turned around two or three times, laughing wordlessly. He slapped Miller on the back again.

"By God, it's about time! By God, Miller! You really ain't a bad feller, are you?" He walked in a tight circle for several minutes, laughing to himself, and speaking senselessly to the other men.

After an instant of elation at Miller's announcement, Andrews felt a curious sadness like a presentiment of nostalgia come over him. He looked at the small campfire burning cheerily against the darkness, and looked beyond the campfire into the darkness. There was the valley that he had come to know as well as the palm of his own hand; he could not see it, but he knew it was there; and there were the wasting corpses of the buffalo for whose hides they had traded their sweat and their time and a part of their strength. The ricks of those hides lay also in the darkness, hidden from his sight; in the morning they would load them on the wagon and leave this place, and he felt that he would never return, though he knew he would have to come back with the others for the hides they could not carry with them. He felt vaguely that he would be leaving something behind, something that might have been precious to him, had he been able to know what it was. That night, after the fire died, he lay in darkness, alone, outside the shelter, and let the spring chill creep through his clothing into his flesh; he slept at last, but in the night he awoke several times, and blinked into the starless dark.

In the first clear light of morning, Schneider roused them from their sleep. As celebration of their last day, they decided to drink what remained of the coffee, which they had been hoarding for several weeks. Charley Hoge made the coffee strong and black; after the weak brew made from reused grounds, the fresh bitter fragrance went to their heads and gave a new strength to their bodies. They yoked the oxen to the wagon, and drew the wagon up to the open area where the hides lay in their tall bales.

While Andrews, Schneider, and Miller boosted the great bales onto the wagon bed, Charley Hoge cleaned their camp area and packed the smoked fish and meat with the other trail goods into the large crate that had stood covered in canvas beside their campsite all winter. Weakened by their long diet of game meat and fish, the three men struggled against the weight of the bales. Six of the huge bales, laid in pairs, covered the bed of the wagon; upon these, the men managed to boost six more, so that the bound hides rose to the height of a man above the sideboards of the wagon. And though they were gasping and half faint from their labor, Miller urged them to pile six more bales upon the twelve, so that at last the hides balanced precariously ten or twelve feet above the spring clip seat which Charley Hoge was to occupy.

"Too many," Schneider gasped, after the last bale had been shoved in place. Breathing hoarsely, his face beneath its grime and smoke paler than his light hair and beard, he moved away from the wagon and looked at its towering load. "It'll never make it down the mountain. It'll tip over the first time it gets off level."

From the pile of goods that Charley Hoge had been sorting beside the wagon, Miller gathered what pieces of rope he could find. He did not answer Schneider. He knotted odd pieces of rope together, and began securing rope to the gussets and eyes along the top of the sideboard. Schneider said:

"Tying them down will just make it worse. And this wagon wasn't meant to carry this heavy a load. Break an axle, and then where'll you be?"

Miller threw a rope over the top of the bales. "We'll steady her as we go down," he said. "And if we take it careful, the axles will hold up." He paused for a moment. "I want us to go back into Butcher's Crossing with a real load. And watch their eyes bug out."

They lashed the hides to the wagon as tightly as they could, straining against the ropes, pulling them so heavily that the hides, flattened, pushed against the sideboards of the wagon and made them bulge outward. When the load was secure they stood away and looked at it, and then looked at the baled hides that remained. Andrews estimated that there were nearly forty of them on the ground.

"Two more wagon loads," Miller said. "We can come back for these later this spring. We're carrying around fifteen hundred hides—and there's better than three thousand here. Say forty-six, forty-seven hundred hides in all. If the price holds up, that's better than eighteen thousand dollars." He grinned flatly at Andrews. "Your share will come to better than seven thousand dollars. That ain't bad for a winter of doing nothing, is it?"

"Come on," Schneider said. "You can count your money when you get it in your hand. Let's finish loading and get out of here."

"You ought to of held out for shares, Fred," Miller said. "You'd of made a lot more money. Let's see—"

"All right," Schneider said. "I ain't complained. I took my chance. And you ain't got your load back to town yet, either."

"Let's see," Miller said. "If you'd held out for a sixth, you'd—"

"All right," Andrews said; his own voice surprised him. He felt a faint anger at Miller rise in him. "I said I'd take care of Schneider. And I'll give him a share above and beyond his salary."

Miller looked at Andrews slowly. He nodded very slightly, as if he recognized something. "Sure, Will. It's yours to do with."

Schneider, his face reddening, looked angrily at Andrews. "No, I thank you. I asked for sixty a month, and I been getting it. Fred Schneider takes care of his self; he don't ask nothing of nobody."

"All right," Andrews said; he grinned a little foolishly. "I'll buy you one big drunk back in Butcher's Crossing."

"I thank you," Schneider said gravely. "I'll be obliged to you for that."

They stowed their camp goods and their smoked food under the high wagon seat, and looked around them to see if anything had been left. Through the trees, the shelter in which they had spent their winter looked small and insufficient for the task it had performed. It would be here, Andrews knew, when they returned later in the spring or summer for the other hides; but in the following seasons, dried by the heat of the sun and cracked in the bitter cold of snow and ice, it would begin to disintegrate, crumble into patches and shreds; until at last it would be no more, and only the stumps of the logs they had set in the ground would remain to show their long winter. He wondered if another man would see it before it rotted in the weather and trickled down into the deep bed of pine needles upon which it stood.

They left the other bales of hides where they were, not bothering to push them back out of sight among the trees. Using the last of his strychnine, Charley Hoge sprinkled the hides to discourage vermin from nesting in the bales. Miller, Andrews, and Schneider saddled their horses, wrapped their blankets and small goods in softened buffalo hides, and strapped these behind their saddles. Charley Hoge clambered atop the high clip seat; at a signal from Miller, he leaned far to one side of the piled bales of hides, unfurled his long bull-whip behind him, and brought it smartly alongside the team of oxen. The splayed leather at the tip cracked loudly, and the crack was followed immediately by Charley Hoge's thin howling shout: "Harrup!" The startled oxen strained against the weight of the wagon, and dug their cloven hooves deep into the earth. The wooden yokes cut into their shoulder flesh, and the wood, strained in the pulling, gave sounds like deep groans. The freshly greased wheels turned on their axles and the wagon inched forward, gaining speed as the oxen found their balance against the weight they pulled. Under the weight of the hides, the wheels sank past their rims in the softened earth and left deep parallel ruts that were dark and heavy in the light yellow-green. Behind them, the men could see the ruts as far as they extended.

At the pass the snow was still fetlock deep; but it was soft, and the oxen made their way through it with comparative ease, though the wagon wheels sank in the wet earth halfway up to their hubs. At the highest point of the pass, precisely between the two peaks that were like the gigantic posts of a ruined gate that let them in and out of the valley, they paused. Schneider and Miller inspected the wagon brake that would keep the wagon from spilling too rapidly down as they descended the mountainside. As they did so, Andrews looked back upon the valley which in a few moments would be gone from his sight. At this distance, the new growth of grass was like a faint green mist that clung to the surface of the earth and glistened in the early morning sun. Andrews could not believe that this same valley had been the one he had seen pounding and furious with the threshings of a thousand dying buffalo; he could not believe that the grass had once been stained and matted with blood; he could not believe that this was the same stretch of land that had been torn by the fury of winter blizzards; he could not believe that a few weeks ago it had been stark and featureless under a blinding cover of white. He looked up and down its length, as far as he could see. Even from this distance, if he strained his eyes, he could see the expanse dotted with the dark carcasses of the buffalo. He turned away from it and pushed his horse over the pass, away from the other men and the wagon which remained immobile at the summit. After a few moments he heard behind him the slow thud of the horses' hooves and the slow creak of the wagon. The party began its long descent.

A few yards beyond the pass, the three men on horseback dismounted and tied their horses loosely together, letting them trail behind them as they made their way down the mountain. The buffalo path, which they had followed up the mountain in the fall, was soft, though not so muddy as the earth had been back in the valley. Because of the softness, the wheels of the wagon had a tendency to slip sideways off the trail whenever it pitched from a level and followed the slope of the mountain; Miller found three lengths of rope in Charley Hoge's goods crate, and secured these lengths high upon the load. As the wagon descended, the three men walked beside it and above it, level with the top of the load, and pulled steadily against the ropes, so that the wagon did not topple over as it angled broadly away from the mountain. Sometimes, when the trail turned sharply, the tottering weight of the high-piled wagon nearly pulled them off their feet; they slid downward on the slick grass, their heels digging for a hold in the earth, their hands burning on the ropes they pulled.

They went down the mountain more slowly than they had come up. Charley Hoge, dwarfed by the hides piled behind him, sat erect upon his wagon seat, angling as the wagon angled, regulating its speed by a judicious mixture of cracking whip and applied hand brake. They stopped frequently; animal and man, weakened by the long winter, were unable to go for long without rest.

Before midday they found a level plateau that extended a short way out from the mountain. They took the bits from their horses' mouths and unyoked the oxen and let them graze on the thick grass that grew among the small rocks that littered the plateau. On a broad flat rock, Charley Hoge cut into equal portions a long strip of smoked venison, and passed the portions among the men. Andrews's hand received the meat limply, and put it to his mouth; but for several minutes he did not eat. Exhaustion pulled at his stomach muscles, sickening him; tiny points darkened and brightened before his eyes, and he lay back on the cool grass. After a while he was able to tear at the tough leather-like meat. His gums, inflamed by the long diet of game, throbbed at the toughness; he let the meat soften on his tongue before he chewed it. After he had forced most of it down his throat, he stood, despite the tiredness that still pulsed in his legs, and looked about him. The mountainside was a riot of varied shade and hue. The dark green of the pine boughs was lightened to a greenish yellow at the tips, where new growth was starting; scarlet and white buds were beginning to open on the wild-berry bushes; and the pale green of new growth on slender aspens shimmered above the silver-white bark of their trunks. All about the ground the pale new grass reflected the light of the sun into the shadowed recesses beneath the great pines, and the dark trunks glowed in that light, faintly, as if the light came from the hidden centers of the trees themselves. He thought that if he listened he could hear the sound of growth. A light breeze rustled among the boughs, and the pine needles whispered as they were rubbed together; from the grass came a mumble of sound as innumerable insects rustled secretly and performed their invisible tasks; deep in the forest a twig snapped beneath the pad of an unseen animal. Andrews breathed deeply of the fragrant air, spiced with the odor of crushed pine needles and musky from the slow decay that worked upward from the earth. in the shadows of the great trees.

Just before noon the men resumed their slow journey downward; Andrews turned back and looked up the mountain they had descended. The trail had wound so erratically that he was no longer sure where he ought to look to find where they had come from. He looked upward, toward where he thought the summit of the mountain might be;

but he could not see it. The trees that surrounded their trail cut off his view, and he could not see where they had been, or gauge how far they had come. He turned again. The trail twisted below him, out of sight. He took his place between Schneider and Miller, and again the group began its torturous descent of the mountain.

The sun beat upon him, and released the stench of his own body and that of the two men on either side of him. Sickened, he turned his head one way and another, trying to get the odor of a fresh breeze. He realized suddenly that he had not bathed since that first afternoon, months before, when he had been soaked by the blood of the buffalo; nor had his clothing been washed, or even removed. All at once his shirt and his trousers were stiff and heavy on his body, and the thought of them unpleasant in his mind. He felt his skin contract from the touch of his own clothing. He shuddered, as if caught in a chill wind, and let his breath come in and out of his opened mouth. And as they more steeply descended the mountain and came nearer to the flat country, the consciousness of his own filth grew within him. At last he was in a kind of nervous agony of which he could give no evidence. When the group rested, Andrews sat apart from the others and held himself rigid so that he could not feel his flesh move against his clothing.

In the middle of the afternoon there came to their ears a low faint roar, as of wind rushing through a tunnel. Andrews paused to listen; on his right, Schneider, who kept his eyes straight ahead on the swaying wagon, bumped into him. Schneider grunted a curse, but did not take his eyes from the wagon, as Andrews moved ahead to an equal distance between Schneider and Miller. Gradually the sound of the roaring became louder; the steadiness and intensity of it made Andrews revise his first impression that it was a wind sweeping upon the edge of the mountain, where the flat land came up to meet it.

Miller turned and grinned at Andrews and Schneider. "Hear that? We ain't got much further to go."

Then Andrews realized that the sound he heard must be the river, swollen with the spring run-off.

The thought of the end of their descent, and of cool

water, quickened their steps and gave them a new strength. Charley Hoge cracked his whip and released his hand brake a few inches. The wagon swayed perilously on the uneven trail; at one point, the wheels on the side facing the three men lifted several inches off the ground; and as Charley Hoge whooped and set his brake, and as the three men pulled desperately on their ropes, the wagon shuddered for an instant before it was pulled back on all four wheels, rocking from one side to another beneath the unbalanced weight of the hides. After that they proceeded somewhat more slowly; but still the imminence of rest conserved their strength, and they did not stop again until they reached the flat moss-covered rock that gently sloped into the river bank.

On the flat bed of rock, they dropped their ropes and sprawled in rest. The rock was cool and moist from the spray flung by the river that ran alongside it, and the sound of the water rushing was so heavy that they had to shout above it.

"High for this time of year," Schneider yelled.

Miller nodded. Andrews squinted against the fine spray. The water flowed from bank to bank, broken at places into whirling ripples by unseen rock deep in the river bed. Here and there, the flowing stream broke into white foam; the foam and stray bits of bark and green leaves rushing upon the surface of the water were the only indications of the speed and thrust that the water gained in its long drop from the mountains. In the early fall, when they had crossed it last, the river had been a thin trickle that barely covered the bed of rock; now it stretched from bank to bank and cut away the earth opposite where they rested. Andrews looked up and down the river; on either side of him, the narrowest part stretched to at least a hundred yards.

Charley Hoge unyoked the oxen and let them join the horses at the edge of the bank. The animals touched their muzzles delicately upon the surface of the rushing water and flung their heads upward as the spray hit their eyes and nostrils.

On the rock, Schneider half crawled and half slid past Andrews and Miller. He knelt beside the river, cupped his hands into the water, and drank noisily from the streaming bowl of his hands. Andrews went across the rock and sat beside him. After Schneider had finished drinking, Andrews let his legs slide over the rock into the river; the force of the water caught him unprepared, and swung his lower body halfway around before he could stiffen his legs against the cold sharp thrust. The water broke in swirls and white riffles around his legs, just below the knees; the cold was like needles, but he did not move his legs. Little by little, holding to the rock behind him, he let his body into the stream; his breath came in gasps from the shock of the cold. Finally, his feet found the rocky bottom of the stream, and he leaned away from the bank toward the water that rushed at him, so that he stood free of the bank, balancéd against the force of the river. He found a knobby protuberance on the rock to his right; he grasped the knob, and let his body fully down into the water. He squatted, submerging himself to his shoulders, holding his breath at the intense cold; but after a moment the cold left him and the feel of the water flowing about his body, washing at the accumulated filth of a winter, was pleasant and soothing, and almost warm. Still tightly grasping the rock with his right hand, he let his body be carried with the rushing of the stream, until at last it lay loose and straight in the course of the water, held near the foaming surface by the river's flow. Nearly weightless, holding to the knob of rock, he lay for several moments in the water, his head turned to one side and his eyes closed.

Above the roar of the water, he heard a noise. He opened his eyes. Schneider squatted on the rock above and to one side of him, grinning widely. His hand cupped, and went into the water; it came up suddenly, and pushed water into Andrews's face. Andrews gasped and drew himself out, bringing his free hand up quickly as he did so, splashing water at Schneider. For several moments, the two men, laughing and sputtering, dashed water toward each other as if they were playing children. Finally Andrews shook his head and sat panting on the rock beside Schneider. A light breeze chilled his skin but there was sunlight to warm him. Later, he knew, his clothes would stiffen on his body; but now they were loose and comfortable to his skin, and he felt almost clean.

"Jesus God," Schneider said, and stretched to lie on the sloping rock. "It's good to be down off that mountain." He turned to Miller. "How long you think we'll be, getting back to Butcher's Crossing?"

"Couple of weeks at the most," Miller said. "We'll go back quicker than we came."

"I ain't hardly going to stop," said Schneider, "except to get my belly full of greens and wash it around with some liquor, and then see that little German girl for a bit. I'm going straight on to St. Louis."

"High living," Miller said. "St. Louis. I didn't know you liked it that high, Fred."

"I didn't either," Schneider said, "until just a minute ago. Man, it takes a winter away from it to give you a taste for living."

Miller got up from the rock and stretched his arms out and up from his sides. "We'd better find our way across this river before it starts getting dark."

While Miller gathered their horses from around the banks where they were cropping at the lush grass, Andrews and Schneider helped Charley Hoge round up the oxen and yoke them to the wagon. By the time they finished, Miller had brought their horses up near them, and, mounted on his own, had found what looked like a crossing. The other men stood side by side on the bank and watched silently as Miller guided his horse into the swift water.

The horse was reluctant to go in; it advanced a few steps into the graveled bed of a shallow eddy and halted, lifting its feet, one by one, and shaking them delicately just above the surface. Miller patted the animal on its shoulder, and ran his fingers through its mane, leaning forward to speak soothingly in its ear. The horse went forward; the water flowed and parted whitely around its fetlocks, and as it advanced the water rose upward, until it flowed around the shanks and then around the knees. Miller led the horse in a zigzag path across the river; when it slipped on the smooth underwater rocks, Miller let it stand still for a moment and soothed it with small pats, speaking softly. In the middle of the river, the water rose above Miller's stirruped feet and submerged belly of the horse, parting on its shoulder and thigh. Very slowly, Miller zigzagged to shallower water; in a few minutes, he was across the river and on dry land. He waved, and then pushed his horse back into the water, zigzagging again so that the lines of his return intersected the lines of his going.

Back on the bank where the others waited, Miller got down from his horse and walked over to them; his water-filled boots squished with each step, and water streamed behind him, darkening the rock.

"It's a good crossing," Miller said. "Nearly flat all the way, and straight across. It's a little deep right in the middle, but the oxen can make it all right; and the wagon's heavy enough to weight itself down."

"All right," Schneider said. "Let's get going."

"Just a minute," Miller said. "Fred, I want you to ride alongside the lead team and guide them across. I'll go in front, you just follow along behind me."

Schneider squinted at him for a few moments, and then shook his head.

"No," he said, "I think maybe I'd better not do it. I never have liked oxen, and they ain't too fond of me. Now if it was mules, I'd say all right. But not oxen."

"There's nothing to it," Miller said. "You just ride a little downstream from them; they'll go right straight across."

Schneider shook his head again. "Besides," he said, "I don't figure it's my job."

Miller nodded. "No," he agreed, "I guess it ain't, rightly speaking. But Charley ain't got a horse."

"You could let him have yours," Schneider said, "and you could double up with Will, here."

"Hell," Miller said, "there ain't no use making a fuss over it. I'll lead them across myself."

"No," Charley Hoge said. The three men turned to him in surprise. Charley Hoge cleared his throat. "No," he said again. "It's my job. And I don't need no horse." He pointed with his good hand to the off-ox in the lead team. "I'll ride that one acrost. That's the best way to do it, anyhow."

Miller looked at him narrowly for a moment. "You feel up to it, Charley?" he asked.

"Sure," Charley Hoge said. He reached into his shirt and pulled out the warped and stained Bible. "The Lord will provide. He'll turn my steps in the right path." He contracted his stomach and thrust the Bible inside his shirt under his belt.

Miller looked at him for another moment, and then abruptly nodded. "All right. You follow straight along behind me, hear?" He turned to Andrews. "Will, you take your horse across now. Go just like I did, only you go straight across. If you find any big rocks, or any big holes, stop your horse and yell out so we can see where they are. It won't take a very big jolt to turn this wagon over."

"All right," Andrews said. "I'll wait for you on the other side."

"Now be careful," Miller said. "Take it slow. Let your horse set her own speed. That water's mighty fast."

"I'll be all right," Andrews said. "You and Charley just take care of the hides."

Andrews walked to his horse and mounted. As he turned toward the river, he saw Charley Hoge pull himself up on one of the oxen. The beast moaned and pulled away from the strange weight, and Charley Hoge patted it on the shoulder. Schneider and Miller watched Andrews as he set his horse into the first shallow.

The horse shuddered beneath him as the water climbed above its fetlocks and swirled about its knees. Andrews set his eyes upon the wet and trampled earth across the river where Miller had emerged, and kept his horse pointed straight toward it. Beneath him he felt the uncertainty of the horse's footing; he tried to make himself loose and passive in the saddle, and slackened the reins. In the middle of the river, the water, sharply cold, came midway between his ankle and his knee; the heavy thrust pressed his leg against the horse's side. As the animal stepped slowly forward, Andrews felt for brief instants the sickening sensation of weightlessness as he and the horse were buoyed and pushed aside by the swift current. The roaring was intense and hollow in his ears; he looked down from the point of land that dipped and swayed in his sight, and saw the water. It was a deep but transparent greenish brown, and it flowed past him in thick ropes and sheeted wedges, in shapes that changed with an incredible complexity before his gaze. The sight dizzied him, and he raised his eyes to look again at the point of earth toward which he aimed.

He reached the shallows without coming across a hole or rock that was likely to cause difficulty for the wagon. When his horse clambered upon dry land, Andrews dismounted and waved to the men who waited on the opposite bank.

Miller, small in the distance that was intensified by the water rushing across it, raised his arm in a stiff response and then let it drop to his side. His horse started forward. After he had gone fifteen or twenty feet into the river, he turned and beckoned to Charley Hoge, who waited astride one of the lead oxen, his oxgoad held high in his good left hand. He let the goad down lightly upon the shoulder of the lead ox, and the team lumbered forward into the shallows. The load of skins swayed as the wagon wheels came off the tiny drop of the bank into the river.

On the bank upstream from the wagon, Schneider waited on his horse, watching intently the progress of the wagon as it went deeper in the swirling river. After a minute, he too turned his horse and followed the wagon, eight or ten yards upstream from it.

When the lead oxen sank to their bellies in the heavy stream, the oxen farthest back, next to the wagon, still had not gone above their knees. Andrews then understood the safety of the crossing; by the time the farthest oxen were insecure and had the struggle to maintain their footing, the other oxen would be in the shallows and could pull the main weight of the wagon; and when the wagon was sunk to its bed, and the sides would receive the full force of the river, all the oxen would be in shallower water, and could maintain a steady pull upon it. He smiled a little at the fear he had not known he had until the instant he lost it, and watched Miller, who had pulled many yards ahead of the lead oxen, hurry his horse through the shallows and up on dry land. Miller dismounted, nodded curtly to Andrews, and stood on the riverbank, guiding Charley Hoge toward him with quick beckoning gestures of both hands.

When the lead oxen were in the shallows within ten feet of the bank, Charley Hoge slipped off the bull he had ridden across and sloshed in the knee-deep water beside them, looking back at the wagon, which was nearing the deepest part of the river. He slowed the oxen and spoke soothingly to the lead team.

Miller said: "Easy, now. Bring them in easy."

Andrews watched the wagon dip toward the hollow in the center of the river. He turned his head a little, and saw that Schneider, still upstream, had pulled up even with the wagon. Water curled about the belly of his horse; Schneider's eyes intently watched the water before him, between the ears of his slowly moving horse. Andrews looked away from Schneider, swinging his gaze upriver, following the dense line of trees that in some spots grew so close to the bank that their trunks were darkened halfway up by the flung spray. But suddenly his gaze fixed itself upon the river. For an instant paralyzed, he raised himself as tall as he could and looked intently at that point that had caught his eye.

A log, splintered at the downstream end, nearly as thick as a man's body and twice as long, bobbed like a matchstick and hurtled forward, half in and half out of the swirling water. Andrews ran to the edge of the bank and shouted, pointing upstream:

"Schneider! Look out! Look out!"

Schneider looked up and cupped his ear toward the faint voice that came across the roaring of the water. Andrews called again, and Schneider leaned forward a little in his saddle, trying to hear.

The splintered end of the log thrust into the side of Schneider's horse with a ripe splitting thud that was clearly audible above the roar of the water. For an instant the horse struggled to keep upright; then the log tore away, and the horse gave a short high scream of agony and fear, and fell sideways toward the wagon; Schneider went into the water as the horse fell. The horse turned completely over, above Schneider, and for an instant the great gaping hole that had been its belly reddened the water around it.

Schneider came up between the fore and hind legs of the horse, facing the men who stood on the bank. For an instant, the men could see his face quite clearly; he was frowning a little, as if vaguely puzzled, and his lips were twisted in a slight grimace of annoyance and contempt. He put out his left hand, as if to push the horse away from him; the horse turned again and one of its hind hooves thudded heavily high on Schneider's head. Schneider stiffened to his full length and quivered as if in a chill; his expression did not change. Then the blood came down solidly over his face like a red mask, and he toppled slowly and stiffly into the water beside his horse.

The horse and the log hit the wagon broadside at almost the same instant. The wagon was pushed sideways over the rocks; the high load swayed, and pulled the wagon; water gathered over the feebly threshing horse, and piled upon the bottom of the wagon bed. With a great groan, the wagon toppled on its side.

As it toppled, Charley Hoge jumped out of the way of the oxen, which were being pulled back into the river by the weight of the overturned wagon. For a moment, the wagon drifted lazily at the middle of the river, held to some stability by the weight of the near oxen, which threshed against their yokes and beat the water to a froth; then, caught more firmly, the wagon scraped against the rock bottom of the river, and swung lazily around, dragging the oxen with it. As the oxen's footholds on the river bed were loosened, the wagon drifted more swiftly away and began to break up on the heavier rocks downstream. The lashing that held the load broke, and buffalo hides exploded in all directions upon the water, and were rapidly borne out of sight. For perhaps a minute, the men who stood on the bank could see the oxen struggling head over heels in the water, and could see the smashed wagon turning and drifting into the distance. Then they could see nothing, though they stood for several minutes more looking downstream where the wagon had disappeared.

Andrews dropped to his hands and knees and swung his head from side to side like a wounded animal. "My God!" he said thickly. "My God, my God!"

"A whole winter's work," Miller said in a flat dead voice. "It took just about two minutes."

Andrews raised his head wildly, and got to his feet. "Schneider," he said. "Schneider. We've got to—"

Miller put his hand on his shoulder. "Take it easy, boy. Won't do no good to worry about Schneider."

Andrews wrung his hands; his voice broke. "But we've got to—"

"Easy," Miller said. "We can't do anything for him. He was dead when he hit the water. And it would be foolish to try to look for him. You saw how fast them oxen was carried down."

Andrews shook his head numbly. He felt his body go loose, and felt his legs shamble away from Miller. "Schneider," he whispered. "Schneider, Schneider."

"He was a blasphemer," Charley Hoge's voice cracked high and thin. Andrews stumbled over to him, and looked blearily down at his face.

Charley Hoge looked unseeingly down the river; his eyes blinked rapidly, and the muscles of his face twitched uncontrolled, as if his face were falling apart. "He was a blasphemer," Charley Hoge said again, and nodded rapidly. He closed his eyes, and clutched at his belly, where his Bible was still strapped. He said in a high thin singsong voice: "He lay with scarlet women and he fornicated and he blasphemed and he took the name of the Lord in vain." He opened his eyes and turned his unseeing face toward Andrews. "It's God's will. God's will be done."

Andrews backed away from him, shaking his head as Charley Hoge nodded his.

"Come on," Miller said. "Let's get out of here. Nothing we can do."

Miller led Charley Hoge up to his horse and helped him to mount behind the saddle. Then he swung himself up and called back to Andrews: "Come on, Will. The sooner we get away from here, the better it'll be."

Andrews nodded, and stumbled toward his horse. But before he mounted he turned and looked again at the river. His eye was caught by something on the opposite bank. It was Schneider's hat, black and sodden and shapeless, caught and held by the water between two rocks that jutted out from the bank.

"There's Schneider's hat," Andrews said. "We ought not to leave it there."

"Come on," Miller said. "It's going to get dark soon."

Andrews mounted his horse and followed Miller and Charley Hoge as they rode slowly away from the river.

PART THREE

I

On a bleak afternoon late in May, three men rode in an easterly direction along the Smoky Hill Trail; a northern wind slanted a fine, cold rain upon them so that they huddled together, their faces turned down and away. For ten days they had come in nearly a straight line across the great plains, and the two horses that carried them were tired; their heads drooped downward, and their bony sides heaved at the exertion of walking on level ground.

Shortly past midafternoon, the sun broke through the slatelike clouds, and the wind died. Steam rose from the mud through which their horses stumbled, and the wet heat stifled the men who sat lethargically on their saddles. On their right were still visible the low-lying trees and bushes that lined the banks of the Smoky Hill River. For several miles they had been off the trail, cutting across the flat country toward Butcher's Crossing.

"Just a few more miles," Miller said. "We'll be there before dark."

Charley Hoge, sitting behind Miller, eased his buttocks on the bony rump of the horse; his good hand was hooked into Miller's belt, and the stump of his right wrist hung loosely at his side. He looked across at Andrews, who rode abreast of Miller; but there was no recognition in his eyes. His lips moved silently, and every now and then his head bobbed quickly, nervously, as if he responded to something that the others did not hear.

A little more than an hour later they were in sight of the humped bank of the narrow stream that cut across the road to Butcher's Crossing. Miller dug his heels into his horse's sides; the horse jumped forward, trotted for a few moments, and then settled into its usual slow gait. Andrews raised himself in his saddle, but he could not see the town above the high banks of the stream. Where they rode now, the rain had not fallen; and the dust of the road, stirred by the slow shuffle of their horses' hooves, rose about them and clung to their damp clothing, and streaked their faces where the sweat ran.

They came up the road over the hump of river bank, and Andrews got a quick glimpse of Butcher's Crossing before they descended into the narrow gulley where the shallow stream ran. It was little fuller than it had been last fall; the water that trickled along its bed was a thick, muddy brown. The men let their horses halt in the middle and drink of the muddy water before they urged them on.

They passed on their left the clump of cottonwoods, scrawny and bare in new leafage; again, Andrews strained his eyes eastward toward Butcher's Crossing. In the late afternoon sun the buildings were ruddy where they were not sharply cast in shadow. A lone horse grazed between themselves and the town; though several hundred yards distant, it raised its head at their approach and trotted away in a short burst of speed.

"Let's turn in here for a minute," Miller said, and jerked his head in the direction of the wagon-track road to their right. "We got things to talk over with McDonald."

"What?" Andrews said. "What do we need to talk to him about?"

"The hides, boy, the hides," Miller said impatiently. "We still got better'n three thousand hides waiting for us where we left them."

"Of course," Andrews said. "For a minute I forgot."

He turned his horse and rode beside Miller upon the twin tracks of earth worn bare by passing wagons. Here and there in the wagon tracks, small tufts of new grass sprouted and spread to the level stretch of grass that covered the prairie.

"Looks like McDonald had a good winter," Miller said. "Look at them hides."

Andrews looked up. Bales of buffalo hides were piled

about the tiny shack that served McDonald as an office, so that as the men rode up they could see only a small section of the warped roof. The bales spread out from the immediate area of the shack and lay irregularly about the edges of the fenced brining pits. Scattered among the bales were a dozen or more wagons; some, upright, blistered and warped in the heat; their wheels were sunk in the earth and grass grew green and strong above their rims. Others were overturned, the metal bands about the spoked wheels showing brilliant spots of rust in the afternoon sun.

Andrews turned to Miller and started to speak, but the expression on Miller's face stayed him. Beneath the black curly beard, Miller's mouth was loose with puzzlement; his large eyes narrowed as they surveyed the scene.

"Something's wrong here," he said, and dismounted from his horse, leaving Charley Hoge seated slackly behind the saddle.

Andrews got off his horse and followed Miller as he threaded his way among the bales of hides toward McDonald's shack.

The door of the shack was loose on its rusted hinges. Miller pushed it open and the two men went inside. Papers lay scattered on the floor, opened ledgers had spilled from untidy piles, and the chair behind McDonald's desk was overturned. Andrews stooped and picked up a sheet of paper from the floor; the writing had been washed away, but the print of a heel mark still showed upon it. He picked up another, and another; all showed the ravages of neglect and weather.

"Looks like Mr. McDonald hasn't been here for some time," Andrews said.

For several moments Miller looked somberly about the room. "Come on," he said abruptly, and turned and clumped across the floor, his feet grinding into the scattered papers. Andrews followed him outside. The men mounted their horses and rode away from the shack toward Butcher's Crossing.

The single street that bisected the group of shacks and buildings that made up the town was nearly deserted. From the blacksmith shop on their right came the slow light clank

of metal striking metal; in the light shadows of the open
shelter there was the vague slow movement of a man's body.
On the left, set back from the road, was the large sleeping
house that lodged many of the hunters during their brief
stays in town; the muslin covering of one of the high windows was torn, and it sagged outward and moved sluggishly
in the light hot breeze. Andrews turned his head. In the
dimness of the livery stable two horses drowsed, standing
upright over empty feed troughs. As they passed Jackson's
Saloon, two men, who had been sitting on the long bench
beside the doorway of the saloon, got slowly up and walked
to the edge of the board walk and watched the three men
on their two horses. Miller looked closely at the men and
then shook his head at Andrews.

"Looks like everybody's asleep or dead," he said. "I don't
even recognize them two."

They stopped their horses in front of Butcher's Hotel,
and wrapped their reins loosely around the hitching post
set several yards away from the walk in front of the building. Before they went inside, they loosened the cinches
under the bellies of their horses and untied their bedrolls
from behind their saddles. During all this Charley Hoge
sat motionless on the rump of Miller's horse. Miller tapped
him on the knee and Charley Hoge turned dully.

"Get down, Charley," Miller said. "We're here."

Charley Hoge did not move; Miller grasped his arm and,
gently, half pulled him down to the ground. With Charley
Hoge walking unsteadily between them, Andrews and
Miller went into the hotel.

The wide lobby was almost completely bare; two straight
chairs, one of them with a splintered back, stood together
against a far wall; a fine patina of dust covered the floor,
the walls, and the ceiling. As they walked across to the
counter of the desk clerk, their steps left distinct prints on
the wood floor.

In the dimness of the enclosing counter an aging man
dressed in rough work clothing dozed in a straight chair
tilted back against a bare desk. Miller slapped his palm
hard on the surface of the counter. The man's rasping
breath caught sharply, his mouth closed, and the chair came

forward; for an instant he glowered sightlessly; then he blinked. He got up and came unsteadily to the counter, yawning and scratching at the gray stubble around his chin.

"What can I do for you?" he mumbled, and yawned again.

"We want two rooms," Miller said evenly, and threw his bedroll across the counter; dust exploded silently upward, and hung in the dim air.

"Two rooms?" the old man said, his eyes focusing upon them. "You want two rooms?"

"How much?" Miller asked. Andrews threw his bedroll down beside Miller's.

"How much?" The man scratched his chin again; a faint rasping came to Andrews's ears. The old man, still looking at them, fumbled beneath the counter and brought up a closed ledger. "I dunno. Dollar apiece sound all right?"

Miller nodded and shoved the ledger, which the old man had opened in front of him, to Andrews. Miller said: "We'll want some tubs and some hot water, and some soap and razors. How much will that be?"

The old man scratched his chin. "Well, now. What're you fellows used to paying for such a chore?"

"I paid two bits last year," Andrews said.

"That sounds reasonable," the old man said. "Two bits apiece. I think I'll be able to heat up some water for you."

"What's the matter with this damn town?" Miller said loudly, and again slapped his palm upon the counter. "Did everybody die?"

The old man shrugged nervously. "I don't know, mister. I only been here a few days, myself. On my way to Denver, and ran out of money. Man said, you take care of this place good, and you keep what you make. That's all I know."

"Then I don't suppose you've heard of a man named McDonald. J. D. McDonald."

"Nope. Like I said, I only been here—"

"All right," Miller said. "Where are our rooms?"

The old man handed them two keys. "Right up the stairs," he said. "The numbers are on the keys."

"Lead the horses over to the livery stable," Miller said. "They need taking care of bad."

"The horses over to the livery stable," the old man repeated. "Yes, sir."

Miller and Andrews picked up their bedrolls and went to the stairs. The dust lay smooth and unbroken on the steps.

"Looks like we're the first customers in a long time," Andrews said.

"Something's wrong," Miller said. With Charley Hoge between them, the three men bumped together going up the stairs. "I don't like the way things feel."

Their rooms were side by side, just off the stairs; the number on Andrews's key was seventeen. As Miller and Charley Hoge started into their room, Andrews said: "If I get through before you do, I'll be outside. I want to look around a little."

Miller nodded, and pushed Charley Hoge before him.

When Will Andrews turned his key in the lock and pushed the door inward, a billow of musty air came from the unused room. He left the door half open and went to the muslin-covered window; the cloth in its wooden frame was clogged with dust. He detached the frame from the window, and set it on the floor beside a wooden rain shutter which showed no sign of having been used against the weather. A warm breeze moved sluggishly through the room.

Andrews unrolled the mattress on the narrow rope bed, and sat on the bare ticking. He removed his shoes, fumbling with the strips of buffalo hide that months before had replaced the original thongs; the soles were worn thin, and the leather of the uppers had cracked through. He held one shoe in his hands and gazed at it for several moments; curiously, he pulled against the leather; it ripped like heavy paper. Quickly, he removed the rest of his clothing, and heaped it in a pile beside the bed; he unstrapped his stained and crumpled money belt and dropped it on the mattress. Naked, he rose from the bed and stood in the center of the room in the amber light that came through the window. He looked down at his bare flesh; it was a dirty, grayish white, like the underbelly of a fish. He pushed

his forefinger along the hairless skin of his belly; dirt came
off in long thin rolls and revealed more dirt beneath. He
shuddered, and went to the washstand near the window.
He took a dusty towel from the rack, shook it out, and
wrapped it around his loins; he went back to the bed and
sat, and waited for the old man to come up with his tub
and water.

The old man, breathing heavily, came up shortly with
two tubs, depositing one in Miller's and Charley Hoge's
room and the other in Andrews's room.

Shoving the tub to the center of the floor, the old man
looked curiously at Andrews, who remained sitting on the
bed.

"By God," he said. "You men sure got a powerful stink
to you. How long since you had a bath?"

Andrews thought for a moment. "Not since last August."

"Where you been?"

"Colorado Territory."

"Oh. Prospecting?"

"Hunting."

"For what?"

Andrews looked at him in tired surprise. "Buffalo."

"Buffalo," the old man said, and nodded vaguely. "I think
I heared once they used to be buffalo up there."

Andrews did not speak. After a moment the old man
sighed and backed toward the door. "Water'll be hot in a
few minutes. Anything else you need, just let me know."

Andrews pointed to the heap of clothing on the floor beside the bed. "You might take these out with you, and get
me some new ones."

The old man picked up the clothing, holding it in one
hand, away from him. Andrews got a bill from his money
belt and put it in the man's other hand.

"What'll I do with these?" the old man asked, moving
the clothing slightly.

"Burn them," Andrews said.

"Burn them," the man repeated. "Any special kind of
clothes you want from the dry goods store?"

"Clean ones," Andrews said.

The old man cackled, and went out of the room; Andrews did not move from the bed until he returned with two buckets of water. He watched as the old man poured them into the tub. From his pockets the old man withdrew a razor, a pair of scissors, and a large bar of yellow soap.

"I had to buy the razor," he said, "but the scissors is mine. I'll bring your clothes up directly."

"Thanks," Andrews said. "And you might as well be heating up some more water."

The old man nodded. "I reckoned this wouldn't get you clean. I've already got some started."

Andrews waited for a few moments after the old man had left the room. Then, holding the soap, he stepped into the lukewarm water and lowered himself. He sloshed water over his upper body and soaped himself vigorously, watching with a kind of ecstasy the dirt fall away in long strips beneath the gritty soap. His body, covered with tiny unhealed insect bites, stung from the strong soap; nevertheless he raked his fingernails roughly across his flesh, working the soap in, and leaving long red welts in crisscrosses on his body. He soaped his hair and beard and watched the black streams of water run back into the tub. His own stench, released by the cleansing he gave himself, rose from the water, and made him hold his breath.

When the old man came back in his room with fresh water, Andrews, naked and dripping grayish water on the bare floor, helped him lug the tub to the open window. They emptied it on the sidewalk below. The water splashed into the street and was immediately absorbed into the dust.

"Whew," the old man said. "That's mighty powerful water." He had brought Andrews's new clothes with him and had tossed them upon the bed before they emptied the water; now he pointed to them. "Hope they fit; it was the nearest I could get to what you throwed away."

"They'll be all right," Andrews said.

He bathed more leisurely, building suds over his body and watching them float on the surface of the water. At last he stepped from the tub and toweled himself dry, marveling at the whiteness of his skin, and slapping it to see the rosy welts appear there. Then he went to the washbasin, where the old man had left the razor and scissors. He raised his eyes to the mirror that was hung crookedly above the basin.

Though he had seen his face dimly and darkly in the pools and streams where they had watered, from the mountains across the great plain, and though he had grown used to the feel upon his face and beneath his fingers of the long tangled beard and hair, he was not prepared for what he saw in the mirror. His beard, still damp from the bath, lay twisted in light brown cords on the lower half of his face, so that it seemed he peered at himself in a mask that made his face like that of anyone he might imagine. The upper half of his face was a bloodless brown, darker than his beard or hair; it had hardened in the weather, so that he could see no expression and no identity where he looked. His hair grew over his ears, and hung nearly to his shoulders. For a long time he stared at himself, turning his head from side to side; then he slowly took up the scissors from the table and started cutting away at his beard.

The scissors were dull, and the strands of hair that he caught and lifted in one hand slipped between the blades so that he had to angle the scissor blades to his face, half cutting and half hacking at the tough, fine hair. When he had reduced the beard to a long stubble, he soaped his face with the yellow soap he had bathed in and drew the razor in short careful strokes over his skin. When he finished, he rinsed the soap from his face and looked at himself again in the mirror. Where the beard had been his flesh was a dead white, startling against the brown of his forehead and cheeks. He flexed the muscles of his face, retracting the mouth in a mirthless grin, and took the skin along his jaw between a thumb and forefinger; it felt numb and lifeless. His whole face was diminished, and it stared palely at him from its tangle of hair. He took the scissors up again, and began hacking away at the hair that lay in thick ropes about his face.

After several minutes, he stood back from the mirror and surveyed his work. His hair was awkwardly and unevenly cut, but it no longer made his face appear that of a child. He brushed together the tufts of hair that had settled on the table, crushed them in his hands, and dropped them out of his window, where they dispersed in the air and floated slowly to the ground, catching the late sunlight in flashing glints and then disappearing as they settled on the sidewalk and the earth below him.

The clothes that the old man had got for him were rough and ill-fitting, but the coarse clean feel of them gave his body a vitality and a sensation of delicacy that it had not had in many months. He turned the bottoms of the sharply creased black broadcloth trousers up over the tops of his stiff new shoes, and opened the top button of the heavy blue shirt. He went out of his room, and in the hall paused before Miller's and Charley Hoge's door. He heard from within the sounds of splashing water. He went down the stairs, through the lobby, and stood on the board sidewalk outside the hotel in the heat and stillness of the late afternoon.

The odd lengths of scrap wood that constituted the sidewalk had warped during the winter, and many of them curved upward from their width, so that Andrews in his new shoes had to walk carefully upon them. He looked up and down the street. To the left of the hotel, east of town, a broad square of packed grassless earth shone in the late rays of the sun. After a moment of thought, Andrews recalled that this was the site of the large army tent that had been the establishment of Joe Long, Barbar. Andrews turned, and walked slowly in the other direction, past the hotel. He walked past a half-dugout that was deserted and crumbling in upon itself, and did not pause until he reached the livery stable. In the dimness of the large stable, the two horses that had brought them into Butcher's Crossing munched slowly over a trough of grain. He started to go into the stable, but he did not. He turned slowly and walked back toward the hotel. He leaned against the doorframe and surveyed that part of the town he could see, and waited for Miller and Charley Hoge to come down to join him.

The sun had gone down, and the diffused tremendous light from the west caught the dusty haze that hung over the town, softening the hard outlines of the buildings, when

Miller and Charley Hoge came out of the hotel and joined Andrews where he stood waiting on the sidewalk. Miller's face, shorn of its black beard, was heavy and white on his massive shoulders; Andrews looked at him with some surprise; except for his torn and filthy clothing, he looked precisely as he had months before, when Andrews had first walked up to him at the table in Jackson's Saloon. It was Charley Hoge who had undergone the most marked change in appearance. His long beard had been clipped as closely as possible with the scissors, though evidently Miller had not risked using a razor; beneath the gray stubble, Charley Hoge's face had lost its lean craftiness; now it was gaunt and vague and drawn; the cheeks were sunken deeply, the eyes were cavernous and wasted, and the mouth had gone slack and loose; the lips moved unevenly over the broken, yellow teeth, but no sound came. Charley Hoge stood inertly beside Miller, his arms hanging at his sides, the stump of his right wrist protruding from his sleeve.

"Come on," Miller said. "We've got to find McDonald."

Andrews nodded, and the three men went off the board sidewalk into the dust of the street, angling across it toward the low long front of Jackson's Saloon. One by one, Miller first and Andrews last, they went into the narrow, low-ceilinged barroom. It was deserted. Only one of the half-dozen or so lanterns that hung from the sooty rafters was lighted, and its dim glow met the light from outside that came through the front door and cast the room into great flat shadows. On the planked bar stood a bottle of whisky, half empty; beside it was an empty glass.

Miller strode to the bar and slapped his hand heavily upon it, causing the empty glass to jump and teeter on its edge. "Hey!" Miller called, and called again: "Hey, bartender!" No one answered his call.

Miller shrugged, took the bottle of whisky by its neck, and poured the glass nearly full. "Here," he said to Charley Hoge, and pushed the glass toward him. "It's on the house."

Charley Hoge, standing beside Andrews, looked for a moment without moving at the drink of whisky. His eyes turned to Miller, and back to the drink again. Then he seemed to fall forward toward the bar, his feet moving just quickly enough to keep the balance of his body. He took the drink unsteadily, sloshing it over his hand and wrist, and put it thirstily to his lips, leaning his head back and taking it in long noisy gulps.

"Take it slow," Miller said, grasping his crippled arm and shaking it. "You ain't had any in a long time."

Charley Hoge shook his arm as if Miller's hand were a fly upon bare skin. He set the glass down empty; his eyes were streaming and he gasped as if he had been running a long distance. Then his face tightened, and paled; he held his breath for an instant; almost nonchalantly, he leaned across the bar and retched upon the floor behind it.

"Too fast," Miller said. "I told you." He poured only an inch of whisky into the glass. "Try her again."

Charley Hoge drank it in a single gulp. He waited for a moment, and then nodded to Miller. Miller filled the glass again. The bottle was almost empty. He waited until Charley Hoge had drunk some more of the whisky; then he emptied the bottle into his glass, and tossed the bottle behind the bar.

"Let's see if there's anybody in the other room," he said.

Again one by one, with Miller in the lead, the three men went through the door that led into the large room next to the bar. The room was dim, lighted only by the flowing dusk that seeped through the narrow windows set high in the walls. Only two of the many tables were occupied; at one of them, across the room, sat two women, who glanced up as the three men walked through the door. Andrews took a step toward them, peering at them through the dimness; they returned his stare dully; he looked away. At the other table were two men, who glanced at them and then returned to a low-voiced conversation. One of the men wore a white shirt and an apron; he was very small and fat with large moustaches and a perfectly round face that glistened in the dimness. Miller clumped across the rough floor and stood beside the table.

"You the bartender?" he asked the small man.

"That's right," the man said.

"I'm looking for McDonald," Miller said. "Where's he staying?"

"Never heard of no McDonald," the bartender said, and turned back to his companion.

"Used to be the hide buyer around here," Miller said. "His place is just out of town, by the creek. Name of J. D. McDonald."

The bartender had not turned again while he was speaking. Miller let his hand fall on the man's shoulder. He squeezed and pulled the man around to face him.

"You pay attention when I'm talking to you," Miller said quietly.

"Yes, sir," the bartender said. He did not move beneath Miller's grasp. Miller loosened his hand.

"Now, did you hear what I said?"

"Yes, sir," the bartender said. He licked his lips, and put one hand to his shoulder and rubbed it. "I heard you. But I never heard of him. I only been here a month or maybe a little more. I don't know anything about any McDonald or any hide buyer."

"All right," Miller said. He stepped back from the man. "You go in the bar and bring us back a bottle of whisky and some eats. My friend here—" he pointed to Charley Hoge—"threw up behind your counter. You'd better clean it up."

"Yes, sir," the bartender said. "All I'll be able to get for you is some fried side meat and warmed-up beans. That be all right?"

Miller nodded and went to a table several feet away from that of the two men. Andrews and Charley Hoge followed behind him.

"That son-of-a-bitch McDonald," Miller said. "He's run out on us. Now we probably won't be able to get any money for those hides we left until we can deliver them."

Andrews said, "Mr. McDonald probably just got tired of the paper work, and took off for a while. There are too many hides back at his place for him just to leave them."

"I don't know," Miller said. "I never trusted him."

"Don't worry," Andrews said, and looked restlessly about him. One of the two women whispered something to her companion, and got up from the table; she fixed a smile on her face and walked loosely across the floor toward

them. Her face was swarthy and thin, and her sparse black
hair was fluffed in wisps about it.

"Honey," she said in a thin voice, looking at all of them,
her lips pulled back over her teeth, "can I get anything for
you? Do you want anything?"

Miller leaned back in his chair, and looked at her with
no expression on his face. He blinked twice, slowly, and
said: "Sit down. You can have a drink when the man brings
the bottle."

The woman sighed and seated herself between Andrews
and Miller. Quickly, expertly, she looked them over with
small black eyes that moved stiffly behind puffed eyelids.
She let the smile loosen on her face.

"Looks like you boys ain't been in town for a long time.
Hunters?"

"Yeah," Miller said. "What's wrong around here? This
town die?"

The bartender came in with a bottle of whisky and three
glasses.

"Honey," the woman said to him, "I left my glass on
the other table, and these gentlemen have asked me to
have a drink with them. Get it for me, will you?"

The bartender grunted, and got her glass from the other
table.

"Do you want my friend to join us?" the woman said,
jerking her thumb in the direction of the table where the
other woman waited torpidly. "We could made up a little
party."

"No," Miller said. "This is all right. Now, what's happened to this town?"

"It's been pretty dead the last few months," the woman
said. "No hunters at all. But you wait. Wait till fall. It'll
pick up again."

Miller grunted. "Hunting go bad?"

She laughed. "Lord, don't ask me. I don't know anything
about that." She winked. "I don't do much talking with the
men; that ain't my line."

"You been here long?" Miller asked.

"Over a year," she said, and nodded sadly. "This little
town's been good to me; I hate to see it slow down."

Andrews cleared his throat. "Are—many of the same girls still here?"

When she did not smile, the skin hung in loose folds on her face. She nodded. "Some. Lots of them have pulled out, though. Not me. This town's been good to me; I aim to stay around for awhile." She drank deeply from the glass of whisky she had poured.

"If you've been around a year," Miller said, "you must have heard of McDonald. The hide buyer. Is he still around?"

The woman coughed and nodded. "Last I heard, he still was."

"Where's he staying?" Miller asked.

"He was at the hotel for a while," she said. "Last I heard, he was staying in the old bunkhouse, out back."

Miller pushed his barely tasted glass of whisky in front of Charley Hoge. "Drink it," he said, "and let's get out of here."

"Ah, come on," the woman said. "I thought we was going to have a little party."

"You take what's left of this bottle," Miller said, "and you and your friend can have a party. We got business."

"Ah, come on, honey," the woman said, and put her hand on Miller's arm. Miller looked at her hand for a moment, and then casually, with a flick of his fingers, brushed it off, as if it were an insect that had dropped there.

"Well," the woman said, and smiled fixedly, "thanks for the bottle." She took its neck in her bony fingers and got up from the table.

"Wait," Andrews said as she started to move away. "There was a girl here last year—her name was Francine. I was wondering if she was still around."

"Francine? Sure. She's still around. But not for long. She's been packing the last few days. You want me to go up and get her?"

"No," Andrews said. "No, thank you. I'll see her later." He leaned back in his chair, and did not look at Miller.

"For God's sake," Miller said. "Schneider was right. You have had that little whore on your mind. I'd almost forgot

about her. Well, you can do what you want about her; but
right now we got more important things."

"Don't you want to wait for our food?" Andrews said.

"You can eat later if you want," Miller said. "Right now,
we get this McDonald business settled."

They roused Charley Hoge from his contemplation of
the empty glass, and went out of the saloon into the dusk.
No lights cut through the growing dark. The men stumbled
over the board sidewalks as they went up the street. Beyond
Jackson's Saloon they turned to their right and made their
way past the outdoor staircase that led to the upper floor
of Jackson's. As they walked, Andrews looked up at the
dark landing and the darker rectangle of the door, and continued looking upward as they passed the building. At the
back he saw through a window the faint glow of a lamp;
but he could see no movement in the room from which
the light came. He stumbled in the thick grass that grew
in the open field over which they walked; thereafter he
looked before him and guided Charley Hoge beside him.

Some two hundred yards from the rear of Jackson's Saloon, across the field in a westerly angle, the low flat-roofed
sleeping house rose vaguely in the dark.

"There's somebody in there," Miller said. "I can see a
light."

A weak glow came from the half-opened door. Miller
went a few steps ahead of the others, and kicked it open.
The three men crowded in; Andrews saw a single huge
room, low-raftered and perfectly square. Twenty or thirty
beds were scattered about the room; some were overturned,
and others were placed at random angles to each other.
None of these held mattresses, and none was occupied. At
the far end of the room, in a corner, a dim lantern burned,
throwing into shadow the shape of a man who sat on the
edge of a bed, hunched over a low table. At the sound of
the men entering, he lifted his head.

"McDonald!" Miller called.

The figure rose from the bed, and backed out of the
light. "Who's that?" he asked in a vague, querulous voice.

The three men advanced toward him, moving through

the scattered bed frames. "It's us, Mr. McDonald," Andrews said.

"Who?" McDonald lowered his head and peered out of the light. "Who's that talking?"

The men came into the dim mass of light cast by the lantern hung from a hook in one of the corner rafters. McDonald came close to them, and peered from one of their faces to another, blinking slowly as his protuberant blue eyes took them in.

"My God!" he said. "Miller. Will Andrews. My God! I'd given you up for dead." He came to Andrews, and grasped both his arms with thin, tight hands. "Will Andrews." His hands trembled on Andrews's arms, and then his whole body began trembling.

"Here," Andrews said. "Sit down, Mr. McDonald. I didn't mean to give you a shock."

"My God!" McDonald said again, and sank upon the edge of the bed; he stared at the three men and shook his head from side to side. "Give me a minute to get over it." After a moment, he straightened. "Wasn't there another one of you? Where's your skinner?"

"Schneider," Miller said. "Schneider's dead."

McDonald nodded. "What happened?"

"Drowned," Miller said. "When we were crossing a river on our way back."

McDonald nodded again, vacantly. "You found your buffalo, then."

"We found them," Miller said. "Just like I told you we would."

"Big kill," McDonald said.

"A big one," Miller said.

"How many hides did you bring back?"

Miller breathed deeply, and sat on the edge of a bed facing McDonald. "None," he said. "We lost them in the river, same time Schneider was killed."

McDonald nodded. "The wagon, too, I guess."

"Everything," Miller said.

McDonald turned to Andrews. "Got cleaned out?"

Andrews said, "Yes. But it doesn't matter."

"No," McDonald said. "I guess not."

"Mr. McDonald," Andrews said. "What's the matter here? Why are you staying in this place? We stopped by your office on the way in. What's happened?"

"What?" McDonald said. He looked at Andrews and blinked. Then he laughed dryly. "It takes a lot of telling. Yes, sir. A lot of telling." He turned to Miller. "So you got nothing to show for your trip. You got snowed in the mountains, I guess. And you got nothing to show for a whole winter."

"We got three thousand hides, winter prime, cached away up in the mountains. They're just waiting. We got something to show." Miller looked at him grimly.

McDonald laughed again. "They'll be a comfort to you in your old age," he said. "And that's all they'll be."

"We got three thousand prime hides," Miller said. "That's better than ten thousand dollars, even after our expense of bringing them back down."

McDonald laughed, and his laughter choked in a fit of coughing. "My God, man. Ain't you got eyes? Ain't you looked around you? Ain't you talked to anyone in this town?"

"We had an agreement," Miller said. "You and me. Four dollars apiece for prime hides. Ain't that right?"

"That's right," McDonald said. "That's dead right. Nobody would argue with that."

"And I aim to hold you to it," Miller said.

"You aim to hold me to it," McDonald said. "By God, I wish you could." He got up from the bed and looked down at the three men who sat opposite him. He turned completely around, and, facing them again, lifted his hands and ran his bony fingers through his thinning hair. Then he held his hands, palms up, out toward the three men. "You can't hold me to nothing. Can't you see that? Because I got nothing. Thirty, forty thousand hides down at the pits that I bought and paid for this last fall. All the money I had. You want them? You can have them for ten cents apiece. You might be able to make a little profit on them—next year, or the year after."

Miller lowered his head and swung it before him, slowly, from side to side.

"You're lying," he said. "I can go to Ellsworth."

"Go on," McDonald shouted. "Go on to Ellsworth. They'll laugh at you. Can't you look at it straight? The bottom's dropped out of the whole market; the hide business is finished. For good." He lowered his head and thrust it close to Miller's. "Just like you're finished, Miller. And your kind."

"You're a liar!" Miller said loudly, and moved back away from him. "We had an agreement, man to man. We worked our guts out for them hides, and you ain't going to back out now."

McDonald moved back and looked at him levelly. His voice was cool; "I don't rightly see how I can keep from it. You can't squeeze juice out of a rock." He nodded. "Funny thing. You're just about seven months too late. If you had got back when you was supposed to, you would have got your money. I had it then. You could have helped ruin me."

"You're lying to me," Miller said, more quietly. "It's some trick of yours. Why, just last year, prime hides—prime hides—"

"That was last year," McDonald said.

"Well, what could go wrong in one year? In just one year?"

"You remember what happened to beaver?" McDonald asked. "You trapped beaver once, didn't you? When they stopped wearing beaver hats you couldn't give the skins away. Well, it looks like everybody that wants one has a buffalo robe; and nobody wants any more. Why they wanted them in the first place, I don't know; you never can really get the stink out of them."

"But in just a year," Miller said.

McDonald shrugged. "It was coming. If I'd been back east, I would have knowed it. . . . If you can wait four or five years, maybe they'll find some way to use the leather. Then your prime hides will be just about as good as easy summer skins. You might get thirty, forty cents apiece for them."

Miller shook his head, as if he had been dazed by a blow. "What about the land you own around here?" he asked. "By God, you can sell off some of that and pay us."

"You don't listen to me, do you?" McDonald said. Then his hands started shaking again. "You want the land? You can have that too." He turned and began scrabbling in a box that lay under his bed. He drew out a sheet of paper and laid it on the table and started scribbling on it with the stub of a pen. "Here. I turn it over to you. You can have it all. But you better set yourself to be a dry-land farmer; because you'll have to keep it; or give it away, like I'm giving it to you."

"The railroad," Miller said. "You used to say when the railroad came through, the land would be like gold."

"Ah, yes," McDonald said. "The railroad. Well, it's coming through. They're laying the tracks now. It'll come through about fifty miles north of here." McDonald laughed again. "You want to hear a funny thing? The hunters are selling buffalo meat to the railroad company—and they're letting the hides lay where they skin them, to rot in the sun. Think of all the buffalo you killed. You could have got maybe five cents a pound for all that meat you let lay for the flies and the timber wolves."

There was a silence.

"I killed the timber wolves," Charley Hoge said. "I killed them with strychnine poison."

As if drugged, Miller looked at McDonald, and then at Andrews, and back to McDonald again.

"So you've got nothing now," Miller said.

"Nothing," McDonald said. "I can see it gives you some satisfaction."

"By God, it does," Miller said. "Except that when you ruin yourself, you ruin us too. You sit back here, and we work our guts out, and you say you'll give us money, like that means anything. And then you ruin yourself and take us down with you. But by God, it's almost worth it. Almost."

"Me ruin you?" McDonald laughed. "You ruin yourself, you and your kind. Every day of your life, everything you do. Nobody can tell *you* what to do. No. You go your own way, stinking the land up with what you kill. You flood the market with hides and ruin the market, and then you come crying to me that I've ruined you." McDonald's voice became anguished. "If you'd just listened—all of you. You're no better than the things you kill."

"Go back," Miller said. "Get out of this country. It doesn't want you."

Breathing heavily, McDonald stood slouched tiredly beneath the lantern; his face was cast in a deep shadow. Miller got up from the bed and pulled Charley Hoge up with him. He walked a few steps away from McDonald, pulling Charley Hoge beside him.

"I'm not through with you yet," he said to McDonald. "I'll see you again."

"All right," McDonald said wearily, "if you think it'll do any good."

Andrews cleared his throat. He said to Miller, "I think I'll stay here and talk to Mr. McDonald for a while."

Miller looked at him impassively for a moment; his black hair blended into the darkness behind him, and his heavy pale face was thrust broodingly out of it.

"Do whatever you want," he said. "It makes no difference to me. Our business is finished." And he turned and walked into the darkness, out the door.

After Miller and Charley Hoge had gone, there were several minutes of silence. McDonald reached up to the lantern and raised the wick so that the light about the two men sharpened and made their features more distinct. Andrews moved the bed on which he had been sitting a little closer to the one upon which McDonald slumped.

"Well," McDonald said, "you had your hunt."

"Yes, sir."

"And you lost your tail, just like I said you would."

Andrews did not speak.

"That was what you wanted, wasn't it?" McDonald asked.

"Maybe it was, in the beginning," Andrews said. "Part of it, at least."

"Young people," McDonald said. "Always wanting to start from scratch. I know. You never figured that someone else knew what you was trying to do, did you?"

"I never thought about it," Andrews said. "Maybe because I didn't know what I was trying to do myself."

"Do you know now?"

Andrews moved restlessly.

"Young people," McDonald said contemptuously. "You always think there's something to find out."

"Yes, sir," Andrews said.

"Well, there's nothing," McDonald said. "You get born, and you nurse on lies, and you get weaned on lies, and you learn fancier lies in school. You live all your life on lies, and then maybe when you're ready to die, it comes to you—that there's nothing, nothing but yourself and what you could have done. Only you ain't done it, because the lies told you there was something else. Then you know you could of had the world, because you're the only one that knows the secret; only then it's too late. You're too old."

"No," Andrews said. A vague terror crept from the darkness that surrounded them, and tightened his voice. "That's not the way it is."

"You ain't learned, then," McDonald said. "You ain't learned yet. . . . Look. You spend nearly a year of your life and sweat, because you have faith in the dream of a fool. And what have you got? Nothing. You kill three, four thousand buffalo, and stack their skins neat; and the buffalo will rot wherever you left them, and the rats will nest in the skins. What have you got to show? A year gone out of your life, a busted wagon that a beaver might use to make a dam with, some calluses on your hands, and the memory of a dead man."

"No," Andrews said. "That's not all. That's not all I have."

"Then what? What have you got?"

Andrews was silent.

"You can't answer. Look at Miller. Knows the country he was in as well as any man alive, and had faith in what he believed was true. What good did it do him? And Charley Hoge with his Bible and his whisky. Did that make your winter any easier, or save your hides? And Schneider. What about Schneider? Was that his name?"

"That was his name," Andrews said.

"And that's all that's left of him," McDonald said. "His

name. And he didn't even come out of it with that for himself." McDonald nodded, not looking at Andrews. "Sure, I know. I came out of it with nothing, too. Because I forgot what I learned a long time ago. I let the lies come back. I had a dream, too, and because it was different from yours and Miller's, I let myself think it wasn't a dream. But now I know, boy. And you don't. And that makes all the difference."

"What will you do now, Mr. McDonald?" Andrews asked; his voice was soft.

"Do?" McDonald straightened on the bed. "Why, I'm going to do what Miller said I should do; I'm going to get out of this country. I'm going back to St. Louis, maybe back to Boston, maybe even to New York. You can't deal with this country as long as you're in it; it's too big, and empty, and it lets the lies come into you. You have to get away from it before you can handle it. And no more dreams; I take what I can get when I can get it, and worry about nothing else."

"I wish you good luck," Andrews said. "I'm sorry it turned out for you the way it did."

"And you?" McDonald asked. "What about you?"

"I don't know yet," Andrews said. "I still don't know."

"You don't have to," McDonald said. "You come back with me. We could do all right together; we both know the country now; away from it, we could do something with it."

Andrews smiled. "Mr. McDonald, you talk like you're putting your faith in me, now."

"No," McDonald said. "It's not that at all. It's just that I hate paper work, and you could take some of it off my hands."

Andrews got up from the bed. "I'll let you know when I've had a little more time," he said. "But thanks for asking me." He gave his hand to McDonald; McDonald shook it limply. "I'll be staying at the hotel; don't leave without looking me up."

"All right, boy." McDonald looked up at him; the lids came down slowly over his bulging eyes, and raised. "I'm pleased you came through it alive."

Andrews turned quickly away from him, and went away

from the thinning circle of light into the darkness of the room and into the wide darkness that waited outside. A thin new moon hung high in the west, giving the dry grass that rustled under his feet a faint, almost invisible glow. He walked slowly over the uneven ground toward the low dark bulk of Jackson's Saloon; the yellow blob of a lighted lamp still showed in a high window near the center of the building.

He had walked past the long upward angling sweep of the stairs, had stepped upon the board sidewalk, had turned, had even made a few steps down the sidewalk beyond the opening of the stairs, before he knew that he was going to walk up them. He stopped on the sidewalk and turned slowly to walk back to where the stairs began. A weakness came into his legs and rose to his upper body, so that his arms hung loosely at his sides. For several moments he did not move. Then, as if beyond his volition, one of his feet rose to find the first step. Slowly, his hands not touching the bannister on his left nor the wall on his right, he went up the stairs. Again, at the landing at the top of the stairs, he paused. He breathed deeply of the warm, smoky air that hung about the town, until the weakness of his body was gathered into his lungs and breathed out upon the air. He fumbled for the door latch, lifted it, and pushed the door inward. He walked through the doorway and closed the door behind him. A hot still air enclosed him and pressed upon his flesh; he blinked his eyes and breathed more heavily. It was several moments before he realized the depth of the darkness in which he stood; he could see nothing; he took a blind step forward to keep his balance.

He found the wall on his left, and let his hand slide lightly over it as he groped his way forward. His hand went over the recesses of two doorways before he came to a door beneath the sill of which a thin line of yellow light seeped. He stood for a moment close to the door, listening; he heard a rustle of movement from within the room, and then silence. He waited for a moment more, and then stood back from the door and closed his loose hand into a fist and rapped upon it, twice. He heard another rustle of clothing and the light bare pad of feet. The door opened a few inches; he could see nothing but the yellow light, which he felt upon his face. Very slowly, the door opened wider, and he saw Francine, a shape against the glow of the lamp behind her, one hand upon the edge of the door and the other clasped at the collar of a loose wrapper that hung nearly to her ankles. He stood stiff and unmoving and waited for her to speak.

"Is it you?" she asked after a long moment. "Is it Will Andrews?"

"Yes," he said, still stiff and unmoving.

"I thought you were dead," she whispered. "Everybody thought you were dead." Still she did not move from the doorway. Andrews stood awkwardly before her and shifted his weight. "Come in," she said. "I didn't mean to keep you standing outside."

He walked into the room, past Francine, and stood near the edge of the thin carpet; he heard the door close behind him. He turned but he did not look directly at her.

"I hope I didn't disturb you," he said. "I know it's late, but we only got in a few hours ago and I wanted to see you."

"You're all right?" Francine asked, coming closer and looking at him in the light. "What happened to you?"

"I'm all right," he said. "We got snowed in; we had to stay in the mountains all winter."

"And the others?" Francine asked.

"Yes," Andrews said. "All except Schneider. He got killed on the way back, while we were crossing a river."

Almost reluctantly, he raised his eyes and looked at her. Her long yellow hair was pulled in a tight braid so that it lay flat against her head; a few thin lines of tiredness ran from the corners of her eyes; her pale lips were parted over her rather large teeth.

"Schneider," she said. "He was the big man that spoke German to me."

"Yes," Andrews said. "That was Schneider."

Francine shivered in the heat of the room. "I didn't like him," she said. "But it's not good to think that he's dead."

"No," Andrews said.

She moved about the room, her fingers trailing along

the carved wood that framed the back of the sofa and restlessly rearranging the knickknacks on the table beside it.
Every now and then she looked up at Andrews and gave
him a quick, puzzled smile. Andrews watched her movements closely, not speaking, hardly breathing.

She laughed low in her throat, and came across the room
to him, where he stood near the door. She touched his
sleeve.

"Come over in the light so I can see you better," she said,
and pulled gently on the cloth of his shirt sleeve.

Andrews let himself be led near to the table beside the
red couch. Francine looked at him closely.

"You haven't changed much," she said. "Your face is
browner. You're older." She caught his forearms in both
her hands, and lifted them, turning his palms upward.
"Your hands," she said sadly, and ran her fingers lightly
over one of his palms. "They're hard now. I remember, they
were so soft."

Andrews swallowed. "You said they would be hard when
I got back. Do you remember?"

"Yes," she said. "I remember."

"That was a long time ago."

"Yes," Francine said. "All winter I've thought you were
dead."

"I'm sorry," he said. "Francine—" He paused, and looked
down at her face. Her pale blue eyes, wide and transparent,
waited for whatever he had to say. He closed his fingers
around her hand. "I've wanted to tell you— All winter, while
we were snowed in, I thought about it."

She did not speak.

"The way I left you that night," he continued. "I wanted
you to know—it wasn't you, it was me. I wanted you to
understand about it."

"I know," Francine said. "You were ashamed. But you
shouldn't have been. It wasn't as important as you thought.
It is—" She shrugged. "It is the way some men are with
love, at first."

"Young men," Andrews said. "You said I was very
young."

"Yes," Francine said, "and you became angry. It is the

way young men are with love. . . . But you should have come back. It would have been all right."

"I know," Andrews said. "But I thought I couldn't. And then I was too far away."

She looked at him closely; she nodded. "You are older," she said again; there was a trace of sadness in her voice. "And I was wrong: you have changed. You have changed so that you can come back."

"Yes," he said. "I have changed that much, at least."

She moved away from him, and turned so that her back was to him, her body outlined sharply by the lamplight. For a long moment there was silence between them.

"Well," Andrews said. "I wanted to see you again, to tell you—" He paused, and did not finish. He started to turn away from her, toward the door.

"Don't go," Francine said. She did not move. "Don't go away again."

"No," Andrews said; he stood still where he had turned. "I won't go away again. I'm sorry. I wasn't trying to make you ask me. I want to stay. I should have—"

"It doesn't matter. I want you to stay. When I thought you were dead, I—" She paused, and shook her head sharply. "You will stay with me for a while." She turned, and shook her head sharply; and the reddish-gold light from the lamp trembled about her hair. "You will stay with me for a while. And you must understand. It's not like it is with the others."

"I know," Andrews said. "Don't talk about it."

They looked at each other without speaking for several moments, making no move toward each other. Then Andrews said: "I'm sorry. It's not the same as it was, is it?"

"No," Francine said. "But it's all right. I'm glad you came back."

She turned away from him and leaned over the lamp. She lowered the wick; still leaning, she looked back over her shoulder at Andrews, and for a long moment studied his face; she did not smile. Then she blew sharply into the lamp chimney and darkness cut across the room. He heard the rustle of Francine's clothing and caught a glimpse of her dim shape as she walked before the window. He heard

the rustle of bedclothing being turned back and heard the
heavier sound of a body sliding upon sheets. For a while
he did not move. Then he fumbled at the buttons of his
shirt as he moved across the room to where Francine waited
in the darkness.

I I

He turned in the darkness, and felt beneath him the bed
sheets dampened by his own sweat. He had awakened suddenly from a deep sleep, and for a moment he did not
know where he was. A slow, regular rasp of breath came
from beside him; he reached out his hand; it touched warm
flesh, and rested there, and moved slightly as the flesh was
moved by its breathing.

For five days and nights Will Andrews had stayed in
the small close room with Francine, emerging from it only
when he took food or drink or purchased some articles of
clothing from the depleted stock of Bradley's Dry Goods
store. After the first night with Francine he lost all consciousness of time, much as he had lost it back in the mountains, during the storm, under his shelter of snow and buffalo hide. In the dim room, with its single window that
remained always curtained, morning became indistinguishable from afternoon; and so long as the lamp was kept
burning, it was difficult for him to tell day from night.

In this close half-world of perpetual twilight he immersed himself. He spoke to Francine infrequently; he
clasped her to him and heard themselves speak only in their
heavy breathing and wordless cries, until at last he thought
he found his only existence there. Beyond the four walls
that surrounded him he could imagine only a nothingness
which was a brightness and a noise that pressed threaten-
ingly against him. If he looked too long and too intently,
the walls themselves seemed to press upon him, and the
objects in his sight—the red couch, the carpet, the knickknacks scattered upon the tables—seemed obscurely to
threaten the comfort he found in the half-darkness where

he lived. Naked in the dark beside the passive body of Francine, with his eyes closed, he seemed to float weightlessly within himself; and even in waking he partook of some of the quality of the deep sleep he found in the moments after his love-making with Francine.

Gradually he came to look upon his frequent and desperate unions with Francine as if they were performed by someone else. As if from a distance, sightlessly, he observed himself and his sensations as he fulfilled his needs upon a body to which, meaninglessly, he attached a name. Sometimes, lying beside Francine, he looked down the pale length of his own body as if it had nothing to do with himself; he touched his chest, where fine hair like down curled sparsely on the white flesh, and wondered at the sensation of his hand brushing lightly above his skin. Beside him, at these moments, Francine seemed hardly to have any relation to him; she was a presence which assuaged a need in him that he barely knew he had, until the need was met. Sometimes, heavy upon her and lost in the darkness of his passion, he was surprised to find within himself qualities of sensation of which he had been unaware; and when he opened his eyes, meeting the eyes of Francine open and wide and unfathomable below him, again he was almost surprised that she was there. Afterward, he remembered the look in her eyes and wondered what she was thinking, what she was feeling, in the close moments of their passion.

And finally this wondering drew his mind and his eye away from the center of his self and focused them upon Francine. Covertly he watched her as she walked about the dim room, clothed loosely in her thin gray wrapper, or as she lay naked on the bed beside him. Not touching her, he let his eyes go over her body, over her round untroubled face framed loosely by the yellow hair that in the dimness was dark upon the bed sheets; over her full breasts that were laced delicately with an intricate network of blue veins; over her gently mounded belly, which flowed beneath the fine light maidenhair caught in the faint gleams of light that seeped into the room; and down the large firm legs that tapered to her small feet. Sometimes he fell quietly asleep gazing at her, and awoke as quietly, his eyes again upon her, but upon her without recognition, so that he searched again her face and her form as if he had not seen them before.

Near the end of the week a restlessness came upon him. No longer content to lie torpidly in the warm dark room, he more and more frequently left it to wander about the single street of Butcher's Crossing. Seldom did he speak to anyone; never did he linger for more than a few minutes at any place he stopped. He was content to let the sunlight seep into him, as he blinked his eyes upon the brightness. He went once to Butcher's Hotel to pick up his bedroll, to pay for his brief lodging there, and to inform the clerk that he would not be back; once he wandered down the road west of town and rested beneath the grove of cottonwood trees, gazing across the area piled with baled hides that had been McDonald's place of business; several times he went into the bar of Jackson's Saloon and took a glass of luke-warm beer. Once, in the bar, he saw Charley Hoge seated at a rear table, alone except for a bottle of whisky and a half-filled glass. Though Andrews stood for several minutes at the bar, sipping his beer, and though Charley Hoge's glance passed him several times, Charley Hoge gave no sign that he saw him.

Andrews walked the length of the bar and sat down at the table; he nodded to Charley Hoge, and spoke in greeting.

Charley Hoge looked at him blankly and did not answer.

"Where's Miller?" Andrews asked.

"Miller?" Charley Hoge shook his head. "Where he always is, down at our dugout by the river."

"Is he taking it pretty bad?"

"What?" Charley Hoge asked.

"About the hides," Andrews said. He put his nearly empty glass before him on the table and turned it idly between his hands. "It must have been a blow to him. I guess I never realized how much this all meant to him."

"Hides?" Charley Hoge said vaguely, and blinked his eyes. "Miller's all right. He's down at the dugout, resting. He'll be along directly."

Andrews started to speak, and then looked closely into the wide blank eyes that stared at him. "Charley," he said, "are you all right?"

A small perplexed frown crossed Charley Hoge's face; then his expression was clear and empty. "Sure. I'm all right." He nodded rapidly. "Let's see, now. You're Will Andrews, ain't you?"

Andrews could not look away from the eyes that seemed to grow larger as they stared at him.

"Miller's looking for you," Charley Hoge went on in a high monotonous voice. "Miller says we're all going somewhere, to kill the buffalo. He knows a place in Colorado. I think he wants to see you."

"Charley," Andrews said; his voice trembled, and he clutched his hands hard around the glass to keep them from shaking. "Charley, get hold of yourself."

"We're going on a hunt," Charley Hoge continued in his singsong voice. "You, and me, and Miller. Miller knows a skinner he can get in Ellsworth. It'll be all right. I'm not afraid to go up there any more. The Lord will provide." He smiled and nodded, and continued nodding toward Andrews, though his eyes had turned downward to his glass of whisky.

"Don't you remember, Charley?" Andrews's voice was hollow. "Don't you remember anything about it?"

"Remember?" Charley Hoge asked.

"The mountains—the hunt—Schneider—"

"That's his name," Charley Hoge said. "Schneider. That's the skinner in Ellsworth that Miller's going to get."

"Don't you remember?" Andrews's voice cracked. "Schneider's dead."

Charley Hoge looked at Andrews, shook his head, and smiled; a drop of spittle gathered on his lower lip, swelled, and coursed into the gray stubble around his chin. "Nobody dies," he said softly. "The Lord will provide."

For another moment Andrews looked deep into Charley Hoge's eyes; dull and blue, they were like bits of empty sky reflected in a dirty pool; there was nothing behind them, nothing to stop Andrews's gaze from going on and on. With a sense almost of horror, Andrews drew back and shook his head with a sharp movement. He got up from the table and backed away; Charley Hoge did not change his empty stare or give any sign that he saw Andrews's movement. Andrews turned and walked quickly out of the bar. On the sidewalk, in the bright sunlight, the sense lingered; his legs were weak and his hands were trembling. Swiftly, unsteadily, he went up the street, turned, and took the stairs that led up the side of Jackson's Saloon to Francine's room.

He opened his eyes wide to the dimness of the room; he was still breathing heavily. Francine, lying on the bed, raised herself on an elbow and looked at him; with that movement, her loose gray wrapper parted and one breast drooped toward her forearm, pale against the gray material. Andrews went quickly to the bed; almost roughly, he pulled the wrapper away from her body and let his hands run swiftly, desperately, over her. A small smile came upon Francine's face; her lids dropped; her hands came to Andrews, fumbled with his clothing, and pulled him down upon her.

Later, as he lay beside her, the tumult within him quieted; he tried to tell her of his meeting with Charley Hoge, and of that sense of horror that the meeting had released in him. It was not, he tried to make her understand, so much a result of his recognition that what Charley Hoge showed him in a blind and enveloping stare was something that each of them—Miller, Charley Hoge, Schneider, and even himself—that each of them had had inside them, all along. It was something—he tried to tell her—that McDonald had spoken of by the flickering light of a lantern in the great empty sleeping house the night they had returned to Butcher's Crossing. It was something that he had seen on Schneider's face as he stood stiff and upright in the middle of the river, just after the horse's hoof had split his skull. It was something—

The faint afterlift of a smile hung on Francine's full, pale lips; she nodded; her hand moved softly, soothingly, over his bare chest.

It was something, he continued, speaking in broken phrases that did not say what he intended, it was something that he had felt even in himself, from moment to moment, during the long trek across the plains, and in the kill of the buffalo at the instant the great animal shuddered and crashed to the ground, and in the hot smothering stench that came with the skinning, and in the vision of whiteness during the snowstorm, and in the trackless view in the aftermath of the storm. Was it in everyone? he asked, without using the words. Did it lurk hidden in everyone, waiting to spring out, waiting to devour and rend, until there was left only the blankness he had seen in the blue stare that Charley Hoge now had to give the world? Or did it wait without, crouched like a timber wolf behind a rock, to spring suddenly and horribly without reason upon anyone who passed it by? Or beyond one's knowledge, did one seek it out, this shape of terror, and pass it by in an obscure, perverse hope that it might spring? At that swift moment in the river, did the splintered log seek the belly of Schneider's horse, and the hoof Schneider's skull? Or was it the other way around, Schneider passing by precisely in search of the gray shape, and finding it? What did it mean? he wanted to know. Where had he been?

He turned on the bed; beside him, Francine had dropped into a light sleep; her breath came gently from her parted lips, and her hands lay loosely curled at her sides. He got up quietly, went across the room, turned the wick of the lamp down, and blew into the chimney, extinguishing the light. Through the single curtained window across from him, a last gray light filtered; outside it was growing dark. He returned to the bed and lay carefully next to Francine, on his side, looking at her.

What did it mean? he asked himself again. Even this, his—he hesitated to call it love—his hunger after Francine, what did it mean? He thought again of Schneider; and suddenly he imagined Schneider in his place, alive, lying beside Francine. Without anger or resentment he saw him lying there, and saw him reach across and fondle Francine's breast. He smiled; for he knew that Schneider would not have questioned, as he was questioning; would not have wondered; would not have let a look from Charley Hoge loose within him these doubts and these fears. With a kind of rough and sour friendliness, he would have taken his pleasure from Francine, and would have gone his way, and would not in any particular manner have thought of her again.

As Francine would not have thought again of him. And, he added suddenly, as Francine probably would not think again of him, Will Andrews, who lay now beside her.

In her sleep, in a whisper, Francine mouthed a word that he could not understand; she smiled, her breath caught, she breathed deeply, and moved a little beside him.

Though he did not want the thought to come to him, he knew that he, too, like Schneider, would leave her, would go his own way; though, unlike Schneider, he would think of her, remember her, in a way that he could not yet predict. He would leave her and he would not know her; he would never know her. Now the darkness was nearly complete in the room; he could barely see her face. With his eyes open in the darkness, he slid his hand down her arm until he found her hand, and lay quietly beside her. He thought of the men who had known her appetite and flesh, as he had known them, and had known nothing else; he thought of those men without resentment. In the dark they were faceless, and they did not speak, and they lay still in their breathing like himself. After a long while, his hand still loosely clasping Francine's hand, he slept.

He woke suddenly, and did not know what caused him to awake. He blinked his eyes in the darkness. Across the room a dim glow flickered at the curtained window, died, and flickered again. A shout, thickened by distance, came into the room; the hooves of a horse thudded in the street outside. Andrews eased himself out of bed and stood for a moment, shaking his head sharply. Another burst of excited voices came up from the street; the wooden sidewalks clattered beneath heavy boots. He found his clothes in the darkness and pulled them on hastily; he listened for other sounds; he heard Francine's regular, undisturbed breathing. He went quickly from the room, easing the door shut behind him, and tiptoed down the dark corridor toward the landing outside the building.

To the west, in the direction of the river, clearly visible above the low buildings of Butcher's Crossing, a flame billowed up out of the darkness. For a moment Andrews clutched the handrail of the stairway in disbelief. The fire came from McDonald's shack. Fanned by a heavy breeze from the west, it lighted the tall grove of cottonwoods across the road from it, so that the light gray trunks and deep green leafage were shown clearly against the darkness around them. The fire illumined its own smoke, which coiled upward in thick black ropes, and were dispersed and carried back toward the town on the breeze; a rank, acrid odor bit into Andrews's nostrils. The clatter of running below him broke into his stillness; he went swiftly down the stairs, stumbled on the board sidewalk, and ran up the dusty road toward the fire.

Even at the point where the wagon-wheel trail turned off the road just above the grove of cottonwoods, he felt the great heat of the fire push against him. He paused there at the twin swaths of worn earth, which were clearly visible in the yellow-red glare of the fire; he was breathing sharply from his running, yet the heavy dregs of sleep were not yet cleared from his mind. Scattered in a wide, irregular semicircle about the flaming shack, fifteen or twenty persons stood, still and small and distinctly outlined against the billowing glare. Singly or in small clusters of two or three, they watched, and did not call out or move; only the dense heavy crackling of the flames came upon the night stillness, and only the great pulsations of the flame moved the men's shadows behind them. Andrews rubbed his hands over his eyes, which were smarting from the haze that settled from the twisting coils of smoke, and ran toward the clusters of people. As he approached them, the intense heat made him turn his face away from the direction he was running, so that he collided with one of the small groups, knocking one of the onlookers aside. The man he bumped against did not look at him; his mouth was open, and his eyes were fixed on the huge blaze, the light of which played upon his face, casting it in deep and changing hues of red.

"What happened?" Andrews gasped.

The man's eyes did not move; he did not speak; he shook his head.

Andrews looked from one face to another and saw no one that he recognized. He went from one person to another, peering into faces that were like distorted masks in the throbbing light.

When he came upon Charley Hoge, cringing before the heat and light and yet crouched as if to spring, he almost did not recognize him. Charley Hoge's mouth was pulled open and awry, as if caught in a cry of terror or ecstasy; and his eyes, streaming from the smoke, were opened wide and unblinking. Andrews could see in them the reduced reflection of the fire, and it seemed almost that the fire was burning there, deep in the vision of Charley Hoge.

Andrews grasped him by the shoulders, and shook him.

"Charley! What happened? How did it start?"

Charley Hoge slid from under his grasp, and darted a few steps away.

"Leave me be," he croaked, his eyes still fixed before him. "Leave me be."

"What happened?" Andrews asked again.

For an instant Charley Hoge turned to him, away from the fire; in the shadow of his brows, his eyes were dull and empty. "The fire," he said. "The fire, the fire."

Andrews started to shake him again; but he paused, his hands lightly resting on Charley Hoge's shoulders. From the crowd came a murmur, low but intense, rising in concert above the hiss and crackle of the flames; he felt more than saw a slight surging forward of the people around him.

He turned in the direction of the movement. For a moment he was blinded by the intensity of the flame—blue and white and yellow-orange, cut through with streaks of black—and his eyes narrowed against the brilliance. Then, among the scattered bales of buffalo hides, high above which the flames turned massively, he saw a dark furious movement. It was Miller, on a horse which reared and screamed in terror at the flames, but which was held under control by the sheer force of Miller's strength. With furious jerks of the reins, which cut the bit deep into the horse's bleeding mouth, and with heavy strokes of his heels against its sides, Miller forced his horse to dart among the scattered bales. For several moments Andrews gaped uncomprehend-

ingly; senselessly, Miller darted up to the very mouth of
the flame, and then let his horse pull away, and darted
close again.

Andrews turned to Charley Hoge. "What's he doing?
He'll kill himself. He—"

Charley Hoge's mouth lifted in a vacant grin. "Watch,"
he said. "Watch him."

Then Andrews saw, and could not comprehend, and then
realized what Miller was doing. Forcing his horse up to
the bales piled close to the burning shack, he was pushing
the piled bales so that they fell into the open mouth of
the flame. Against those bales which lay singly upon the
ground, he forced the breast of his horse, and raked the
flanks relentlessly, so that the bale was pushed along the
ground into the edge of the holocaust.

A cry came from Andrews's dry throat. "The fool!" he
shouted. "He's crazy! He'll kill himself!" And he started to
move forward.

"Leave him be," Charley Hoge said. His voice was high
and clear and suddenly sharp. "Leave him be," he said
again. "It's his fire. Leave him be."

Andrews halted and turned upon Charley Hoge. "You
mean— Did he set it?"

Charley Hoge nodded. "It's Miller's fire. You leave him
be."

After the first involuntary surge forward, the townspeople
had not moved. Now they stood still, and watched Miller
gallop recklessly among the smoking bales. Andrews
slumped forward, weak and helpless. Like the others, he
watched Miller in his wild riding.

After he had tumbled the hides nearest the shack into
the fire, Miller rode somewhat away from the flames,
leaped off his horse, and tied the reins to the tongue of
one of the abandoned wagons that littered the area. A
dark figure, shapeless in the outer edges of the firelight, he
scuttled to one of the bales that lay on its side near the
wagon. He stooped, and in the shadow became indistinguishable from the bale. He straightened, and the shapes
became distinct, the bale moving upward as he straightened, seeming to the men who watched a huge appendage

of his shoulders. For an instant, he swayed beneath the gigantic shape; then he lurched forward, and ran, halting abruptly at the side of the wagon, so that his burden toppled forward off his shoulders and crashed into the bed of the wagon, which swayed for a moment beneath the impact. Again and again, Miller ranged about the wagon, gathering the bales, swaying beneath their weight, lurching, and running with bent knees to the wagon.

"My God!" one of the townspeople behind Andrews said. "Them bales must weigh three, four hundred pounds."

No one else spoke.

After Miller had boosted the fourth bale upon the wagon, he returned to his horse, unwound a length of rope from his saddle horn, and looped it around the apex of the oaken triangle that secured the wagon tongue to the frame. With the loose end of the rope in his hand, he returned to his horse, mounted it, and wound the end of the rope twice around his saddle horn. He shouted to the horse and dug his heels sharply into its sides; the horse strained forward; the rope tautened, and the wagon tongue lifted beneath the tension. Miller shouted again and slapped his palm on the horse's rump; the sound of the slap cracked above the hiss and rumble of the fire. The wheels moved slowly, screeching on the rusted axles. Again Miller shouted, and dug his heels into the horse; the wagon moved more swiftly; the horse's breath came in heavy groans and its hooves cut the dry earth. Then wagon and horse, as if released from a catapult, careened across the flat earth. Miller yelled once more, and guided horse and wagon straight toward the flame that grew from the shack and the piled hides. At the instant before it seemed that man and horse would plunge into the yellow-hot heart of the fire, Miller swerved his horse suddenly aside, unwinding in a rapid motion the rope from his saddle horn, so that the wagon, unloosed, plunged in its own momentum into the heart of the fire, spewing sparks over an area a hundred feet in diameter. For several moments after the wagon with its load of hides crashed into it, the fire darkened, as if the fury of the assault had extinguished it; then as the wagon caught, it flamed more furiously; and the townspeople drew back several steps before the intensity of the heat.

Behind him Andrews heard the sound of running feet and a shout that was almost a scream, high and animal in its intensity. Dully, he turned. McDonald, his black frock coat flared out at the sides, his arms flailing at random in the air, his sparse hair disheveled, was running toward the knotted bunches of townspeople around the fire—but his eyes looked beyond them wildly, fixed upon his burning office and his smoldering hides. He broke through the group of men, and would have continued running beyond them, had not Andrews caught him and held him back.

"My God!" McDonald said. "It's burning!" He looked wildly around him, at the still and silent men. "Why doesn't somebody do something?"

"There's nothing they can do," Andrews said. "Just stand easy here. You'll get hurt."

Then McDonald saw Miller dragging another wagonload of hides into the widening circle of flames. He turned questioningly to Andrews.

"That's Miller," he said. "What's he doing?" And then, still looking at Andrews, his jaw went slack and his eyes, beneath their tangled brows, widened. "No," McDonald said hoarsely, and shook his head like a wounded beast, from side to side. "No, no. Miller. Did he—"

Andrews nodded.

Another cry, almost of agony, came from McDonald's throat. He twisted away from Andrews, and with hands clenched into fists held like clubs above his head, he ran across the smoldering field toward Miller. On his horse, Miller turned to meet him; his smoke-blackened face broke in a wide and mirthless grin. He waited until McDonald was almost upon him, his fists raised impotently to strike out; then Miller dug his heels into the horse's flanks, dodging away, so that McDonald struck at air. He drew his horse to a halt several yards away from where he had waited; McDonald turned and ran toward him again. Laughing now, Miller spurred away; and again McDonald beat his fists upon emptiness. For perhaps three minutes the two men moved jerkily like marionettes in the open

space before the great fire, McDonald, almost sobbing between his clenched yellow teeth, chasing stubbornly and
futilely after Miller, and Miller, his lips drawn back in a
humorless grimace, always a few feet out of his reach.

Then, suddenly, McDonald stood still; his arms dropped
loosely at his sides and he gave Miller a quiet, almost
contemplative look, and shook his head. His shoulders
slumped; with his knees sagging, he turned away and
walked across to where Andrews and Charley Hoge stood.
His face was streaked with soot and one eyebrow was singed
where a flying ember had caught.

Andrews said: "He doesn't know what he's doing, Mr.
McDonald. It looks like he has gone crazy."

McDonald nodded. "Looks like it."

"And besides," Andrews went on, "you said yourself the
hides weren't worth anything."

"It's not that," McDonald said quietly. "It's not that
they were worth anything. But they were mine."

The three men stood, silent and almost unconcerned,
and watched Miller lug the bales and hides and pull the
wagons up to stoke the fire. They did not look at each
other; they did not speak. With an interest that appeared
nearly detached, McDonald watched Miller drag the
wagons and send them crashing into the ruins of other
wagons that stood in stark skeletal shapes within the fire.
Bale after bale, wagon after wagon went upon the flaming
heap, until the fire was more than twice its original size.
It took Miller nearly an hour to complete his task. When
the last wagon with its load of bales went smashing into
the fire, Miller turned and rode slowly up to the three men
who stood together, watching him.

He pulled his horse to a halt; the beast stopped suddenly
in its tracks, its sides heaving so violently that Miller's legs
moved perceptibly above their stirrups; from its mouth,
wrenched and torn by the bit between its teeth, blood
dropped and gathered in the dust. The horse is blown,
thought Andrews distantly; it won't live till daylight.

Miller's face was blacked by the smoke; his eyebrows
were almost completely burned away, and his hair was
crisped and scorched; a long red welt that was beginning to

form into a blister lay across his forehead. For a long while Miller looked over his horse's bowed head, his eyes somberly upon McDonald. Then his lips drew back over his white teeth, and he laughed gratingly, deep in his throat. He looked from McDonald to Charley Hoge to Andrews, and then back to McDonald again. The grin slowly came off his face. The four men looked at one another, moving their eyes slowly and searchingly across the faces about them. They did not move, and they did not speak.

We have something to say to each other, Andrews thought dimly, but we don't know what it is; we have something we ought to say.

He opened his mouth, and put his hand out, and moved toward Miller, as if to speak. Miller glanced down at him; his glance was casual and distant and empty, without recognition. He loosened himself in his saddle, dug his heels into the horse's flanks; the horse leaped forward. The movement caught Andrews unprepared; he stood, his arm still held out, upraised. The horse's chest caught him on his left shoulder and spun him around; he stumbled but he did not go to the ground. When his vision cleared, he saw Miller, hunched over the horse, riding unsteadily into the distance and the darkness. As Miller went away, Charley Hoge moved from the two men and shambled after him. For several moments after they had gone into the darkness, and after the pounding of hooves had died in the distance, Andrews stood and looked in the direction they had gone. He turned to McDonald; they looked at each other in silence. After a while McDonald shook his head, and he, too, walked away.

III

Near dawn a chill came into the air and pressed lightly against the backs of the few people who remained to watch the smoldering remains of the fire. They moved forward a few steps to the edge of the great scorched circle. Small flames licked about the charred timbers of the shack, blue upon the black-and-gray ash, and tipped with light yellow; dozens of smoldering heaps that had been baled hides and that had collapsed upon themselves, glowed a dull, uneven red, and sent thick twists of smoke up into the darkness. The uneven flames illumined the site faintly so that each man who remained stood apart, anonymous in his little portion of shadow. The acrid and rotten smell of the burned hides grew more intense as the eastward breeze lessened. One by one, the men who had waited out the fire turned and made their ways back to Butcher's Crossing with a quietness that seemed almost deliberate.

At last only Will Andrews remained. He moved toward one of the charred bales; it appeared to have been blackened but not consumed by the fire. He kicked it idly and it collapsed, falling upon itself in a soft explosion of ash. Near the center of the scorched circle, in which he now stood, one of the timbers burned through with a faint snap; for an instant, the flames rose as if their extinguished fury were renewing itself. Until the brief rekindling spent itself, Andrews stood and gazed with an absent fixity upon the fire. He thought of Miller, and of the sudden blankness that had come upon his face in the instant before he had spurred his horse away from the holocaust he had started; he remembered the sharpness of Miller's image, limned and defined and starkly identified against the furious blaze that he had labored to feed; and he remembered the merging into darkness of that same stiff figure, as Miller rode away from them on his dying horse. He remembered Charley Hoge, and the image of the fire burning like a vision of hell in his empty eyes; and he remembered the quick, awkward shift of Charley Hoge's body as he turned to follow Miller, as he turned away from the fire, from the townspeople, from the town itself, to follow all that remained to him of the world. And he remembered McDonald, and his flailing against a dark animal shape that would not remain still to receive his fury, a shape that had betrayed a faith that McDonald would not acknowledge; he remembered the sudden slump of McDonald's body when he ceased his vain pursuit and the distant, almost

quizzical, look upon his face as he stared before him, as if
to search the meaning of his fury.

In the east, above the horizon, the first faint gray of
dawn dulled the sky. Andrews moved, his limbs stiff from
his long vigil at the fire, turning away from the fire to walk
in the lifting darkness back to his room in Butcher's
Crossing.

Francine was still asleep. During the night she had
thrown aside her covers, and lay now in her nakedness
sprawled awkwardly upon the bed, a pale shape that seemed
to glow out of the dark. Andrews went very quietly to the
window and drew back the curtains. The out-of-doors
stretched vast and colorless before him, thickened and unreal in the gray haze that had begun to take on the faintest
tinge of pink from the light in the east. He turned from
the window and walked back to the bed where Francine
lay; he stood above her.

Her hair, lusterless in the morning light, lay in tangles
about her face; her mouth was half open, and she breathed
heavily in sleep; tiny wrinkles that spread from her eyes
were barely visible in the light; an oily film of sweat
covered the flesh that sagged in its repose. He had not seen
her before as he saw her now, caught in the ugliness of
sleep; or if he had, he had not let his eyes stay upon her.
But seeing her now, defenseless in sleep and in the innocence of sleep, a friendly and unguarded pity came over
him. It seemed to him that he had never looked at her
before, had never seen a part of her that he was seeing
now; he remembered the first night he had come to her
room, months before, and his rush of pity for her in the
humiliations, the coarsenesses she had schooled herself to
endure. Now that pity seemed to him contemptible and
mean.

No, he had not seen her before. Again he turned to the
open window. The flat land beyond Butcher's Crossing lay
open and clear in the crisp gray light that swelled from the
east. Already, on the eastern coast, the sun was up, glinting
on the rocks that lined the northern bays, and catching the
wings of gulls that wheeled in the high salt air; already it
lighted the empty streets of Boston, and shone upon the

steeples of the empty churches along Boylston Street and St. James Avenue, on Arlington and Berkeley and Clarendon; it shone through the high windows of his father's house, lighting rooms in which no one moved.

A sense of sorrow that was like a foretaste of grief spread upon his mind; he thought of his father, a thin austere figure that moved before the eye of his mind like a stranger, and then faded impalpably into a gray mist. He closed his eyes in a spasm of regret and pity, and perceived sharply the darkness he brought on by that small motion of his lids. He knew that he would not go back. He would not return with McDonald to his home, to the country that had given him birth, had raised him in the shape he occupied and the condition that he had only begun to recognize, and that had relinquished him to a wilderness in which he had thought to find a truer shape of himself. No, he would never return.

As if balancing himself finely at the edge of an abyss, he turned from the window and looked again at the sleeping figure of Francine. He could hardly recall, now, the passion that had drawn him to this room and this flesh, as if by a subtle magnetism; nor could he recall the force of that other passion which had impelled him halfway across a continent into a wilderness where he had dreamed he could find, as in a vision, his unalterable self. Almost without regret, he could admit now the vanity from which those passions had sprung.

It was that nothingness of which McDonald had spoken back in the sleeping house as he stood beneath the lantern that flickered weakly against the darkness; it was the bright blue emptiness of Charley Hoge's stare, into which he had glimpsed and of which he had tried to tell Francine; it was the contemptuous look that Schneider had given the river just before the hoof had blanked his face; it was the blind enduring set of Miller's face before the white drive of storm in the mountains; it was the hollow glint in Charley Hoge's eyes, when Charley Hoge turned from the dying fire to follow Miller into the night; it was the open despair that ripped McDonald's face into a livid mask during his frenzied pursuit of Miller in the holocaust of the hides; it was what he saw now in Francine's sleeping face that sagged inertly on her pillow.

He looked once more at Francine, and wished to reach out gently and touch her young, aging face. But he did not do so, for fear that he would awaken her. Very quietly he went to the corner of the room and took his bedroll up. From the money belt that lay upon it, he took out two bills, and stuffed them in his pocket; the rest of the bills he neatly piled on the table beside the couch. Wherever Francine went, she would need the money; she would need it to buy a new rug, and curtains for her windows. Once again he looked at her; across the room, in the large bed, she seemed very small. He went quietly across to the door, and did not look back.

Streaks of red lay in soft banks in the east. In the stillness of the deserted street he walked across to the livery stable and got his horse, awakening the stableman to give him one of the bills he had kept. He saddled his horse quickly in the dim light of the stable, mounted, and turned to wave to the stableman; but he had gone back to sleep. He rode out of the stable and down the dusty street of Butcher's Crossing; the clop of his horse's hooves was muffled in the thick dust. He looked on either side of him at what remained of Butcher's Crossing. Soon there would be nothing here; the timbered buildings would be torn down for what material could be salvaged, the sod huts would wash away in the weather, and the prairie grass would slowly creep upon the roadway. Even now, in the light of the early sun, the town was like a small ruin; the light caught upon the edges of the buildings and intensified a bareness that was already there.

He rode past the still smoldering ruins of McDonald's shack and past the cottonwood grove that stood on the right. He crossed the narrow river and brought his horse to a halt. He turned. A thin edge of sun flamed above the eastern horizon. He turned again and looked at the flat country before him, where his shadow lay long and level, broken at the edges by the crisp new prairie grass. His horse's reins were tough and slick in his hands; he was acutely aware of the rocklike smoothness of the saddle he sat in, of the gentle swelling movement of the horse's sides as it took in air and expelled it. He breathed deeply of the fragrant air that rose from the new grass and mingled with the musty sweat of his horse. He gathered the reins firmly in one hand, touched his horse's flanks with his heels, and rode into the open country.

Except for the general direction he took, he did not know where he was going; but he knew that it would come to him later in the day. He rode forward without hurry, and felt behind him the sun slowly rise and harden the air.